Her friends were there to help her get revenge. All she had to do was decide…

They walked into the house, all trying to take in this bizarre conversation. To each of them, the notion of getting Phillip's revenge was both frightening and enticing.

"I'm not saying that this makes any sense at all, but let's say we agree with that—you know seeking vengeance—how do we do it?" asked Chuck.

"Who knows?" said Rita. "But the reason we've all been walking around like zombies since we found out that Crotty ruined JoAnne's life is because we feel helpless. We haven't decided to settle the score. We first need to agree it's something we want to do. Jo, we want to do this, don't we?"

JoAnne and Phillip DiMatteo led an ideal life in their small Italian neighborhood. They were respected business owners and pillars of their community, with a large circle of good friends. But when Phillip unseats oafish and corrupt Mayor Michael Crotty and his political machine, the DiMatteo's idyllic lives are forever changed. After Phillip tragically and mysteriously dies, JoAnne turns to the shelter of her best friends for support and comfort. Together they are soon confronted with information about Phillip's untimely death which they simply can't ignore. Living together in a stately house, named The Settlement, the ladies bring ingenuity to a new level in creating an elaborate sting to get corrupt Mayor Crotty out of office and into jail. Orchestrating every aspect of Operation Out 'n' In, they assemble and direct a disparate cast of quirky characters, who turn settling a score into an art form...

KUDOS for *The Settlement*

In *The Settlement* by Ken Bessette, JoAnne DiMatteo has just lost her husband Phillip under mysterious circumstances. The only thing she knows for sure is that his death was caused, directly or indirectly, by his corrupt political rival, Mayor Michal Crotty and his political machine that has ruled their small town for decades. When Phillip unseats him as mayor, Crotty is determined to get even and destroys their business, reputation, and lives. After Phillip's death, JoAnne wants revenge, and she and her close friends, living together in a mansion called The Settlement, come up with a plan to get Crotty and his cronies out of office and into jail. It takes getting revenge to a whole new level. Now all they have to do is pull it off. Fun, creative, and refreshingly unique, this is a story you will want to read over and over again, just for the pure enjoyment. ~ *Taylor Jones, The Review Team of Taylor Jones & Regan Murphy*

The Settlement by Ken Bessette is the story of four women bent on revenge. When JoAnne DiMatteo's husband Phillip decides to run for mayor of their town and unseat the corrupt political machine currently in power, he has no idea what he is getting into. Phillip wins the election, but his and JoAnne's lives are turned upside down by the ex-mayor and his cohorts. Then Phillip dies mysteriously, the corrupt mayor is back in office, and JoAnne has finally had enough. With her life destroyed, she moves in with three women friends in a house called The Settlement. Bent on revenge, she decides to take down the powers-that-be who she feels are responsible for Phillip's death. The four women, along with several friends, set up Operation In and Out, an elaborate sting to get the corrupt mayor out of office and into jail, turning getting revenge into an art form...I loved this book! Well written, clever, creative, and fun, *The Settlement* will make you laugh, make you cry, and make you feel good right down to your toes. A truly delightful book. ~ *Regan Murphy, The Review Team of Taylor Jones & Regan Murphy*

The

Settlement

Ken Bessette

A Black Opal Books Publication

GENRE: MYSTERY-DETECTIVE/SUSPENSE/WOMEN SLEUTHS

THE SETTLEMENT
Copyright © 2019 by Ken Bessette
Cover Design by Ken Bessette
All cover art copyright © 2019
All Rights Reserved
Print ISBN: 9781644371039

First Publication: MARCH 2019

Published by Black Opal Books **http://www.blackopalbooks.com**

For Diane

"One should forgive one's enemies,
but not before they are hanged"
~ Heinrich Heine

Chapter 1

With her head down and her face resting in both hands, JoAnne DiMatteo sat in a large wing chair a few steps to the right of a closed casket. On top of the casket was a photo of Phillip DiMatteo, her deceased husband, taken many years prior. It showed Phillip standing behind the counter, at the DiMatteo Family Pharmacy, as he was being handed a ridiculously large cardboard cut-out of a key by his father, Peter. It was taken on the day that Peter retired and Phillip took over the pharmacy. It had been the proudest day of Phillip's life and for him, a moment of pure joy. JoAnne wanted to remember him that way—she also wanted everyone coming to the wake to remember him that way.

Phillip and JoAnne had spent the better part of their married lives owning and operating the DiMatteo Family Pharmacy. In the old neighborhood of South Troy where it was located, it was known familiarly as the "Fam Pharm." Phillip began work there, the day after he graduated from the Albany College of Pharmacy, under the tutelage and direction of his father who had started the business before Phillip was born. JoAnne began working there as a billing clerk soon after she and Phillip married. She later earned her pharmacy degree from the same college as Phillip and together they ran the business for nearly thirty years.

John Martone, second generation owner of Martone's Funeral Home in South Troy, stood quietly, well off to the side of the casket. He had personally driven JoAnne to the funeral home an hour before the wake would begin. She had

said she wanted some private time with Phillip before everyone came.

She spent much of that time remembering her days with
Phillip at the Fam Pharm before he got into politics. That
life she loved so much totally revolved around Phillip and
the pharmacy. Now, both were gone forever.

In her solitude, she wondered whether she could have
done more to change the course of these horrible events.
Should she have insisted that Phillip get more help? Should
she have intervened when his behavior began to get so hor-
ribly erratic? Should she have somehow stopped him from
getting into politics in the first place? Could she have done
anything to save her husband and best friend? She despaired
that her "mistake" at the pharmacy had begun his agony and
now hers.

The county coroner had been slow to issue a definitive
statement regarding Phillip's death. Clearly it was the result
of the massive injuries he sustained when his car was
smashed by a freight train traveling at sixty miles per hour.
What was not clear to anyone was what Phillip was doing
out there in the middle of the night on the railroad crossing
at Rackley Road—a crossing that led only to a long-
abandoned farm. The newspaper account diplomatically
steered clear of calling it a suicide. Based on interviews
with JoAnne, Phillip's doctor, the train operator, Police
Chief Roberts, and others who had been in contact with
Phillip in the preceding weeks, the report strongly suggested that Phillip's fateful crossing of the tracks at Rackley
Road that night could well have been the result of drug-
induced night wandering. By all accounts of Phillip's recent
behavior, it appeared as though he was literally asleep at the
wheel on the train tracks.

But as she sat quietly beside him for the very last time,
JoAnne was not so sure that it was an accident. She was
horrified to think that he had taken his own life, but she was
painfully aware of how deeply saddened and depressed he
was. He had blamed himself for the sorrow they had both

endured over the pharmacy scandal. He felt disgraced and ashamed and was devastated that he had brought down such feelings on JoAnne as well.

She realized that she might never know if he was on the train tracks that night by accident or by plan. But oddly, it didn't seem to matter much to her. Either way, Phillip was gone because of a series of events that were brought on by his involvement in politics and the pain they both endured as a result. While she felt that there was no hope of ever definitively knowing exactly why Phillip was on Rackley Road that night, in JoAnne's mind, it really didn't matter. He was dead because of Michael Crotty.

With his head lowered and hands clasped behind him, John Martone slowly stepped toward JoAnne. His approach snapped her out of her thoughts. She looked up at him and smiled a tired but sincere smile. Martone sat on the arm of her chair. He bent toward her, kissing her softly on the cheek.

"Jo, it's four o'clock. There's a long line outside already, and we should open the door soon."

"Are there really a lot of people coming, John?" she said almost hopefully.

"The line is huge already. It's already halfway down Fifteenth Street," he said as he put his hand on her shoulder. "Listen to me, Jo. This is going to be a long night. There are going to be more people coming than you can imagine. I want you to know that no matter how long this takes, I'm going to be right here with you. And it's okay to…you know…take a little break every now and then. Marie will be in the office and will be there for you any time you need to take a little time for yourself. Believe me, everybody will understand. Promise you'll take a break every once in a while if you need to, all right? Will you promise me you'll do that?"

"I'm glad people are coming, John." JoAnne had a charming way of not answering questions she did not want to by just pretending they were never even asked. "It shows how much they respect Phillip. I want them all to know how much Phillip and I appreciate them coming." Even four days after the crash, JoAnne was still talking about Phillip in the present.

They both stood up. JoAnne nervously brushed at the front of her simple black dress as though to ensure her proper appearance. Phillip was watching, she thought. She surveyed the room. "So many flowers. So many, many people sent flowers," she said to no one in particular.

As Martone walked out to open the front door of the funeral home, JoAnne motioned over the two women who had been standing silently in the back of the room. Her two closest friends in world, Rita Russo and Pat Bocketti, had been by her side almost constantly since the news about Phillip had broken. They had tried to persuade her to stay with them at the house they shared in the South Troy Hill section but instead JoAnne stayed alone in her own house, alone with her thoughts of Phillip.

Seeing JoAnne's beckoning move, Rita gave Pat a nudge. "Come on, Patty. Here we go," she said as they hurriedly moved to take their position on either side of her.

The calling hours were scheduled from four to eight p.m., with the funeral service set for nine a.m. the following morning at Saint Paul's Church, the same church in which Phillip and JoAnne had both been baptized and had been married when they were both twenty-two years old.

For three solid hours, family, friends, local politicians, business leaders, police and fire department officials, and countless associates of both Phillip and JoAnne packed the funeral home. It was by far the largest turnout for a wake to be seen at the Martone Funeral Home in many years. John Martone and his wife Marie skillfully and diplomatically handled the crowds while Rita and Pat stood faithfully at JoAnne's side, trying to keep the well-intended but tediously repetitious condolences to a minimum. JoAnne mouthed the words "Thank you" to them about every five minutes.

All things considered, the wake went off mostly as

planned. JoAnne was completely gracious to everyone who passed through the line and was overwhelmed by the outpouring of support. She was gratified and, in a way, relieved by the extraordinary turnout. It was a type of vindication for herself and for Phillip. The outpouring of support was, to her and to everyone in attendance, a sign that the fog of shame that had fallen on the DiMatteos had been lifted. JoAnne stood stoically and bravely hour after hour and took no breaks. She sincerely thanked everyone who passed by for their support and repeated over and over again how blessed she was to have had Phillip by her side for so many years and how proud she was to have been his wife. The wake was, like the DiMatteos themselves, ordered and dignified almost in its entirety. Almost.

Slightly after seven, as JoAnne, Rita, and Pat stood facing the room and the seemingly endless line of people that snaked its way back through the funeral home and out the door, Rita took note of some commotion at the far-end entrance which led from the Martone living quarters. Emerging from the door were Marie Martone and Mayor Michael Crotty, along with his ever-present top aide, Bruno Kreider. They were moving directly toward the front, down the aisle of chairs filled with attendees who sat for a time after going through the line.

The mayor and Kreider had come in through the private entrance to the Martone residence, effectively avoiding what was still a lengthy wait outside. Crotty moved directly toward JoAnne wearing a transparently fake look of sadness. As Marie followed them toward the front of the room, Rita's eyes widened and blazed in their direction. Marie saw Rita's reaction and mouthed to her, "What am I gonna do?"

Crotty strode confidently forward, with Kreider close behind, nodding solemnly to all who noticed him entering. As he neared the casket, Rita broke ranks from the receiving line to intercept the approaching mayor. She reached him several feet away and firmly grasped his arm, effectively steering him toward an empty space around the corner of the viewing room.

"You got a special pass on you there, jackass? Perhaps neither you nor your dopey sidekick here noticed that there's a line," she said to him with fire in her eyes. "Now be a good boy and go stand at the end of it."

"Well hello, Mrs. White," Crotty said in a sarcastic reference to Rita's former husband, Joe White.

"It's Ms. Russo to you, butt-head."

Kreider took a step to move between Rita and Crotty. "Now, Rita, let's not make a scene here."

"Shut up, Kreider," Rita snapped back before returning her attention back to Crotty. "And you're the one creating a scene by just showing up in the first place. Everybody knows you hated Phillip and you showing up at his wake is ridiculously phony, even by your slimy standards. Now why don't you and your little toady go outside and get in line behind those people who are here for the right reasons. Hopefully, it's so long we can close the doors before you get back in."

Crotty sported a calm smile as Rita chided him, well aware that half of the people in the room were witnessing this. In a low tone he said, "I'm glad to see that Mrs. Di-Matteo has hired a security team. Maybe she should have gotten one for her husband." Kreider let out an audible derisive snort at Crotty's comeback.

"You bastard," Rita snarled as Crotty gave a little smiling nod in the direction of two passersby as though this conversation was all routine.

Kreider stepped closer. "Rita, insofar as this is a public facility and several of the mayor's police friends are present, you may do well to just allow him to express his condolences, and then we can be on our way without you being handcuffed."

Rita knew she could not actually stop Crotty from being there, but she did want to lay down some ground rules. "If you say one single thing to upset JoAnne, I'll reach into your mouth and rip out your tongue," Rita replied, mimicking Crotty's phony smile. "And you, Kreider, you need to just shut the hell up."

Gesturing gently with his hand toward JoAnne, Crotty said, "Shall we?"

As they approached, JoAnne saw Crotty coming. She immediately turned and sat in the wing chair for the first time all night. Pat had not been able to hear the confrontation between Crotty and Rita but knew that there had indeed been one and that it probably did not go well. She moved closer to JoAnne as if for moral support. Martone had also noticed what had transpired and hurried toward them. He wanted nothing to go wrong and quietly halted the line of well-wishers to create some space between them and Jo-Anne.

Crotty extended his hand toward JoAnne as he approached. "I'm terribly sorry for your loss, Mrs. DiMatteo," he said a bit too loudly.

"Thank you," JoAnne said, looking up but not actually at Crotty. When she purposely did not get out of her chair or extend her hand to Crotty, he casually raised his arm up as though he were wiping away a tear. Rita and Pat both noticed and admired JoAnne's ability to send messages without actually doing anything.

Unfazed, Crotty pressed on. "If there is anything I or my office can do to help you in this horrible time, please be sure to—"

"I know you're a very busy man, Mr. Mayor, so don't feel obliged to stay too long," JoAnne abruptly said, interrupting him in mid-sentence. "And please, by all means, don't take time away from your work with the city to come to the funeral tomorrow. Surely both Phillip and I would think that best."

Pat and Rita had all they could do to not cheer out loud at JoAnne's elegant way of dismissing Crotty.

Crotty nodded, stepped back, and moved toward Phillip's casket to stand for a moment, pretending to offer up a prayer. After a few seconds, he noticed Rita approaching. He made a half-hearted sign of the cross and walked toward the rear of the room, nodding and gesturing diplomatically to the many still seated in the folding chairs, but to no one in particular. Kreider was close behind as they exited the same way as they entered.

As soon as they left the room, JoAnne got up out of the chair to again resume her courtesies to those in the long line that remained.

"Rat bastard," Rita whispered in Pat's ear.

"You're too kind," Pat whispered back.

⌘

JoAnne spent the next several days alone, tormented and still in disbelief that Phillip was gone. She spent far too much time wondering what could have been. In her lonely hours, she blamed herself for allowing Phillip to get involved in Troy politics and she got angry at herself for actually helping him win the election. She wished she had just followed her instincts and convinced Phillip to not get involved. She missed him deeply.

As her lonely hours turned into lonely days, JoAnne found herself lost in her memories. She let herself become absorbed in detailed flashbacks of the unforeseeable twists and turns her life with him had taken since Phillip decided to take on Michael Crotty and the Democratic Machine by running for mayor.

Up until that time, their lives together had been all that she had ever dreamed of. She and Phillip were happy each day to be running the Fam Pharm and to be around their many friends. They took pride in their successful business and in being able to provide a valuable service to their South Troy neighbors. They took a personal interest in all of their customers and were ubiquitous in the community. They donated generously to every call for support.

The Fam Pharm van, which delivered prescriptions to

the elderly and homebound, was on the road around town all day, every day. On the counter of the pharmacy was a large glass jar labeled, "Change for our Neighborhood," into which customers could make a contribution. Every month, the DiMatteos would count the donations, match the amount, and use the funds to pay for prescriptions for those in need of help.

Phillip was president of the local Marconi Club for many years, and JoAnne was the first female chairperson of the Troy Rotary Club. They were "patrons" of the Troy Music Hall, the South Troy Boys and Girls Club, the United Way of Troy, and founding members of the South Troy Neighborhood Watch Program. If ever there were true pillars of any community, Phillip and JoAnne were that in theirs. They loved what they were doing to make a difference.

And so, it was with great trepidation that JoAnne learned that Phillip had been approached by a number of local business owners and the Republican Party to run against six-term Mayor Michael Crotty. With a city-wide voter registration that was nearly eighty percent Democrat, Democrats had held power in Troy for nearly forty years.

Crotty, a career politician with no discernible skill set, began his career by winning a seat on the city council at the age of twenty-four with the backing of the Democratic Party. That support came as a reward for Crotty being a member and then Chairman of the Young Democrats—the "farm team" for future Troy politicians, dedicated solely to perpetuating political control. To be elected to any position in Troy politics, one only needed to get the Democratic endorsement. In most elections, that candidate ran unopposed.

Such was the case with Crotty when, at the age of thirty-six, he was first elected Mayor of Troy, thus becoming forever in debt to the democratic machine. He was tapped by the party after the four-term sitting mayor, Pat Powers, dropped dead while holding sway at his "reserved" bar stool at the far end of the Excalibar. The Excalibar was the home-away-from-home for all Democratic politicians in the city where, for decades, deals were made and the machine rolled on.

On that fateful night, Mayor Powers suddenly started to cough, wheeze, and clutch his throat after downing a clam shooter. He fell off his bar stool and choked to death on the floor while two dozen regulars looked on. No one stepped in to aid the choking mayor, and he died well before the EMTs arrived. The talk of who the new mayor might be began even before Powers's body arrived at the morgue.

After a few days of bickering, the party leaders unanimously chose Michael Crotty to succeed Powers, mostly based on his unique ability to play the role of flunky for the old-line party officials. They recognized that Crotty had just the right combination of loyalty and obliviousness to do whatever they wanted and to blithely take the fall if anything turned bad.

As usual, the leadership's political instincts were spot on. Over the remainder of Powers's term, Crotty proved to be willing to bend, break, fake, flaunt, or otherwise ignore both the law and any sense of propriety in ruling the city. If anything surprised them about his tenure, it was his uncanny knack of finding new ways to spread corruption even deeper into the fabric of the city.

Michael Crotty epitomized how and why the system worked in Troy for so many years. The party leaders easily controlled him, and the populace dared not cross him. His prowess at retribution became legendary and feared, his willingness to do anything to stay in power knew no bounds. The patronage system was his natural habitat.

Running unopposed, Crotty was re-elected six consecutive times over the following twelve years. As the party, the system, and the Crotty "machine" rolled on, it seemed inconceivable to the Democratic leadership that anyone would even dare run against him, and they believed that no one could unseat him.

For the first time in decades, their political instincts were wrong.

The Crotty regime had gotten clearly out of hand over his time in office. Since Crotty was only forty-eight years old, previously quiet but fed-up city residents and business leaders alike knew that things would continually get worse and that, without serious opposition, he would remain mayor for years to come. Crotty never really bothered to campaign in any of elections, but shortly before his so-called "campaign for re-election" for his seventh term began, a small but determined group of carefully selected Troy business leaders began to quietly meet to discuss what amounted to a secret attack on city hall. Among them was Phillip DiMatteo.

What started out as a series of complaint sessions about local government in general, and Crotty in particular, soon escalated into a genuinely hopeful series of serious meetings about ending the decades-long corruption that was smothering the city. The group, twelve in all, was comprised of well-intended, well-connected, well-respected, and wealthy business leaders, who went from wishing, to hoping, to planning for Crotty's defeat in the upcoming election. The meetings became more frequent and more focused. The group had a clear goal: to defeat Crotty and rid city hall of corruption. They called themselves "The Gang of Twelve."

They believed they could succeed because of several assumptions which they discussed at length: that Crotty was a crook—and nobody likes a crook except other crooks—and a majority of the people were not crooks. Despite the fact that eighty percent of the voters in the city were registered Democrats, only an extremely small percentage of them cared much for Crotty and very few of them actually voted in the mayoral elections since everyone assumed that the conclusions were foregone.

The Gang also believed that the ethnic neighborhoods of Troy, unlike the inner city, would overwhelmingly support the right candidate if they thought there was a reasonable chance to unseat the machine. Lastly, they were certain that the Crotty government had no clue as to how to actually run a campaign against a legitimate contender since they had never had to do so.

These fundamentals caused the group to believe that a strong, last minute, well-funded, and organized campaign founded on overthrowing corruption in government and led by a respected and trusted candidate, well known in the neighborhoods, could succeed. Phillip DiMatteo was their unanimous choice to be that candidate. The entire Gang, including Phillip, were excited by the potential of unseating Crotty. They also knew that before that could happen, Phillip would have to get JoAnne to agree to have him run. Above all else, Phillip and JoAnne were a team. Looking back, JoAnne vividly recalled Phillip's rather clumsy effort to get her on board…

ℰ✺ℰℱ

"Are you ever going to ask me about all those meetings I've been going to at Fippi's?" he said to JoAnne one evening while clearing the table after dinner.

Fippi Casella was the owner of a beer distributorship located in South Troy. It had a large employee lunch room in the back and The Gang of Twelve had been secretly meeting there for weeks.

"You know I don't ask questions like that," JoAnne replied in a matter-of-fact way, without looking up from the newspaper.

Each night, JoAnne would prepare dinner while Phillip looked at the paper. After dinner, Phillip would clear the table while JoAnne read the paper.

"I just thought you'd be curious, that's all. I've been spending a lot of time there lately. Aren't you curious?" he asked, clearly begging the question.

"Did you see in the paper that Maggie Ormond's boy, Joey, made the dean's list at Rutgers? Joey Ormond is in college. I can't believe it. I remember him when he was a little boy. He always got earaches, remember? Maggie was in the shop this morning, did you see her?"

"Uh, no. No, I didn't," Phillip replied, annoyed that Jo-Anne had not taken the bait about the meetings at Casella's. "I'm going back to Fippi's again Friday night for a while. I just thought you should know."

With that, JoAnne folded the paper and looked up at Phillip as he returned to the table. "Okay fine, it's obvious you're dying to get me to ask. So, darling, I've been meaning to ask you, what's been going on at all those meetings you been going to at Fippi's?" she said, in a pleasant and playfully sarcastic tone.

It unnerved Phillip sometimes how easily she could read him. "Well, since you asked," he said with a wry smile. "I've been meeting with a working group—I guess you'd call it that—to see if we can do something about getting Michael Crotty out of office."

JoAnne's eyes widened as she took off her reading glasses and looked up at Phillip. This clearly got her attention. "You mean other than by feeding him some clam shooters at Excalibar?"

They both grinned.

"Yes, some way other than that."

"And?"

"We think he can be beaten in the November election by the right candidate with the right team behind him."

"Behind him?" she asked as though to mock Phillip's political incorrectness.

"Of course, I mean him or her. But we've actually been thinking of a him."

"What him?"

"Well..." He paused as though reluctant to answer.

JoAnne's mouth fell wide open. "Oh, no, don't even tell me that you mean him as in you! No, no, no, no! Don't you dare stand there in my presence and tell me that you've totally lost your mind."

Phillip knew that the game was on and there was no

turning back now. "Now wait, Jo. Don't get all opinionated before you hear the plan."

"The plan? Plan? Phillip, my love, no matter what the plan is, if it involves you running for mayor, I hate it!" She was getting louder but not angry.

"Without even hearing it, you hate it?"

"Yes, that's exactly right. Without even hearing the plan, I hate it. Do you know why? Let me explain, Phillip. If the plan is bad, you lose, and Crotty will make our lives miserable forever for running against him. If the plan is good, you win and then you'll actually have to be mayor. How can either of these be good for you, or for us? What about the business? Win or lose, we are all doomed if you so much as even enter this race. Please don't tell me we're diving into the political cesspool. Please, I beg you, don't tell me that. I'll follow you to the end of the earth, Phillip, but please don't get us involved in politics. You know I think it's all slimy. I hate politics!"

Phillip was in awe of how she had assessed the situation so quickly and given him a logical and legitimate reason why he should not get involved before he had even asked the question. But he was prepared. "You're exactly right—"

"Thank you," she interrupted. "Now did you say you did or didn't see Maggie Ormond come into the store today? And by the way, is Rutgers in New Jersey? I think it is."

Phillip was having none of JoAnne's ploy of changing the subject. "What I meant was, you're exactly right about Crotty and his band of merry crooks being slimy. I agree. But that's the point! They're slimy politicians who need to be removed from office. That's why this is important. I think—no, we all think—that I can run them out. And we think it's worth the effort."

For several seconds nothing was said. JoAnne was holding her head with her hands, just staring at nothing. Finally, she got up from the table and went around to where Phillip was still sitting. From behind him, she wrapped her arms around his shoulders and kissed the top of his head. In a gentle voice, she said, "Phillip, honey, if you've already decided you're going to do this, tell me now and don't insult me by pretending I have some say in it. Will you do that for me?"

He nodded as a sign that he understood. "I need you to help me to decide what to do. And then I need you to help me to live with that decision, whatever it is."

She walked slowly toward the kitchen and, without looking back, she said, "We'll talk about the plan, but not tonight. Tomorrow after dinner we'll talk about it. Not tonight. Tonight, I'd just like some wine. Be a doll and break open a bottle of Pinot, will you? Let's the two of us drink a little wine and talk about the weather."

As brief and indecisive as this first conversation was, the one the following night was extremely long and quite decisive. Phillip spoke passionately about the frustration with the Crotty administration. JoAnne learned who was involved with The Gang of Twelve. She listened intently to the logic of why Crotty was vulnerable. She heard the strategy and finally, how Phillip had carefully been chosen to be the face of reform for the city. They discussed it all in great detail.

JoAnne, in turn, voiced her concern about retribution in the event of a failed attempt. She was also quite concerned about Phillip actually winning, becoming mayor, and effectively leaving her to run the Fam Pharm. She was worried about the demands on his time and general wear and tear on him both mentally and physically. And the mere thought of getting involved with politics was abhorrent to her. They discussed her concerns, likewise, in great detail.

No matter how hard she tried to see Phillip's perspective, deep down, JoAnne hated the idea. But she could tell that this was something that Phillip felt a calling to do, something he needed to do. Yes, Phillip had asked her opinion as to what he should do, but she knew that for his sake what she needed to do was different from what she wanted to do.

In the end, Phillip said, "Let's do this, Jo."

She sighed an exaggerated sigh. "This is a mistake, Phillip. I absolutely hate politics and the idea of you getting involved in this, but I admire you for wanting to make a difference. If this is what you really want, we'll do it. We'll do it together," she said.

Phillip smiled a knowing smile. "You're the best," he said while gently gripping her hand.

JoAnne got up and looked toward the ceiling as though she was looking for divine intervention. "You're not going to actually win, are you?" she asked somewhat playfully.

"I might."

"I was afraid you were going to say that."

☙❧❦

The Gang of Twelve put all of their energies behind Phillip's campaign, which hit the ground running and caught a shocked Crotty and his cohorts flatfooted. The well-funded and organized DiMatteo campaign plan worked exactly as planned. They had accurately calculated Crotty's weaknesses and exploited them. Phillip ran on a platform of anti-corruption and vowed to clean up city government and its system of favoritism, fear mongering, and cronyism. They worked the neighborhoods hard, going door to door to get out the vote.

As reluctant as she was to get involved in politics, JoAnne hit the campaign circuit along with Phillip. She focused on women's issues and getting out the female vote. She appeared and gave speeches everywhere and anywhere she could and consistently depicted Crotty as being, as she called it, "female oblivious," pointing out that there were exactly zero women in leadership positions in Crotty's government.

As a part of his agreement with JoAnne about running for office, Phillip publicly vowed to be a one-term mayor whose sole purpose during his term would be to rid the government of corruption and return the election process to one of a true democracy. The campaign depicted Phillip as the best and maybe last chance to clean up city hall. By the time the Crotty camp realized they were in trouble, it was too late. They had no idea how to respond to a serious challenge.

On election day, there was a huge turnout from the neighborhoods. Women, especially, who had never voted in the past, overwhelmingly supported Phillip and, by inference, JoAnne. Predictably, there was a small turnout from the inner city. As the Gang had assumed, the crooks were outnumbered and, when given a real chance to topple the regime, the people did it. Phillip won the election handily. He would be the first non-Democratic mayor in four decades.

While the people of Troy felt it was a new day and the dawn of something good, JoAnne felt her life—a life that she loved—would never be the same. She was right.

Chapter 2

I believe it was that great philosopher, Anonymous, who once said, 'Be careful what you wish for, you just might get it,'" bellowed Maurice "Mo" Wheeler, the second-generation owner of Wheeler's Quick Step, the city's only shoe repair shop. He was the unofficial chairman of the Gang of Twelve. His opening statement brought nervous laughter all around.

The Gang, including Mayor-Elect DiMatteo, assembled the night after the election in their regular meeting place at Casella's beer distributorship.

"I hope none of you are too hungover after last night," Wheeler continued, generating more nervous laughter. "I suppose the first order of business is to confirm our agreement with Phillip to continue to support him and recognize that our work is just beginning. All in favor of standing with Phillip as he begins the work of cleaning up the governmental mess, please signify by saying 'aye.'"

"Aye," came the thunderous and unanimous response.

"The 'ayes' have it. Phillip, we're with you all the way. How can we help?"

Everyone was jubilant—everyone, seemingly, except Phillip who stood slowly and shook his head as though to suggest that he really did not know how to answer that question. Plan A was to beat Crotty. Beyond that, he had not done much actual planning. Since the moment he realized that he might in fact become the next mayor, Phillip's lone thought beyond the election was that if he did win, his only chance for success would come if the Gang could stay intact and become his unofficial kitchen cabinet. So, as he contemplated the monumental tasks that lay ahead, he was glad, at least, to have the support of every person in that room.

"First," he began, "I believe it was also that great philosopher, Anonymous, who also said, 'Be careful of asking how you can help, somebody just might tell you.'"

"You're scarin' us, Phillip," Fippi joked.

"Good," Philip replied with a slight grin. "Now that I have your attention, let me tell you what I think lies ahead of us.

The meeting that night went on for several hours as Phillip outlined the myriad problems he foresaw. He noted that virtually everyone in the existing city hall bureaucracy was a Crotty appointee and beneficiary of the very system the Gang wanted to clean up. They would not be helpful. He talked of how difficult it would be to even find all of the problems that existed, let alone clean them up.

"They've been screwing with this for four decades," said an impassioned Phillip. "And let's give credit where it's due. They're damned good at it, and they'll do everything possible to stop us from succeeding in cleaning this mess up."

The discussion touched on all aspects of running the city: public safety, planning, zoning, economic development, public works. They all agreed that the entire atmosphere of government had to change.

But in the midst of all the talk about overhauling the very essence of day-to-day life in city hall, Mo Wheeler, always the pragmatist, issued a sobering warning.

"Before everybody goes all Batman here and runs all the bad guys out of Gotham City, let's not forget that come January somebody's still got to do the actual work. We're with you all the way, Phillip, but I don't think any of us here want to be driving snow plows or fixing broken water pipes in the middle of the night after we've gotten rid of all of the employees."

Wheeler's words were a reminder to everyone of the task that lay before them. They all felt a bit overwhelmed but were not dismayed in the least.

Phillip rubbed his face with both hands and stretched as he stood up. "It's getting late, my friends, let's say we wrap it up for tonight. Are we okay to meet here again next Tuesday night? We've got a little time before my term starts, but not much and Crotty will spend that time laying land mines all over the place. I really need you guys now."

Jack Catranis, owner of the Red Door Restaurant, had said little all night but then made a slight hand gesture toward Phillip as to indicate that he wanted to say something.

"Jack, you've been quiet for the last couple of hours. That's not like you. What's on your mind?"

"Everything has all been pretty positive so far. I hate to bring this up but I feel like I gotta do it," Catranis said softly.

"We're all big boys here, Jack. What's on your mind?"

Catranis shuffled in his seat. "When are we going to talk about the backlash?"

Phillip crooked his head, not immediately grasping what Catranis was talking about.

"You know, the backlash," Catranis repeated. "Backlash from the Crotty people. We haven't talked about it but we all know those bastards are not going to let us ruin their game without making us pay the price. We've been a secret society up to now and we all feel safe here during our meetings. But trust me, they're soon going to know what we've been up to. They're going to find out everything we've been doing and what we're going to be doing to help you. And I think we all understand that we're going to pay a price for this coup. All of us—especially you, Phillip. We need to talk about protecting ourselves."

The entire Gang knew that Catranis was right. It was the one thing that had gone unsaid but everyone knew needed saying. Retribution was coming.

"Fair point, Jack," Phillip replied. "Unfortunately, it's a

fair point. Let's give that a little thought before the next meeting and make it the first item on our next agenda. In the meantime, let's all just watch our backs."

❧❧❧

As inept as the Democratic leadership was at conducting a legitimate campaign against Phillip, they proved quite good at counterattacking. While the Gang of Twelve was meeting to plan their new government, the old guard was regrouping. Phillip DiMatteo may have been elected mayor, but the city council still consisted of eight Democrats and one lone Independent member from the Hill Section. Those council members, along with the back-room political hacks and hangers-on, were ripping mad, and they now had a cause: get back at DiMatteo and his confidants and send a message that anyone who dared to challenge the system would pay a steep price. They believed the empire had to strike back, and they acted quickly.

Just days after the election, Dan Robbins, the least-tenured of the at-large Democratic city council members, suddenly announced that he was resigning his seat on the council at the beginning of the January term in order to spend more time with his family. It was clear to everyone that Robbin's declaration of the need to spend more time with his family was code for, "I'm resigning because I have to but don't ask me why." Robbins did his best to conceal the fact that he was being forced to resign his seat but was only moderately successful at hiding his anger.

The council immediately called an emergency session in order to elect Robbins's successor. To no one's surprise, they unanimously elected Michael Crotty to complete the vacant term. In a hastily called press conference, Crotty read a prepared statement which, in part, mentioned how pleased he was to be able to continue his work on behalf of the people of Troy and to work side-by-side with Mayor DiMatteo. Everyone, including Phillip, knew exactly what had just transpired. City government was not going to change without a fight of epic proportions. The regime was launching a counterattack and wanted their point man back in the game. The message could not have been more clear. The war was on, and even though they had just been defeated in the election, Michael Crotty and the machine were back on the attack.

Phillip, with the Gang orchestrating every move, undertook every possible step that did not require council approval to change how things got done. He replaced old political appointees as quickly as he could. He aggressively went after the system of "pay-to-play" that was the fabric of how the government ran. The authority of the mayor's office, which had expanded greatly under Crotty, worked to Phillip's benefit. He was able to unilaterally make some changes to how the government ran, but everything was in chaos. Scores of employees were dismissed while others resigned in support of Crotty. Those who remained were uncooperative at best as word spread quickly that Crotty and the old guard were fighting back and those who remained loyal to them would somehow, someday, be rewarded.

The simplest functions of government went undone. There were excruciatingly long delays in public works activity. Normal services were interrupted, and some abandoned outright. A majority of the city employees were effectively on strike, but still being paid. The so-called "Blue Flu" plagued the police and fire service. Things deteriorated so quickly and badly that even those who hated Crotty and his administration began to believe that a corrupt government was better than one that couldn't even provide basic services. The city may have historically been managed by crooks, people thought, but at least things got done. It soon became clear that Phillip's administration would not be able to effectively run the city amid these conditions.

Phillip was distraught. He and the Gang felt overwhelmed by the difficulties they were facing in managing even basic functions. Soon, discussions of their grand plans to improve the system took a back seat to simply getting by. This was not what they had in mind during those exciting times in the meetings at Casella's. Mo Wheeler's joke about having to plow city streets personally was fast becoming a reality. Phillip's days and the continuing meetings of the Gang were consumed by addressing mounting problems for which they received little help in overcoming.

On top of all of these growing problems, the Democrats piled even more. The city council launched a series of lawsuits against Phillip, which challenged his authority to make many of the changes he had already made. These suits were without any real legal merit but still had to be defended, further pulling DiMatteo off task and adding to his frustration. The pending legal action stalled Phillip's actions to affect change. Meanwhile, none of the new mayor's initiatives which had to come before the council were getting approved. Directives that he was able to issue without council approval were mostly just being ignored. He spent his days essentially alone in his city hall office, and each new day brought with it even more problems that he had to face without any real allies inside the government to help tackle them.

Less than six weeks after taking office, Phillip had become discouraged and at times distraught, thinking that his ideas and those of the Gang were never going to succeed. Secretly, he regretted getting involved at all. He kept remembering JoAnne's very first take on the whole idea, and he regretted not listening to her.

Then, as if Crotty and the others sensed Phillip's weakening resolve, the backlash Jack Catranis warned of began. One morning, shortly after beginning their daily distribution runs, all four of Fippi Casella's beer trucks experienced engine trouble almost simultaneously. The truck engines hesitated, sputtered, and then just shut down. It was later determined that sugar had been poured into the truck's gas tanks overnight. The repairs were expensive and took days to

complete. After one of his regular morning swims at the
South Troy YMCA pool, Mo Wheeler returned to his locker
to find the lock missing along with all of his clothes, wallet,
cell phone and car keys. The YMCA attendant apologized
and said that could not explain how that had happened, but
Mo knew.

One member of the Gang had the front window of his
home smashed by a brick in the middle of the night. The
brick had a note on it attached by a rubber band. "More to
come," it read. Another received a phone call one night after midnight from someone pretending to be from St.
Mary's Hospital saying that his son had been in an auto accident. He and his panic-stricken wife rushed to the ER only
to find that the call was a hoax. Later, police traced the call
back to the pay phone at the Excalibar, but they had no suspects.

The street in front of Jack Catranis's Red Door Tavern
was suddenly shut down for water main repairs. The water
main was not broken and the repairs were, according to the
Department of Public Works, preventative in nature. Those
repairs and the necessary street repaving directly in front of
the restaurant parking lot effectively closed the Red Door
for five days.

Phillip and the Gang of Twelve understood how and why
these things were happening, but their anger was overshad-
owed by their feeling of helplessness. In truth, more than
anything, they felt afraid.

As a part of his defense against the backlash discussed
by the Gang, Mayor DiMatteo had swiftly reappointed
Jackie Roberts as Police Chief. The Gang felt that Roberts
was a "career cop" rather than a Crotty toady and hoped
that Roberts would somehow be helpful to them when
things got ugly.

After each of the unfortunate occurrences that befell the
Gang members, Phillip pleaded with Roberts to aggressively pursue any crimes that had been committed. They both
knew why these things were happening and who was be-

hind them but while Roberts went through the protocols of investigation no suspects ever turned up in any of these events.

At Phillip's urging, Roberts assigned patrolmen to keep watch over every member of the Gang. It did not help. In fact, as though a point was being made, one night the Fam Pharm Van was broken into and its contents spilled onto the street right in front of the pharmacy during a change in shifts of the police officers specifically assigned to watch the building.

Phillip was frustrated and felt personally responsible for the crimes that were being committed on his closest allies. He also feared that the backlash would continue and worsen as the days went on. He knew he had to do something to protect himself and his allies.

One evening he called Crotty at this home.

"Michael, this is Phillip DiMatteo. I'm sorry for bothering you at home."

"Mayor DiMatteo! How are you? Listen, not a problem. I've told you many times, don't hesitate to call me any time. What can I do for you?"

Phillip reminded himself that he would need to tolerate Crotty's phony pleasantries it if he were to get anywhere. "Michael, I'd like to have a private meeting with you sometime very soon."

"Private meeting? Well, well. A private audience with the mayor. I'm honored. To what do I owe this privilege?"

"Can we agree to meet and I'll tell you what's on my mind then?"

"Sure thing, Mayor, I'll drop by your office first thing tomorrow. Would that work?"

"No, actually, that won't work. I want to meet you off campus, if you know what I mean. Tomorrow morning is good but let's meet at the Downtown Diner around ten." Phillip knew that the diner would be almost empty at that time.

"Sounds ominous, Mayor. Sounds a little secretive for an

open-government guy like you," Crotty said. "Can you at least give me a hint of what the topic is? You know, so I can be prepared to help."

Phillip knew he was being toyed with. Crotty knew what this would be about and was likely expecting it.

"All right, Michael, I want to talk to you about the recent, shall we say, crime wave that's befallen the city. In particular, I want to discuss the crimes against some of my associates."

"Oh, yeah, sorry to hear about the string of bad luck. Funny how those things happen. I'm sure I know nothing about any crimes but if you think I can help, I'll be happy to talk about it."

"Tomorrow morning, then. At the diner. Ten o'clock. And, Michael, leave Kreider at home," Phillip said.

"I'm lovin' it, Phil. Mano a mano is my kind of..." Phillip heard Crotty saying as he hung up the phone.

ఌౝఌౝ

The Downtown Diner was a local landmark in the city and was the busiest place in town between the hours of six and nine a.m. but, as Phillip knew, by ten, it was always pretty much cleared out of customers until lunch time.

Phillip arrived at the diner shortly before ten, asked the waitress for a cup of coffee, and took a seat in the booth located back toward the emergency exit. The only other customer was sitting at the counter and took no notice of Phillip coming in.

Phillip sipped his coffee and mentally went over how he would approach Crotty about the backlash. He knew Crotty would be late just to prove, at least to his own petty thinking, who was really in charge. Phillip was determined not to be unnerved by this or any of Crotty's games. He had more important things to accomplish than playing one-upmanship with an oaf.

His singular goal was to see what could be done to establish a truce with Crotty. While he was not about to fall into the old Crotty pay-to-play trap, he felt that he at least needed to make an attempt to protect his friends from further harm.

At ten-ten a.m. Crotty bounded into the diner. "Hello, sweetheart," he bellowed as he waved at Donna Marx, the diner's waitress.

"Good morning, Mayor," Donna responded with a tired wave back. "Little late today, aren't you?"

"Mayor? Did you just call me mayor? Wait a sec there, good looking, that's the mayor over there," he said in an overly loud voice while pointing in Phillip's direction in the back booth. "I'm a has-been. That's your new mayor."

"Whatever," said Donna. "You want anything?"

Crotty stopped abruptly and looked back at Donna. "What I want from you isn't on the menu," he replied with an exaggerated wink.

"Come on, I got stuff to do. You want your regular?"

"Nope, nothing. I got no time for that. I've got an important meeting with the mayor," he yelled back as he reached the booth where Phillip was waiting.

Donna disappeared through the swinging doors that led into the kitchen, and the remaining customer left. Phillip and Crotty were alone in the diner, just as Phillip had hoped.

"Hello, Michael," Phillip began in as pleasant a tone as he could muster as Crotty reached the booth.

"Don't get up," said Crotty although Phillip had made no move to do so.

With difficulty, Crotty squeezed all 290 pounds of himself into the booth. Phillip smirked at Crotty's struggle to fit in the booth. As he looked up he remembered how the Gang used to refer to the Crotty "uniform." Every single day of his life, no matter what the occasion, Crotty wore gray pants, a white shirt that was far too tight at the neck, a navy-blue blazer with cheap bronze-colored buttons, and either a blue or red regimental striped tie. He apparently had two ties, one of the Gang members had once observed.

Crotty lost his pleasant demeanor as soon as he sat down. He was suddenly all business. "I got a feeling we're not here for the cuisine. What's on your mind, Phil?"

No one ever referred to Phillip DiMatteo as Phil, not even JoAnne or his closest friends. More games, Phillip thought.

"Do you want to have at it or do we have to pretend for a while you don't know why we're here?" Phillip started.

"It's your booth, use it any way you want. Either way, I'm all ears."

Hardly, Phillip thought, noticing Crotty's gut squashed up against the booth table. "Okay, Michael, I suppose play time is over. I want to talk about getting you and your thugs to stop the assaults you've orchestrated against my friends. I know you're a business man, so I want to discuss a deal wherein you stop harassing people who side with me."

"Well, I'm sure I have no idea what you're talking about, my friend." Crotty said, struggling to reposition himself in the booth. His previously coy and playful mood had disappeared. "But let's say, just for grins, that I did. Explain how me stopping something is a deal? That sounds to me like you get what you want, and I get nothing. Maybe in Italy, that's what you wops call a deal, but in the good ole' US of A that doesn't sound like a deal. That sounds more like you just telling me what to do. I don't think it's going to work that way."

"Maybe we should start by stopping the ethnic slurs," replied Phillip, unable to restrain himself. *This is not off to a good start*, he thought.

"Sure, sure, whatever," Crotty shrugged. "No offense. You know now that I'm no longer mayor, my political correctness skills are fading. Anyway, let's talk about your so-called deal. Let me repeat: assuming I did know what you are talking about—which I again vehemently deny—what would I get in exchange for me stopping those things which I know absolutely nothing about? You know, in order to make this an actual deal, how would it work?"

"Well, for starters, I could get Chief Roberts to abandon those leads he's following which will likely soon turn into related arrests and prosecution." Phillip was lying about leads but hoping that Crotty would not know that.

"Chief Roberts? Do you mean Jackie Roberts? The guy I like to refer to as Barney fucking Fife?" Crotty said incredulously. "Jackie Roberts couldn't find a criminal if you took him on a field trip to death row. Get serious, Phil. Don't try blowing that smoke up my ass. And don't tell me you dragged me to this secret meeting to talk about a truce and that's all you got. Honestly, now that I think of it, I'm more than a little pissed that you made me come all the way over here and that's your deal. That's your deal? You get what you want and I get squat? Jackie Roberts? Christ," Crotty said, shaking his head.

Phillip knew that he was foolish to think that Crotty would be intimidated by this bluff. "I have connections in law enforcement well beyond this city, Michael. I won't hesitate to turn this over to the state police. And I won't hesitate to get the news people involved in this either." He found himself making up scenarios as he went along. He should have been better prepared, he thought.

Crotty laughed out loud. "Oh, yeah. The state troopers are going to drop everything and descend upon the city to find some kid who threw a rock through a window. And they're going to call in the fucking national guard to find the skivvies old man Wheeler got stolen out of a locker." He was on a roll and kept getting louder. "The news people too? Oh no, not the cub reporters. When Jimmy fucking Olsen comes knocking on my door asking about prank ER phone calls, I'm gonna fold up like a cheap suitcase. I confess, Jimmy, you got me!" Crotty boomed, holding out his hands in mockery as though ready to be handcuffed.

"And if Jackie Roberts or Jimmy Olsen or Lois Lane don't get me, can Superman be far behind? What else you got, Mr. Mayor, city hall waterboarding?"

They stared at each other across the booth.

Phillip was ashamed at himself for allowing Crotty to so quickly and clearly take the upper hand. He instinctively tried to go back on the offensive. "I thought you said you didn't know anything about these crimes," Phillip said, struggling for some sort of comeback.

Crotty smiled smugly and squeezed himself out of the booth, slowly pulling at the lapels of his "uniform" jacket. He stood, menacingly put his hands on the table while leaning in on Phillip. In a quiet and sinister tone said, "You wanna know what I know Mister Big-shot Pisan Mayor? I'll tell you what I know. I know that you and your grease-ball friends had your fun in the campaign, and now you're going to pay the price for that. I also know that you've only begun to understand how big a price that is and already your sphincter is getting tight. That's what I know. The only thing I'm not quite sure about is how long it will take you to crumble. You will, you know, it's just a matter of time. You're not dickin' around counting pills in the back of your stinking tiny-ass drug store any more. This time you fucked with the wrong guy. You're going down, Phil, and going down hard. Now be sure to let me know when you've had enough. In the meantime, quit wasting my time with your bullshit threats."

As Crotty headed toward the door he threw a kiss toward Donna who had just come out of the kitchen.

"See ya 'round, Mayor," she said.

"Later, Dollface," he said with a broad smile. "And tell that lucky husband of yours that if doesn't treat you right, I'm coming to steal you away from him."

"Yeah, yeah, go on," Donna waved as though shooing him away.

Phillip sat motionless for several minutes. He knew that things had just gotten considerably worse.

Chapter 3

While Phillip struggled with the mounting problems at city hall, things at the Fam Pharm were difficult but manageable for JoAnne. Phillip tried to stay engaged in the business but, for all practical purposes, she was running it alone. In the early days of his term, he made a point to be home for dinner as much as possible and instead of reading the newspapers after dinner, they talked about the pharmacy business instead—never about politics. But soon even those conversations became few and far between. The enormous undertaking of managing a city in political turmoil and the continuing meetings with the Gang of Twelve took up almost all of Phillip's time and energy. He often had to skip dinner with JoAnne and, when he did come home at night, he had little energy to get involved with the family business. JoAnne knew this and generally just left him alone.

Despite, or perhaps because of Phillip's absence, the Fam Pharm employees—sixteen in all, including two other licensed pharmacists—were as committed as JoAnne to keeping the business thriving. They were all determined to pay back Phillip and JoAnne for the kindness and generosity they had always shown them. Everyone at Fam Pharm had worked there for years. Seven of them had never worked anywhere else. They relished getting more involved in the success of Fam Pharm.

In truth, over the previous few years, Phillip's role in the business had become more ceremonial than functional. He was the face of Fam Pharm, but everyone knew that JoAnne was running the business. This was especially true after Phillip was elected mayor.

After becoming mayor, it became Phillip's habit to come to the pharmacy at lunch time almost every Tuesday and Thursday to visit with everyone and to try to keep involved with its goings on. He tried to keep his schedule open on those days so that he could at least spend lunch time with them. On his way from city hall to the pharmacy, he would stop at the delicatessen down the street to pick up lunch for everyone, and they all genuinely looked forward to seeing him. Even employees who were not scheduled to work on those days often stopped by for lunch when Phillip was coming in.

He was their father-figure and their friend. They loved his visits. While they ate lunch in the back room, JoAnne worked the counter and answered the phone. She had everything under control, but already was looking forward to the time when Phillip could get out of politics and get back to the business and his extended family at Fam Pharm. "One term," he had promised.

After lunch on each of his visits, Phillip would spend a few minutes checking the store's receipts and going over the orders and inventory, which JoAnne meticulously handled.

Ostensibly, he was keeping an eye on things. He would open his mail, ask about customers and their health issues, and generally try to stay engaged. He would routinely complain about rising prices and how hard it was to make a profit.

JoAnne would say "Yes, Phillip" this and "No, Phillip" that and, in short order, ask, as only JoAnne could, "Shouldn't you be off running the city?"

Everyone, even Phillip, would smile an understanding smile when she said that and off he would go. They loved this little routine but, as the weeks went on and City Hall problems mounted, Phillip began spending less and less time at the pharmacy.

❦❧❦

On one such day in early spring, after going through his mail, Phillip simply walked out the front door without so much as saying goodbye to anyone. JoAnne and the staff all thought how unusual it was for Phillip, of all people, to do that. He was never, ever rude. They all shrugged it off, assuming he was just preoccupied with the ongoing turmoil at city hall. Knowing Phillip's every move and mannerism, JoAnne sensed a problem but, typically, knew that if Phillip wanted her to know something, he would tell her sooner or later.

When he returned to city hall that day, he brought back with him an envelope from the state attorney general's office that had come to him at the pharmacy. It was marked *CONFIDENTIAL.*

JoAnne had seen the envelope earlier in the day but gave it little notice, thinking it had to do with government issues and was mistakenly sent to the pharmacy instead of city hall. Such was not uncommon.

When he arrived at his office, he closed the door and re-read the contents of the envelope. It was what appeared to be a form letter from the Medicaid fraud control unit (MFCU) of the attorney general's office, informing Phillip that The DiMatteo Family Pharmacy had been randomly selected for an audit of its records. It specified that the unit was investigating what it called "widespread, systematic, and fraudulent practices that had been uncovered involving overcharging customers by certain pharmacies across the state." Specifically, it went on to say, "This practice involves an illegal overcharging for prescriptions covered by Medicaid resulting in higher amounts paid for such prescriptions, by both the Medicaid office as well as by customers who make co-payments as a percentage of the total charge." The letter reminded all recipients of their legal obligation to cooperate with investigators by providing any and all records of Medicaid prescriptions filled during the previous six years and that "Any attempt to impede the investigation or otherwise falsify or destroy such records is punishable by fine, loss of license, imprisonment, or any combination thereof." The letter instructed Phillip to await subsequent contact from the MFCU within the next two months as to when the investigation would commence. It closed with assurances that these investigations were routine and in no way a claim or suggestion of actual wrongdoing.

When he finished re-reading the letter, he slammed it onto his desk. "Routine, my ass," he whispered. "You son of a bitch, Crotty."

෴

Since his disastrous meeting with Crotty in the diner, the dirty tricks seemed to have centered on Phillip and away from the others. In addition to the incident involving the Fam Pharm van, the mailbox in front of his home had been run over by a snow plow, somehow his garbage was no longer being picked up, and the sign in the city hall parking lot which read *Reserved for the Mayor* had vanished. Their home phone rang so many times in the middle of the night that they had the number changed. He and JoAnne knew it was all harassment. JoAnne called it "hazing." She was good natured about it, but Phillip knew that she was concerned.

When the letter concerning the audit appeared, Phillip was certain that it was more of the same. It was just Crotty somehow getting a mid-level bureaucrat to harass him. But he feared that the "hazing" was getting more threatening and more serious with each passing day. He easily shrugged off missing parking signs and broken mailboxes. But now Crotty was coming after his business.

Phillip was not the least bit concerned about Fam Pharm being found guilty of any wrongdoing. He didn't know exactly what the audit would focus on, but he knew they would find nothing wrong. He did dread the thought of Jo-Anne having to go through a tedious audit process. She was stressed enough just running the business, he thought.

He wondered if he might be able to make this problem just go away. Maybe he could pull some strings somewhere. It would be at least two months before an audit would begin, so he chose to not tell JoAnne about the letter right away. He'd find a way to keep her out of this and take care of it quietly himself.

It occurred to him that he would soon be attending the annual meeting of the New York Conference of Mayors being held in New York City. From reading the conference registration materials, he knew that the attorney general was not only the keynote speaker at the opening luncheon but was also scheduled to hold a private breakfast the following day for first-time mayors. Phillip thought that since the MFCU was an arm of the state attorney general's office, perhaps he could have a conversation about this "hazing" with the AG himself. For the first time, he thought about using his "office" to make something happen that otherwise should not happen. "Fight politics with politics," he reasoned.

こうこう

Phillip found the two-day mayor's conference boring. The AG's opening speech was a canned litany of things he had done to rid Wall Street and the banking sector of corruption, and how his "posse" of deputies would make the cities of New York State a better place to live.

The rest of the day was no more than a series of receptions at which career politicians glad-handed, told tales of their personal triumphs, and drank too much. There were several so-called education sessions scheduled in an attempt to legitimize the time and taxpayer expense of the conference, but in fact very few mayors actually attended these

sessions. It took Phillip no time at all to see that this conference was a typical political boondoggle and a total waste of
his time. He quickly regretted not spending the weekend at
home with JoAnne instead of being there. He did, however,
really want to try to get the AG's ear the next morning.

He was greatly disappointed to find that the attorney
general sent one of his deputies to the breakfast meeting in
his place, citing a schedule conflict. As the deputy droned
on and on about ethics in government, Phillip thought how
it was the career politicians, not the newly-elected ones,
who needed the "Ethics 101" speeches. When the breakfast
session concluded, he decided to go back to his room, pack
up, and go home early. The only real reason he had gone to
the conference in the first place—to speak personally with
the attorney general—was no longer possible. He decided
that he would leave the conference, get home by noon, and
spend the rest of that Sunday catching up with JoAnne instead of wasting it in New York City. He called home to let
JoAnne know he was coming back. When she did not answer their home phone, he called her cell phone.

"Hey, Jo, it's me. This thing is a total waste of time. I
can be home in a few hours. What are you up to?"

"Oh, it's you. I didn't expect to hear from you until tonight. You're coming home? Good, I'm glad! I spent all day
yesterday at the shop and was just on my way back. I decided that since you were going to be playing Mr. Big Shot
with all of your mayor buddies, I'd spend the time cleaning
out the pharmacy back closet."

"My mayor buddies?" Phillip said sarcastically.

"You know I'm just teasing. I'm sorry you're unhappy
about how the meeting is going. I really am. Get in your car
and come home. I'm sick of cleaning out the storeroom anyhow, and I'd love to see you early. Let's have a date
night." They always referred to their rare quiet times together as "date nights."

"Deal," Phillip replied. "I'll see you in a few hours." As
he got into his car to drive back home, he was excited by

the prospect of leaving and of date night with JoAnne. But he also knew that he still had done nothing about the upcoming audit of Fam Pharm.

෴

A week later, Phillip bounded into the pharmacy on a cold but sunny afternoon carrying the box of sandwiches. "Anybody hungry?" he called out as he headed toward the lunch room.

The staff greeted him with their usual exuberance, and they had their normal pleasant lunch, talking a little about the business but mostly about the goings on in their personal lives, in which Phillip always took great interest. JoAnne took up her position at the counter while Phillip "held court" with the staff in the lunch room. He noticed that she didn't greet him with her normal hug and kiss on the cheek, but he thought little of it.

After lunch, as usual, he went into the back office to rummage around the business paperwork and open the mail. JoAnne came into the office and closed the door. By the look on her face Phillip knew that she had something serious on her mind. She sat across the desk from him with an envelope in her hand.

"There was a letter in today's mail. It was addressed to you but it got into my pile. I opened it by accident. It's from the Medicaid fraud control unit." She tossed it in front of him. "It's about the audit they're conducting here in two weeks. It said it was a follow-up to their earlier notification. What notification, Phillip? I didn't hear about any earlier notification. When did you plan on telling me about this? Since when do you not tell me about stuff like this? Tell me what's going on."

Phillip was stunned. Her questions were coming in rapid-fire fashion, and her tone was uncharacteristically aggressive. The audit notice had come far earlier than it should have.

He still had not been able to do anything about getting rid of the problem as he had hoped he could do. He should have told JoAnne about it, but he hadn't, and now she was furious.

"It's Crotty, Jo. It's nothing more than another round of harassment by those sons of bitches. This is no big deal, and I didn't want to trouble you with it. I was going to take care of this myself and keep you out of it. You know I try to keep you out of politics. This is just politics."

"No, no, no," she fired back. "This is business! We don't keep business secrets, Phillip. Maybe Crotty is behind this. Maybe it is all politics, but it's still business and you should have told me."

Phillip knew she was right. "I'm sorry," was the best he could muster.

JoAnne stood up and just stared at him for the longest time. Phillip didn't quite know what more to say.

"I'm sorry, Jo. I'm sorry this is happening. I'm sorry I didn't tell you. I'm sorry I got us into this. I'm sorry I ever ran for office," he said.

JoAnne just turned and moved toward the door.

"I'll deal with it," she said as she walked out. "You go save the city. I'll deal with it like I have to deal with everything else around here." Her words stung Phillip but he knew that everything she said was true.

⋇⋇⋇

The New York State MFCU consisted of hundreds of auditors, investigators, prosecutors, and support staff all funded almost entirely by the recoupment of fines and penalties from those found guilty of Medicaid fraud. So prevalent was Medicaid fraud in New York that the MFCU was the single largest unit in the AG department's criminal division. It investigated any and all known claims and suspicions of fraud within the Medicaid system which ranged from the largest of the so-called "Medicaid Mills" to smaller incidents, especially those which involved taking advantage of the elderly or the disabled. In addition, the Unit—as it was called—conducted routine and random audits of Medicaid service suppliers and providers, including pharmacies.

A typical audit of a pharmacy, depending on its size and the scope of the investigation, involved from one to three auditors essentially setting up camp at the business for several days and requiring the owners to produce any and all records, receipts, documents, or procedures they asked for. The auditors were well schooled at being matter of fact, uncommunicative and thorough. They knew what they were looking for and they knew how to find it.

The general procedure when they arrived at an audit was to inform the owners of the focus of their investigation and give them a list of required information which owners must provide immediately.

The owner was also required to provide a suitable and private place on premises for the auditors to conduct their work and be available throughout the audit to answer any questions that may arise.

On the day of Fam Pharm's audit two auditors, one male and one female, both in their mid-twenties and dressed in suits, arrived at ten a.m. at the front counter. Through the window of the back office where they had been nervously waiting all morning, Phillip and JoAnne saw them enter and were taken aback by how young they appeared to be.

"I've got ties older than them," Phillip whispered.

"Don't let that fool you. It's the young ones who feel like they have something to prove," JoAnne said as she moved out of the office to introduce herself and Phillip. The auditors each showed their identification badges and handed business cards to JoAnne and Phillip.

"Mr. and Mrs. DiMatteo, I am Colin Stanley and this is Sheila Albright. We are here to conduct an audit on behalf of the state Medicaid fraud control unit pursuant to the notice which you have received. If you would be so kind as to show us to where we will be situated, we'd like to begin immediately."

"Of course," JoAnne said as she motioned them toward the lunch room in the back where they would be temporarily housed. "Can I offer you any—"

"We're fine, thank you," Albright interrupted.

Young as well as rude, Phillip thought.

As soon as they had all entered the lunch room, Stanley informed Phillip and JoAnne of the scope of the investigation and assured them that it was routine. Albright handed JoAnne a preliminary list of the documents they would need to conduct the investigation. "This list," she said, "may or may not be all that we need. When each item is provided to us we will verify its receipt by initialing the bottom of the front page and one of you will need to sign a guarantee that none of required information has been altered or destroyed as a result of our inquiry."

"I'll need just a few minutes to get all of this pulled together. Shall I start at the top of the list?" asked JoAnne.

"Of course," Stanley replied.

JoAnne wondered momentarily whether "of course" referred to taking a few minutes or starting at the top of the list. *No matter*, she thought, as she went toward the back closet where most of the required records were kept.

"Are you sure I can't get either of you anything?" asked Phillip politely.

"No." Stanley said. "We'll let you know if we need anything else." Sensing he was being dismissed, Phillip nodded and went back to his office.

For two days, Stanley and Albright shuffled papers, took notes on yellow legal pads, and spoke softly into hand-held recorders behind the closed door of the lunch room. JoAnn provided them with everything they asked for and answered the occasional question about Fam Pharm procedures. Despite her frequent diplomatic inquiries as to how things were going, the auditors made it very clear to her that they were not telling her anything about their findings.

They revealed only that the audit was focusing on the practice known as "shorting" where a pharmacy purposely and repeatedly dispenses prescriptions a few pills short of the labeled prescription. Particularly with high-count prescriptions, the assumption is that the customer will not actually count the number of pills dispensed and not notice the shortage. Over time this results in more frequent prescription refills, which cost the Medicaid system millions, not to mention the higher prescription costs for customers who have coinsurance or copay obligations. JoAnne was highly insulted by the mere suggestion that shorting had gone on at the Fam Pharm and somewhat aghast that this was being done by any pharmacist.

Phillip decided that he would not just pace around while the audit was going on. JoAnne was perfectly able to—in fact better able to—provide the auditors with what they wanted and answer any questions they had. As the audit progressed, he busied himself back at city hall, having made JoAnne promise to call him if anything happened or at least when they were finished with what he began calling the "Inquisition." JoAnne was relieved that Phillip stayed out of the way. She feared his hostility toward the entire thing would somehow make things worse.

Late in the afternoon of their second day at the pharmacy, Albright came out of the lunch room. "Mrs. DiMatteo, we have a question for you, can we see you for a moment?"

"Of course, what is it?"

"Inside, please, ma'am."

When she went back into the lunch room, Stanley closed the door.

"Mrs. DiMatteo, we've asked you for the records of your filled prescriptions but you've only provided them for the past three years. We need to see six years, or more, if you have them. But at least six."

"Six? I only keep the last three years."

"You have many other records going back past that," Albright said.

"Well, for some things, yes. But I'm running out of space in the store room and there are just a million of these little prescription sheets. I've been cleaning out around here lately. I looked in the state pharmacy manual. It said we only needed to keep old prescription records for three years. I specifically looked that up before I tossed the old records."

Stanley leaned over the table to reach for a document. JoAnne could see the cover sheet. The document Stanley had in his hand was called the New York State Medicaid Program Pharmacy Manual Policy Guidelines. He flipped to a page that was marked with a paper clip and handed it to JoAnne. She noticed a section highlighted with a yellow marker. "The Medicaid Department has its own requirements, Mrs. DiMatteo," Stanley said tersely. "It's six. What you said is perhaps true for general pharmacy records but the Medicaid rules are separate."

JoAnne was panic stricken. Her eyes flashed across the highlighted section.

"In addition to the record keeping requirements in the general information section of this manual, pharmacies must keep on file the signed prescription or fiscal order for which Medicaid payment is claimed. These signed prescriptions and fiscal orders must be kept on file for six years."

Without looking up, JoAnne said softly, "I thought it was three."

After several seconds, Albright said, "It's six—six years."

Stanley removed his glasses and rubbed his eyes. "Mrs. DiMatteo, did you just tell us that you recently got rid of some old prescription copies?" He stressed the word, "recently."

"Yes, I just did it a couple of weeks ago. I thought it was three. Honestly, I thought the requirement was three years. I even looked it up," she exhorted again.

"And when you say, 'got rid of,' do you mean that they were destroyed?"

"Yes."

"And did you say that you did this recently?" Stanley pressed.

"Yes, just a few weeks ago. I needed the space...."

"Are you sure you didn't put them somewhere else where they can be retrieved—like in storage maybe?" said Albright, almost as though even she was troubled by what was occurring.

"No. Oh, God, I wish I had," said JoAnne who was by now noticeably flushed. "I boxed up about fifteen years' worth of old stuff we were keeping and had the shredder company come and get them. You have to believe me. I thought the requirement was three years. Is this going to be an issue?"

Albright was taking nearly verbatim notes of JoAnne's words on her legal pad. She stopped and said, "Mrs. Di-Matteo, according to your testimony, you said—"

"Testimony!" JoAnne interrupted, "Am I on trial here?"

Stanley held up a hand as though to calm the escalating tension. "No, no, wait. Testimony is not the right word. What Miss Albright was getting at is that you have apparently destroyed information that was a part of our investigation, and you did that after receiving clear notice not to do so. The original letter specifically outlined these requirements and the penalties involved. You just told us that you destroyed some of the records after you received that notice. I'm afraid that could be a problem."

"Wait, wait, wait!" JoAnne said in a panic. "When I shredded that stuff, I didn't know anything about this audit. Phillip never told me about this." While she was not actually on trial, JoAnne found herself testifying in her own defense. "It was an honest mistake," she said to no one in particular and began to cry. "I didn't know about this audit when I shredded those records. I thought it was three years. I swear it. I swear that's true."

"Are you saying you didn't receive the original notice?" asked Albright.

"Phillip received it," JoAnne said in a muffled voice as her hands were covering her face. "He didn't tell me. I didn't know there was going to be an audit. I didn't know the requirement was six years. I didn't know!"

Stanley and Albright said nothing in response and began to pack up their belongings.

JoAnne went and sat alone in a chair in the corner of the room. "What happens now? Where are you going?"

"Mrs. DiMatteo, due to this development we've gone as far as we can go with this audit. We're now required to turn this over to our investigation division. There is a different part of the unit that handles missing records. They will be in touch."

JoAnne sat with her face buried in her hands. Without saying anything further Stanley and Albright were gone.

මාමාම

"Mr. Hale, Mr. Watkins is on his way," the receptionist said to Phillip who was seated beside JoAnne in the waiting room of Watkins, Waldon, and James, LLC. Phillip had arranged a meeting with Attorney J.C. Watkins but asked that for privacy reasons, it be booked under the name of Phillip Hale. Watkins understood why confidentiality was especially important in a case involving a public figure like Phillip.

"JoAnne, Phillip, please come in," Watkins said as he entered the waiting room and escorted them into his office.

For more than twenty years, Watkins, Waldon, and James was the most highly regarded defender of every major case of Medicaid fraud brought by the Albany Regional Office of the MFCU. Watkins, in particular, had made a career defending these cases and was regarded as one of the best in the business. Even within the MFCU itself, it was conceded that nobody on earth had a better grasp of the system than J.C. Watkins, including the auditors and investigators themselves.

Watkins sat across from the DiMatteos at an impressively large conference table. "I've read the complaint and the statement that JoAnne gave to the investigation unit. I've also had a little off-the-record chat with some people I know at the unit."

"We've done nothing wrong, Mr. Watkins," JoAnne blurted out, "at least not on purpose."

Watkins nodded and smiled knowingly at her. "Let me start by saying to both of you that I absolutely believe that this was a simple clerical error you made, and your timing was nothing more than an unfortunate mistake—an honest mistake. We don't have to spend one second of our time here convincing me that you are anything but totally innocent."

"Thank you," they both replied simultaneously.

"The investigation people are writing up the complaint right now and they filled me in on the details. It's perfectly clear to me that there was no willful misconduct on your part."

"So," Phillip continued, "you can get this taken care of? If we need to pay a little fine or something, I understand, but—"

"Let me put this out there right now," Watkins interrupted Phillip in mid-sentence, "so we can all look at it the same way. If you were John and Mary Doe, I could pretty much guarantee you that, with two phone calls, I could have this matter resolved before nightfall. This clearly was a clerical error and not some attempt to purposely destroy records. You know that, I know that, and actually the unit knows that. But the problem is that your name is not Doe, it's DiMatteo, as in Mayor DiMatteo. And in the process of becoming Mayor DiMatteo, you have seriously annoyed pretty much every politician in the city of Troy. And they do not want this to go away. The higher-ups at the MFCU know that this case is radioactive. They can't be seen as doing anything to...shall we say?...accommodate a politician."

Phillip was shocked by this. Again, he had underestimated Crotty. "Are you telling me that Michael Crotty and his goons know about this? How in hell did that happen?"

"I don't exactly know," replied Watkins. "But I assure you they not only know about this, they've already let the unit know that this one is going to be watched very closely. To be honest, the unit people don't know what to do with this. They believe that JoAnne made an honest mistake, but the whole thing took on a new dimension when the records got destroyed after you got warned to not do that. When that happened, a routine audit quickly turned into a potential case of purposeful evidence tampering. It got kicked upstairs and, unfortunately, your political opponents were standing at the top of the stairs."

"Michael Crotty put them up to this, J.C. He's responsible for this. It's political payback! JoAnne did nothing wrong," Phillip cried out in frustration.

"Phillip, I have no doubt all of that's true," said Watkins in a calming tone. "I'm sure this was politically motivated but now that the issue of records destruction has come up, their little harassment game has taken on a whole new dimension, and they're going to seize that opportunity."

"Somebody's leaking this information to Crotty," said Phillip.

"I suppose so. But however that happened is not our concern right now. Right now we've got to minimize this damage and get out of this as best we can."

"What's the worst-case scenario?" asked JoAnne.

Watkins hesitated. He did not want to alarm his clients but JoAnne had asked him a clear question.

"By the book, we're looking at a significant fine, and as much as I don't want to scare anybody, you could lose your license. Worst case? We could also be looking at jail time."

"Jail?" Phillip yelled. "They're gonna put a sitting mayor in jail for mistakenly shredding a bunch of old prescriptions?" he asked incredulously.

Watkins slowly closed his eyes and rubbed them. "Phillip, it was JoAnne who shredded the records."

❧❧❧

Phillip spent the succeeding days in despair. This was all his fault, he thought. If only he had paid more attention to the business, if only he had told JoAnne about the audit in the first place, if only he hadn't gotten involved in politics. If only...

He essentially ignored the issues at city hall and canceled most of the meetings on his schedule, including two successive meetings of the Gang of Twelve. He spent most of his time alone in his city hall office, talking to no one about the dilemma he had put JoAnne in. He did not even tell any of the Gang about the audit, but they all knew something was terribly wrong. Phillip was losing his spirit, and everyone around him sensed it.

JoAnne kept up her regular schedule at the Fam Pharm, pretending that all was well. She was her usual pleasant self with the staff and all of the customers. She tried to act naturally, but when she was alone, she was despondent. She and Phillip barely spoke to one another.

Watkins had promised that he would pull every string he could with the unit to minimize the damage, but he reminded them that both Phillip's notoriety and public perception were weighing heavily on the outcome. While they waited, in hopes that somehow Watkins could give them the help they needed, things got even worse.

On a rainy Monday morning, Phillip insisted on driving JoAnne to the Fam Pharm. He didn't want to have her drive in the bad weather or have to get wet running from the parking lot into the pharmacy.

As JoAnne was getting out of the car in front of the pharmacy, Tammy Braman, who worked the counter each morning, came running toward the car with a rain jacket held over her head. She practically pushed JoAnne back into the passenger seat and hopped in the back.

"Jo, you and Phillip can't come into the shop. There are

two guys from the news in there, and they have cameras and everything. They won't leave. Did you see the paper today?"

They hadn't.

Tammy showed them a copy. The *Troy Register* newspaper had reported the entire incident of the investigation. It detailed how an audit had been conducted regarding Medicaid fraud, how records had been destroyed, and how Jo-Anne and Phillip could be facing indictment. It "speculated" that the indictment may charge the Fam Pharm, as well as the mayor himself and his wife, with fraudulently conspiring to overcharge Medicaid and its customers, especially the elderly and the poor. It also suggested that JoAnne may be charged with destroying evidence to cover up the conspiracy.

They were devastated.

They let Tammy out of the car and Phillip drove immediately to Watkins's Albany office. Watkins had seen the story and brought the DiMatteos into his office as soon as he heard them in the waiting room.

"I've already contacted my guy at the MFCU. I'm meeting with him in an hour. We've got to get a settlement, and we need it right away," Watkins said before Phillip and Jo-Anne even sat down. "The longer this story goes on, the harder it's going to be to get the unit to settle. They're still nowhere near getting an indictment, but we need to settle before the heat gets turned up any higher. This newspaper story is a huge problem for us."

"Like what? What kind of a settlement?" Phillip said. "And how did this story get out in the first place? Don't we have any right to privacy?"

"Obviously, your political opponents have a mole at the unit, and they also have a friendly reporter at the paper. This is all politics, Phillip. You know that. I know that. But your enemies see an opportunity here, and they've put the unit under extreme pressure to throw the book at you. They purposely got the press involved to tighten the screws even more. So they're breathing down the unit's neck, and they're also trying to apply even more pressure by leaking the story."

"You said we need a settlement. What kind of settlement?" Phillip repeated his earlier question.

Watkins felt terrible that he didn't think he was going to be able to help them any more than to negotiate a settlement in an attempt to salvage something. He lowered his tone. "We have to prevent an indictment of JoAnne, keep her out of jail, and keep both of you out of the poorhouse. At this point, I'm thinking any deal we can get that accomplishes those things is about as good as it's going to get. This is way out of control."

ℰↃℰↃ

As Watkins worked to mitigate the damage, the scandal proliferated. Alex Cord, the *Troy Register* reporter who had broken the story, kept the heat on with almost daily updates. Other news outlets were not able to generate any details on their own but Cord was clearly able to do just that, and the story stayed alive under his byline. Cord clearly had a source of information that none of the other news organizations had and was parlaying this inside information into his own notoriety.

Seemingly every day he was able to uncover and write about behind-the-scenes maneuvering allegedly taking place to extract the DiMatteos from their difficulties with the MFCU. J.C. Watkins was incensed that this information was being leaked and threatened the unit with a countersuit if the leaks continued. After the threat by Watkins, Cord's stories did not stop. They just became more speculative about the negotiations, still citing anonymous sources reportedly "close to these negotiations."

The more Cord kept the story going and insinuating that a political deal was being worked out, the harder it was for Watkins to keep the government from throwing the book at his clients. As time went by, Watkins sensed that he was running out of room to maneuver.

All the while, Phillip's ability to manage city hall was lessening. Those few allies he had soon began to distance themselves from him for fear of being caught up in this scandal. Besides being totally preoccupied by the scandal, Phillip genuinely feared that JoAnne would end up being the one who paid the highest price for his foolish foray into Troy politics. He kept hearing Watkins's words during the meeting a few weeks earlier: "Phillip, it was JoAnne who shredded the records."

He also flashed back to the day at the diner when Crotty guaranteed that Phillip was going down—hard—and that sooner or later he would give up. In his despair, he began to sense that that time had come. Nothing, he thought, was worth having JoAnne pay the price for his political lark. By attacking her, his political opponents had found his most vulnerable point. By attacking JoAnne, they had successfully made Phillip understand that he had had enough.

With his administration in ruins, his reputation in shamble, and with a growing fear for his wife's very freedom, Phillip called Watkins.

"Anything new, J.C.?"

"No, not since we last talked. I know both you and JoAnne said that the unit's original proposal was out of the question but just between you and me, I'm starting to get concerned that their next deal will be even worse for us."

"The newspaper stories are hurting us."

"Killing us, Phillip. I've complained to everybody who will listen, including the paper's editor himself. He's standing by the stories and the sources. Every time another article about our negotiations is written, the more hard-nosed the unit people get."

"We're not going to get out of this are we, J.C.?"

"Not without paying a public price, no. But I still think we can keep this out of court."

"I think it's time, J.C. The fine, the licenses, and city

hall. That was their proposed deal, correct?"

"That's what they put on the table last week, yes."

"No admission of any wrong-doing on our part and it's over. Correct?"

"Yes, in a nutshell that's their offer, Phillip."

"I'll talk to JoAnne."

"Okay. Good. And Philip?"

"Yes."

"Do it today."

ඏඏ

On the morning of June first, five months to the day after Phillip DiMatteo took the oath of office to become mayor of Troy, Alex Cord broke the story in the morning paper that the mayor had resigned. Cord's story did not miss the opportunity to note that the man who ran his campaign based on ridding the city of corruption had resigned under a cloud of suspicion that his resignation was part of a back room deal to save himself and his wife.

Citing his same anonymous source, Cord reported that while the DiMatteos admitted to no guilt in the investigation, in exchange for surrendering their pharmaceutical licenses and paying a fine of $250,000, the investigation would be closed and JoAnne DiMatteo would not be prosecuted for destruction of records in the matter. The story stopped short of saying that Phillip's resignation was a part of the deal but it certainly implied that it was.

The AG's office made no comment, except to say that it was an appropriate conclusion to the matter.

In a statement issued by the mayor's office, Phillip thanked all those who had supported him and indicated that he was resigning to spare the city any additional notoriety in the matter and to concentrate on supporting his wife during this difficult time.

The DiMatteos hastily departed on a trip to Europe, a trip that they had talked about taking for years but for which

they never had the time. Before departing, they left instructions with their accountant to begin the process of creating
an employee stock ownership program through which they
would transfer ownership of the Fam Pharm to their employees in exchange for a one-time payment of one dollar.

Chapter 4

The city charter contained provisions to deal with the resignation or death of a sitting mayor. These provisions were clearly designed to give the city council de-facto control over determining the next mayor. It allowed the council to set the date for a city-wide election to fill the unexpired mayoral term. It also allowed the council to put forth its own nominee for that election and to appoint an interim mayor. The shortest time period allowable between a mayor's death or resignation and an interim election was ninety days. Candidates not put forth by the council were required to submit a petition, signed by a minimum of thirty percent of all registered voters, sixty days prior to the election. Clearly these provisions were designed to make it virtually impossible for an outside candidate to get on the ballot or to have time to launch a viable campaign against the council's nominee.

The council wasted no time in seizing the opportunity created by Phillip DiMatteo's resignation. It was not only quick to act, but it was clearly prepared to do so. On the very evening of Phillip's resignation, the council held a special meeting. Long-time council president Danny Burgess had huddled all that afternoon with council members preparing for the meeting. He used his prerogative to conduct this meeting in closed session with only elected council members and Tom Abernathy, the city clerk, in attendance.

Every council member had been fully briefed beforehand as to what was about to happen and how it would happen.

Burgess made it clear to all members that anything other than unanimous support for the succession plan would be considered an act of disloyalty.

ↄ∙ↄ∙ↄ

The meeting lasted three minutes. The script had been followed to the letter. In three minutes, the council had regained absolute control of the city and undone everything that Phillip DiMatteo and the Gang of Twelve had worked to achieve, everything they had sacrificed so much for. All in three minutes.

When the doors to the council chamber swung open, Burgess led the members out to a small crowd waiting in the outside corridor, comprised mostly of council family members and aides as well as a few members of the media who were still playing catch up with this quickly unfolding story. Burgess stood in front of the group and held up both hands as though to quiet them. When he was satisfied that he had everyone's attention he said, "My friends and fellow citizens of this fine city, I wish to report to you that in exercise of the obligations that were unfortunately thrust upon us by the untimely and scandalous resignation of the former mayor, the council members have set a date for a special election ninety days from today. In addition, we have received the necessary support from this council to place the name of Michael Crotty in nomination for this election and have appointed Mr. Crotty to serve as acting mayor in the interim."

While this announcement came as no surprise to anyone in attendance, it was met with thunderous applause from all of the hand-picked attendees. Crotty, standing to Burgess's immediate right, sported a beaming smile and blew several exaggerated kisses at the crowd. Burgess whispered in Crotty's ear. Crotty nodded and stepped forward toward the microphones being thrust out by the media. He took a piece of paper from the pocket of his blue blazer and began reading.

"I am indeed humbled and honored by the trust the council has placed in me to bring our city back to its former prominence and to begin anew the process of making our government function on behalf of all of our citizens as we have done in the past. I can assure you that the climate of dysfunction that our good city has experienced during the past several months is now over and that, with your help, we can get Troy back on the right track. In the days ahead, I welcome your thoughts and ideas on initiatives that can guide us to a brighter future."

Crotty folded up the prepared statement, looked up and smiled glibly. Going off script, he added, "and to get us started back on the right track, I hope you will all join us at a little gathering being held tonight over at Excalibar."

With that, the Crotty regime was back in business. As well-wishers crowded around Crotty, the rest of the council engaged in a round of handshaking and backslapping. They were excited and delighted that normalcy was returning to their political way of life. The Machine had bounced back from defeat and retaken control.

A few local television and print media reporters converged on Crotty to get quotes to accompany their stories on the return of Michael Crotty. Among them was long-time city hall political reporter for the *Troy Register*, Alex Cord. Seeing Cord in the back of the emerging pack of reporters, Crotty yelled to him above the simultaneous questions being hurled his way.

"Alex!" He motioned to Cord to come forward. Cord made his way around the crowd and was greeted by Crotty, who took him aside and whispered in his ear, "Don't bother fighting this crowd of idiots and asking a bunch of dumb questions, I'll give you all the time you need later at Excalibar."

Cord smiled and nodded and extracted himself from the crowd.

"Okay, what do you want to know?" Crotty asked the remaining reporters.

The council members who were still present held their collective breath as they were all too well aware that an unscripted Michael Crotty was a ticking PR time bomb waiting to explode. The questions were shouted as cameras rolled.

"Have you spoken to Phillip DiMatteo about his resignation?"

"No, I haven't. This is all happening pretty fast. I'm as surprised as anyone by all of these events. But I'd be happy to meet with Mr. DiMatteo. I have great respect for him."

"You really didn't know that you were going to be selected by the council tonight?" came a question which seemed more like an accusation.

Even after years in office, Crotty hadn't learned how to avoid questions he did not want to answer. Instead of simply evading difficult media questions as politicians usually did, Crotty's approach was to just lie instead.

"No, no I didn't. As I said, this comes as a total surprise to me."

"The meeting didn't take very long. Apparently there was not much discussion of this behind those closed doors tonight," came another comment from a reporter.

"Sometimes doing the right thing doesn't take that long," commented Crotty, making no attempt to hide his smugness.

"Were you aware that Mr. DiMatteo was going to resign last night?"

"Well, let me just say this. Given the legal trouble that his wife was in, I'm not surprised he resigned."

"Are you saying that he had to resign to save his wife from jail?"

"I didn't say that, you did," Crotty said smugly.

"It looks like a plea deal may have been struck so that if the mayor resigned, his wife would not be prosecuted. Were you a part of those negotiations?"

Before Crotty could answer, Danny Burgess stepped in front of him and said, "Listen everyone, this is an occasion to talk about a new day for our government so let's all focus on Troy's future, not its past. The mayor and all of us up here are moving forward and have nothing to say about the previous administration's problems."

With that, Burgess grabbed Crotty by the arm and began to move him away from the reporters. It was clear that the impromptu press conference was over.

As Burgess pulled Crotty out of earshot of the reporters he said, "Michael, it's time for you to shut up and get out of here."

"Sorry, everybody, I can't answer any more of your questions. I don't want to say anything that would get Mr. DiMatteo into any more trouble than he already is in," Crotty yelled over his shoulder as he was ushered away by Burgess back into the now empty council chamber.

Once inside, Burgess closed the door behind them. "Jesus, Michael. Are you nuts taking reporter questions about the DiMatteo deal? What the hell is wrong with you?"

"Ah, shit, Danny, relax. I didn't admit to anything, and I'm never gonna admit to anything. I'm too smart for that. You and I both know what happened here, and I don't see anything wrong with letting everybody think it happened because that bastard DiMatteo and his merry band of assholes decided to fuck with us. If that's what everybody thinks, great! Maybe in the future people will think twice about crossing us."

"Dammit, Michael, we absolutely cannot get the press thinking we cooked this whole thing. We got our revenge on DiMatteo. Let's just take that as a win and not play any games that could backfire on us later. We won, Michael, we won! Please just shut up about it."

Crotty smiled and gave Burgess a playful slap on the shoulder. "Sure, Danny. Whatever you say. Now let's get out of here and go hoist a couple at Excalibar."

"Oh, and that reminds me," a clearly frustrated Burgess said. "What in hell were you thinking inviting everybody to Excalibar? You invited everybody to a party with TV cameras rolling. Now it's going to be all over the news tonight and it's going to look like we're celebrating DiMatteo's downfall."

"We are Danny, we are," replied Crotty.

Burgess just shook his head. "I need a drink."

On their way out the back door, a clearly euphoric Crotty said to Burgess, "Oh, hey, Danny. I had an idea about my first official act tomorrow. I'm going to order a new sign to put up at the end of the bridge that everybody will see when they come into the city."

"Sign?" said Burgess.

"Yeah, I want to put up a gigantic sign saying, 'Welcome to Troy where payback is a bitch.' What do you think? Catchy huh?"

෨෨෨

Excalibar was located on Third Street in the heart of the city about two and a half blocks from city hall. It was housed in a three-story turn-of-the-century brownstone with apartments on the upper three levels. The bar itself was situated in what was once the building's basement. It was accessed by stepping down four steps to an entrance door which was next to a large glass window that could barely be seen when walking by on the street. The window was adorned by a stencil of the name, Excalibar, appearing in a crude Medieval-looking typeface alongside an image of a knight, presumably King Arthur, pulling a bottle of beer out of a large stone. In the lower corner of the window it read: Brian Crawley, Prop.

The long, dimly lit L-shaped bar was vintage prohibition-era in its ornateness. Its dark mahogany surface was marred by time as was the brass foot rail. The view from the bar out the front window revealed only the legs, from roughly the knees down, of people walking by on the street.

In the months following Phillip DiMatteo's victory, the regular flow of Democratic politicians and hangers-on frequenting the Excalibar had slowed to a trickle. Somehow the bar seemed to remind the old guard of what they had lost. Those who did stop in on occasion did so mostly out of habit or just to say hello to Brian Crawley, the long-time owner. Michael Crotty had not taken up his regular seat at the far end of the bar since he lost the election. It was in that seat that he spent the night of his loss to Phillip DiMatteo watching the election returns on television. It was from that seat which he made the phone call to Phillip on election night conceding the election. The place simply held too many bad memories of an election, gone wrong, for the Machine faithful and Crotty in particular.

But on the night of Crotty's resumption of power, the mood at Excalibar reminded everyone of the good old times. It was no coincidence that Excalibar had been chosen as the site of the celebration. Insofar that it was once the symbol of Troy's former political power base, holding the event there was a metaphor for the political machine's return. To Brian Crawley, the events of that night meant that he was back in business too. In celebration of this, Crawley provided an open bar and a huge buffet in the back room.

While Crotty had publicly extended an invitation to everyone, clearly this was meant to be an insiders-only affair—a gathering of the loyalists. There were two "greeters" at the top of the stairs leading down into Excalibar who controlled access, allowing in only a predetermined list of party regulars, family and friends to enter.

Two of the first to arrive after the Council meeting events had ended were a young newswoman from the local TV affiliate and her cameraman. They were met by the greeters at the top of the stairs.

"Hi, I'm Liz Allen from TV Five news, and this is my camera man, Don. We'd like to get a little film for the eleven o'clock story we're airing tonight."

"Oh, sorry, ma'am," said one of the greeters. "I'm afraid that the legal maximum capacity of the bar has been reached. You can't go in."

"Wait, we're like the first people here," replied Allen incredulously. Her cameraman bent down to street level to look inside.

"There's hardly anybody in there," he said.

"Not so," said the greeter. "There's a big crowd in there already. You just can't see them all. It's a capacity crowd, sorry. City ordinance."

"Do you mind if I just go down the stairs to take a peek in?"

"Yes, I do mind."

"Why don't you just say there's no press allowed?" replied Don.

"I'm only going to say this one more time: The legal maximum capacity of the bar has been reached, and I can't allow you in. You should leave now," said the greeter tersely.

As the disgruntled reporter and cameraman started to walk away, Councilman Chris Doring and his wife arrived and were immediately waved in by the second greeter. As they went down the stairs, Liz Allen hurried back and said, "What happened to the legal limit? How come those two can get in and we can't?"

"Well you see, ma'am, there's a back door to the bar and two people just exited right after you two walked away so we let in two more—it happens."

"That's bullshit," she replied. "Let's go, Don, it's clear we're not welcome here. We'll just report it that way. That's what I'm going to report, you know," she yelled to the greeter.

"I don't really care what you report, lady," he replied.

As they walked away the second time, they noticed reporter Alex Cord walk right by them and say something to the two greeters. Cord was immediately allowed down the stairs.

"How does that happen? Isn't he a newspaper guy?" Don said.

"That's Alex Cord," replied Allen. "He's been a toady

for these creeps for a long, long time. If you write whatever Crotty likes to see in print, you obviously get access that real reporters don't get."

By the time the eleven o'clock news appeared on the Excalibar's television, the celebration had been in full swing for hours. Everybody was in a celebratory mood, none more so than Michael Crotty, who was holding sway in his reclaimed regular spot at the end of the bar. The crowd got quiet as the lead story began on TV. It started with excerpts of the DiMatteo resignation statement followed by a report on the appointment of Michael Crotty as acting mayor. The Excalibar crowd cheered loudly when Crotty was shown in front of the council chamber. Liz Allen reported on not being allowed into the party. She suggested that the event was as much a celebration of DiMatteo's demise as it was of Crotty's reassumption of power and that, in keeping with the secretive nature of all of the night's activities, the event was closed to them.

"And the bitch wonders why we don't invite her to come in to eat and drink for free," yelled out Crotty as the news story concluded.

Everyone cheered.

Crotty was, by then, quite intoxicated. One could always tell how much he had to drink by how loud he had gotten. It was well known that the more Crotty drank, the louder he got.

After the news segment was over, the party started to wind down and attendees began to stop by to say goodnight to Crotty before leaving. Crotty was disappointed that the celebration was over and urged people to stay. He was clearly basking in the new glow of attention he was getting. Nonetheless, the crowd was quickly thinning out after the news report aired.

Around that time, Alex Cord caught Crotty's attention and pointed at his wrist watch. "When can we get some time together, Mayor?" he said to Crotty.

Crotty had told Cord that they could spend some private

time together so that Cord could get whatever he needed to round out the story he'd write for the next day's paper.

During the course of the evening, Cord had spent considerable time alone at one of the booths in the back working on the story of DiMatteo and what had happened at the council meeting. But he wanted to get a few private moments from Crotty so that his story would again contain details no other news outlet had. It was getting late and Cord still had much work remaining to polish his story by the overnight deadline.

"Oh, yeah, Alex," Crotty said, his speech clearly getting more garbled as the night wore on. "Ten minutes. Gimme ten more minutes, okay?"

Crotty took up a position near the door to shake everyone's hand one more time as the bar cleared out. When only a few people remained at the far end of the bar and Brian Crawley was busy cleaning up, Crotty moved over toward the booth where Cord sat working on his story. Cord was startled by the noise of Crotty knocking over a barstool he was using to steady himself as he approached. Cord was not entirely optimistic that he would get anything useful from a clearly inebriated Crotty, but he was not about to pass up the private interview time he had waited all night for.

Crotty took off his blue blazer and hung it on the hook on the side of the booth as he plunked himself heavily into the seat. "So, amigo, some day, huh? Sorry it took so long to sit with you. Everybody's been bending my ear all night, you know? Let me make it up to you. Ask me anything you want, and I promise I won't bullshit you like I do the rest of your reporter pals. By the way, do you know that bitch reporter, Liz Allen? Who put the bug up her ass anyhow?"

"No, I don't know her," Cord quickly responded, not wanting to get into anything that would delay this any longer.

At that moment, Bruno Kreider, Crotty's long-time aide, saw the two together in the booth. While Kreider trusted that Cord would be discreet as he always was with things

Crotty said, he was especially cautious given Crotty's state of intoxication. He quickly went to the booth.

"Mr. Mayor, I think it's time we wrap this up. Sorry Alex."

Cord gave Kreider a disapproving glance. "The mayor agreed to give me a moment of private time, Bruno," Cord said. "I've waited all night for this."

"Yeah," Crotty said to Kreider. "Alex has been pretty good to us lately, Bruno, so let's let him have his fun too."

"I'll stay while you two chat," Kreider said.

"I don't think we need a censor," Cord said dismissively.

"Yeah, he's right," slurred Crotty. "Instead of sitting around here, go figure out how the fuck we're going to get home tonight. You're in no better shape to drive than I am."

Kreider shook his head and turned to walk away. "Five minutes," he said.

Alone again with Crotty, Cord returned to reporting mode. "Mr. Mayor, I'd just like to spend a minute or two rounding out some of the details of what happened today."

"Sure, Alex, sure. But let me first ask you, do you wanna know what happened or you wanna know what really happened?" Crotty said with a bleary-eyed wink.

Cord was well aware of Crotty's blurred state of mind but sensed that he was in a mood to be more forthcoming than usual, even for Michael Crotty.

"Well, sir—" he began.

"Fer Chrissake, Alex, just for tonight can you not be so damned formal? Let's just relax for once. Are we on or off the record here?"

"Well I don't really know. That's pretty much up to you."

"Listen, I've been feeding you juicy shit for a long, long time and I know that you are...what, judocious?...about what you write."

"You mean judicious. Yes, I am judicious about what I learn from you," Cord said, diplomatically correcting Crotty's slur.

"Yeah, jud-i-cious. What'd I say, 'jud-o-cious'? My mistake," he laughed. "Jud-o-ocious. I don't know shit about judo," he said and roared, laughing at his own joke. "Sorry, musta' been something I drank," he added, again laughing out loud. "Okay, let's get serious. I'll answer any question you have and leave it up to you not to write anything that makes me look bad. You're good at that, Cord. I trust ya. But make it snappy, goddamn Bruno is going to have a shit-fit if we take too long."

"Sure, okay. I'll make this quick," Cord began. "Let's start with the question that reporter asked you earlier about what you knew about Phillip DiMatteo's troubles and when you knew about them. Did you know DiMatteo was going to resign and was his resignation a part of a deal to keep his wife out of jail?"

"Of course, I knew. Of course, I did. I knew all about it!" Crotty said in an overly loud voice. "Look, Alex, would it shock you if I told you that I not only knew about it, but I cooked up the whole damn thing?" he said in a slightly lower tone.

"Cooked up?"

"Yes, cooked up." Crotty was clearly ready to brag about his accomplishments. He took a dazed look around him as if to make sure nobody was listening. Cord knew that even by Crotty's normal loose-lipped standards, he clearly was in the mood for braggadocio.

"Tell me," he said, leading the witness. "You said something about cooking up this whole thing."

"Me and Danny Burgess and Al Moradian and a couple of other council members set up DiMatteo and made him resign. We set him up and took him down. Then we greased everybody on the council so that we could make me acting mayor and hold the next election so fast that none of DiMatteo's wop buddies would have the time or the balls to put up a fight against us. Plain and simple. There, I said it. We cooked up this whole thing and it worked to perfection. Actually, it worked even better than we thought."

"What do you mean?" asked Cord. He had learned a long time ago that when you were interviewing somebody just dying to spill their guts you kept them talking simply by asking questions vague enough to allow them to say whatever was on their mind. Cord knew he was taking advantage of Crotty's drunken state, but he did not want to pass up an opportunity to get everything possible out of this interview.

"I mean. What I mean is..." Crotty's voice trailed off. He had clearly lost his train of thought. He looked like he was fading fast.

"You were saying how you set up DiMatteo and it worked out better than you even thought it would."

"Yeah, yeah. That's what I was saying. Anyway, you remember the fraud investigation of his rinky-dink pharmacy, don't you? Of course, you do. We fed you the goddamn story, Alex. You ran with it and we even fed you the shit about the deal. You even wrote the story in a way so that the deal looked like a smelly one. And let me tell you, my friend, you putting that in the paper and flogging it like you did kept the story alive. It kept the pressure on DiMatteo till he bailed like he was on the freekin' Titanic. Listen amigo, I'm forever in your...your..."

"My debt?" added Cord, leading Crotty to continue.

"Yeah, that's right. I'm forever in your debt. And that's why I'm going to continue to give you what you need to keep scooping all of those other dip-shit reporters out there. I'm going to make you a star!"

"How did it turn out better than you thought it would?" Crotty pressed hard, worried that Kreider would return and cut off the conversation.

"It turned out better because his wife fucked up. Now I don't believe for a second that she shredded those records on purpose, but it sure could look that way. That was a huge break for us. That, with your help, is what made a little deal seem like a big deal. That was a huge break for us."

"How? I don't think I understand."

"Let me talk real slow so you can follow this. I'm the one who got one of my pals in the AG's office to audit the DiMatteos in the first place but I was just doing that to bust his balls. Kinda' like we did to his buddies. You know the crank calls, the rocks through windows. Saba...saba..."

"Sabotaging?"

"Yea, sabotaging those beer trucks, shit like that. We were just trying to teach them a lesson. We were just screwing with them."

"We?"

"I told you, me and Danny and Al. And Ernie Weeks and Ed Cross were in on it too. We cooked up all that stuff. Remember that Watergate story with those guys doing all of that shit to Nixon's opponents? They called them dirty tricks. We love that shit and we even started calling them dirty tricks. Getting the DiMatteos' business audited was just another dirty trick, but it turned out that DiMatteo's ole' lady made a little boo boo when she trashed some records by mistake. When my inspector buddy told me about that, the whole thing just fell into place. I figured we could pounce on her little screw up. If I leaked the information to the press—to you—the story would stay alive. It did, and it sounded way worse than it actually was. After that it was a simple matter of making a few phone calls to make sure the AG's office wouldn't sweep this under the carpet, and the next thing you know, DiMatteo's falling on his sword to keep his wife out of jail. I told him a long time ago that sooner or later he'd regret fucking with me and that's exactly what happened. He got what he had coming, that's all. Thanks to a little dirty trick, a few political favors I called in, a little luck, and you helping to publicly drag DiMatteo and his wife through the muddy street, I took his ass down—like I told him I would."

Cord was stunned by all of this. Yes, Crotty had given him information about the DiMatteo audit and the legal issues, but Crotty and Kreider had been giving Cord access to inside information for years. He had no idea that Crotty,

Burgess, and the others had set the DiMatteos up. The real story was that this was all a vengeance plot to ruin a political opponent.

He sat silently processing what he had just heard. This was a political conspiracy and he had just gotten the head conspirator to admit to it—brag about it, actually. And then it occurred to him that in a way, he had let himself become part of that conspiracy by using every bit of information Crotty and Kreider had secretly provided him to keep the pressure mounting on the DiMatteos. It came as no surprise to him that Crotty and the others would stoop this low, but he felt sick to his stomach when he thought about being used to disgrace and ruin Phillip and JoAnne DiMatteo.

The only question he had remaining was not of Crotty but of himself. What was he going to do with this information? That was all he thought about as he sat in silence in the booth across from Mayor Michael Crotty who, Cord noticed, had fallen sound asleep in the booth across from him, still sitting upright, his chin on his chest.

The silence was broken when Brian Crawley came to the booth and shook Crotty awake. "Mayor, listen, it's time for me to close up, and you have a big day tomorrow. Johnny O'Keefe is waiting outside to drive you and Bruno home. Bruno asked me to come and fetch you."

"Johnny O'Keefe? Did you say, Johnny O'Keefe is taking me home?" Crotty perked up. "Oh, oh, Johnny O. That must mean it's time to go," he sang out. He repeated his little rhyme again as he extracted himself from the booth with Crawley's help. "Oh, oh, Johnny O. That must mean it's time to go," he sang over and over again.

Crawley helped Crotty out of the booth but with great difficulty. "Steady as she goes, Mayor," he said as he guided Crotty toward the door.

Before exiting Crotty looked back toward the booth. "Gotta go, Alex. And you gotta go write a story. Go easy on me, amigo. And don't write anything that I'm gonna have to deny tomorrow," he said with a wink at Cord.

Crawley helped Crotty into the waiting car as Cord stood outside Excalibar alone in the night. As the car drove off, Cord began the six-block walk to his apartment, thinking only about what Crotty had just told him, how he had been used to help ruin the lives of Phillip and JoAnne DiMatteo and to take down the mayor of Troy. The sensational information he had received just moments before was ringing in his ears. And now that he had the information, he had no idea what to do next, except to regret that he had ever heard it in the first place.

The story of the mayor's resignation, the scheduled special election, and Crotty's appointment headlined the following day's newspaper under the byline of Alex Cord. As usual, Cord's story contained certain behind the scenes details that others did not but made no mention of anything that he learned while sitting in the booth with Crotty.

There was also no mention of the fact that after filing his story, Cord sat alone in his apartment all night without sleeping, regretting that he had allowed himself to become a contributor to political corruption. He felt ashamed of himself, disgusted with Crotty, and horrible for being a party—however unwittingly—to the ruination of the DiMatteos. Little did he know that his anguish would grow far worse when, only a short time later, he would be covering the story of Phillip DiMatteo's death on Rackley Road.

Chapter 5

Shortly after Phillip's funeral the county coroner concluded that Phillip had died of massive internal injuries incurred in the train accident, and that his fateful crossing of the tracks at Rackley Road that night was more than likely the direct result of his drug and alcohol-induced night wandering. It was, in the end, ruled an accidental death.

Due to Phillip's prominence in the community, the tragic nature of his death and the unfortunate notoriety the Di-Matteos had gained in the Medicaid fraud matter, the coroner's finding was a widely followed local story. It even garnered some national attention.

The *Troy Register* filed frequent stories, all written by Alex Cord, on the accident and its aftermath and ultimately on the cause of death. It all was big news in the city, and the entire matter captured everyone's attention. The paper, which had a long history of coziness with the Democratic machine and had chosen to not endorse Phillip's Mayoral campaign, nonetheless published an editorial which praised Phillip, for his efforts to be of service to the city and called his death a tragedy, the likes of which the city had not seen in years. The overriding public sentiment was sympathetic toward Phillip, and even more so toward JoAnne. Most believed that the episode of the pharmacy investigation was completely overblown and that the DiMatteos were the only real victims.

JoAnne found solace in the knowledge that she and Phillip apparently had been exonerated in the public's view.

Certainly, the outpouring of public support at both Phillip's wake and funeral was gratifying to her. Still, she missed him terribly and was haunted by her own uncertainty as to whether or not Phillip's death was really an accident. On one level, that uncertainty haunted her—on another, she really did not want to know the truth. In her mind, either way, Phillip died at the hand of Michael Crotty and the political machine.

In the days that followed, JoAnne, like Phillip had before his death, became a recluse. She deeply missed him and her extended family at the pharmacy, and she even missed the day-to-day grind of running the business, all of which had given her life meaning and a sense of accomplishment. She was fifty-four years old, sad, and alone with her thoughts of what might have been if only they had stayed out of politics.

෴

"Jesus God Almighty, there she is!" JoAnne heard from the outside as she went to open her front door after hearing a knock.

It was Rita Russo peering through the door window standing next to Pat Bocketti. She opened the door without saying anything to her two guests.

As she entered, Rita continued. "Jo, you're scaring the crap out of us. You're not even answering your phone."

JoAnne sighed as they went into the living room. "I'm just tired of everybody wanting to talk to me about…you know…about everything."

Pat walked around the house, raising the window blinds. "Honey, you at least gotta get some light in here. Really, I know it's only been a week, but this place looks like a cave."

"A depressing cave, at that," Rita continued. "And that's exactly why we're here."

"Well, plus to make sure you're okay," Pat added quickly.

"Yeah, of course," Rita said almost apologetically. "But the fact is it's pretty clear to me that you're not okay, and you can't spend your days pacing around this living room. You can't be hanging around here day in and day out with all of these…you know…all of these reminders." Rita was trying to be gentle and choose her words carefully, which always was difficult for her.

JoAnne was used to Rita's abruptness and also quite adept at dealing with it. "Of course, I can, Rita. If pacing around this living room all day long is what I want to do, of course I can. And if I want to do it in the dark then I'll do it in the dark."

Rita shook her head in frustration. "You talk to her, Patty. Maybe if she hears our idea from you, she'll pay more attention."

"Idea?" JoAnne said. "What idea?"

Pat took JoAnne by both hands and gently led her to the sofa, where they sat facing each other, Pat still holding Jo-Anne's hands.

"Jo, Rita and I have talked a lot about this, and we think you should come live with us at The Settlement, at least for a while. It doesn't have to be permanent. Just try it for a while until things sort of calm down."

"Me? Come live at The Settlement? Oh, I don't think so," JoAnne said almost to herself as she got up and walked toward the kitchen. Clearly, this idea had never even crossed her mind. "I don't think so."

Rita followed her into the kitchen with Pat right behind. "We think it's a great idea. Don't we, Patty? We've been talking about this for the past two days, Jo. We love this idea."

JoAnne went to the sink and began filling the tea kettle with water. "I'm so rude," she said. "I didn't offer you any tea. Do you want some tea? I'm going to have some tea. Want some?"

Rita pressed on. "Oh, no. We're on to that old trick, sweetie. Forget the tea. Now why don't you pull some of your things together and head up the hill with us. We can get the rest of what you need later. C'mon, let's get it in gear. This is a great idea—and you know it."

Pat jumped in. "Let's slow down. We need to give Jo a chance to think about this a little." She moved toward Jo-Anne, took the kettle out of her hand, and put it back on the stove top. "This really is a good idea—good for you and good for us."

"Us?" JoAnne said skeptically. "How is taking in a total-ly depressed and ruined old lady good for you?"

Pat hesitated. "Well, quite honestly, I'm looking for someone else to live up there with me who will help me put up with her," she said with a wink and a smile that both Jo-Anne and Rita could see. She was always good at lightening the tension. "Will you at least think about it?"

"Yeah, at least think about it, okay?" Rita added, clearly slowing down her assault. "That's all we're asking. Just think about it."

JoAnne let out an audible sigh. "I don't know." After a long pause she offered a slight ray of hope. "You've really talked about this?"

"We have," Rita and Pat said simultaneously, sensing that JoAnne was at least considering it. "A lot," Pat added. "And we really like this idea, Jo. It's just the two of us up there in that great big house right now, and we'd love some company."

"We think it will be good for you, JoAnne," Rita said softly. "And we also think it will be fun. Believe me, honey, a little fun wouldn't hurt you right now."

"I'll think about it," JoAnne said. "Now let's have some tea."

᭒᭒᭒᭒

The Settlement was the name Rita Russo had given to her house. It was a 5,000-square-foot colonial-style home built on four acres of property in the Troy Hill Section. She and her former husband, Joe White, had lived in the house after having it custom built several years after they were married. They lived there together for less than three years before their legal separation and their uncontested divorce one year later.

Joe White was the owner of an auto dealership known as White Mercedes, which he always referred to as the largest Mercedes dealership in "the entire area." While the dealership was quite large and undeniably successful, Joe took great pains to never define "the entire area." His competitors joked that this meant the entire area between his ears which, given Joe's ultra-large ego, was thought to be quite large indeed.

Joe was a larger-than-life, gregarious fellow whom everyone recognized from the many White Mercedes TV commercials which aired in and around Troy for years. He "starred" in every one of his ads and always appeared sitting in or standing beside, of course, a white Mercedes-Benz. At the end of every commercial, Joe would be heard saying, "No matter what color Mercedes you want, get a White Mercedes." He thought that was enormously clever and was always quick to tell everyone that he had thought it up all by himself.

He was also known for the numerous donations he made all around Troy, all of which resulted in his name being prominently associated with them. There was the Joe White Little League Field, the Joe White Biking Trail, the Joe White Boat Launch, and the Joe White Town Park. He generously supported all of the Troy City Council members in their re-election campaigns, as well as the Democratic candidate for mayor. Joe White was the contribution darling of every political incumbent in every election—as long as they were sure to win. He also contributed to every cause that needed money, as long as he could somehow affix his name to it.

While most everyone thought of Joe as a self-promoting braggart, when Rita Russo met him while working as a cocktail waitress at Troy Bowl, she fell hard for his bravado and was thoroughly impressed by his willingness to throw his money around. Being a bowling alley waitress was not what Rita had dreamed of doing all of her life, but as a pretty girl who was adept at playing to the men around her, she made great money in tips.

White Mercedes sponsored teams in the men's leagues three nights a week and Joe liked to drop by Troy Bowl on nights when his teams were bowling. Even though he didn't bowl, on his way in he would slip into his own bowling shirt with *White Mercedes* embroidered on the back. He loved to hang with the boys and buy a few beers for his team. He especially loved flirting with Rita.

Rita, then in her late twenties, had seen the likes of Joe many times over but she secretly feared that spending all of her time in a bowling alley was not the best way to find her knight in shining armor. While she could see through Joe's bravado, she seemed nevertheless to be oddly attracted to him and always gave him special attention when he came in. He reveled in their coy banter and her flirtations. In return, he was a very generous tipper.

Deep inside, Rita knew that it was Joe's lifestyle and the excitement that seemed to accompany him everywhere that most attracted her. In truth, she enjoyed the "buzz" that he generated more than Joe himself, but despite that, they began dating. Joe treated Rita with a level of attention she had never experienced before and she loved it. After dating for less than a year, she said "yes" to his proposal to go spend a week in Las Vegas and get married.

She quit her job at the bowling alley and instead focused her life almost entirely on escorting Joe to the endless functions he attended. Joe was proud to show off his bride and, mostly to her quiet dismay, referred to her publicly as his "arm candy." At first, she was flattered by all of the attention he gave her and seemed fine with Joe's normal way of depicting her more as an escort than as his wife. She was pretty and she knew it and was generally happy to, as Joe called it, "glam up" for a night out. Joe thoroughly encouraged Rita to play the role of his sexy bride and even once tried to convince her to appear in one of his commercials draped across the hood of a White Mercedes clad in a white bikini. At that suggestion, she drew the line. "Hire somebody else to do that, Joe," she said. "I don't want to put some bimbo out of work."

For nearly a decade, Joe and Rita White were a ubiquitous couple out and about around the city. Privately, Joe rarely displayed any real respect or affection for her. He flattered her incessantly but deep-down Rita sensed that Joe didn't really love her—he just loved having her around. Their marriage was clearly one of convenience, but it seemed to suit them both. Secretly, they both knew that they were using each other more than in love with each other. Joe used Rita to show off; she used him as a means of lavish support and an escape of sorts from her otherwise dull life.

Thus it was a fairly easy thing for her to deal with finding out that Joe was gay or, as she technically gathered, that he was bisexual. But after she saw the pictures, she never again thought of him as anything but gay.

The pictures, four in all, were sent to her in an otherwise unmarked envelope. There was no accompanying note just an envelope addressed to her, marked *PERSONAL*, containing four photographs.

Each of the photos showed Joe wearing a bra, garter belt, stockings, and high-heels in a hotel room with a teenage boy who was wearing only boxer shorts and a broad smile. Each successive picture she looked at was more and more graphic, and more and more repulsive to her.

For most of their marriage, especially over the previous year, she and Joe engaged in very infrequent sex and few, if any, displays of affection. But that her husband was gay was something she never considered, and the photos absolutely shocked her.

It was one thing to find out that her husband was gay—it

was quite another to actually see graphic evidence of it in the photographs.

"Oh my God!" she heard herself say aloud as she stared at the pictures that day. The photos fell from her hand onto the floor as her mind went numb. But she was snapped back to reality when the phone rang. As things happen, it was Joe calling.

"Hey, baby, something's come up. I can't make it in time to go the Hart's birthday bash tonight. I'll call them and beg off. That party was going to be a drag anyway."

She could hear his words but thought for a moment that she was in the middle of a bad dream sequence, especially when he used the term drag to describe the party.

"Hey, you there? Rita, can you hear me?" he asked when she said nothing.

Her instincts took over and as though she was having an out-of-body experience she heard herself say, "Drag? Did you say it was going to be a drag, Joe? You mean drag as in no fun or drag as in fun?"

"What?" Joe replied. "Rita, babe, what are you talking about?"

"Ya know, drag as in fun. Fun, Joe, fun. Drag fun. Like you have when you get dressed up in drag to go out on a date with young boys. That kind of fun."

"Boys? What boys? What are you talking about?"

"The boys like the one in the pictures I just got in the mail, Joe."

Her words seemed to echo in his ear and were met by a prolonged silence.

"You still alive, Joe?"

"Oh, Jesus. Pictures?" Joe said, otherwise unable to respond.

"I doubt his name is Jesus. But I do know one thing for sure. I've never been so disgusted in my life. Two things, now that I think of it: I'm disgusted beyond belief, and you're not going to weasel out of this. The pictures don't lie, Joe. We're through."

Click.

Rita had always prided herself on being a survivor. She was also quite decisive when need be. As soon as she hung up on Joe, her plan to get him out of her life rapidly took shape. It was as though she had been planning this for years. Certainly, she had never foreseen this exact scenario, but she had thought before about how their marriage would end. Somehow, she knew that at one point or another—for one reason or another—Joe would do something to ruin their marriage. She had always assumed it would be over Joe's infidelity, just not with a man—a boy, no less.

Without putting down the phone after hanging up on Joe, she called the South Troy Lock Shop. "Artie, this is Rita White."

"Hey, Rita. Long time no. How's everythin—"

"Don't ask a lot of questions Artie, just do what I'm going to tell you," Rita quickly interrupted. "I need you to do this right away, okay?"

"Whoa, Rita, slow down. Do what? What's up?" replied Artie Costello, South Troy Lock Shop owner.

"I need you to stop whatever you're doing and come to my house right now. Bring your truck and all your stuff, too. I need to you completely change the locks on all of my house doors. And I need you to figure out how to kill the automatic garage door opener. Change the code, rip out the wires, whatever. I need this place secured."

"Secured from what? Rita, what's going on here?"

"Secured from that asshole husband of mine," she shot back.

"What? From Joe? Hey wait, Rita, you know I love you and all that, but I don't want to get in the middle of something between you and Joe. What in hell happened?"

"I'm sorry, Artie. I'm sorry to bark at you." She calmed her tone. "Look, this is between me and Joe, and I'm not trying to get you mixed up in it. But I need your help, dammit. Are you going to help me or not? I need my locks changed right now, and if you don't do it, I'll find somebody who will. If Joe gets pissed at you for doing this, I'll tell him I lied to you about our house being broken into or something. I'll take care of Joe. Will you come, Artie? Now?"

"Aw, shit, Rita," Costello said.

"You coming or not Artie?

"I'll be up in fifteen minutes."

Rita knew that in reality whether she changed the locks or not, Joe would not have the nerve to come home after what had just happened. He knew Rita well enough to stay away from her when she was mad, and she had never been this mad in her life. Joe was so unraveled and so afraid at that point that he wouldn't dare come anywhere near Rita.

But her instincts were to act decisively and aggressively. She knew that Costello would cover his own butt by telling Joe about changing the locks. He did a lot of business with White Mercedes and would probably call Joe immediately. She wanted Joe to know she was fighting back. She wanted to quickly put him back on his heels and keep him there for a long, long time. Within an hour, all of the door locks had been changed along with the garage door codes.

That evening, after White Mercedes was closed, Rita called the dealership and got into Joe's voicemail.

"Okay, asshole, let me tell you how this is gonna work. You give me everything I want, and I keep your scummy little secret safe. But keep in mind that if you don't give me everything that I want, I will make your sorry existence a miserable hell. Now pay attention because I am not going to repeat myself. If your creepy little mind gets confused by any of this, just replay the freakin' tape.

"Duke is going to pack up all of your shit from the house on Saturday. Call his cell at five p.m. and he'll bring it to wherever you tell him to. If you don't call on Saturday at five, he's taking it all to the dump. Don't you dare try to see me or call me—ever. It's over between you and me, Joe. Period, end of story. My lawyer will be in touch. Do what he tells you to do or, I swear to God, the disgusting pictures of you and your little boy-toy will be all over the internet, and I'll blow you and your bullshit business to kingdom come."

Click.

By the next morning, Rita had somewhat gotten over the shock of what she had seen in the photographs, although she would never be able to erase those images from her memory. Each time the thought entered her mind about somehow trying to forgive Joe, those images came back to her, and she became more steadfast than before. She quickly began to realize that she was not actually all that upset about having to end her marriage. It really was a sham anyway, she thought. In fact, having thought more about it, she saw this as a best-case scenario for her: get rid of what was bad about Joe—namely, Joe himself, and keep what was good about Joe—namely, his money. And once she got over the shock of the photographs, she was almost happy to learn about Joe's fancy for young boys. It somehow suggested to her that the lack of intimacy between her and Joe was not due to her own lack of attractiveness. It was a strange way of looking at things, she knew, but it somehow consoled her.

She was still not entirely certain who had sent her the photographs, although she had a good idea. For many months, if not years, Rita suspected that Joe was having an affair. Other than the occasional pat on her behind and harmless flirting, there had been little intimacy in their marriage for a long, long time. She had noted that Joe's late-night meetings "that can't be avoided" had grown more and more frequent and that he was always completely evasive in explaining their nature or any details.

"Just boring business stuff," he would say after his late-night returns back home.

While she didn't much care where he was or who he was with, she suspected they were dalliances on his part, and she had casually mentioned such to Duke Bennett. Bennett was an employee at White Mercedes whose prime responsibility was to take care of things at their home and to take care of whatever Rita wanted or needed. In the process, Duke and Rita became close over the years, and Rita considered him a loyal confidant. In mentioning her suspicions about Joe, she once asked Duke to let her know if ever he came across any information in that regard that might be "of interest" to her.

On the morning after her blow up with Joe, Duke came to the house to fix a clogged drain in the kitchen sink. Rita heard him enter through the back door and begin working on the drain.

"Hi, Duke, you're up and out early today," she said as she entered the kitchen.

"Lots going on today, Miss Rita. If you don't need me this afternoon, Donnie and I got a little side job we need to do."

"All I need today is to get this sink fixed, thanks," Rita said as she puttered in the kitchen.

"It's probably just a little clog. I'll have this taken care of in a few minutes. I'll be around all day tomorrow probably. I think I'm gonna clean out the garage and get a few other things done out in the shed," Duke said as he began work on the sink.

"Duke, speaking of Donnie, have you or your associates been taking any pictures lately?"

After a very long pause, Duke replied without turning around, "Pictures, ma'am? I'm sure I don't know what you're talking about."

Rita immediately sensed by his tone of voice and careful choice of words that Duke was being purposely evasive.

"Is Mr. White here?" he asked.

"Joe is gone and will not be returning, Duke. Not to-day—not ever."

Duke said nothing and continued to work on the drain.

Rita continued. "It seems my suspicion that he was...let's just say...playing around on me turned out to be real."

"Sorry to hear that," Duke said, again without looking at

Rita. It was clear to her that Duke knew exactly what she was talking about.

"Was it you who sent me the pictures, Duke?"

Duke stopped and finally looked at her. He got out from under the sink and wiped his hands on a towel as he thought about his response. "Miss Rita, you know how our deal works. You ask, I do. That's it. I never ask you why you want something done and you never ask me how I get it done. That's our arrangement, right?"

"It is," she said. "Yes, it is."

"I think it works best like that, don't you?"

Rita moved closer and gently grabbed Duke by the arm. "I do understand that, Duke, and yes, it does work best that way. I'm sorry I asked. But I want you to know that I had no idea how bad—how totally awful—this thing with Joe was going to turn out to be and now that I've found out, I'll forever be grateful to you for how you helped me with this and for how discreet you and your friends are. You will be discreet about this won't you, Duke?"

"Just wait a few minutes and run some hot water down that drain. It should be fine now. Let me know if you need anything else." As he headed toward the door, he stopped for a moment. "You don't need to worry about me talking about stuff like this, Donnie neither. We're both real good at doing what we do and not giving any details to anybody."

"I didn't mean to suggest—"

"Not a problem, Miss Rita. None of this is a problem for me. I'm just sorry it happened. Let me know if I can help out with whatever comes next, no matter what it is. You gonna be okay, Miss Rita?"

"I'll be fine, Duke. I'll be fine."

ↄﻉↄﻉↄ

Within a few days, Rita arranged to meet with a local divorce attorney named Carl Campbell. She was careful not to tell Campbell the exact nature of the evidence she had on

Joe. She told him only that it was adultery-related and that proof of Joe's infidelity was indisputable. Technically accurate, she thought. Perhaps her explanation was missing an important detail or two, but it was technically accurate.

At first, Campbell was reluctant to take Rita as a client against Joe. He expressed more than a little concern that Joe's connections with city hall and around town could become a problem for someone representing Rita against him in a legal matter. He was afraid things would get messy.

Rita convinced him otherwise. "Mr. Campbell, let me give you two good reasons why you should represent me. First, Joe White has a ton of money and, as I think you are well aware, is a creep. Given that, I would think that it would give you some measure of satisfaction to extract a bunch of money from this creep's pocket. Second, this is going to be a slam-dunk case for you. I assure you that Joe White will give me a divorce and anything I ask for. He's going to go quietly and do it on my terms. This is going to be low-hanging fruit for you, Mr. Campbell. Joe White is even going to pay your legal fees so don't be shy with your bill. He can afford it."

Campbell smiled. "Are you going to tell me what you've got on him?"

"That won't be necessary. He knows what I have and that's all that counts. Believe me, he'll do whatever it takes to keep me quiet about it. You'll handle this for me, won't you?"

Campbell rose to shake Rita's hand. "Should I assume he'll be using Alan Hotchkiss to represent him?"

"Probably. Hotchkiss handles everything Joe screws up."

"I'll get started on this right away. You'll hear from me soon. I'll call Hotchkiss. If you're right about them rolling over on this, once I get that sense from him, we'll talk about exactly what it is that you want."

"Perfect," she said. On her way out the door, Rita reached into her handbag and handed Campbell a sealed envelope. It contained the photographs.

"Here, keep this in a very safe place. It's everything we need to nail Joe White's ass to the door. I don't want it hanging around my house." she said. "We may need it someday but I seriously doubt it. Never open this unless I tell you to or I turn up dead. In that case, the killer's picture is in the envelope and the motive will be apparent," she said with a wry smile.

"It's that good?" Campbell said with a raised eyebrow.

"It's that good," Rita said as she shook his hand good-bye.

✂✄

In a quiet and amicable agreement, Joe and Rita White were quickly granted a legal separation and a year later received an uncontested divorce. Neither Rita nor Joe ever offered a public explanation. "Irreconcilable differences" is what they both always called it.

In the agreement, Rita received sole ownership of the marital household and all of its contents, along with a new Mercedes-Benz S550, ten percent of all future profits of White Mercedes, calculated and paid monthly and subject to audit upon demand, and "other considerations, cash or otherwise, which from time to time she may require to maintain the lifestyle to which she was accustomed." For her part, Rita agreed to never divulge any information regarding Joe which would serve to impair his business and/or stature in the community so long as Joe abided by all of the terms of the agreement.

Even Carl Campbell was totally amazed that White had so quickly and willingly agreed to all of this, especially the open-ended "other considerations" clause.

"This is a home run," he once said to Rita.

"Grand Slam," she said, "he's still getting off easy, and he knows it."

After Joe quickly agreed to these terms, the agreement was immediately finalized. Rita's first action was to take steps to reclaim the legal name of Rita Russo. Her second was to have the new white Mercedes S550 painted black. Her third was to order a large custom-made bronze sign to be affixed to the top of the gate guarding the entrance to the property. It read "The Settlement."

☙❧❧

On a cold snowy Monday morning, about a week after JoAnne had promised to give more thought to Rita and Pat's idea about staying with them, a Ford F-150 pickup truck appeared in her driveway. Two men emerged from the truck and noticed JoAnne peering out the front window from behind the curtain.

The driver of the vehicle, a round-faced husky man in his mid-thirties with short blond hair, came toward the door lifting his collar up against the weather. His passenger, an immense dark-skinned Jamaican of a similar age, waited inside the truck.

Before the man reached the front door, JoAnne had come to open it. "Oh, it's awful out there. Please come in and invite your friend in too," she urged.

"Aw, it's not so bad. We don't want to mess up your carpet," he said while stopping short of the doorway. "I'm Duke Bennett. Miss Russo said you would be expecting me."

"Yes, hello, Duke. Nice to meet you," JoAnne said while holding the door open against the wind. "If you don't want to come in, then just go around to the garage. I'll open the door. My things are all there."

"You got it," replied Duke as he headed toward the garage, motioning for the Jamaican to follow.

As the door opened, JoAnne met the two of them. "At least come inside the garage, it's cold and snowy out there."

"Ma'am, this is Donnie Moore," Duke said as they stepped inside.

"Mrs. DiMatteo," Donnie nodded his head at JoAnne as

he tipped the bill of his baseball hat. She felt dwarfed standing with these two very large men.

She pointed to a corner of the garage where four boxes were neatly sealed and stacked. "I don't have that much to bring. Rita said I really didn't need any household things. No bed or furniture or things like that, just some clothes and a few personal things. I'm sorry to drag both of you out on a miserable day like this."

Donnie immediately moved toward the boxes. Duke responded. "Really, ma'am, that's not a problem at all. And no, you don't need anything more than your clothes and things like that. Miss Russo's home is pretty well equipped."

"Of course," JoAnne said. She had been to The Settlement many times and knew that he was right. "It most certainly is," she said.

Duke just politely nodded. "After Donnie and I load up the boxes, he's going to drive the pickup and I'm going to drive you in your car to the house. The two of us came so you wouldn't have to drive in this weather. The roads are pretty bad. If you go grab your coat, we can get going."

"Oh, my goodness," JoAnne gushed a little. "You two are so wonderful."

"Let's get you out of the cold, ma'am," Duke said as he picked up one of the remaining boxes and headed toward the pickup.

As Duke and JoAnne drove up the driveway leading to The Settlement, she noticed the door to the three-car garage open. She could see Rita and Pat standing in the rear of the garage. They were waving and smiling as though JoAnne was an arriving dignitary. Duke parked JoAnne's car next to the black Mercedes S550. Donnie backed the pickup into the remaining spot in the three-car garage.

Rita and Pat were clapping their hands like schoolgirls as they rushed up to JoAnne's car. They both quickly hugged JoAnne and escorted her into the kitchen as Duke and Donnie could be heard bringing the boxes to an upstairs bedroom. On the table in the kitchen were three cups of tea and a small home-made cake with icing on top spelling out "Welcome, JoAnne."

"You two are unbelievable," she said with tears in her eyes. "I'm so grateful."

"You're gonna love it here, Jo. And we're gonna love you being here," said Rita.

JoAnne smiled and said, "A little while. That's all we agreed to. I'm only staying a little while."

"Fine, fine," Rita said. "We'll talk about that later. Let's have some cake."

They enjoyed their tea and cake. Duke and Donnie politely declined the invitation to join them and left.

Pat got up to start clearing the table and said to JoAnne, "You know, that's what I said too."

JoAnne gave Pat a quizzical look. "What?"

"That's what I said, too," Pat repeated. "I'm only staying a little while. That's what I said—what, Rita—five years ago?"

"Almost six," said Rita. "But who's counting?"

Pat playfully stuck her tongue out at Rita.

They all laughed and spent the afternoon arranging JoAnne's closet, bedroom, and bathroom. The Settlement was a wonderful place, and JoAnne felt lucky to be there with such close friends. In a way, she felt that by leaving her home she was leaving Phillip behind. In a way, she felt she needed to do exactly that.

That night she lay in her new bed surrounded by the comfort of her best friends living together in the same house. She thought how, for the first time in a month, she had spent the entire day without grieving—not once. For the first time in a long, long time she felt happy again.

Chapter 6

The Marconi Club was the name given to any number of social clubs scattered across America and other countries that were established in honor of the Italian inventor and Nobel physicist, Guglielmo Marconi, who was widely known as the inventor of the wireless telegraph system. At the time of the founding of most of these clubs, Marconi was one of Italy's most renowned men and his name became synonymous with Italian ethnic pride.

In the United States, Marconi Clubs sprang up during the waves of Italian immigration in the early part of the 1900s as a meeting place for people of Italian descent to preserve and promote their cultural heritage in the community. As was most often the case, especially just before and after World War I, waves of immigrants followed their ethnic forerunners to America seeking a new way of life; often settling in the same small communities, where they lived and worked mostly as laborers and merchants. Such was the case with the many Italian immigrants who came to settle in the southern part of Troy, New York. By the mid-1920s and for the decades that followed, South Troy was predominantly an Italian neighborhood where residents enjoyed what the new world had to offer, all the while staying true to their ethnic roots and customs.

Following the lead of similar neighborhoods across America, the Italians of South Troy established their own Marconi Club in 1935 during the height of The Great Depression. Its original founders, thirty-one Italian men in all, convinced the city to provide them with a one-hundred-year

rent-and-tax-free lease on a long-abandoned red brick
school house. They used their own meager savings and their
own highly skilled labor to turn the building into a focal
point for ethnic life in South Troy. For its part, the city encouraged the neighborhood development that the Marconi
Club and all the hard-working Italian families brought to
the area.

Fittingly, on April 25, 1935, the day of Guglielmo Marconi's sixty-first birthday, the South Troy Marconi Club
opened its doors with a simultaneous raising of both the
Italian and the American flags. Its first president, Alfonso
Giordano, read a congratulatory letter from Mr. Marconi
himself. In South Troy in the year 1935, the letter could be
read aloud in its original Italian language and be understood
by all in attendance.

While not strictly closed to others the club was, for all
intents and purposes, a men's club—specifically, an Italian
men's club. It contained a bar, a card room and a pool
room, and two sparsely but nicely appointed sleeping rooms
upstairs where regulars often "slept it off" rather than navigate home after a late night. The large schoolyard situated
in the back was set up for outdoor games of horseshoes and
bocce, and a large barbecue pit was erected for use at family
gatherings, held mostly on Sunday afternoons and holidays—most notably Marconi's birthday in the spring and
Columbus Day in the fall.

During the middle part of the century, the club's popularity grew. It became the center of activity in South Troy,
if not all of Troy. Over the years, it relaxed its men-only
attitude, and it opened its doors to women and to people of
all ethnicity. But its board of directors, still populated exclusively by Italian men, made certain that the club remained focused on its original purpose of propagating Italian heritage.

Throughout its history, the club served as not only a center for ethnic social life, but also one which aimed to give
back to the community through various charitable activities.

The club and its members were quite proud of these efforts. It maintained a standing group, known as the Good Deeds Committee, whose sole purpose was to consider acts of charity to be carried out on behalf of members and their families. Over the years the Good Deeds' efforts provided scholarships, funding for funeral and burial services, rent payment assistance to poorer members, and even some personal loans which often were never repaid. It worked with local vendors to offer discounted services to members who had become disabled or unemployed and even hired a mediator to settle community disputes.

The club was extremely well funded by local businesses and by membership support. And despite the fact that it became one of the more lucrative operations in the city, it benefited greatly from its rent-free and tax-exempt status. Over time it underwent a series of significant improvements, opened a fabulously popular restaurant, installed state-of-the-art equipment, and was appointed with the finest decor and furnishings of the time.

Through the latter half of the century the club's growth continued as second-generation members maintained its proud traditions and assumed leadership positions on the board of directors. While it still maintained its Italian roots and subtle ethnic biases, by the turn of the century, its well-advertised "open door" policy made the Troy Marconi Club the center of the social universe in the South Troy neighborhood and beyond.

ℰℐℰℐ

In the Spring of 2000, the club decided to employ Pat and Bobby Bocketti as a full-time management team. While the club had engaged many employees and outside vendors to run its events in the past, the business side was always handled by volunteers who served on its board of directors. The enormous success of The Marconi Grill—as its restaurant became known—the wildly popular and lucrative social and holiday events held at the club, and its very large membership base allowed them to afford to employ full-time managers to continue the growth and popularity of the facility.

Pat and Bobby Bocketti were the perfect couple to run the Marconi Club. They both were born and raised in South Troy. They dated throughout high school, were married in St. Paul's Catholic Church, and had an apartment above the Fulton Street Meat Market. Bobby was a cook at the nearby Red Door Restaurant and Pat worked part-time at the local consignment shop. Bobby's grandfather, Roberto Bocketti Sr., was one of the original founders of the club.

As co-managers of the club they also served as permanent hosts, managed the growing staff, and greatly improved the already very successful Marconi Grill. They employed a restaurant and bar staff along with others to help keep the place clean and maintain the grounds. They hired a bookkeeper/receptionist/restaurant hostess named Angie Zablocky, who everyone joked was selected just to prove that the place was really open to non-Italians. The club renovated the upstairs sleeping quarters, turning it into a fully equipped and comfortable apartment where Pat and Bobby took up residence.

For five years this arrangement allowed the club to rise in popularity and stature. The South Troy community became even more close-knit with the Marconi Club as its epicenter. Every Friday and Saturday night and on most holidays, the Grill hosted a virtual who's-who of local business leaders and common folk alike. Under Pat and Bobby's direction, The Marconi Grill was the most popular place in the area growing more and more so with each passing day.

Things all changed on a warm July night in 2005. That night the Grill, as everyone called it, had its usual large crowd for dinner and afterward at the bar. The packed restaurant included all of the regulars and the evening was, as always, being expertly orchestrated by Pat, Bobby, and Angie along with the weekend staff.

JoAnne and Phillip DiMatteo arrived around eight that night. Angie seated them at a table with Joyce and Anthony Mashuta along with Marconi Club President Jimmy Mariano and his wife Judy. Within minutes, Rita Russo arrived and made her way toward one of the two remaining seats at their reserved table. Phillip thought how much he preferred this seating arrangement to their former one when Joe White sat in the now-vacant chair. It had been three years since the White's divorce. Joe wisely steered clear of the club whenever there was a chance that Rita might be there. Nobody at the club seemed to miss his presence.

As was his custom after preparing the last dinner and while the wait staff was finishing clearing all the tables, Bobby came out of the kitchen to join the others who lingered at the bar. Pat let the regular bartender go home and took up her position behind the bar. To encourage patrons to linger after dinner, the club had what it referred to as Late Happy Hour from nine to ten with all drinks offered at half-price. There was a nice crowd that evening enjoying Late Happy Hour.

As was often the case, Phillip did not drink after dinner, but gladly encouraged JoAnne to enjoy the time by having one more glass of wine with her friends. He was happy to stay so that she could do that and, as he often did, declared himself designated driver for anyone who drank too much and needed a ride home. That night he had already agreed to drive Rita home as he often did.

At around nine-fifty, Angie had finished her work and came out to the bar. She handed Pat the nightly restaurant credit card receipts and cash and said goodnight to everyone. As she was leaving, Phillip said, "Okay, Rita, the last bus up the hill is leaving in ten minutes. Let's get it going."

"Killjoy," she said playfully in Phillip's direction without looking at him. Looking at JoAnne, she said, "Does he ever lighten up?"

"Now, don't blame Phillip," Bobby said, as he got up from the bar and made his way around to do last-minute clean-up so that Pat could start cashing out the bar. "It's closing time. You got room in your car for the rest of this crew, Phillip?" he joked. "Take 'em all with you. This joint's closing. Good night, everybody," he said as he began to wash and rinse the glasses in the bar sink. It was closing time.

After hugs and handshakes all around, Phillip, JoAnne, Rita, and the remaining four customers left together. Bobby went back into the kitchen while Pat stayed behind the bar to cash it out.

At about ten-ten, a few minutes after everyone had left, Pat heard the front door open. Unconcerned, she looked out from behind the bar, assuming she would see one of the regulars who had returned to retrieve something left behind. She did not recognize the man who entered.

He was a scraggly-looking, overly-thin white male in his twenties wearing cut-off jeans and a red tee-shirt. His wild red hair and wide eyes made him seem deranged. He raised his arm and pointed a handgun at Pat as he moved toward her.

"Don't make a sound," the man said in a low but menacing tone. "Shhh," he said while holding his index finger to his lips.

"Oh, God, no," Pat whispered. "Okay, okay. Here, I've got all our money right here." She was grabbing at the cash she had neatly piled in front of her as she counted the nightly receipts. She snatched up the piles and nervously placed them on the bar, then backed away. "Take it and go, please take it and go," she said in a hushed tone. "Please, it's all right here—all of it."

The intruder kept pointing the gun at Pat as he moved toward the piles of cash. At that very moment, the door at the end of the bar leading to the kitchen swung open as Bobby emerged drying his hands on his white apron. He had heard the front door open.

"Let me guess, Pauly's car won't start again. Am I right?" he said as he walked around the corner of the bar.

Pat stood frozen. The gunman was about twenty feet away as Bobby rounded the corner of the bar. Before another word was spoken and before even noticing the intruder, Bobby was hit in the chest by a single shot. Pat let out a scream as Bobby went down at the very spot where just minutes before he stood while enjoying a beer with his friends. The gunman snatched up some of the cash and ran out the door.

Bobby bled out on the floor while Pat held his head in her arms.

☙❧

The South Troy Marconi Club was never the same after that night. On the day after the shooting, the board of directors decided that the club would be closed indefinitely. Bobby's wake and funeral were delayed several days while a traumatized Pat remained hospitalized. She was unable to attend the wake and appeared for the first time since the shooting at the church for Bobby's funeral mass. No one in South Troy would soon forget the scene of Pat following Bobby's casket down the aisle with JoAnne and Rita holding her under each arm. St. Paul's Church, where Bobby and Pat Bocketti had been baptized and were later married, was packed for his funeral. Most of the local businesses closed that morning and every flag in the city flew at half-mast.

The entire neighborhood mourned Bobby's death and in the aftermath of the shooting, despite repeated efforts to find a way to carry on the "life" of the club, no one was able to imagine how the Marconi Club could continue to operate. Nobody could even foresee a time when they would be able to walk into the front door of the club without seeing the image of Bobby and Pat on the floor by the main bar, his life taken away and hers ruined.

With its beloved management team gone and its spirit decimated by the senseless murder of Bobby, the South

Troy Marconi Club was shut down. On the large panel of glass on the door leading into the club, a sign was placed which read:

The Marconi Club is closed for an indefinite period of time as we all mourn the loss of Robert J. Bocketti who was senselessly murdered here on July 24, 2005. We may reopen at some future date but not likely any time soon. May God bless Bobby Bocketti.

James Mariano, President

A short time after the funeral, Pat began the long process of recovery and life without Bobby when she moved into The Settlement with Rita for, "just a little while."

Chapter 7

It's open, Duke!" Rita yelled toward the front door of The Settlement after hearing the doorbell ring. She and JoAnne remained seated at the breakfast table while Pat sprang up and headed toward the coffee pot.

"Coffee, Duke?" Pat said even before Duke reached the kitchen.

"Love some," he said as he entered. It was nine a.m. and he was, as always, exactly on time. "Good morning, ladies. Everybody sleep well?" he said.

"Here, sit. Sit down," Pat said cheerily as she cleared a place for Duke to join them at the table.

He was there to bring JoAnne to her house to gather up some more of her belongings. It was to be the second such trip they would make since JoAnne moved in.

"I'm ready whenever you are, Miss JoAnne," Duke said as he sat next to Rita at the table.

He always respectfully referred to the ladies in the house as miss or ma'am. He referred to them collectively as The Ladies.

On more than one occasion JoAnne had commented on how helpful and polite Duke always was. "Why do I feel like I'm in a scene from *Driving Miss Daisy*?" she said, smiling at Duke.

"Oops, I forgot my little chauffeur's cap," he countered. "Should I go back and get it?"

Rita gave him a playful slap on the arm. "You just wish you were as good as Morgan Freeman."

"I think they're both wonderful," JoAnne said.

"Hear that, Miss Rita? I'm wonderful," he said, standing up and taking an exaggerated bow.

It had been a week since JoAnne moved in and, while she had never actually said it, as far as she was concerned, she saw no reason to go back to live at home. The Settlement was a beautiful and spacious home, and she was thrilled to be in the constant company of her best friends. Instead of living alone among all of the reminders of her past life, she now looked forward to the prospect of starting a new one amid such safety and friendship.

Pat and Rita had sensed her growing comfort level with this new arrangement. As JoAnne went to the closet near the door to get her coat, Rita followed her.

"Why don't we all go this time? That way, we can get everything you're going to need...you know...for a long time," Rita said. "Stay at least through the holidays, at least through Christmas."

"Yes, be with us for Christmas, Jo," Pat pleaded. "You can help us decorate. You always loved decorating—" She stopped herself, not wanting to bring up Christmases past.

"We were so busy after the election last year we didn't even put up a tree," JoAnne said softly, almost to herself. She looked toward Duke as she put on her coat. "Is it cold out today? How cold is it? I don't need a hat or anything, do I?"

Before Duke could respond, Rita pressed on. JoAnne had tried to change the subject but had not said no to the prospect of an extended stay. "Duke, you got time today? We may be needing to make more than one trip."

"All the time you need," he said without hesitation.

"Where did you find this man?" JoAnne said with a smile as she tugged on her gloves.

JoAnne had not said no. To Rita, that was a "yes."

"Come on. We're all going," Rita said to Pat.

"Well, if Duke has time and you two don't have anything better to do, fine. We'll bring back more this time," JoAnne relented.

Rita rushed toward the coat closet. "The three of us will go in Joe Black. You follow us in the truck, Duke." Joe Black was the name Rita had given to her repainted Mercedes S550. She thoroughly enjoyed naming things in ways that would annoy Joe White.

They spent the rest of the morning packing most of JoAnne's personal belongings to bring to The Settlement. She purposely left behind nearly everything that would serve as a reminder of the life she was trying to move past, everything except for a photograph of Phillip standing behind the counter of the Fam Pharm being handed a large cardboard cut-out key from his father—the same photo that sat on Phillip's closed coffin. She did not intend to actually hang the picture anywhere at The Settlement. She just could not leave it behind.

On their second and final trip back, JoAnne was quiet as she thought about some of the things she had not brought along. It occurred to her that it was more than things she was leaving behind. It was a former life. For most of the trip, this thought saddened her but as the car climbed up Congress Street toward the Hill Section and as her new surroundings came into view, she began to think more about her future than her past.

The car turned down a side road, and she could see in the distance the quaint old wooden covered bridge which crossed a small creek just a short distance from The Settlement.

For some reason, she remembered the Dr. Seuss quote which she had first heard many years ago as a child and which she so often had repeated to Phillip: "Don't cry because it's over, smile because it happened." She smiled.

As the car emerged on the other side of the bridge, Rita turned to JoAnne and said softly, "Nice day for crossing bridges, don't you think?"

Still smiling, JoAnne said, "Yes. I think it is."

ℰᴖℯᴖ

Life at The Settlement was better than JoAnne could have imagined. The initial feeling of being just a temporary visitor quickly turned into a sense of real belonging. Pat and Rita went about their own daily routines and left JoAnne to develop her own. At their urging, she gradually began to get out more. She took on some volunteer work, first at the information desk at St. Mary's hospital and then helping out at the South Troy consignment shop where Pat had once worked. She even began to go back to visit all of her friends at the pharmacy from time to time. To no one's surprise, JoAnne soon began to show up at the pharmacy once a week around lunch time. She would pick up lunch at the delicatessen on her way—just like Phillip used to do—and thoroughly enjoyed her visits with the staff who were now all part owners of the pharmacy, thanks to her and Phillip.

It had been a long time since JoAnne felt comfortable enough to go out in public without having the feeling that everyone was watching her and talking about her behind her back. With the constant support of her new housemates, the reassurance of her friends at the pharmacy, and the community overwhelmingly welcoming her back into it, she was re-energized.

While the three generally went their own ways during the day, they made a point of all getting together for dinner each night. They looked forward to this time together, during which they talked about their day, caught up on local goings on, and had light-hearted conversations about whatever was on their minds. On occasion, they would discuss matters related to running The Settlement—business issues, Rita called them. These discussions were Rita's way of trying to make Pat and JoAnne feel included. After all, it was her house and her money that was funding it all.

"I want to start thinking of what we need to do around here this spring," Rita said one night during dinner. "I know it's still a few months away, but we need to get a projects list going. I don't think that landscaper we had last year did a very good job with the cleanup, so maybe we should try somebody else. I also think we have to have the driveway sealed. And then, I was thinking of having a hot tub put in on the back porch. It would be a hoot to have cocktail hour in a spa." She stopped and waited for a reaction to her last suggestion.

Hearing the comment about the hot tub made Pat and JoAnne stop what they were doing. "Yeah, I can just see the three of us putting on our bikinis, hopping into a hot tub, and drinking cosmos every night," Pat said sarcastically.

"Is she serious?" JoAnne said to Pat as though Rita was not sitting right there.

"It's hard to say," Pat said.

"Good idea," JoAnne joked as she got out of her chair and began to pick up the dishes from the table. "But just get a small one, just big enough for yourself, right, Pat?"

"Okay," Rita finally said. "Okay, Jo. No spa. A pool then—let's put in a swimming pool!"

JoAnne didn't even respond to Rita's playfulness. It was clear she had something else on her mind. "This is as good a time as any to bring this up," she said ominously. "Can we talk about money for a minute?"

"We're not allowed to talk about money, Rita won't allow it," Pat said abruptly. "Believe me, I've tried that."

"Pat's right, we don't talk about money," Rita said as though to close the subject.

"No, really," JoAnne persisted. "I've been here for over a month and I've yet to pay a penny for anything. You two have been so wonderful to take me in like you did, and I love you both for that, but I feel like a freeloader. When do I pay my—my rent?"

"Oh boy," Pat injected while shaking her head as though to try to stop the conversation. "Jo, don't go there, trust me."

"But I have to pay something! Rita, I know you got this house from Joe, but it's got to be costing a fortune to maintain it. You've got Margaret coming in to clean twice a week, you've got landscapers and snow plowers, we have food delivered three times a week from McCarroll's Market, and some guy named Ozzie comes to pick up and deliver laundry every Friday. Who has food delivered to their house? Who has a laundry service?" JoAnne was getting more and more animated. "And what about Duke? He's like a valet, a driver, and handyman all rolled into one. Every single time we need anything done, he's here in ten minutes. How do you pay for all this? I have to pay something!"

Rita smiled in Pat's direction and then at JoAnne. "Okay, Jo, calm down," she began. "Of course, you deserve an answer and I certainly appreciate your willingness to contribute. But I'm only going to talk to you about this once, and once only. Pat will now be hearing this for the second time."

"I'll go get us all some tea," Pat said while leaving the dining room.

Rita got up from her seat across from JoAnne and moved to one right next to her. "Okay, let me tell you the way this works. Believe me, it works just fine this way. It will come as no surprise to you that all of this is funded by Joe White," she began. "Joe was quite generous in our divorce settlement and will continue to be quite generous. I can tell you that money is not, and will not ever be, an issue here. The only thing I won't talk about is why he was so generous. I will tell you, though, that it was in his best interests to be generous when we divorced and, more to the point, it is in his best interests to continue to be generous. And, Jo, in case you're feeling sorry for the creep, my generous ex is not going to the poorhouse any time soon. For some reason which I can't understand, people buy a lot of cars from him. They buy a lot of really expensive cars, and he can easily afford what he's paying me—easily.

"So, my dear," Rita concluded as Pat re-entered the dining room with three cups of tea, "that's how all of this is being paid for and that's how all of this will continue to be paid for. Like I told Pat a long time ago when she asked the same question and made the same offer, thanks but no thanks. Joe's picking up the tab."

With that and as though to end the conversation, Rita got up and returned to her regular seat at the table. Before she sat down she smiled broadly at JoAnne. "And that's why we should get a hot tub."

JoAnne didn't comment on Rita's attempt to change the mood. She still had something on her mind. "Can I ask you one more question about money?" JoAnne said shyly.

"One," said Rita. "But, if you ask me again about paying rent—"

"No, not that, but it is about money, and I've been meaning to talk to you both about this. Now seems the right time."

"Of course, you can," Rita said in a capitulating tone.

"Do you have a money problem, Jo?" asked Pat.

"No, no. Nothing like that. At least I don't think so. It's just that a few days ago, Julius Sloan called and asked if I could stop in to see him. I have an appointment with him on Friday afternoon. You know Julius, don't you?"

"He's the money guy, right?" asked Pat.

"Yes," JoAnne explained. "He runs the Sloan Group. It's that financial management company downtown."

"Wasn't he the money guy for Phillip's campaign?" asked Rita.

"Yes, that's him," JoAnne continued. "And he was also Phillip's personal money manager for as long as I can remember. Now that the will and trust are settled, he wants to talk about our investments."

"If there is problem, we can handle it," Rita assured her.

"No," JoAnne responded quickly. "I'm pretty sure there isn't a problem. In fact, when Julius called he made sure to tell me five times that this is not about a problem. It's just that, with Phillip gone, he needs me to make some decisions about what to do with the money. He asked me if I knew about Phillip's portfolio. I told him that I knew there was one but that Phillip handled all of that himself. That's what Julius assumed so he wants to talk with me about it going forward. He told me it was substantial. He specifically used the word, substantial. I'm actually glad he called, because I also have no idea what to do with the money from Phillip's life insurance. I got the check last week and just deposited it in the bank. I probably should invest it or something, but this is just one of those things that I always had Phillip handle."

"How much money are we talking about here?" Rita asked.

"Rita, really, I don't think that's any of our business," Pat admonished.

But JoAnne jumped right in. "No, that's fine. I don't have any secrets from you two. And I really do need to talk about this. I got the life insurance check this week, and it's a half million dollars. A half million dollars!" she repeated. "And I really don't know how much we have in our investments. I know Phillip has been dealing with Julius for a long time, but we never talked about it. I have no idea."

"Oh my," said Pat.

"Anyway, I guess that's my point here," JoAnne continued. "I have all that insurance money just sitting in the bank and now I think Julius is going to tell me there's a lot more. I'd like you two to come with me to that meeting. I certainly trust Julius but he's probably going to ask me what I want to do with this money, however much it is, and he doesn't even know about the life insurance money. I wish you two would help me with this. Can you come with me?"

"Of course, we'll come," Pat said instantly. "But to tell you the truth, Bobby and I never had enough money to invest in anything, so I don't know how I can help."

"Well, I'm pretty good at spending money," Rita added, "but I don't know much about investing. Can we trust Sloan?"

"Oh, I think so," JoAnne said. "Phillip certainly trusted

him for a long time. And Julius stuck with us during our problems when almost everyone else couldn't get far enough away from us. Yes, I trust him."

"Okay then," Rita said. "Let's go see what he has to say."

"Good, thanks. Thank you both," JoAnne said as she got up to finish clearing the dinner table.

"Now that that's settled, can we talk about getting a pool?" said Rita with a pretend whine. "And we can hire a cabana boy too!"

JoAnne grabbed a dinner roll from the basket and playfully tossed it at Rita.

❡❡❡

That Friday afternoon, Duke Bennett double-parked Joe Black in front of the downtown office of The Sloan Group. JoAnne, Pat, and Rita got out and headed toward the building.

"Call my cell when you're ready, and I'll pick you up right here," he said.

Julius Sloan had handled the DiMatteos' finances for nearly thirty years—almost exclusively through monthly meetings with Phillip. Throughout their marriage, JoAnne had taken care of the family finances when it came to banking, bill-paying, and household spending, but when it came to investing, she always let Phillip handle those matters with Julius.

She was aware that since the day he took ownership of Fam Pharm, Phillip had been a steady investor, regularly taking a part of the monthly salaries they drew from the business and investing a portion of it with The Sloan Group. As far as she knew, none of that money had ever been taken out of his brokerage account, but she and Phillip had never discussed it.

She imagined that if there had been a problem with the

account, sooner or later Phillip would have told her. He never did.

She had a fleeting concern that Phillip had perhaps drawn from the account to pay the MFCU audit fine, but she kept reminding herself that Sloan kept using the word "substantial" in describing the investment portfolio. Yet, she was nervous about the meeting. She felt better that her friends were with her.

"I hope you don't mind that I have my close friends with me, Julius," JoAnne said as Sloan accompanied them to his well-appointed conference room.

"Of course not," he said. "Rita, Pat, nice to see you both again, it's been a while." The last time they had seen each other was at Phillip's funeral.

Sloan was as devastated as anyone by Phillip's death. He was a member of the Gang of Twelve and had spent countless hours with Phillip during the highest and lowest points of his life. With Phillip now gone, Sloan and all of the others in his immediate circle, especially the Gang of Twelve members, felt it was their job to do whatever they could to help JoAnne get beyond this tragedy. Separating his personal love for Phillip and JoAnne from the business at hand was difficult for him, but he moved immediately into it after a few pleasantries.

"Jo, I would not have asked you to come here today if it wasn't essential that we talk about the portfolio that Phillip has left behind. You are now the sole owner. Rita and Pat, I hope you won't be offended when I make sure that JoAnne knows we'll be discussing highly personal financial matters today that I would otherwise consider private."

"Of course," they both said at the same time.

"Julius," JoAnne quickly interjected, "investing was always something I left to Phillip. I've asked my two closest friends to be with me today as I expect you'll be asking me some difficult questions. Please be assured that there is nothing I want to keep secret from either Pat or Rita."

"Thank you," Sloan said while sliding a report he had in

his hand across the table to JoAnne. "This is the year-end report summarizing Phillip's—excuse me, your—portfolio. As you will see from this report, Phillip was a wise investor. I only wish all of my clients were as conscientious and as successful in their efforts as he was."

JoAnne's eyes scanned the page, but it was just a cover sheet. She slid it slightly across to her left so that Rita and Pat could see it too. They all haphazardly looked across the page for the bottom line which wasn't there.

"Before we look at this in detail, let me explain to you how we operated. This will make more sense if I put it in context." With that, Sloan began a summary explanation of a process that he and Phillip followed for nearly thirty years. "Phillip was a remarkably disciplined investor. Years ago, he began transferring money into this brokerage account on a very regular basis. He started doing this soon after he took over the pharmacy."

"Yes," JoAnne agreed. "We thought we should invest a little bit each month."

"I was always under the impression that you were aware of these transactions, JoAnne."

"I was. But only to the extent that I knew he was saving for our future and what amounts he was investing, but we never really talked about the results very much. On occasion, I'd ask him how things were going, especially when there was news of the stock market going badly. But he would always say that the two of you had everything under control. It was under control, wasn't it, Julius?"

Sloan smiled across the table at JoAnne. "Very much so," he assured her. "Let me go on. At the end of every month, and I mean every month, he would make a deposit into the brokerage account. For the first several years that amount was five hundred dollars. After a while it became more, and then more, and then more. I presumed that as things went better and better at Fam Pharm, you could afford increased investing."

"I know that the monthly amount we put in went up over

the years but I honestly did not pay that much attention," JoAnne said almost apologetically.

"He did that every month, without fail, for almost twenty-five years," said Sloan admirably. "I know precisely the amount of actual money that went into the account because he had me keep track of it separately so it would not get mixed in with earnings which he always reinvested. Knowing exactly how much of his own money he was actually putting into the account was the key to his success."

At that point, Sloan took a note pad and wrote the figure $494,850. He turned the pad so it was facing the three ladies. "This is the total."

"Oh, wow," said JoAnne, looking wide-eyed at Pat and Rita. "That's a nice sum of money. And this report tells me where it's invested, right?" JoAnne said as she began thumbing through the pages of the report.

"Jo," Sloan said, shaking his head. "You won't find that number anywhere on these reports. That's the amount that, over the years, Phillip put in. That's the amount he invested over the years, not what it's worth today." Sloan paused for a moment to let this sink in. "What the investments are worth today is on the last page."

JoAnne quickly flipped the report to the last page as Rita and Pat practically knocked each other over, craning to see over her shoulder.

"Jesus!" said Rita. "Jesus, Mary, and Joseph."

"What—what?" Pat said, not being able to see the numbers. JoAnne stared at Sloan.

"How is this possible, Julius?" JoAnne asked, not really comprehending the figure she was looking at.

"That's what I'm trying to explain," Sloan went on. "Phillip's plan was ridiculously simple and incredibly smart at the same time. He was partly lucky, but mostly it worked because he was so damned disciplined. If you notice in this report, right now he's only invested in seven different stocks—seven. Over the years we actually purchased many, many different stocks but if their value went down, we sold them right away. As long as any stock's value stayed higher than the amount he put into it, we kept it.

"He would move money into his brokerage account at the end of each month. I would purchase for him an equal dollar amount in each of the stocks he owned or new ones he wanted to buy. I would then keep track of the amount of money he actually put into each stock, and that would become his stop-loss."

"Stop-loss?" said Pat.

"Yes," Sloan continued. "Phillip believe that over time one could do well in the stock market by staying invested in just a few companies that succeed, and that he could limit or nearly eliminate losses by selling others as soon as they stopped being profitable."

"Isn't that what everybody does?" asked Rita.

"No!" Sloan said emphatically. "Most investors speculate too much or try to time the market. They buy and sell—sell and buy. Phillip never did that. Most of the time we only bought more shares of what he already owned. Every so often, maybe once or twice a year we bought something new, usually a new company stock that we thought would have long-term success. We'd watch it carefully for a few weeks but would sell it as soon as the value went below his stop-loss—below how much he had invested. Sometime we'd only keep a stock for a month and then we'd dump it. His losses were next to nothing. And with some stocks, that never happened. Their values went up and down like all stock values do over time but in the cases of these stocks we've kept, their values never fell below the amount he had invested in them. Those are the ones we kept. We bought and sold a number of different stocks over the years, but we kept only seven through this entire process. He's owned this batch of seven for a long time.

"Each of them has been a huge winner for a long, long time. Remember, Phillip started putting his money into these companies in the 1980s and has been doing it ever since. He was buying Apple stock when it was selling for under ten dollars a share. And yes, the price of that stock has gone way up and way down over the years, but never has the total value fallen below what he had put into it. So, he never sold any of his shares. He just kept buying new ones and keeping track of how much of your money he put into them. Today that stock is worth about forty times the amount he put into it over the years. He's been buying Berkshire Hathaway for more than twenty years and he's never sold a single share. That stock alone has had an average annual gain of almost twenty percent. His stop-loss number never got hit on these stocks, so they were never sold. In fact, he kept buying them. Extraordinary discipline."

JoAnne was shocked at the numbers she was looking at but not by the fact that Phillip was a disciplined investor. Phillip was always disciplined.

"Perhaps we got lucky with some of these picks," Sloan continued. "But these returns are really the result of extraordinary discipline." He slowly rolled his chair back from his desk and planted his hands on the arm rests as though to let his words sink in. "And now, as you see at the bottom of page five there, the value of this portfolio is just a bit over eight million dollars."

"Oh—my—good—God," Rita said with her hand over her mouth.

"Million?" Pat cried out.

"Eight," said Sloan.

JoAnne looked up from the page at Sloan. She was expressionless but Sloan noted that her eyelids were blinking rapidly.

"Some time—not today, but some time—we should talk again," Sloan said with a comforting smile. "I know this is a lot for you to digest right now. But we should talk about locking in some if not all of these enormous profits. You don't need to speculate in the market as much as Phillip did now that…"

"Now that things have changed?" offered JoAnne.

"Jo, Phillip did this all for you. In our discussions I would often ask him about his investing goals, about what he was really trying to accomplish. He would always say the same thing. He'd always say, 'My only goal is to make sure JoAnne will be financially secure forever.' So now that things have changed, let's make sure Phillip's goal is reached. I think we should get you out of the speculation of the stock market and lock this money down. That way you'll have over eight million dollars absolutely secured for you, no matter what. That way both you and I will accomplish Phillip's goal once and for all."

"I couldn't begin to imagine how to even come close to spending all that money," JoAnne said.

"That's the whole idea," Sloan replied.

ᘒᘒᘒ

When they got to the sidewalk, Duke had the car waiting in a nearby parking spot. When he saw them, he hopped out of the car to open the doors for them. They all piled into the car, and Duke drove off. For the first few minutes, nobody said anything.

Rita broke the silence by starting to laugh out loud. "Oh—my—good—God," she said again.

"What?" Duke said. "Oh my good God, what?"

JoAnne was just staring out the side window in the back seat. She was still in shock over what she had just learned.

"I know what you're thinking, Rita," Pat said. "Go ahead. Go on. I know you're gonna say it."

"What?" JoAnne and Duke both said.

Rita turned around to look at Pat and JoAnne in the back seat. "Swimming pool and a hot tub! And a cabana boy"

"Only if I can help pay for it," JoAnne said with sheepish grin.

"Help? Oh no, honey," Rita replied. "This time you're buying!"

Chapter 8

A nor'easter is the term given to large-scale storms that occurred along the East Coast of the US and Canada. They were noted for causing severe flooding along the coastline and for their damaging winds. Anyone who lived in any of the northern coastal states understood that, when a nor'easter occurred during the winter months, it was best to prepare for at least a full day of blizzard conditions, followed by several days of digging out from the snow. It was not unusual for a nor'easter to leave a foot or more of snow along with sub-zero temperatures in its path. Since they were so large and followed fairly predictable paths, a nor'easter forecast got the attention of everyone living along the East Coast.

"Happy Valentine's Day, ladies!" Duke announced as he came through the door into the kitchen as Pat was making a large pot of beef stew. Rita and JoAnne came into the kitchen when they heard him arrive.

"I bought you ladies something for V-Day," he proudly announced as he plunked a big red heart-shaped box of chocolates on the table and handed a bouquet of flowers to Pat. "You ready for the storm? They say it's going to be big one. Maybe instead of flowers, I should have bought you snowshoes or something."

"You shouldn't have gotten us anything, Duke. We're getting a little old for Valentines," JoAnne added.

"Speak for yourself, JoAnne," Rita chided. "What are you doing here today?" she asked Duke. "I wasn't expecting you."

"I just came by to wish you a happy V-Day and to make sure you're ready for this storm. Could be a doozy. They said on TV this morning that we could lose power and all that. Are you all set?"

"We've got food, clothing, shelter, and now you, Duke," Pat said. "What else is there?"

"That should do it, Miss Pat. But seriously, I'm gonna put together a box of stuff and leave it right in the living room so you know where it is. You know: candles, batteries, a radio, stuff like that. You got bottled water, right? And I'm going to build up the fireplace so all you got to do is light it up in case you lose power, and I'll stack loads of wood on the side over there. Matches, you'll need matches," Duke said while rummaging through his coat pockets. "Now if you need anything you don't have in the house right now, just say so pretty soon so I can go and get it for you in time. We need some matches," Duke said, continuing his hurried preparations.

"I think we're all good here, Duke," said Rita. "Pat? Jo? Need anything?"

"It's already started snowing," said JoAnne, looking out the kitchen window.

"Oh, boy, they said it wouldn't get here until later," Duke could be heard saying as he headed out to the garage to get firewood. He came back carrying a large pile. "That wind is whipping up already. I gotta get a move on and get off this hill before it gets worse. I swear, the weather is a lot worse up here than downtown," he said as the wind began to rattle the windows. He began stacking the wood in the fireplace.

Pat, still looking out the window at the front driveway, yelled from the next room. "Why don't you just stay here tonight, Duke? It's snowing already."

"No, but thanks, Miss Pat," Duke replied. I'll get back down the hill okay. The pickup is pretty good in the snow. I got a little time before it starts piling up too bad."

Rita, having heard Pat's suggestion, walked toward

Duke as he finished stacking the logs. "That's a good idea! Stay here tonight, why don't you? It's already snowing like mad out there."

"No, really, I've driven in a lot worse than this. I'll be fine."

By then Pat and JoAnne had joined them in the living room. JoAnne looked at Rita and was rapidly nodding her head as though to encourage Rita to have Duke stay.

"Okay," Rita continued. "But let me ask you something. If I told you that we all wanted you to stay with us tonight during this storm in case we needed help with something, would you do it?"

Duke got up from in front of the fireplace and brushed his hands together. "Well…"

"We really would feel better if you stayed with us during this storm. You never know what's going to happen," Rita added. "And besides, we're going to need you first thing tomorrow to help us dig out. Why not just park your truck in the garage right now and sit out the storm with us? We've got lots of room."

Pat jumped right in. "I've got a huge pot of beef stew on the stove. Wouldn't you rather have a nice dinner with us than go back out in this?"

"And we'll sit around the fire. We'll drink some brandy tonight," said JoAnne. "Besides, it's time I get to know you better anyhow and what better time than during a blizzard? Stay, Duke. Stay with us tonight."

It actually all sounded good to Duke. He had nowhere else to go that night and always hated having to dig out his truck from the city streets after snow storms.

"If you ladies insist…" he said.

"We insist!" Rita, Pat and JoAnne all said simultaneously

ෙෙෙ

As the storm intensified outside, Duke and the ladies enjoyed dinner around a candlelit table. This was a rare and welcomed treat for Duke who otherwise lived alone in a small apartment in the city. He was grateful for the company and the nice meal and quite happy to not be sitting out the storm alone in his small apartment. He mentioned several times how great it would be to not have to shovel his truck out in the morning. He wished that he was dressed a little better as he was being hosted by the ladies in such nice surroundings. The ladies were not concerned in the least about Duke's appearance. They were genuinely glad he stayed, and they all felt safer that he was with them during the storm.

After dinner, Rita arranged four chairs near the fireplace. Duke lit the fire and JoAnne poured four glasses of brandy. As they sat in a semi-circle facing the fireplace, the conversation remained lighthearted. The wind was howling outside as they talked about spring projects at The Settlement, Jo-Anne's volunteer work, Duke's life in a small apartment in downtown Troy and, of course, the nor'easter. The conversation was occasionally interrupted by periods of silence as they sipped their brandy and stared at the fire while the wind howled outside.

It was early evening as JoAnne got up and reached for the brandy bottle. "One more?" she asked.

"One, just one more for me," answered Pat. "Three is my limit."

"I don't have a limit," offered Rita.

Duke got up. "Sure. I'm not going anywhere. Should I crank up the fire again?"

"Absolutely," declared Rita.

Duke went to the garage and came back with another arm full of firewood. After pouring another round of brandy into each of their glasses, JoAnne settled back into her chair. As they watched while Duke rebuild the fire, she said, "Rita, where did you find this man?"

"Who me?" Duke said.

"Yes, you. I've been here now…what?…a couple of

months? Almost every day you appear out of nowhere and drive us where we need to go, deliver whatever we need delivered, fix anything that needs fixing, take care of the property, you name it. Then you disappear for a while and come back any time any of us needs anything. Today when we're getting hit with a huge snow storm, you show up to take care of us. Rita, where did you find this man?"

Rita looked at Duke and smiled a knowing smile. "Shall I tell her where I found you, or will you, Duke?"

"Aw, you're a much better story teller than I am, ma'am. Besides, I'm afraid the brandy will make me say something I maybe shouldn't."

"Oh, come on. No secrets. I thought we agreed we'd have no secrets," JoAnne added somewhat playfully.

Rita quickly jumped in. "You're right, Jo, no secrets. But Duke likes it better when not everything about him is known to everybody. Right, Duke?"

"Well, yeah, sort of but I don't want Miss JoAnne thinking I'm some sort of suspicious character."

"But you are some sort of a suspicious character, Duke," Pat said. "I mean that in a good way, though. I think you like being a little suspicious—in a good way—and honestly I like that about you too."

"Sometimes it's better that way," he said. "Isn't that so, Miss Rita?"

Rita winked at Duke and said to JoAnne, "Well, if you must know I actually didn't find Duke—Joe White found him. Long story short, Duke worked for Joe at the dealership, and I stole him away. There, did I miss anything?"

"I'm fine if you want to leave it at that," Duke said.

"Not so fast," said JoAnne. "I want to hear it all. I've got all night."

"Fine, if you insist," Rita said, pretending to be exasperated before continuing. "As you are well aware, Duke here is the guy who keeps The Settlement going."

"I learned that right away," JoAnne agreed.

"He keeps it supplied and in good shape. He keeps all of

us safe, like he's doing tonight—thank you very much, Duke," she said, nodding in his direction. Pat and JoAnne playfully clapped their hands in agreement.

"My pleasure, I'm sure," he said as he took a fake bow.

"As I was saying, Duke is not only great for The Settlement, he was actually a part of the settlement, that is, my settlement with my former husband. Duke worked for Joe and part of his job was to help around this house since Joe was always too busy or otherwise incapable of doing what needed to be done around here. Frankly, I found it way better to have Duke around than Joe, so when we divorced, I insisted that I get to keep Duke as part of the agreement. Joe pays him to take care of us and The Settlement. It's a perfect situation."

"That's incredible! That's the best deal I've ever heard of," said a clearly impressed JoAnne. "So, you actually work for White Mercedes?"

Duke nodded. "Well, yes and no. I get paid by White Mercedes but I really only work for Miss Rita and now you and Miss Pat."

"You don't even have to show up at White Mercedes?" asked JoAnne.

Duke smirked a little. "Well, that's not exactly right. Actually, I do go to White Mercedes every now and then to have Joe Black serviced and the tires rotated. Oh, and to pick up my paycheck."

"Even that's on Joe. Even the car service is free!" Pat yelled out for emphasis. "Do you believe that?"

"I gotta hand it to you, Rita, that's brilliant!" said JoAnne, still amazed by this arrangement.

"Hell hath no fury like a woman scorned," replied Rita.

"I should say so," agreed JoAnne. "I think this is a wonderful arrangement."

"Oh, so do I," Duke added, "I tell all of my buddies that I'm on retainer like some hot-shot lawyer.'"

"How does it feel to be a kept man?" Rita said playfully.

"Works for me," he said.

A howling wind and the sound of sleet on the windows caught their attention and temporarily reminded them of the raging nor'easter outside.

Duke moved toward the fire to rearrange the logs. He abruptly stopped and turned toward JoAnne. Clearly something had occurred to him.

"Now, Miss JoAnne, I don't want you to think I'm lazy 'cause I'm not here all the time. I don't want you to think I'm just lying around whenever I'm not here."

"Of course not," she assured him. But she really did not know what else he might be doing when he wasn't at the house.

"No, really. I do a lot of, you know, side work. Whenever I'm not needed here or not doing something for you ladies, I keep pretty busy doing side work."

"Of course, you do," JoAnne said although instantly realizing that she had sounded a bit patronizing.

Sensing the same, Duke persisted. "No, really. I have a couple of buddies. One works construction and the other used to be a tugboat guy but he retired early. We work together doing side jobs that we drum up however we can. We work as a team. But we have an understanding: for me, my work for Miss Rita takes precedence over any side jobs. So whenever I'm needed—here I am!"

"You and your buddies you do what? Things like construction jobs?" JoAnne asked.

"Well, yes, sort of," Duke said while giving an odd look toward Rita that JoAnne did not notice. Rita just gave Duke a quick head shake as if to tell Duke not to go there.

Recalling the day when she first met Duke, JoAnne said, "That day you came to help me move my things here for the first time, you had a young man with you. Is he one of the associates you mentioned?"

"Oh, yeah," recalled Duke. "That was Donnie Moore. He's one of my...what did you call him? Yeah, he's one of my associates. Yeah, Donnie is my associate. I needed help that day to drive your car 'cause we didn't want you to have to drive in the snow so I got Donnie to come. He's from Jamaica. Nicest guy in the world."

"He's a big boy," JoAnne said. "Bigger than you, even."

"We're all big boys, Miss JoAnne. That comes in handy sometimes. You never know. And when you put the three of us together, there's pretty much nothing we can't get done. And there's nothing we wouldn't do for Miss Rita."

"Have you ever heard of such a sweet arrangement?" Pat asked JoAnne.

"I surely have not," JoAnne replied with emphasis.

"As I said, works for me," Duke added with a big smile.

"Me too," said Rita.

They toasted to that and to their friendship as the fire warmed the house against the ferocious storm outside. To JoAnne, that feeling of warmth and protection seemed to be a metaphor for the second life she had begun at The Settlement.

ভওভ

The Valentine's Day nor'easter was a potent but fast moving one. By early the next morning, as was often the case with such storms after they passed, the sun was shining brightly and the clear blue sky belied the fierceness of the previous night's storm. Nearly a foot of fresh snow blanketed the area.

At just before seven-thirty a.m., the private snow plow service had already finished clearing the long driveway leading into The Settlement. Duke was up and out to check the grounds for any damage and to shovel the walkway. JoAnne came into the kitchen. Rita and Pat were already on their second cup of coffee.

"Did the plow wake you up?" Pat asked.

"Yes, but this is way past my normal wakeup time anyway. I guess brandy makes me tired," she said. "Any big damage from the storm?" she asked Rita.

"I don't think so. Duke's out there now checking things

out, and we didn't lose power. I think everything's fine."

"Still," JoAnne said, "I felt better last night having him around just in case."

"Duke's a good man," agreed Pat.

The ringing phone brought an audible "uh-oh" from Rita.

"Who calls on Saturday morning at seven-thirty?" said Pat, somewhat annoyed.

Rita got up and headed toward the phone in the living room. "I hope it's not Chuck."

"Chuck?" JoAnne said to Pat as Rita went to take the call in another room.

"Sister Charles," Pat replied. "Rita calls her Chuck."

"No, don't tell me that," JoAnne responded, apparently aghast at Rita's disrespect toward her sister, who JoAnne knew to be a Catholic nun. "How is she anyhow? I haven't seen her in years. Is she still a teacher?"

"Yes, in Philadelphia," Pat said.

"Why did Rita say she hoped it wasn't her on the phone?"

"She's been having some issues lately, and Rita thinks things are getting out of hand."

"Issues? What kind of issues?"

Pat got up from the table. "I really should let Rita tell you about that. It's a touchy subject. Besides, maybe it's not even her on the phone."

JoAnne let it go and decided to go upstairs to take a shower. When she returned about thirty minutes later, Rita had just finished the phone call and come back to the kitchen. She did not look happy.

"Was that your sister? Is everything okay?" JoAnne asked.

Rita took a sip of her now-cold coffee. "Yes and no. Yes, that was my sister and no everything's not okay. It seems our little sorority house is about to get a new sister. I hope you girls don't mind, but Chuck is coming to stay with us for a while."

"Of course, we don't mind," said JoAnne. "What's going on? I hope she's not sick or something."

Rita didn't answer; instead she headed toward the front door. Pat and JoAnne soon heard her calling for Duke to come inside. They both stood in the kitchen doorway to listen as Duke came in after stomping snow from his boots.

"Nasty storm last night but a nice morning outside, Miss Rita. The sunshine's blinding off the new snow, kinda pretty though. Need me for something?"

"Unfortunately, I do," she replied. "Do you think the roads will be cleared soon?"

"Main roads, yes. I think the storm passed about three this morning. They've probably been plowing all night, and this bright sun will help a lot. Side roads will still probably be a little tricky, but it shouldn't be bad at all. Where we heading?"

"Philadelphia."

"Sister Charles?" Duke asked immediately.

"Why else would we go to Philadelphia, Duke?" Rita was clearly agitated.

"I was just wondering because she normally doesn't visit us in the winter—her teaching school and all that," Duke explained.

"Well, there's nothing normal about what's going on," Rita said in a much calmer tone. "Sorry to snap at you. Come on, we gotta go get her and her stuff."

Every year since Rita's divorce, Sister Charles—or Chuck as Rita and only Rita referred to her—visited The Settlement for six weeks during the summer on what she referred to as her vacation. She lived in a convent in Philadelphia, and Duke would drive her back and forth on her visits. She and Duke had developed a great relationship over the years which centered on the baseball rivalry between her Philadelphia Phillies and his New York Mets, as well as her persistence in convincing Duke to expand his horizons by reading more than the sports pages. Mindful of Duke's somewhat limited inclination to sit still for very long, she got Duke to read classic short stories. Over the years, she sent to him a variety of classic stories by authors that she thought would suit his taste: Hemingway, O. Henry, Salinger, Updike, and others. During their drives back and forth between Troy and Philadelphia and throughout her vacation stays at The Settlement, she and Duke spent hours talking about these stories and, of course, baseball.

"Did you say Sister Charles and her stuff? What kind of stuff?" Duke asked.

"I did, but it probably won't be much. Somebody who has spent her whole life as a nun can still travel pretty light. We should still take the truck. Who knows what she'll be bringing? Duke, I know this is really short notice so if you can't make it, I understand. I can go get her in the Mercedes and you can go get her stuff some other time. Either way, I'm leaving to get her right now. My sister is not staying in some damned shelter, that's for sure. A shelter—Jesus!"

Pat could no longer stand the suspense. "Rita, we're delighted that Sister Charles is coming to stay with us but please tell us what's going on. Is she okay?"

"She's leaving the damned convent! That's what's going on. Right now, as we speak, she's headed out the door. She's quitting, or resigning, or going AWOL, whatever you call it when somebody decides to leave a damned convent. She called to tell me she was going to stay in some shelter and that's just not going to happen to my sister. I told her to pack up her stuff, and I'd be there around noon. Jesus, did she have to pick the day after a damned snowstorm to become a runaway?" Rita hurried toward the closet to get her coat.

"I'll go get the truck," Duke said as he headed toward the garage.

Rita turned to Pat and JoAnne who were still standing in the kitchen doorway trying to absorb what was happening. "I'm sorry, I'm crazed about this," she said. "Patty, please fill JoAnne in on what's going on as best you can. You can pretty much figure out what's happened. Apparently,

Chuck's visit with the Mother Superior yesterday didn't go well. If the roads are okay we'll be back for dinner. And Pat, tell JoAnne everything—all of it."

With that, Rita was gone.

Pat had been made aware of the on-going drama that had been playing out over the past several weeks in the life of Sister Charles. She did the best she could to relate to Jo-Anne what had happened.

୧୬୧୬

Charleen Russo entered the Sisters of St. Joseph Convent Albany Province immediately after high school. Her vocation to become a Catholic nun was clear to her as far back as she could remember. Throughout her Catholic school education, she had been drawn to the sisterhood, having been deeply influenced by the camaraderie that the Sisters of St. Joseph displayed and the dedication they showed toward educating their students. Charleen was a brilliant student throughout high school and upon entering the order of nuns right after graduation, soon distinguished herself while an undergraduate at the College of St. Rose in Albany, NY. There she was accepted into the Accelerated BA/MA Program and in five years received both her Bachelor of Arts and Master of Arts degrees in English Literature.

At St. Rose, she assimilated so easily into the campus community that it often surprised fellow students to learn that she was a convent novice. Unlike most other sisters who were among the students there, Charleen Russo, in addition to being a distinguished literature student, gained a reputation as a campus activist who regularly participated in and organized events for various causes. She headed the campus hunger network as well as the coalition in support of unwed mothers. She was ubiquitous at virtually every event conducted on behalf of the poor by the Albany office of Catholic Charities.

However, to the quiet chagrin of convent and diocesan

leadership but to the delight of local organizers, the soon-to-be sister was an outspoken supporter of various civil rights causes, among which included support of gay and lesbian groups—causes that mainstream Catholicism generally steered clear of.

Such activism periodically received quiet but stern rebukes from her superiors, but she was always careful to come ever so close to the lines of convent propriety without actually crossing them.

She graduated with honors from St. Rose, receiving the Faulkner award for most outstanding student in the English Department's Masters Degree program. Shortly thereafter, she took her final vows to enter the order of the Sisters of St. Joseph and took the name Sister Charles.

As a part of her transition to full status as a Catholic nun, she applied for and received a teaching position at Troy Catholic, her high school alma mater, where she quickly distinguished herself as a gifted English teacher with a passion for education and for mentoring students. Her clear love for teaching literature and her compassionate approach to her students soon made Sister Charles a favorite member of the faculty among the students at Troy Catholic. She worked tirelessly, splitting her time between teaching and convent duties, all while continuing her advocacy work.

Despite comfortably settling into all of these roles, it was with great joy that several years later, she accepted an offer by the Order to take a position at East Philadelphia Catholic Preparatory Academy. Catholic Prep, as it was known, was an institution which attracted some of the most gifted high school students from the Western Pennsylvania and Southern New Jersey areas.

It was unique among Catholic schools for many reasons. Unlike most private schools, it was fully enrolled at all times and accepted only the best and brightest students who could handle its high academic standards. If ever there was an "Ivy League" of high schools, Catholic Prep would be in it. Virtually, every graduate went on to a prestigious college—most on academic scholarships. Over the years, many of its graduates went on to lucrative careers in business and academics. As a result, Catholic Prep was exceptionally well endowed. Only children of wealthy families were charged tuition and even those students had to pass its strenuous academic requirements to be admitted. The academy was also unusual in that it had an exceptionally high number of Catholic priests and nuns on its faculty. It was a haven for the true academicians from among the Jesuit Order of priests and the Order of the Sisters of St. Joseph.

Sister Charles was honored to have been asked to join the faculty at Catholic Prep and jumped at the opportunity to go there, despite having to leave behind her fellow sisters at the convent, her students at Troy Catholic who loved her, and of course, her own sister Rita with whom she had always remained very close.

Her sense of honor in being recruited to the Catholic Prep faculty was somewhat diminished by her sense that, in a way, she was being "honorably discharged" from Troy Catholic. Her continued advocacy for individuals and causes not normally associated with Catholicism were a growing irritant to the Church hierarchy and her convent superiors. She was well aware that her outside activities were a constant source of aggravation to them, and it was because of this awareness that she welcomed the opportunity to go to Catholic Prep. She felt that her liberal views on certain societal issues would find greater acceptance there. She was hopeful that her focus on academics rather than on strict Catholic teachings would at least be better tolerated there.

Sister Charles immediately fit in at Catholic Prep, and it was there that she really hit her stride bringing the gift of literature to serious students and being an advocate for the rights of students—roles she cherished and considered her life's purpose. Unfortunately for her, it was also there where she finally crossed the lines of propriety which she had previously been able to avoid.

Catholic Prep, as an institution, was indeed more understanding of gray areas between strict Catholic teachings and modern-day sensibilities. It was not, however, immune from the pressures of the Church hierarchy, especially when Church doctrine got publicly criticized by a nun.

In only her third year at Catholic Prep, Sister Charles found herself embroiled in a controversy which began as what appeared to be a silly prank but soon escalated into an all-out public debate.

One of her students, a junior named Kelly Walters, brought a date to the Junior Prom. When Kelly signed up for the prom, she entered her date's name, Chris Oswald. But Kelly failed to mention that Chris was a female friend of hers from her hometown of Mount Laurel, New Jersey. Kelly was bringing her "girlfriend" to the prom.

On the night of the prom, several faculty members were in attendance as chaperones, including Sister Charles. An immediate buzz went around the gymnasium as Kelly and Chris mingled with attendees who all seemed genuinely enthralled with the unorthodox couple.

The Catholic Prep Principal, a Jesuit Priest named Reverend James Dolan, was clearly not amused and immediately sought out Sister Charles, whom he knew to be one of Kelly's teachers and mentors. Sister Charles, always the peacekeeper, convinced Dolan to not make too much of it, insisting that the girls were just having fun. Kelly was, she explained, a wonderful girl who simply liked to stand out. Dolan reluctantly let it go but kept a close watch on Kelly and Chris all night.

It seemed as though nothing more would come of the matter until the end of the night when the prom-goers voted Kelly and Chris "Queen and Queen" of the prom, and they were paraded up on stage to accept their cardboard crowns. The crowd wildly applauded their approval of this selection as Kelly took to the microphone and cheerily thanked everyone for their vote.

Then with the entire assembly looking on, she proceeded to give Chris a great big long kiss before they marched out of the gym holding hands and waving to a cheering crowd.

The following Monday morning, Kelly was called to Father Dolan's office. She was immediately suspended and informed that Dolan would be seeking School Board approval to have her expelled for engaging in homosexual conduct. Kelly knew that bringing Chris to the prom would not sit well with many of the religious members of the faculty. She also presumed that the "Queen and Queen" sequence of events and the on-stage kiss was certainly not going to help, but she assumed it would only result in some sort of reprimand—not a suspension and certainly not expulsion.

Sister Charles had feared for the worst after witnessing the prom event and tried a pre-emptive strike by stopping by to see Father Dolan before class that morning. Dolan's door was closed when she got there and he did not answer her knock.

News of Kelly's suspension and potential expulsion rocketed through the school that day as countless students appealed to Sister Charles to come to Kelly's aid. Sister Charles camped outside Father Dolan's office after classes that day, waiting for him to emerge.

"I know why you're here, Sister Charles. Don't bother," Dolan said as he walked by her and out the door.

She followed close behind.

"I'd like you to reconsider, Father. Can we talk?"

He stopped, turned, and faced her. "This is up to the board of directors now, and you're wasting your breath on me. I want her out! And you need to be very careful to not get on the wrong side on this one, Sister Charles. Be very careful." Dolan then walked away.

Less than a week later, the board met to consider Kelly Walter's expulsion from Catholic Prep. She was allowed to appear on her own behalf and to select one other person to do likewise. She chose Sister Charles.

Father Dolan was already edgy the night of the meeting and became visibly agitated by the sight of Sister Charles appearing on Kelly's behalf. He had warned her. Despite Dolan's clear irritation over her presence, Sister Charles launched into a well-rehearsed defense of Kelly Walters. She recited Kelly's exemplary record as a model student with a history of doing charitable work. She depicted the incident at the prom as just "kids being kids" and called upon the board members to show compassion and forgiveness as a sign of their own Christian values and those of the school. Finally, she diplomatically but forcefully reminded the board that there was no school policy against bringing a member of one's own gender to a school function. She pleaded with them to lift Kelly's suspension and allow her to continue as a student.

In response, Dolan, acting more as a prosecutor than a principal, was totally dismissive of Kelly's academic and charitable record. He conceded that there indeed was nothing in the school's code of conduct which prohibited someone from bringing someone of the same sex to a school function, however, citing the Church's clear prohibitions against homosexual conduct, he insisted that the coronation kiss, witnessed by everyone, was a homosexual act. Kelly should be expelled from Catholic Prep, he argued.

Each board member then had their say. From the tone of their comments, Sister Charles was somewhat optimistic. She felt that only a few of the nine members were firmly standing with Dolan against Kelly.

Before putting the matter to a vote, Kelly was then given an opportunity to address the board. Sister Charles felt that all Kelly would need to do was to explain that she understood that her actions were wrong and would not happen again. If she did that convincingly, Sister Charles assumed, she would be allowed to stay at Catholic Prep.

Kelly began her well-thought-out response by thanking Sister Charles for her support which showed the true nature of Christian values. She then slowly and methodically characterized her life, since childhood, as one which was dedicated to those same values as well as to academic excellence. She was thoughtful and eloquent—Sister Charles and several of the board members smiled compassionately at her as she spoke. All was going well.

Then, in closing and without hesitation or wavering in the slightest, Kelly informed the board that she was, in fact, gay and that, under no circumstances, would she apologize for being gay or for what she did at the prom—not then, not ever.

Board members, particularly those who moments before seemed ready to overlook Kelly's transgression, were visibly shocked by her pronouncement. The room fell silent.

Kelly then again thanked Sister Charles for her support and stood up. Staring directly at Reverend Dolan, she defiantly asked, "If Jesus accepts me as being gay, why don't you?"

After she and Sister Charles left the room, the Board voted to expel her by a vote of nine to zero.

ఆఅఆ

Kelly's pronouncement had come as a complete surprise to Sister Charles. Even after the prom incident, it hadn't occurred to her that Kelly actually was gay. She thought that the entire episode was a lark, and that Kelly would simply apologize, be reinstated, and the entire incident would be over.

Sister Charles's emotions over these occurrences ran the gamut. She felt that she was unfairly blindsided by Kelly who did not tell her what she was going to do. She felt used by Kelly, who had to know that publicly proclaiming her homosexuality would definitely result in her expulsion from Catholic Prep. But mostly she felt admiration for Kelly's courage in not compromising what she believed in. She was saddened that a bright and promising student's life was being ruined for standing up for her beliefs and angered that an unforgiving and intolerant group of individuals pretending to be Christian would do such a thing.

"That's when the wheels really came off," Pat said as she went on relating the story to JoAnne.

"You mean it gets worse?"

"A lot worse," Pat answered. "Sister Charles decided that it was not going to end there. She turned it into a cause."

"She and Rita are about as different as two sisters can be, but I guess they both share the same genes when it comes to fighting back," JoAnne said.

"Oh, boy. Did she ever fight back," Pat continued. "First, she circulated a petition around the school to get Kelly reinstated and got it signed by almost every student and a fair amount of faculty members. She delivered it to the principal who not only turned her away but threatened her position on the faculty if she persisted. And then the convent superior got wind of it all and essentially forbade Sister Charles from pursuing it."

"Let me guess," said JoAnne. "That got her even madder."

"It sure did! She went straight to the bishop's office with the petition and wrote a formal complaint that Reverend Dolan and the board of directors were acting in a manner that was against Church teachings of tolerance and forgiveness."

JoAnne closed her eyes and shook her head. "She went to the bishop?"

"She told Rita what she was going to do and even Rita told her that she was going off the deep end. What Rita didn't know was that going to the bishop was not the end of it. Of course, the bishop refused to talk to Sister Charles, which made her even madder. So she organized a demonstration: signs, songs, the whole works. She picketed the bishop's residence for God's sake. She got a lot of support from students, parents, and, not surprisingly, a Philadelphia gay rights group and the National Organization of Women."

"Oh, no," said JoAnne who grew more and more shocked.

"Oh, yes," Pat continued. "And once word of those groups getting involved spread, a writer from the Philadelphia newspaper came to the demonstration to cover the story. He covered the event and interviewed both Kelly and Sister Charles. Kelly was defiant and—here's where it really got crazy—in the interview, Sister Charles announced that she too was gay."

"What!" JoAnne practically shrieked.

"Yep, right there in front of a reporter with a recorder going, she told the world that she was homosexual. Apparently, she made a huge point about being what she called a 'non-practicing lesbian' but that very important part of the story never made it into print."

"Non-practicing lesbian?" JoAnne said. "Does that mean what I think—what I hope it means?"

"Yeah, I think so. I guess it means that she doesn't actually have sex but if she ever did—"

"That's what I thought," JoAnne interrupted, not wanting to get too far into that discussion. "And they can throw somebody out of a convent for that? I've honestly never thought about this before, but it would be hard for me to imagine that Sister Charles is the first gay nun."

"I would hardly think so," agreed Pat. "But she surely is the first one to declare it to a newspaper reporter while picketing the bishop's residence."

"Fair point," agreed JoAnne.

"Besides, I don't think she got thrown out of the convent, I think they sort of coaxed her out."

"Either way, I think it's awful," JoAnne said, "and I can't wait to tell her how proud I am of her for standing her ground. It's just too bad that the school and the students had to lose such a wonderful person."

"Their loss is going to be our gain," said Pat. "Now let's go get our little sorority house ready to welcome another sister. Or should I say, former sister?"

Chapter 9

The sound of the garage door opening alerted Pat and JoAnne that Rita and Duke had returned, presumably along with Sister Charles and her belongings. It was well after dark and the round trip had taken more than ten hours. Pat and JoAnne were relieved. It had been a nervous day for them as they waited. They were nervous about the travel conditions after the storm but they were mostly nervous about the state of mind that both Rita and Sister Charles would be in. Rita had left in somewhat of a rage and was clearly not happy about what had happened. They assumed that Sister Charles would be devastated. They had prepared themselves for a good deal of tension around The Settlement and had discussed how they would help both Rita and Sister Charles get over this entire episode.

The door into the house from the garage swung open. Sister Charles was the first to enter. She was dressed plainly and had her hair pulled back, piled under a Philadelphia Phillies baseball cap. Otherwise, she looked like a slightly graying version of Rita. Though a few years apart in age, they looked very similar.

"Patty! So great to see you again," Sister Charles said excitedly as she practically ran across the room to give Pat a big hug. She quickly turned to JoAnne and opened her arms. "JoAnne, Rita told me everything. First, please know that I'm so sorry for what you've gone through. Rita has told me all about it. But I was very excited to hear that you were living here. What a great day this has turned out to be!" She was absolutely gushing with enthusiasm.

Pat and JoAnne reciprocated with long hugs but neither said a word. They were not prepared for this, expecting a totally different demeanor from Sister Charles, considering what she had just gone through.

As Rita and Duke followed into the house, JoAnne noticed Rita holding her hands and arms out to each side, shaking her head. "She has not shut up for one second in the past five hours. I don't know how she can go five hours without breathing. Duke, do you remember her even taking a breath?"

"We had a lot of catching up to do," replied Duke with his typical diplomacy.

"I don't know what was worse: listening to her yammering about Philadelphia sports teams or her and Duke going on and on about Sherlock Holmes stories for hours on end."

"I just finished an entire book of Arthur Conan Doyle stories and me and Sister Charles had not had a chance to talk about them yet," Duke said as he struggled to carry in two large suitcases. "Do I put these bags up in Sister's regular room?"

"No," Rita quickly replied. "She's staying in the garage until she calms down."

"Stop it, Rita," admonished Pat. "Yes, Duke, please take them upstairs. Your regular room is all set up for you, Sister."

"Thank you, Pat," Sister Charles said as she headed upstairs.

"Duke, will you stay for dinner?" asked JoAnne.

"Thanks, no. I'd love to but I haven't been home in a couple of days. I'm gonna leave you ladies alone tonight. I'm sure you got lots to talk about."

A few moments later, Duke came back down. "Miss Rita, I'm going to just leave the rest of her things in the garage. I'll be back tomorrow and you can tell me where you want them. Goodnight, ladies."

"Thank you, Duke," said Rita sincerely. "I really appreciate you doing this for us today."

"No problem," he replied and moved toward the garage.

"And thanks for staying with us last night," JoAnne added.

"Again, my pleasure. Actually, I had fun last night and today too. Sister Charles is a rip!" he said before leaving.

Rita, Pat, and JoAnne were alone in the kitchen and could hear the sounds of their new resident putting away her things upstairs. They could hear her singing.

"God Almighty! She's singing that annoying theme song from Welcome Back, Kotter. Shoot me now," Rita said. "I'm calling the convent right now to see if they'll take her back."

"Stop it," Pat admonished.

"She does seem to be managing this extremely well, don't you think, Rita?" JoAnne asked.

"I'll say. Honestly, I don't get it. She's sure not acting like someone who has just left behind twenty-five years of work and dedication. I don't know if she's in denial or on drugs or what in hell's going on."

"She's really not going back?" asked Pat.

"Nope. She's had it. She does not feel wanted or appreciated and refuses to pretend anymore that she's okay with hypocrisy. She's going to start fresh, doing what, I have no idea. But if I know Chuck, in about two weeks she'll be knee deep in some new project or cause. Believe me, my sister never has a problem keeping occupied. Maybe she'll save the whales, or the planet, or all of God's furry creatures. I don't know what she'll do. What I do know is that she's not sorry for taking her stand, and there's no turning back for her."

"Good for her," Pat said.

"She'll make the best of it," added JoAnne.

"Oh yes, she will," Rita replied. "I only hope she doesn't make us all crazy at the same time. She's still badgering Duke to get him to read more and then—get this—she started in on me about dating. She told me I need to get back into the dating scene. Can you believe it? A gay nun telling me I need to date more. I can't imagine what's next."

"I heard that!" Sister Charles said as she was entering the room.

"Oh, Sister, you're done upstairs. Good, let's have some dinner," said Pat.

"Patty, everything smells wonderful. Thank you so much," Sister Charles said. "But before we go sit down, first let's get rid of the elephant that will surely join us in the room if I don't do this. Rita, do the ladies know the story?"

"Yes, they do."

"The whole story?"

"Yes, Pat filled JoAnne in today."

"All of it? Even the part about—"

"Yes, Chuck. All—of—it!" Rita interrupted.

"Good. Now that you've all heard the story, let's agree that after tonight, nothing more will be said of the entire matter. Can we do that?"

"The less, the better, as far as I'm concerned," said Rita.

"Good," Chuck said, "but before that happens, I want to clear the air. I'm sure you all have some questions about a lot of things. I want to give everyone a chance to ask questions. I always did this with my students before every test I gave. It was amazing how much they would learn that way. Everybody has to ask at least one question. Pat, you start."

Pat did clearly not expect this. "Oh, dear. Can I go last?"

"No," Rita said.

"Well, let's see. Um. Well, okay, I have a question. Now that you're not a nun any more, I presume we should stop calling you Sister Charles. So what should we call you? Will you be Charleen again?"

Rita laughed out loud. "Good one, Patty!" she said. "Let me answer that. We're not calling her Charleen. Maybe we should call her The Fleeing Nun."

"I didn't ask you," Pat replied dismissively. "That's awful." She turned to Sister Charles who was clearly amused by Rita's joke.

"Well, technically, I'm still a nun, even though I left the convent. By rule, I have two weeks to change my mind. But believe me, I won't be changing my mind, so as far as I'm concerned, starting now I should no longer be called Sister Charles. The Fleeing Nun sounds a little undignified but no one has called me Charleen in twenty-five years so, in honor of my sister who took me in from the cold—quite literally—I'm good with Chuck. From now on, I'm Chuck."

JoAnne began to snicker.

"What?" said Rita. "What's wrong with that? I've been calling her that forever."

"I know and that is really fine with me. I was just thinking that Duke will be calling her Miss Chuck. Sounds funny."

"You gotta love that!" Rita roared her approval. "Good morning, Miss Chuck. How's Miss Chuck today? What can I do for you today, Miss Chuck. That's perfect!"

"Done!" Chuck said. "Chuck it is—I'm good with that. Okay, JoAnne, you get the next question."

"Me? Well, Chuck—Oh, that doesn't sound right at all."

"Go on, JoAnne. You'll get used to it," Chuck said.

"Okay maybe, but not right this moment. Anyway, I'm impressed by how well you seem to be coping with what had to be an earth-shaking experience for you. Maybe I can learn from how you've dealt with your situation so I can deal better with my own. How on earth did you go through what you went through and, in no time, seem to be perfectly fine about it?"

"Thank you, JoAnne. I'm really glad you noticed that and that you asked. Clearly, I have given this whole thing—leaving the convent—a lot of thought. It was really pretty easy for me to come to terms with it once I realized that by leaving the convent, I wasn't leaving God. I believe that I have been put on this earth to help others, and to encourage them to help others, who will, in turn, help others, and so on and so on. That's what God wants me to do and that's what I'll do. A long time ago, I chose to do that in the structure of a convent but recently that structure seemed to be getting in the way of what I need to do, so I left. But I didn't leave God. I didn't leave teaching. I didn't stop trying to help others. I just moved on. I just changed addresses, thanks to my little sister Rita over there."

Rita smiled and winked at Chuck from across the table. She was proud of her big sister and delighted that after so many years, they would again be living in the same house.

"I'm proud of you," Rita said.

Chuck smiled back at Rita. "JoAnne, I know a lot has happened to you too and you are struggling with it. If I might suggest, you didn't stop being the wonderful person you've always been. You didn't stop being a bright, energetic, and loving person. You just changed your address, just like me and just like Patty."

"Thank you," JoAnne said quietly, "that's a good way to look at things, a very good way."

There followed a long pause in the conversation as Chuck's words seemed to resonate in the dining room. Pat broke the silence by starting to pass food around the table.

"Not so fast," Rita said. "I didn't get to ask my question and, besides, I think the elephant is still in the room."

"Uh-oh," said JoAnne, not even looking up.

"Go ahead, Rita," Chuck said, fully knowing what was coming.

"I think all of us girls who will now be living with you under the same roof would like to have certain assurances that you intend to remain...what did you call it? Oh yeah, a non-practicing lesbian."

"Rita!" both Pat and JoAnne shrieked simultaneously in protest.

At the same time, Rita and Chuck began laughing out loud.

"No, really," Rita persisted, clearly just giving her sister a hard time. "What's your answer?"

"Rita, stop it!" demanded JoAnne. "None of us care about that."

"JoAnne, it's quite okay, I know Rita just does things like this to give me a hard time," Chuck said.

"Well Chuck…" Rita said.

Chuck paused for the longest time before smiling and saying, "I'm a little old to start practicing anything. Does that mean I can stay, Mother Superior," she said, winking at Rita.

"Unless I'm mistaken, I think I just heard the elephant leave the room. Let's eat," said Rita.

The rest of the dinner conversation was animated, light, and cheery. Mostly they talked of old acquaintances and growing up in South Troy. There was no mention of any of their respective travails or to any of the psychological baggage each of them had brought to The Settlement. They had all taken vastly different routes on their way, but there the four of them were: happy to be moving on, happy to be together, happy to be focused on the future.

そのそ

In short order, Chuck's influence on The Settlement became clear and ever-present. Rita clearly enjoyed having her big sister around. Pat and JoAnne seemed changed too. They were each inspired by Chuck's ability to deal with her issues and used this as inspiration to get beyond their own. The mood at The Settlement was peaceful, collegial, and universally positive. Rita had a small plaque made up that was hung by the front door which read, *Drama Free Zone*.

Chuck's influence went far beyond mood alteration. She quickly began to instill a certain order to the goings on in the big house on the hill. She convinced the others to hold regular meetings every Wednesday evening. It was at these meetings when they would discuss business matters regarding life at The Settlement.

They began referring to the group as the board of directors. Rita once playfully accused her of trying to turn the household into a convent but, on the whole, they all welcomed the structure Chuck brought into the house.

Each meeting had an agenda. Chuck was chairperson and their rules were such that everything they agreed upon needed a clear majority—three out of four—to be approved. Rita objected to this rule initially but, much to the amusement of the others, her objection was overruled by a vote of three to one.

At the start, this somewhat structured approach seemed a bit awkward but soon they all began to look forward to the Wednesday night meetings. JoAnne and Pat, especially, welcomed a clearer sense of belonging and contribution that the meetings provided.

The Wednesday night meetings became quite productive and formed the backbone of Settlement structure. Soon everything was running so smoothly that Rita began getting bored. "We've got to do something to introduce a little more fun into this place," she said one Wednesday night. "This is all good but we have to have some more fun."

The others agreed and began to regularly discuss having more fun. They started going out to dinner and movies, they went on field trips to museums and to vineyards, they often accompanied Chuck to benefit events with which she had become involved. They even discussed taking a cruise. While these things were generally fine and acceptable to everyone, they soon agreed that these were just activities.

"I think we're confusing activity with progress," JoAnne once said. "I think we're doing things but not really getting anywhere. I'm all in favor of doing things, but I think what we're looking for is doing things that are meaningful."

Deep down, they felt that they could do something better with their efforts, something truly meaningful and much more fun.

With that, they began to search for something that would bring enjoyment into their lives and accomplish something important at the same time. Little did they know, at the time, that they did not really have to try to find it. It would soon find them.

☙❧☙

"JoAnne!" Rita called out as she came into the den where JoAnne was reading the newspaper. "The phone—it's for you."

"Me?"

"Yes, it's Alex Cord, the reporter for the *Troy Register*."

"What does he want? How does he even know I'm here?"

JoAnne picked up the phone. "This is JoAnne Di-Matteo."

"Mrs. DiMatteo, this is Alex Cord. I'm really sorry to bother you."

"How did you know I was here?"

"I didn't, actually. I called Ms. Russo, hoping she would know how to reach you and she told me."

JoAnne gave a quick look of disapproval toward Rita. She was not a fan of Alex Cord after the way he handled the story of the audit of Fam Pharm and always seemed to side with Mayor Crotty and the Democrats.

"What can I do for you, Mr. Cord?" she said coldly.

"Mrs. DiMatteo, I'd like to talk to you. There is an issue that I've been thinking about for a long, long time, and I need to talk to you about it."

"Go ahead, Mr. Cord. What's your issue?"

"Well actually, I'm calling in hopes of setting up a time when I can see you in person."

"I don't have any information to give you, Mr. Cord. And if I can be blunt, even if I did, you'd be about the last person I'd give it to."

"Please, Mrs. DiMatteo, I don't want information from you. I have information to give to you, information that I think is important for you to know. I want to talk to you but not over the phone. It's important—important to me, and I think important to you as well."

"Mr. Cord, I'm sure this is about my husband and everything that has happened to us. I hope you can understand that I really don't want to talk about any of that, especially to a newspaper reporter. Don't take this personally, but I really have nothing more to say about it, and to be totally honest, I've spent the last few months trying to get some closure on the whole matter. I don't want to talk about it."

"I'm not doing a story, ma'am. This has nothing to do with me being a reporter. In fact, I'm trying to help and I think what I have to say to you will actually help you get the closure you deserve."

"I'm sure I don't understand."

"Please let me meet with you so I can explain. It will only take a few minutes and I'll meet you anywhere, anytime you want."

JoAnne really didn't want to revisit any of the horrible occurrences of the past several months, but she was more than a little curious about what Cord could possibly say that would help her. The thought crossed her mind that while Cord did what she felt was a hatchet job on them during their troubles, his story on Phillip's death and its aftermath showed some compassion, and it was he who reported on the possibility that Phillip was a victim in this whole affair.

"All right, Mr. Cord. I'll see you but if you want to meet with me it will have to be in the presence of my friends here. If you want to talk, come to Ms. Russo's residence next Wednesday night at seven p.m."

"It might be best if it were just the two of us."

"My friends and I will meet you Wednesday night at seven. If that is not acceptable to you, Mr. Cord, then my answer is no."

"I'll be there," he said before saying goodbye.

JoAnne briefed the others on her conversation with Alex Cord. They all agreed that she should hear him out and that they would be at her side during the conversation.

"I'll have Duke close by just in case Cord steps out of bounds or we otherwise want to get rid of that creep," Rita said.

こうこう

As Cord's car pulled up the driveway just before seven, Duke ambled off the front porch to greet him. Cord was not expecting this and did not know who it was that was approaching his car. He opened the car window just a crack.

"I'm here to see Mrs. DiMatteo. I believe she is expecting me."

"Alex Cord, I presume?"

"Yes. Mrs. DiMatteo is expecting me," Cord repeated. It was clear that he was somewhat unnerved by this greeting, which was the desired effect Duke was looking for.

"Leave your car right here and come with me."

Cord put the car in park, got out, and walked behind Duke as they headed toward the front door. Before entering the house, Duke said, "I'll be right out here in case any of the ladies need me." His tone was purposely menacing. "And Mr. Cord?"

"Yes?"

"The ladies mean a lot to me. I don't know exactly why you are here, and I'd hate to see them disturbed by your visit. Are you hearing me, Mr. Cord?"

"Uh, yes, I understand. Thanks," said Cord as he went toward the door.

Rita greeted Cord at the door, led him to the dining room, and handled the introductions while JoAnne sat stoically at the head of the table. Cord was offered a seat at the opposite end. He was clearly nervous.

"What is it that you wanted to talk about, Mr. Cord?" JoAnne said curtly.

Over the next ten minutes, Cord told an incredible and horrifying story to JoAnne and her friends. In a clearly rehearsed monologue, he began by telling them that as soon as he could find another job, he'd be resigning from the newspaper and would be trying to find another way to earn a living. The events surrounding the tragic story of Phillip

DiMatteo had convinced him that he could no longer be a part of covering politics and that he was ashamed of how he was duped into being a part of it. He kept referring to a "cover-up."

He told, in great detail, what he knew about Crotty's behind-the-scenes orchestration of the dirty tricks that were done to the members of the Gang of Twelve and how he looked the other way in his reporting of those events. He outlined case after case of how Crotty and others among the Democratic leadership on the city council had made shady deals for their own profit—how they had strong-armed contractors, vendors, and common people alike into actions that benefitted them and them alone.

At one point, JoAnne interrupted Cord's monologue. "Excuse me, Mr. Cord, but if the information you have amounts to telling me that Mayor Crotty is a despicable politician, I'm afraid this is not news to me."

"I understand," Cord replied. "If I may continue for just a few more moments?"

JoAnne reluctantly nodded.

Cord then removed from his jacket a notepad which contained the notes he had taken on the night of his interview with Crotty at The Excalibar. Cord used those notes to detail the meeting he had on the night of the election with a clearly intoxicated Michael Crotty.

He explained how Crotty had taken full credit for causing the original audit of Fam Pharm. Then, seizing the opportunity created by JoAnne's honest mistake, how Crotty had bragged to Cord about forcing the attorney general's office to pursue the case against JoAnne in order to get Phillip to resign in disgrace.

Cord detailed how Crotty had both orchestrated and reveled in Phillip's demise and repeatedly called it political payback. He repeated Crotty's bragging words about the payback he had visited upon Wheeler, Casella, and the others. Using quotes from the conversation with Crotty, Cord laid out the entire scenario of Crotty's vengeance against

Phillip. The word "vengeance" echoed in JoAnne's ears.

When he had finished his chronicling of Crotty's despicable actions against Phillip, JoAnne, and the Gang of Twelve, Cord told them how ashamed he was for having been tricked into proliferating the Fam Pharm story in the newspaper. In every way, he felt that he was responsible for allowing it to happen and, in fact, felt that he was complicit in illegal acts. He confessed how ashamed he was for not exposing Crotty and allowing his corruption to continue unabated for so long.

He said that coming forward to JoAnne was the only thing he thought he could do to even come remotely close to "saving his soul." He apologized profusely to JoAnne but did not ask for her forgiveness. "That would be asking too much," he said.

Throughout Cord's monologue, the ladies sat in silence. When he was finished, everyone looked at JoAnne. She was crying. Chuck and Pat felt deeply sorry for her. Rita was infuriated. They all instinctively sensed that JoAnne should be the next to speak so they waited while she composed herself.

"It's admirable that you have admitted all of this to us, Mr. Cord," she finally said.

"It's the very, very least I can do, Mrs. DiMatteo. I can't begin to put into words how truly sorry I am. I know that there is nothing that I can ever do to make it up to you but if I could, I would."

"Can I ask you a simple question, Mr. Cord?" Chuck asked.

"Of course."

"Why don't you just put this all in the newspaper? And why aren't you telling this to the police instead of us?"

"I have certainly thought of that, long and hard. But let me assure you that these guys are extremely good at covering their tracks. There's no way that I could ever prove any of these things—just no way. Crotty has his wagons circled pretty tight, and he'd just deny everything and accuse me of making up the story. It would be my word against all of theirs, and I'd just end up getting sued or worse, if you know what I mean."

"Or both," Rita conceded.

"Exactly," Cord said. "Thank you for your time, Mrs. DiMatteo. In some way I hope this helps you to piece together what was an awful chain of events. Telling you this was something I just had to do. Your husband was a good man. I wish there was a way I could make it up to you and to Phillip. I wish you well." With that, the meeting was over, but its aftermath was just beginning.

૮ઝૡ૩

In the days that followed, the gray cloud of Cord's revelation hung over life at The Settlement. JoAnne stayed in her room most of the time while the others simply tried to keep busy. There was little talk in the house and no joy to be found anywhere. Indeed, drama had come to the Drama Free Zone. Despite the fact that not a single conversation was had among them regarding what Cord had said, they all had independently arrived at the very same conclusion: whether Phillip's death was accidental or self-inflicted no longer mattered. Either way, Michael Crotty was the real cause of Phillip's death and of JoAnne's great sadness.

Chapter 10

Sundays at The Settlement were set aside as a time of togetherness, especially since Chuck had arrived. They would all attend ten o'clock mass together at St. Paul's Church and then go the Sunday brunch at the Italian-American Club in nearby Albany.

On the Sunday after the meeting with Alex Cord, they quietly assembled at the front door and left for church at nine-forty-five a.m. Cord's revelations about Crotty still seemed to hang in the air but neither separately nor as a group had they talked about it. In the car ride, Pat suddenly started the conversation.

"Today at Church I'm going to pray that we find a way to get past this. It's not doing any of us any good to just go from day to day ignoring the fact that we—all of us—have to move past this. We have to do something to deal with this issue so that it stops consuming all of us. I'm going to pray that we find it."

"Well said, Patty," said Chuck. "And I agree that showing faith in each other and in God is a good place to start."

"Would it be okay if I prayed that Crotty gets struck dead by lightning?" Rita said as she drove.

"Rita, really..." Pat chided.

"I'm serious," Rita said. And as though days of frustration were finally being vented all at once, she turned and said in a very loud voice, "As sure as we're all sitting here, Michael Crotty killed Phillip, and we can't let him get away with it! There. I said it. You can pray all you want about moving on, but I'm not moving on until that bastard pays for killing Phillip. I'm gonna pray that the bastard dies a slow and painful death."

"I'm not sure God will be answering prayers for vengeance," Chuck said.

"Chuck, you pray for what you want, and I'll pray for what I want. I want that son of a bitch to pay."

JoAnne said nothing. She stared out the window in the back of Joe Black. She was in tears.

After mass, they arrived at the Sunday Brunch which was, as usual, very crowded. Many regulars and old acquaintances were there, including some of the former Marconi Club members from South Troy who would travel on Sundays and religious holidays to the Italian American Club for brunch after mass.

For Pat, seeing those people was a difficult reminder of her days with Bobby at the Marconi Club, but she was always happy to see her old friends.

So too it was difficult for JoAnne, especially on that particular Sunday.

"JoAnne, it's so good to see you," said Fippi Casella, Phillip's friend and confidant from the Gang of Twelve days. He had not seen or spoken to JoAnne since Phillip's funeral. "It's been a long time. I had heard you were in good company living up on the hill. Ladies..." he said, nodding politely to the other three. "And, Sister Charles, how great it is to have you back in town."

"Thank you, Fippi. It's good to be back."

"I'll bet this is an especially tough day for you, Jo," he said as he made his way around the table, giving awkward but well-intended hugs to each of them.

"You remember," she replied.

"Of course, I remember. You bet I do. Once, many years ago, I forgot Phillip's birthday and he never let me live it down."

"Oh, Jo. We didn't know," said Pat, speaking for the others as well who were not aware that it was Phillip's birthday.

"I didn't mean to, you know, bring up a tough subject," Fippi said apologetically.

"Not a sore subject at all, Fippi. Thank you for remembering," JoAnne said.

"Phillip will never be forgotten Jo, not by me, not by any of us," he said. "I gotta get going. Happy Birthday, Phillip," Fippi said as he pointed toward the sky and made the sign of the cross before leaving the table.

"Nice man," JoAnne said, breaking the awkward silence at the table.

Rita, Pat, and Chuck were all impressed by yet another demonstration of JoAnne's grace under trying circumstances. The matter of Alex Cord's revelation had to be haunting JoAnne, especially that day—Phillip's birthday—yet she remained the picture of grace and composure.

On their drive back to The Settlement, again it was Pat who brought the ever-present subject back into focus.

"I prayed for help today in Church like I said I would. I prayed today that we find a way to get JoAnne the peace she deserves. I even threw in your request too, Rita."

"I'm quite sure that God has more important things to do than help me find peace of mind. And I'm absolutely certain he's got better things to do than deal with the likes of Michael Crotty," JoAnne said softly.

"Like what?" Rita snapped. She was still enraged every time she thought of Crotty.

"I think God answered my prayer today," Pat went on. "Do you believe that's possible, Chuck?"

"I certainly believe that prayers do get answered. Yes, I believe that's possible."

"So what's the answer?" Rita asked skeptically. "Did God tell you that we could kill Michael Crotty? Please tell me he gave that the okay."

"Not exactly, Rita, but funny you should say that," Pat went on. "For some reason, out of the clear blue a thought popped into my mind. I remembered what Bobby always used to say to men at the Marconi bar who had stayed late and were worried their wives were going to be mad if they stayed any later. He would always say, 'better to ask for forgiveness than to ask for permission.' I have no idea why that popped into my head today. Maybe it was divine intervention, maybe it was Bobby speaking to me. Maybe it was a response to my prayers. I don't know."

"I don't get it," Rita said. "How is that answering your prayers?"

"I was thinking about what Chuck said about God not answering a prayer for vengeance," Pat continued. "That's when Bobby's expression about not asking for permission popped into my head."

"What are you talking about?" asked Rita.

"Well, think about it," Pat continued. "Chuck said that God was not likely to answer prayers asking for revenge. Okay maybe so, but I'm thinking that if we do get revenge, he will forgive us. We shouldn't be asking God for permission to get peace for JoAnne. But if we do find a way—"

"Good point!" Rita banged her hand against the steering wheel. "That's an excellent point. Chuck, you're always talking about God being forgiving, and you're the most forgiving person I ever met. I'll bet you didn't ask God's permission to leave the convent, but I'll bet you asked for forgiveness. Am I right? Do you think God has forgiven you?"

Chuck thought for a moment. As the other three looked at her she finally said, "I think so. Yes, I think so. In fact, I know so! Now that you mention it, that's exactly what happened. I didn't ask God for permission to leave the convent but I did ask for forgiveness. And I believe I have been forgiven. I know I have!"

Rita slammed her hand on the steering wheel again as they rolled into the driveway. "We'll get our revenge on that bastard, Crotty, and after we do, we'll just ask for forgiveness."

"This is preposterous," said JoAnne derisively.

"I don't think so. I don't think it's preposterous at all," injected Pat. "Chuck?"

"This is certainly a bit of a convolution of the whole notion of forgiveness, but as I think about it, it has a certain logic to it."

"See, Jo!" Rita said excitedly.

"Now hold on," said Chuck as an afterthought. "We can't just kill somebody and ask for forgiveness. That's not how it works."

"Of course not," said Pat. "But there has to be a way to do what we need to do without breaking any laws, or even any of the Commandments, for that matter."

They walked into the house, all trying to take in this bizarre conversation. To each of them, the notion of getting Phillip's revenge was both frightening and enticing.

"I'm not saying that this makes any sense at all, but let's say we agree with that—you know seeking vengeance—how do we do it?" asked Chuck.

"Who knows?" said Rita. "But the reason we've all been walking around like zombies since we found out that Crotty ruined JoAnne's life is because we feel helpless. We haven't decided to settle the score. We first need to agree it's something we want to do. Jo, we want to do this, don't we?"

"Does anyone want coffee?" said JoAnne.

They all understood JoAnne's response. They also all knew that this was not the time to force the issue on her. It was Phillip's birthday.

"I say we each have a Mimosa instead of coffee and toast Phillip's birthday," said Rita as though to suggest that they put the matter aside for the time being.

That, they did.

Nothing more was said on the issue for the following few days but on Wednesday, at breakfast, Pat casually suggested that at that night's meeting time be given to continuing the discussion begun after Sunday Mass. Rita quickly agreed and both Chuck and JoAnne said that they wouldn't object to it. They all had thought about little else since that day. Each questioned the convoluted logic involved and certainly had no idea how they could get revenge against Crotty. But at the same time each—even JoAnne—allowed themselves the simple pleasure of dreaming that they could. It was time to resolve the issue one way or the other.

Rita and Pat were skeptical that Chuck and JoAnne would agree to be a part of anything that would even remotely be payback for Crotty's role in Phillip's death but they were both determined to do just that.

That afternoon, Pat announced that she wanted to go to the bakery to get a special dessert for after that night's meeting. Rita offered to drive Pat. While they did drive to the bakery and pick up some cannoli, the trip itself was a ruse for them to have a private conversation about the discussion they would all be having later.

"JoAnne won't agree to anything that's illegal and Chuck won't agree to anything that's immoral and neither will agree to anything that's unethical," Rita said on the way to the bakery. "I think they both would like to see Crotty pay for killing Phillip, but I don't think they'll have the stomach to actually make it happen."

"I don't think we should do any of those things either," said Pat. "Chuck is right. We can't just kidnap and torture the guy. Even if God forgave us, we'd still go to prison. And, under no circumstances, can we do anything that makes JoAnne uncomfortable."

"I know, but I don't see how we can get back at Crotty by staying on the high road. This will have to get a little messy at some point or it's all pointless."

"I'm not sure that either Chuck or Jo will go down the revenge road at all."

"Don't sell Chuck short," said Rita. "She's an ex-nun but she's still Italian."

"Agreed," Pat said in response, "but I'm afraid JoAnne is just too…"

"Proper?" added Rita. "Yes, she is proper but she's also Italian and, it's sad to say, a widow."

On the way back from the bakery Rita and Pat agreed on

the go-in strategy they would employ. Whatever they proposed to do about Crotty, they knew it would be important to get Chuck to give the plan what they referred to as her "blessing" and in the end, they would simply have to get JoAnne on board. They agreed on a frontal attack and then, if and when JoAnne or Chuck objected, they would fall back. But at least by going in aggressively, it would be clear that they were serious about getting revenge.

The meeting that night utilized the regular agenda. They handled each topic in the normal fashion, except that they sped through the regular agenda in a cursory manner. They all knew that the main event would begin after all other items had been handled.

After the last item of other business was dispensed with, Pat brought in the tray of cannoli they had picked up earlier at the bakery. JoAnne let out an audible sigh as if to demonstrate that she was uncomfortable with the discussion that she knew was coming.

Chuck thanked Pat for the cannoli and said, "Under Miscellaneous, I think we agreed that we would discuss the matter which came up last Sunday and specifically whether or not we would like to respond in any way to the revelations made to us by Mr. Cord. So, I'd like to ask if anyone has any ideas or proposals they'd like for us to consider. I suppose the question before us is two-fold: Will we respond to the allegations against Michael Crotty made by Alex Cord and, if so, how? I know that each of us, in her own way, has wrestled with this question all week. Would anyone like to start the conversation?"

Per their earlier agreement, Rita and Pat waited a moment to see if JoAnne would give any indication of how she would feel about going after Crotty but she sat expressionless and said nothing.

"I have an idea," said Rita firmly.

"Go ahead," Chuck said, not at all surprised that Rita would be prepared.

"I suggest that we firmly agree that we are absolutely

going to right the wrong perpetrated upon JoAnne and Phillip. And I further think that we should agree to use every physical, mental, emotional, and financial recourse at our disposal to take that rat bastard Michael Crotty down and make him pay dearly for what he has done. In short, do whatever it takes to bring Crotty down."

"I agree with that. I definitely agree," Pat said instantly.

Chuck, playing the role as chairman of the group, responded, "Well, that's all fine but it's a little vague on definition. I think, if Rita agrees, that we need to specify how we define 'bring Crotty down.' How will we measure our success if we do this?" After a moment's pause, she said, "It seems to me that good revenge should consist of getting Crotty out of office and in jail. Personally, I think that just killing him is not good enough. It's not enough suffering and, besides, I'm pretty sure that getting God's forgiveness for a killing is going to be hard."

Rita was elated. Clearly, Chuck was buying into the idea of getting revenge. "I agree," she blurted out.

"Me too," Pat said. "I like that!"

They all looked at JoAnne. She shook her head and covered her eyes with her hands in disbelief at what she was hearing. While it appeared that everyone, including Chuck, was in favor of going after Crotty, the final decision was to be hers. She had said nothing during the discussion that would give a hint of what she was thinking.

"First," she finally began, "let me say that outside of my dear Phillip, never in my life have I ever felt so close to or loved by anyone such as the feeling I'm getting from all of you right now. I know that this entire idea, as bizarre as it is, is all about you doing everything you can to support me. Thank you all so much for that. But I have to say that I think what you are proposing is just plain crazy. It's crazy for four ordinary women like us from South Troy to be talking about taking on Michael Crotty and his gang of political cronies. It's crazy for us to think we could pull something like this off, whatever it is that we'd actually try. It's also

crazy for us to be accepting the notion that getting forgiveness instead of permission is okay. I understand that
this is your way of supporting me and supporting Phillip,
and I love you for that more than I can ever say or repay."

"I hear you, JoAnne, and I understand," Chuck responded. "But I think we all know that this is really up to you.
Whatever you decide, you know that we're behind you one
hundred percent. We need to know what you think about
this, no matter how crazy it sounds."

JoAnne was prepared to say no. She still thought this
idea was crazy. But she sat for a second and wondered what
Phillip would think. She often did that when making decisions. As the thought of Phillip crossed her mind, her thinking began to change. She remembered Crotty's phony display of sorrow at the wake. The thought of seeing Crotty
pretending to shed a tear at Phillip's coffin sickened her.
She recalled all of the terrible tales of corruption told to
them by Alex Cord. She recalled how disrespectful Crotty
had been toward Phillip.

Most importantly, she remembered that it was his actions
that caused Phillip's death in the first place. And she knew
that, no matter what actually happened with Phillip that
night on the tracks, he would not have been there in the first
place were it not for what Michael Crotty had done to him.
For all intents and purposes, Michael Crotty had killed Phillip.

Filled with those thoughts, suddenly, she heard her own
voice say aloud, "I agree. I just had a little spiritual meeting
with Phillip, and I know that he would do this for me if
things were the other way around. Phillip and I both vote
yes. We want Crotty out of office and in jail. And we also
would appreciate an apology. Yes, that's right, an apology.
Ladies, we've been talking a lot lately about finding good
causes to support and having more fun. I think that the ruination of Michael Crotty is a very good cause, and I also
think that it will be great fun to make that happen. Oh, and
while we're at it, I also want an apology!" she repeated.

eɔeɔ

With the agreement to avenge the harm inflicted by Michael Crotty, the four friends became of one mind, energized by the challenge of their cause. Rita wrote the words "Out n' In" on a note pad and posted it on the refrigerator door to remind everyone of the goal. Although they still had no idea how they would pull it off, they were of one mind to get Crotty both out of office and in jail.

They talked about Operation Out 'n' In almost incessantly during the following days, not bothering to wait for their normal Wednesday night "business" meetings. It was the topic of conversation at dinner, as they passed in the hallways, as they went about their normal activities. Despite this obsession, as time passed, the details remained so elusive that they soon began to think they were being naive to believe that they could take Crotty and his cohorts down. Despite being clear and unified on their goals, they were quite divided on how to reach them. The more they talked about it, the more these divisions became frustrating.

After a week of this frustration, Rita resorted to confiding in Duke. After all, she thought, who better to consult with on such matters? Duke and his cohorts always seemed to be able to get things done, no matter what type of things needed doing. She told him the entire story and hoped that he, and maybe his group of nefarious co-workers, could perhaps come up with an idea as to how to get back at Crotty. Duke, in turn, engaged his "associates" in such conversations.

They energetically put forth a number of suggestions which were relayed to Rita but, even to her, somehow their ideas always sounded more like criminal operations than anything else. The modus operandi they normally employed, while generally effective, could not pass the unwritten but understood "smell test" of the ladies. Plus, despite her outward bravado, Rita would never ask Duke to do anything that could later land him in jail.

It seemed, after a week or more of constant thought, they all were beginning to think that Operation Out 'n' In was just a silly and undoable idea. After several days had passed, Duke popped in the back door one morning while the ladies were at the breakfast table. He had come to get Joe Black and bring it in for service.

"You look tired, Duke," Pat said while pouring him a cup of coffee.

"I am a little. I got this weird thought last night and it kept me up thinking about it."

The ladies went about their business only paying slight attention to the conversation. Their attention was piqued when he went on to say, "I was thinking about the Operation. I had an idea you ladies might actually like—probably a dumb one though."

"We haven't had any ideas lately, Duke, dumb or otherwise. Let's hear it," urged Pat.

"It's just a general idea. Not specific," he went on.

"Spill it, Duke," Rita said casually, not expecting much.

"I got to thinking about one of the stories that Miss Chuck got me to read. It was one written by that Edgar Poe guy."

"Edgar Allan Poe," Chuck added, although not in a correcting or condescending way. "Everybody refers to him by his full name."

"Yeah, that's the one, Miss Chuck."

"Good idea, Duke. I like it already. We cut out Crotty's heart and hide it under the floor, right?" Rita said jokingly. "Or maybe lay him down under a swinging pendulum and wait for it to cut open his fat belly."

"Good one, Miss Rita. I get the joke, but no. Those are not the stories I was thinking about. I was thinking more of the story called *The Purloined Letter*. I read that one last week. It was a pretty cool story, and I've been thinking about it a lot."

Of course, Chuck knew the story but the others could recall only the name, not the story itself.

"Tell the story, Duke," said Chuck. "And tell us how you think that relates to what we've been struggling with."

Duke pulled back one of the chairs at the table and sat sipping his coffee.

"Well, in this story, there's a real important letter that gets stolen, and the detective...I forget what they called him. It's French, I think."

"The Prefect," Chuck said.

"Yeah, Prefect. Anyhow this Prefect guy needs to find the letter, and he knows it's hidden in some guy's house. I forget how he knows that but it doesn't matter. He and the police spend days, looking all over this house for the letter but can't find it. They tear out the walls and rip up the floors. They take apart the furniture, dump all the drawers. They turn the place upside-down but still can't find the letter. So the cops put up a reward for anyone who can help find the letter. This other guy named Dupin is an amateur detective or something—a Sherlock Holmes type of guy, I guess—and in no time he finds the letter and gets the reward. The letter was in the house all along, just sitting out in plain sight. Right, Miss Chuck?"

"Yes, that's right. That's basically how the story goes. But how do you think this is related to Operation Out 'n' In?"

"Well, I think that the point of the story is all about how Dupin figured it out. He figured that the guy hiding the letter would figure that the detectives looking for it would think that it would be hidden in some really tricky place in the house. So he hid the letter out in plain sight and the cops, looking in all the hard places, never found it. Dupin knew the guy hiding the letter was pretty smart and would do that, so he found it right away."

Duke took another sip of coffee.

"I'm not sure I see where this is going," said Pat.

"I was thinking," replied Duke, "maybe our situation

here is just the opposite of that story. In the story, the guy hiding the letter was really smart so Dupin figured a really smart guy would hide it right out in the open. Maybe we've been trying too hard to come up with a scheme to take Crotty down that's too complicated. In this case, Crotty is pretty stupid. Maybe all we have to do is lay a trap for him and put it right under his nose. He won't be smart enough to see it."

The ladies all sat, just taking in what Duke had just said. They looked at him and then at each other and then at him again.

"Anyway, for what it's worth, that's what I was thinking about," Duke said, getting up from the table. "I know it's just maybe a crazy thought but it should not be that hard to get a dumb person to do something so dumb that he gets run out of office and in jail. I gotta go take the car in for service."

"Wait, Duke," Rita said. "Maybe we should talk about this some more. Maybe you're on to something. Why don't you call your associates, maybe invite them to dinner tonight?"

"This could get fun," Duke said with a wry smile.

Chapter 11

A week later, Duke's pickup truck rolled up to the curb and parked right behind Jimmy Mariano's car in front of the Marconi Club on Van Schaick Avenue. At seven forty-five a.m. on a Monday, the dead-end street was otherwise deserted. They both got out when Duke arrived and stood together on the sidewalk for a moment gazing up at the front door and at the sign that Jimmy, as club president, had posted years before on the inside glass.

"Morning, Jimmy," Duke said.

"Morning."

The sign brought back many bad memories for Jimmy and was a sad reminder that the club never recovered from that horrible night. "God bless Bobby Bocketti," he said softly, reading the words he had written almost six years before.

"Has anybody been in here since?" asked Duke.

"Some. Me and some of the old board members stop in once in a while just to make sure there's no vagrants or wild animals wrecking the joint. We winterized the place pretty good and turned everything off. We keep it heated in the winter to keep everything from freezing up, and we had to replace a few busted windows over time. It's not in bad shape really—considering. I guess we always hoped that someday we'd reopen it but, you know, time has a way of slipping by."

"It does," agreed Duke as Jimmy unlocked the door and they both went inside.

In a way, it seemed like time had stood still all those

years since the club had closed. Things had been cleaned up
after the night of the shooting and, over time, everything
had been removed from the bar, kitchen, and restaurant and
stored in the attic.

The same had been done with the office area, game
room, restrooms, and the upstairs apartment where Bobby
and Pat had lived. But, otherwise, it appeared as it did those
many years ago.

Jimmy was careful to walk around the area on the floor
where Bobby had fallen. It was easy to see that area. So
much scrubbing had been done to clean up the blood that
the wooden floor boards were washed to a neutral color.
Duke noticed the area and avoided walking on it as well.

"It'll be interesting to see what Frank says about how
much fixing up will be needed," Jimmy said as he and Duke
walked into the empty dining room. Their footsteps made a
hollow-sounding echo. Jimmy went to the large windows
and began opening the drapes to let in some light. From one
he noticed a brown panel truck pull up. It was marked,
"Frank Fallon General Contractor."

"Frank's here," Jimmy said as he went toward the door
to let him in. He and Frank Fallon shook hands.

"Frank, this is Duke," was all Jimmy said by way of introduction.

Fallon nodded at Duke as he shook his hand but said
nothing. The three entered the bar area.

"Long time since I been in here. Thinking about opening
'er up again are you, Jimmy?"

"It's time," answered Jimmy.

"Glad to hear it. I miss the place."

"I think everybody does," added Duke.

"Mind me asking, what brings you here, Duke?" Fallon
asked, in his typical no-nonsense way.

"I asked Duke to help us out with the remodeling,
Frank," Jimmy answered. "He's sort of volunteered to be
the go-between for us. I don't really have the time. I got a
day job, you know?"

Frank just nodded but it was obvious he did not really understand. For the next hour, the three walked through the entirety of the Marconi Club, discussing what needed to be done to be able to reopen it. From the conversation, it was clear that Duke, not Jimmy, was making the decisions. Fallon took detailed notes on a room-by-room basis. When they had finished the walk-through, they found themselves back at the bar area.

"Big job, but overall it's not in bad shape," Frank said. "Most of the rooms are just going to need fresh paint and maybe new windows. Same with the kitchen, but some of the equipment is probably going to need replacing, and we'll have to check the plumbing and the electric. Moving this bar area is the biggest issue. You sure you want to do that?"

"We're sure," Jimmy said. "We can't have this area look anything like it did. We don't want anybody walking in and imagining Bobby lying on the floor, you know?"

Frank just nodded again. "What kind of budget are we looking at?"

"Whatever it takes, but not a penny more," Duke answered.

"What kind of timeframe we looking at?"

"Month," Duke replied.

"Month?" said Frank. "Jesus, that's a little tight."

"Six weeks, tops. We want to open on the twenty-fifth of next month," Jimmy said.

"Jesus, Jimmy," Frank said as he poured over his notes. "There's a lot to do. It's gonna depend on how quick I can bring my subs in. I'm going to need a bunch of subs, and I'm afraid of ripping up that bar and finding bad stuff underneath."

"Frank, write it up. Factor in whatever help you need. Whatever amount we agree on, I'll up it by twenty-five percent if you get it done on time," said Duke. "If you don't think you can get it done, let me know right now, and we'll talk to someone else."

Fallon was still confused and looked at Duke with noticeable suspicion. He was surprised when Jimmy had contacted him about renovating the club in the first place. Now he had no idea why, after it had sat dormant for years, there was such a push to get the club back open so soon. And he was totally confused as to why Duke was seemingly calling all of the shots.

"You good with all this, Jimmy?"

"I am, Frank. In case you're wondering about money issues, I'll be signing everything on behalf of the club. If you need some assurances, I'll give you a copy of the line of credit letter I got from Troy Savings Bank."

"No, no. I trust you, Jimmy. Don't get me wrong."

Duke was impressed with Jimmy for pulling off that bluff. There was no line of credit, and there never would be one.

"How long will it take you to put together an estimate?" asked Duke.

"I can get you a figure on the big stuff by tomorrow. Add-ons can be done on the fly. If something huge turns up in the process, we'll have to talk about that later. No offense, Duke, but since I'm going to be laying out a fair amount of cash and making commitments to a bunch of subs, I need club approval on everything. Jimmy has to sign everything and approve any run-ups, not you."

"Understood," said Duke. "If we take your bid, we'll spot you half up front. Can we meet here tomorrow then?"

"You are in a hurry, aren't you?" said Frank. "End of the day tomorrow. I can be here at four o'clock."

Duke looked at Jimmy. "Okay, Jimmy?"

"Four o'clock."

༺༻

Within days, the Marconi Club was a beehive of activity, the likes of which had not been seen on Van Schaick Avenue in a long time.

The sign on the door, which years ago announced the club's closing, was gone.

Each morning, Frank Fallon's panel truck appeared at seven a.m. as did Duke's pickup. Duke would always bring coffee and hard rolls for him and Frank as they started each day with an update before the subcontractors arrived. Frank was still totally unclear as to who Duke was and how he had become the leader of this project. But since Jimmy Mariano was agreeing to everything Duke wanted done, and Duke had become quite helpful to Frank as the project went on and issues arose, they got along well.

It certainly helped with Frank's acceptance of Duke when, a week into the project, Duke handed him a $10,000 cash advance.

Fallon, determined to get his twenty-five percent bonus for bringing the project in on time, assembled a team of subcontractors: plumbers, painters, carpenters, electricians, window installers, and an interior decorating company who would all share in the bonus if the timetable was met. Each morning, they, along with Fallon's regular crew, converged on the club and worked well into the night—the allure of the bonus was highly motivating to all of them. Two weeks into the job, they were running ahead of schedule.

The apartment rooms upstairs were repainted and the bathrooms were upgraded. The downstairs office, meeting room, and game room were freshly painted as well, and the hardwood floors were resurfaced. The main restrooms downstairs were completely remodeled and, by the start of week three, the main bar was moved to the opposite side of the room. Movers had come to resurrect the furnishings that had been kept in the basement, and that which was not salvageable was replaced with new pieces.

As week four of the project began, Duke and Jimmy were ecstatic over the pace of the improvements. Several members of the previous club board of directors had come to see the improvements, and they even held their first meeting in years in the renovated meeting room. The Marconi Club was starting to look like its old self again, most thought, even better.

While it was clear that the club was preparing to reopen, the locals remained perplexed that nothing was being said about a reopening. Jimmy Mariano and other board members were mum about it, and the less they said, the more curious people became. Many of the former club members had come by to see what was going on inside but only the board members and the contractors were allowed in. A new sign had been posted on the entry door glass replacing the old notice of closure. It simply read:

The Marconi Club is preparing to renew its commitment to the ideals upon which it was founded.

This somewhat cryptic message only served to heighten the local curiosity level. The work being done at the club became the topic of much conversation everywhere around Troy. It created so much buzz that the curiosity even reached city hall.

☙❧☙

Michael Crotty was, above all else, a creature of habit. He wore the same "uniform" each day: blue blazer, gray pants, white shirt, and regimental striped tie. He was picked up in front of his house on Dowd Street each morning by his long-time assistant, Bruno Kreider. Kreider used his personal car for the morning pick-ups but whenever they traveled on official business they used a car belonging to the city bearing the NY vanity license plate: *MR MAYOR*. Crotty rarely drove himself anywhere.

Each day, Crotty and Kreider would travel the five blocks to the Downtown Diner where they would sit in the booth at the far end. Kreider would have two cups of coffee, and Crotty would have the "breakfast special" created just for him, consisting of three scrambled eggs, bacon, three pancakes, and a large glass of chocolate milk. Crotty would flirt with Donna, the waitress, and say hello to every single person in the diner, one by one, as he came in. At the end of each brief conversation, he would always say, "Don't forget to let me know how I can help you." By the time he had made the rounds, Donna had put the breakfast special down at his seat in the booth. It was a process that was repeated with precision each and every morning.

"It sounds like they're getting ready to reopen the Marconi Club," Kreider said one morning after Crotty had taken his place in the booth.

"I heard somebody talking about that the other day," Crotty said with a mouthful of pancakes.

"They've been renovating it all month but nobody's saying anything about it."

"We should have voided their lease a long time ago," mumbled Crotty.

"That would not have been smart. Pissing off the Italians is normally not a good thing to do."

"Screw them," Crotty said while wiping a drop of maple syrup from his tie. "Is that nitwit Mariano still running the joint?"

"I guess. But nobody's saying anything about what they're up to."

"Probably because nobody cares."

"Maybe, but I don't like it."

Kreider's comment seemed to suggest to Crotty that the club's reopening was something that he should care about. He put down his fork. "Why don't you like it? Who cares what they do?"

"I can't really say. It's just that I think there were a lot of...let's say...bad feelings about the whole deal with Di-Matteo, and I don't like the fact that all of his supporters will have a new place to come together and bitch about us."

"Let 'em bitch, Bruno. Italians are morons, but they're not totally stupid. They won't soon forget what happened the last time one of their pals decided to fuck with us. Let them have their little hangout. Relax."

"Maybe. I just don't like the smell of it, that's all."

"Well then, go find out what's going on. Sniff around. Ask some questions. Somebody had to get a permit to do all that work, find out who put it in and what it says. Call Mariano. Call your buddy Alex Cord. He's the professional snoop, ask him."

"Maybe I will—just to see what's what."

"Relax, Bruno. You worry too much."

"Maybe."

"Come on, I'm done. Let's get out of here," Crotty said while squeezing himself out of the booth. "See ya, doll," he said to Donna as he was leaving.

She had left them no check for breakfast. She never did.

He left no tip. He never did.

☙❧☙

The renovations at the Marconi Club were finished several days ahead of schedule. At the end of the final walkthrough, Jimmy and Duke thanked Fallon for bringing the project in on time and on budget. Fallon was paid in full, including his twenty-five percent bonus. He thought it curious that Duke paid everything in cash rather than a check from the Marconi Club, but during the course of the project, Fallon had learned that it was best to not ask a lot of questions. Besides, for a lot of reasons, he and his subcontractors loved being paid in cash.

The next night, just after dark, Jimmy Mariano arrived at the club, opened the doors, and turned on every single light in the place. He had seen the project's progress from time to time but this was really the first time that he stood alone, with the place fully lit up, admiring how beautiful the club looked. It was even better than before, he thought.

A few minutes later, Joe Black rolled up to the front of the club where Duke's truck was already parked. Duke was standing at the entrance to the parking lot, having taken down the chain that had been blocking it for years. As he waved at the car, it made its way into the lot in the rear out of sight from the street. Rita, Pat, JoAnne, and Chuck all got out and walked around with Duke to the front steps.

Rita and JoAnne instinctively stood on either side of Pat, each holding her by the arm as they all stood at the foot of the wide stone stairway leading up to the entrance. They were excited that the Marconi Club had been restored to its once-proud-and-beautiful appearance, but more so they were also filled with apprehension as Pat Bocketti was about to return to the place where she and Bobby had lived and worked, the place where she watched him die in her arms the last time she was there.

"You sure you're up to this?" Rita said, breaking the silence.

"It's time," Pat said softly. "Lead the way, Duke."

Mariano welcomed them at the door and led them through the glass entryway into the bar area. They all stood there for a moment, saying nothing. Pat looked directly toward the area where Bobby had fallen but it was difficult to locate the exact spot since everything in the room had been reversed. The bar had been moved to the right side of the room and the old bar area was now covered with cafe tables and chairs. The tables formed an arc around a circular platform that had been built on the spot where Bobby had died.

The platform was about six feet in diameter and about two feet high. On it was a round carpet with oriental decoration around the perimeter in the center of which was woven the image of a lit candle. The platform had no visible function except to serve as a centerpiece around which the tables were situated. While its function was not apparent, its intention was. Pat immediately identified the area and approached it slowly. The others followed closely behind but stayed back as Pat took in the image of the candle. After a moment, she turned, wiped at her eyes, and forced a slight smile.

"It's beautiful," she said.

"We raised it up so nobody would walk there, Miss Pat," offered Duke.

"Was this your idea, Duke?" she asked quietly.

"Well, we all sort of talked about it."

"It was his idea," Jimmy said.

"It's sort of like that eternal flame thing they did for President Kennedy," Duke explained. "If you don't think it's right, Miss Pat, it's out of here tomorrow."

"It's perfect," she said and gave Duke a hug.

Everyone, including Jimmy Mariano, had tears in their eyes. "You're a strong woman, Patty," Jimmy said while walking toward the dining room so as not to be seen crying himself.

"Let's see what else you have to show us, Duke," Jo-Anne said, changing the mood.

"Yes, let's see it all," said Chuck.

The women were amazed and excited by what they saw. They all remembered what the club had looked like and marveled at how much better it appeared, compared to what they remembered. With all of the repairs made, the fresh paint, new decor and furnishings, the Marconi Club was again a sight to behold. As they did their walkthrough, the entrance into each successive room elicited a new round of superlatives from the women.

"I don't suppose you want to see the upstairs apartment," Duke said softly.

"You all can go up," said Pat. "I'll stay here." As strong as she was, she was not about to re-enter the apartment she and Bobby shared.

"I'm sure it's as nice as the rest of the place," said Rita.

None of them went up.

"This is truly wonderful," gushed Chuck as they made their way back toward the front.

"Reminds me of the good old days," Rita added, emphasizing the word, "good."

"It does," agreed Pat. "It really, really does."

"Thank you, Jimmy, and you, Duke," said JoAnne.

"No, thank you," said Jimmy. "If not for you ladies, none of this would have happened—maybe not ever."

"We really should get going, ma'am," Duke said to Rita. "I'm afraid somebody's going to see you ladies in here."

"Yes, we should," Rita agreed. "When are we expecting Mister…" She paused, trying to remember a name.

"Geracitano," Duke said. "Joseph Geracitano. He'll be moving in, probably tomorrow or the next day."

"He's ready for this?" JoAnne said, seeking assurances from Duke.

"He can't wait."

"Game on!" said Rita as she led them out the door.

∽∾∽

Across town, at around the same time, Bruno Kreider noticed Alex Cord come down the stairs and enter the Excalibar. He waved from the far end as Cord strained to see into the dimly lit bar.

Alex Cord first met Bruno Kreider shortly after Kreider had graduated from college with a degree in communications. Kreider's uncle was one of the Democratic organizers in the city's sixth ward whose sole duty it was to visit the home of every person who moved into the ward to make certain that they enrolled as a Democrat and voted in the next election.

While Bruno Kreider had absolutely no demonstrable skill set, he was hired straight out of college as a favor to his uncle to become "special assistant to the mayor" during Michael Crotty's second term. While the job had no real purpose or description, Kreider quickly became a Crotty favorite by being a willing gofer with a seemingly endless appetite for performing any and every task Crotty assigned him. He later redefined the role for himself and became Crotty's closest confidant, skilled at handling all of the mayor's dirty work. With no political or social skills of his own, Crotty relied heavily on Kreider's knack for political expediency. He and Crotty were almost inseparable, and Alex Cord learned early on that Kreider was involved with, if not the mastermind of, everything that Crotty did.

So when Cord was asked by Kreider to meet him that night at Excalibar, he knew full well it was not a social visit.

"Over here. Alex, over here," Kreider called out as he saw Cord enter the bar.

Cord made his way to the far end of the bar where Kreider was sitting. They shook hands.

"Can I buy you a drink?"

"Depends," answered Cord.

"On what?'

"On whether or not I'm working here tonight."

"Oh, hell no, Alex. This is a social visit. You're off the clock. Have a drink."

"I'll just have a Budweiser, Bruno."

Kreider signaled to Brian Crawley behind the bar. "Brian, give our reporter friend here a Bud. Put it on my tab."

For the next several minutes, Kreider made small talk with Cord about trivial occurrences at city hall and the hailstorm that had hit the area the night before.

"You a Yankee fan?" Kreider asked, pointing up at the baseball game on the TV over the bar.

"I don't watch much baseball," Cord replied.

He was well aware that this small talk was all a lead-in to the real reason he had been invited to see Kreider. After they each finished their beer and he ordered another, Kreider casually got to the point.

"Oh, Alex, speaking of what's going on in our fair city, what's this I hear about the Marconi Club getting ready to reopen?"

"Don't know much about it," Cord said equally casually.

"C'mon, you know everything going on in this town, Alex. What's going on over there?"

"I understand they've done some renovations, and they're looking like they're about to reopen the place," was all Cord offered.

"And?"

"And nothing. That's all I know."

Kreider put down his drink and gave Cord a look with an upturned eyebrow.

"That's not like you, Alex. There's stuff going on in our city, and you're not on top of it? You're slipping, pal."

"I didn't see it as a big deal, and it has nothing to do with my area of responsibility with the paper. Why do you care, anyway? Is that why you asked me here tonight? You know something I don't?"

"Maybe. Look, Alex, it's no secret that the relationship between the Italian Americans and our administration is not...shall we say?...all that cordial. Now this has nothing to do with anything that the mayor is interested in, but you know me, I'm curious, that's all. It would be interesting to know what's going on over there. Call it a defensive move on my part."

"What are you defending against?" Cord asked.

Kreider laughed. "I'm defending against everything. That's my job, you know that. Just think of this as me doing my job by trying to find out some otherwise useless information."

"I really have nothing, Bruno. Honestly, I got nothing for you on this."

"That won't do." Kreider said as he got up from the bar stool and walked toward the men's room. He was clearly perturbed.

When Kreider returned, Cord said, "Look Bruno, I think I'm gonna go, okay? If you brought me here to find out about the Marconi Club, you just wasted our time. I got nothing."

"Alex, I gotta tell you that I think you're holding back on me and that makes me a little cranky. Permit me to re-mind you that our office, and me in particular, have been feeding you inside shit for you to use in your paper for a long, long time. It's been a good working relationship, wouldn't you agree?"

"I'd say it's worked for both sides."

"Exactly! Now I would never, ever ask you to do something that's outside of simple reporting, something outside of your job description. But as I see it, you keeping me informed is a big part of your job description."

"Really?" Cord said skeptically. "Keeping you informed is my job? How's that?"

"I look at it this way. The more you are informed, the better you can do your job. Am I right? And as you are well aware, the more that you keep me informed, the more I keep you informed. So it follows that keeping me informed is a part of your job description. No?"

Cord was simultaneously amused and aghast at Kreider's logic but not surprised at all by it. They had had this type of relationship for many years. Kreider apparently thought it necessary to remind Cord of it every now and then.

"I'll see what I can find out, but what exactly do you want to know?"

"Just the basics, for now. I'm probably seeing ghosts where there are none, but I'll be honest with you. I got my ass in a great big crack a while ago when I didn't keep track of what was going on all the while DiMatteo's crowd was plotting and scheming over there in Fippi Casella's beer joint, right under my fucking nose. The next thing we know, my guy gets beat in an election. I am not going to let something like that happen again. The mayor holds me personally responsible for keeping him informed of what he needs to know, especially when it comes to an election."

"So you think that the Marconi Club is the next meeting place for a plot to overthrow Crotty?" Cord said, sounding incredulous.

"I don't think that, no. But let's just say, I get suspicious whenever two or more Italians get together and start talking about anything that has to do with this city."

"Jesus, Bruno. When did you start reading conspiracy novels?" Cord said in an attempt to lighten the mood.

"When I was ten."

"I'll poke around a little. If I find anything out that

sounds like it might interest you, I'll let you know."

"That's the spirit, Cord!" Kreider said loudly, giving Cord a little slap on the back. "Brian, get us one more," he yelled across the bar.

"No, I gotta go, Bruno," Cord said. Clearly this last conversation was the reason Kreider had wanted to talk, and Cord saw no reason to stick around.

"Suit yourself. Brian, just me," he said to the bartender. "I think somebody was just jaywalking on State Street and Alex has to go cover the story," Kreider said mockingly.

After this last remark, it occurred to Cord that Kreider had been hanging around Michael Crotty for too long. He let the slight go. "See you around, Bruno."

Chapter 12

Donna put down the mayor's breakfast before he had even finished his routine glad-handing and gotten to his booth. She poured a cup of coffee for Bruno Kreider, who paid no attention to her. He was reading the morning paper when the mayor sat down. After squeezing himself into the booth, Crotty began to attack the pancakes. "Starvin' today," he said with a mouthful.

"I saw Alex Cord last night," Kreider said.

"So?"

"You suggested I should talk to him about the Marconi Club."

"Well?"

"He told me he didn't know anything about it."

"Do you believe him?"

"Maybe. It's not like the reopening of Yankee Stadium or anything. He didn't think it was that big a deal. He said he'd poke around."

"He's a load," Crotty grunted. "I swear if we didn't feed him information, he'd never write another story."

"He's got some sources. Let's let him do his thing."

"Did he tell you about the grand reopening ceremony?" Crotty asked without looking up from his plate.

"No, he didn't. What grand reopening?" Kreider said nervously. "Nobody has said anything about a grand opening. Who told you that?"

"Bruno, if I'm going to get all of my information from people in this stinking diner, why do I need you?"

"What? What did you hear?"

Just then Donna came by to top off Kreider's coffee cup.

"The good looking one, here, she told me," Crotty said, pointing up at her with his fork. "Tell him what you told me about the Marconi Club."

"Gene Boticelli was talking about it at the counter this morning. He said he got an invitation in the mail to go attend their grand reopening Sunday afternoon."

"This Sunday? Who got invited? Why didn't we know about this?" asked Kreider.

"Maybe it's because you're not Italian, Bruno," said Donna smugly.

Crotty laughed out loud as she walked away. "She's a pip, ain't she?" he said, shaking his head in an exaggerated way.

Kreider pulled out his cell phone and called Alex Cord's number. Cord did not answer, and the call was put into his voice mail.

"Alex, this is Bruno. I just heard that the Marconi Club is having an opening bash this Sunday afternoon. I'm a bit pissed that I didn't hear about this from you. Maybe you should grab your trusty press pass and get over there." Kreider put down his cell phone. "Now I have to tell him where to look for his information. Jesus."

"Both of you are fucking clueless, you know that?" said Crotty as he finished his milk and wiped the chocolate mustache from his upper lip. "Forget Cord, maybe you should go yourself. Get in there yourself and see what they're up to."

"I'm not Italian, remember? I'm sure they just invited their pals."

"Do I have to do all the thinking today? Christ, Bruno, we're dealing with a bunch of guidos. You gotta speak their language, you know? Make them an offer they can't refuse. Like in the stinking *Godfather* movies," Crotty said, amusing himself.

"Like what? Offer what?"

"Simple. Just write up one of those bullshit mayoral

proclamations like we do every time some kid opens up a
Kool Aid stand around here. Declare Sunday to be fucking
Wop Day or something like that. It don't matter what it
says. Tell that moron Mariano that you want to come and
issue a proclamation on my behalf. Tell him I can't make it.
He can't say no even if he wants to. Go and read the fucking thing to them and while you're there find out what's
what and bring me a list of everybody who attends—
especially any of those bastards who took a run at us last
time."

"I'm on it," said Kreider.

℘℘℘

Guglielmo Marconi himself could not have asked for a
finer spring afternoon than the Sunday of the reopening of
the Troy Marconi Club. Van Schaick Avenue and the surrounding area experienced more traffic on that one day than
it had in the previous year combined. Every club member at
the time of its closing was mailed a formal invitation to the
reception which was to be followed by the introduction of
"a prestigious new member" and a review of the club's
plans for the future. The reception was to be free of charge
to all past members and other invited guests with attendees
asked to make a donation to the re-established Marconi
Club Scholarship Fund.

The club's exterior was festooned with American and
Italian flags along with balloons and streamers. Club President Jimmy Mariano stood at the front steps with all of the
other members of the board of directors, forming a receiving line. Inside, a fairly lavish lunch buffet had been catered
in and there was free beer and wine. Nearly all of the 155
invitees from the old membership list showed up, even on
such short notice, and the newly renovated bar, lounge, and
dining area were filled to capacity as the ceremonies began
at three p.m.

A ten-foot stepladder was brought in on which Jimmy

Mariano had to climb up to be seen and heard above the crowd.

Someone yelled, "That's as close to heaven as you're ever gonna get, Jimmy."

The mood was festive, and Mariano had a hard time getting everyone's attention as he balanced himself near the top of the stepladder. He held a microphone in one hand and put his notes on the top step of the ladder.

When he had gotten everyone's attention he welcomed everybody to the reopening of the Marconi Club and read from the official stated purposes of the club and the ideals that its founders had established years before. He only briefly alluded to the reasons for the club's closing and did that only to mention that the reopening had the full support of Bobby Bocketti's widow, Pat, who was unable to attend.

Mariano thanked and introduced the board members, each of whom received a warm reception. He introduced state assemblyman and club member, Don Cantori, who was on hand as were many of the local business owners who had made significant contributions to the scholarship fund. Each was acknowledged with applause. In jest, Cantori made a playful attempt to yank Jimmy off the ladder.

"Still jealous of the people at the top, Assemblyman?" Jimmy joked.

Everyone laughed.

Mariano shuffled his notes yet again while holding the microphone under his chin. Everyone roared when they clearly heard him say, "Oh shit!" as the notes he had so carefully scripted fell out of his hands, cascading onto the floor. "Well, screw it," he said. "I'll just wing it."

Applause all around.

"I also want to introduce Mr. Bruno Kreider, Special Assistant to Mayor Crotty, who has a proclamation to deliver."

As Kreider proceeded toward Jimmy, a polite but noticeably tepid smattering of applause could be heard. As Kreider reached the ladder, Jimmy made no move to come down so that the mayor's representative could climb up to be seen. Jimmy also made no move to hand over the microphone.

Kreider, a rather short and indistinguishable man, was not visible to anyone except those standing in his immediate vicinity. He began, as loudly as he could, to read several "Whereas" paragraphs of the proclamation, few of which could heard by anyone. He finished in as loud a voice as he could muster with a declaration that the day be officially known as Marconi Day in the City of Troy.

To his great surprise and puzzlement, the proclamation was met at first with total silence and then, as word of what he had just said spread across the room, there rose a chorus of laughter. His head spun as he tried to comprehend what was happening. He knew that the crowd was not going to be overly appreciative of anything coming from the mayor, but he was stunned by this reception. Why was everybody laughing? Were they laughing at him? Was it what he just said? Did he say something wrong?

Mario Valentini, one of the older members of the club, couldn't resist. He reached up and took the microphone from Jimmy's hand. "Hear that everyone?" he blared. "Our thoughtful mayor has decided that April twenty-fifth is Marconi Day. Well, thank you so much, Mayor."

Everyone roared hysterically.

A clearly embarrassed Kreider handed the proclamation copy up to Mariano, who was still atop the ladder, and quickly headed toward the door. He still did not understand what had happened. He had personally written it and scribbled Crotty's signature on the bottom. While he had not shown it to anyone beforehand, he knew that it read correctly. Kreider had no idea what was so funny. In his embarrassment, he hurriedly gave a cursory wave to the raucous crowd and left.

What Kreider did not know, of course, was that the grand reopening of the Marconi Club was being held on that day for a very specific reason. April twenty-fifth was Guglielmo Marconi's birthday and, as such, had long been rec-

ognized by Marconi Clubs everywhere as their most cele-
brated day of the year. Kreider had, with much fanfare, just
publicly declared it to be Marconi Day on what had, to Italians, been Marconi Day for decades. Everyone was greatly
amused by this—everyone except Bruno Kreider.

Alex Cord stood alone in the back of the room as he had
most of the afternoon. "Moron," he mumbled as he watched
Kreider beat a hasty retreat.

Jimmy took back the microphone from Mario Valentini,
who was still in hysterics. It took Jimmy several seconds to
compose himself and calm down everyone in the room.
"Mario, remind me to send the mayor an Italian calendar,"
he said into the microphone, not being able to resist one last
dig at Kreider's gaff.

When some semblance of order was restored, Jimmy
soldiered on. He began to fill everyone in on the club's plan
to again become the center of what he called "Italian values" in the city. He announced the schedule of events which
would be highlighted by the two main festivals of days past:
Columbus Day in the fall and, he said, not being able to re-
frain from taking one more shot at Kreider, "I guess in hon-
or of the mayor's proclamation we're actually having a
Marconi Day celebration next year too and it will be on
Marconi Day!"

The crowd let out the loudest cheer of the afternoon.

"Now, before this gets even more out of hand," Jimmy
continued, "let me introduce to you our most distinguished
guest."

With that, a man who appeared to be in his early thirties,
dressed in an expensive-looking double-breasted gray pin-
stripe suit could be seen coming down the stairs from the
upstairs living quarters. He wore a white shirt and a purple
silk tie with a matching pocket scarf. He was perfectly
groomed and stood out among the more casually-dressed
attendees. As he glided gracefully forward, he could be seen
straightening his tie and tugging at his monogramed shirt
cuffs. When he reached the ladder, Mariano continued.

"Ladies and gentlemen, this day—this wonderful day—and the reopening of our beloved club would not have happened were it not for one man. You perhaps have been wondering why we decided to reopen the club and also wondering how we have been able to do it in such a magnificent way—how we have been able to afford all this," Jimmy said while sprawling out both arms as though to display the beautiful new surroundings. "The man I am about to introduce is, like all of us, a proud Italian. He's a proud Italian who came to this area recently and heard about the hard times that had befallen our club and the void in our neighborhood that was created when we had to close our doors. He heard about hard-working people like so many of us, who grew up in the shadow of this place and who called it our home-away-from-home, people who lost a big part of their lives when the Marconi Club closed.

"He heard about the Italian kids in our neighborhood who could not go to college because our scholarship program was discontinued. He heard about the loss that we felt when we no longer had a place to break bread together, to drink together, to have festivals together, to play together, or a place where we could honor and maintain our heritage. This man's own childhood and upbringing made him aware of how much our club was missed by all of us, and he knew he had to do something to bring it all back. He believes in the ideals of the Marconi Club and respects the work of our founding members and all those who kept the club going through all of those tough years. So much so does he believe in what we all believe that he recently came to us with an offer to help us bring it all back.

"Now, out of respect for him we cannot and will not go into all of the details of this arrangement. In the end, none of that is important. What is important is that our club is alive again, and the Italian heritage so dear to all of us will live in our neighborhood. Please welcome the man who made it all happen, Mr. Joseph Geracitano."

The members were amazed by what they had just heard.

They all looked at each other as if to say, "Who?" Nobody had ever seen or heard of this man before yet Jimmy was heralding him as the savior of the Marconi Club and the new poster boy for Italian heritage in Troy.

Jimmy climbed down from the ladder and handed Geracitano the microphone. Despite begin overdressed for climbing ladders, he grabbed the microphone and gamely climbed most of the way up so that he could be seen by everyone. The applause increased as he did.

"I'm not scared of much, but I am a little nervous on a ladder," he was overheard saying as made his way up. "Thank you everyone and thank you, Jimmy, for that very kind introduction. I only have a couple of things to say. I'm not that big on giving speeches. First, I want to thank you all for coming to this great occasion. Surely Guglielmo Marconi is smiling down on us this day as the sunshine outside clearly demonstrates. It would be my honor to meet every one of you as I honestly hope to do today and in the days ahead. As Jimmy said in his very kind introduction, I'm here today and happy to be a part of the reawakening of the club because I believe in what it stands for, and I believe in the goodwill of all of you, its wonderful members." He paused for effect just as he had rehearsed and was pleased that this was met with applause.

"I would also like to thank President Mariano and the board members for their support of my efforts here and let them know that I appreciate them offering to me an honorary membership in this fine club." More applause. "While my given name is Joseph Anthony Geracitano, I prefer to be called what I have been called by my friends since growing up in my own Italian neighborhood. Please call me Joey G. or just plain Joey. In closing, I hope to be getting to know all of you very soon and hope you all come back to the club regularly as I plan on being here regularly too. Thank you."

The crowd reaction was polite but lacked its earlier enthusiasm. They had expected to learn much, much more about this otherwise unknown and unexpected benefactor.

After Jimmy's tantalizing introduction, all they really learned about him was his name.

Jimmy took the microphone and went back up the ladder. It was time for him to wrap up the formal part of the program and allow the members to mingle and enjoy the buffet. He then made a tactical error. "Before we close the official part of our program today, does anyone have any questions or comments they want to make?" he said almost as a throw-away line of conclusion. A hand was raised from the middle of the room. Another long-time member and former board member, John Paladino, had his hand in the air.

"Comment, John?" Jimmy asked hesitantly.

"Not really a comment but a question."

"What is it?"

"Well, back in the day," Paladino said in a loud voice, "every time a new member came into the club, he was asked to tell us about himself and members got to ask him some questions about his background and such. Since Mr. Geracitano is a new member, and I guess a real important one at that, I think we'd all like to hear more about him."

The crowd seemed to concur with Paladino's comment as it elicited a great deal of applause.

"Well, John, this is sort of a different occasion, and I think people are getting a little hungry and thirsty, so why don't we save that for another time," Jimmy quickly replied. It was clear that he had not expected this and was trying to avoid it. But he was stuck.

"We got time, Jimmy. Let's hear about our new guy," came a different voice from the crowd. "Yeah, Joey G. tell us about yourself," came another.

Jimmy was unnerved. The program had been tightly scripted and didn't include putting out any detailed information about Geracitano. Jimmy assumed that Joey G. had not prepared for any such event. As he was contemplating how to deflect this without seeming evasive, Geracitano reached up and took the microphone from his hands.

"Happy to, sir," he said. "If you don't mind, I'll do it from down here this time. I'm a little afraid of heights," he joked to lighten up what he sensed was a little tension growing in the room. At that point, Joey happened to glance toward Duke Bennett who had appeared halfway down the stairs with a worried look on his face. Duke had been listening from the upstairs apartment all afternoon, not wanting to be seen, but this made him too nervous to not come and take a look. Geracitano gave Duke a little wink of assurance.

Duke remained concerned. This was not in the plan and he had no idea how Joey would handle it.

"I kept it short earlier because I don't want to bore all of you with the details of my past. But since you asked, let me give you the highlights, such as they are—kinda' boring actually. Well, let's see…I was born at a very young age," he said, pausing to wait for the joke to sink in. He was glad when he heard a few laughs. "Seriously, since the name Geracitano is a bit of a mouthful especially to non-Italians, I am often called Joey G., or just plain Joey, either way. I am thirty-seven years old, and I have two younger brothers, Michael and Al—for purposes of trying to endear myself and my family to everybody here, I'll add that Al's real name is Alfonse." He paused again and got more reassurance when he saw some smiles from the crowd. "Anyway, my dad was a stone mason and my mom took care of us and our little house in Bayside, Queens. It was a pretty normal childhood for me and my brothers—like the Cleavers—you know the Cleavers from *Leave It To Beaver*. Except my family had more style," he said with a wry smile, "and my mom made a better red sauce than Beaver's mom." Joey was hitting his stride to the amusement and interest of all of the members.

"I went to St. Anthony's school in Bayside until I was eleven when unfortunately, my parents were both killed in a hit-and-run accident while on their way to church." Joey paused to let the audible "ooohs" and "oh nos" from the

crowd sink in before going on. "Me and my brothers moved
in with my Aunt Marie and Uncle Pete out on Long Island
but they were very poor. We were so poor, we couldn't
even afford to pay attention." Joey again paused waiting for
his little joke to be picked up. Getting little reaction, he
immediately smiled and went on. "Anyway, by the time I
got to high school, I was helping bring in money for Aunt
Marie and Uncle Pete by being a runner at the Hempstead
Italian-American Club. For those of you who don't know
what a runner is, it's a kid who hangs around a men's club
and runs errands for the members. I would bring them
drinks, get them cigars, empty ashtrays, run their numbers,
things like that. All legal stuff…well, mostly legal stuff. I
made pretty good tip money there, which I always handed
over to my aunt and uncle, to help support us. I did that for
a few years until one day I foolishly talked back to one of
the men who was giving me a hard time about my acne
which I had pretty bad in those days. That turned out to be a
huge mistake since the guy that I talked back to apparently
did not like backtalk, especially from little snot-nosed kids
like me. He took out a handgun and shot me in the foot."

The Marconi Club crowd was captivated by this story as
Joey went on. Duke and Jimmy were incredulous. Where
was this all coming from?

"I got taken to the emergency room, and I told the doc-
tors I got shot in a hunting accident. Nobody believed that,
of course, since few people actually hunt in Hempstead,
especially with a thirty-eight. They knew I was covering for
somebody, which they understood, and everyone at the club
appreciated, especially the guy who shot me. He later gave
me two large for keeping my mouth shut. Anyway, I had
surgery done on my foot, coincidentally by an Italian sur-
geon, Doctor Vumbacco, who lived on the North Shore. He
was really rich and felt bad for me when I told him my story. He took me into his home and I became a part of his
family. Beautiful home, North Shore, Long Island no less."

Joey paused and smiled a little toward the stairs where

Duke stood, still in shock over what he was hearing. The entire story that Joey was telling was totally made up and, Duke thought, was getting more and more implausible the longer Joey went on. Yet on he went.

"Should I stop now?" Joey said.

"No! Go on," yelled someone from the crowd. Everybody applauded their agreement.

"Anyway, the Doc—I called him Doc—started bringing me to the North Shore Marconi Club where the members treated me so nice I couldn't believe it. They had a scholarship fund, just like you folks do here, and I ended up going to NYU on the Marconi Club scholarship where I studied finance. When I graduated from NYU, one of the club members, who was a big shot on Wall Street, offered me a job. It turns out I had a knack for securities trading and luckily got in at the right time. I started making a ton of money and made more and more every year. That went on for five years.

"As you may have heard some of those security trading firms eventually ran into a few problems and went bankrupt, but before that happened I had made an obscene amount of money. I made so much money I'm embarrassed to tell you. But by then I had had it with that business anyway. What I was doing was a little too...I don't know...not right, if you know what I mean. Not illegal exactly, just not right. Anyway, by that time, I had made enough money to live on for a long, long time so I decided to get out of Dodge. I moved upstate.

"The point of me telling you all this is that, because of what Doc Vumbacco and the other men at the North Shore Marconi Club did for me, I vowed to someday pay back their generosity. When I heard about the problems here at the Troy Marconi Club, I remembered that vow. I called Jimmy Mariano and the rest, as they say, is history."

There was total silence in the room. Nobody had any idea where the mysterious Joey had come from but certainly no one could have foreseen the amazing tale they had just heard. To a person, they all stood motionless, including Duke who was still at the base of the stairs in disbelief at what he had just heard.

"And that's my story," Joey said.

"And you're sticking to it, right?" yelled Mario Valentini.

"Any questions?" Joey replied. "Then let's eat!"

The rest of the afternoon went according to plan. Joey G. was the center of attention and carried himself admirably. He met scores of members who all were friendly and appreciative toward him. Jimmy was at his side throughout and was both amazed and impressed at how Joey had handled the entire afternoon. Of all the people Geracitano had met that day, no one seemed anything but pleased to meet him. Of course, not a single one actually believed his incredible story. And not a single one questioned it.

After the festivities concluded and Jimmy and Joey personally said goodbye to every last person, Jimmy locked the door and went back into the bar with Joey. Duke had come back down the stairs and poured himself a beer when they got to the bar.

"That was the single most incredible bunch of bullshit I have ever heard," Duke said as he quickly polished off the beer.

"What?" said Joey as he took off his suit jacket and loosened his tie.

"That story! That stuff about your parents being killed, you getting shot, and making all that money on Wall Street. Was any part of that even remotely true?" asked Jimmy.

"Of course not," Joey said almost dismissively, "not a single word of it."

"Joey, I don't know how smart it was to make up all that shit," said Duke. "We didn't talk about doing any of that."

"Come on, Duke, you were there! I had to say something. What did you want me to do tell everybody I was an ex rabbi or something? An artist maybe? A magician? A proctologist? What was I supposed to say?"

"Maybe you should have told everybody that you got dropped on your head, got amnesia, and can't remember anything about your past. That would have been more believable."

"You don't get it, do you?" Joey asked.

Just then there was a knock on the door and Jimmy went to see who it was. It was Mario Valentini. A few seconds later Jimmy reappeared at the bar with Mario.

"Mario has one more question, Joey."

"Hey, Mario, go home, go home, the beer's all gone," Joey said cheerily. "Kidding—just kidding, my friend. What can I do for you?"

Mario moved closer to Joey, stood for a moment, looking at him and said, "Your life story you told us today...Goodfellas, right? Spider. The kid in the movie, Goodfellas. The gofer kid who got shot in the foot. Am I right?"

Joey smiled at Mario. "Good catch, Mario," he said with a wry smile. "But the stuff about Wall Street I made up myself."

"I knew it!" Mario exclaimed as though he had just figured out the meaning of life. "I knew when you were telling that story it reminded me of something. Your story was just like the kid in that gangster movie. I knew it. I knew you were making that shit up. Beautiful!" he said as he walked toward the door, shaking his head. "That was beautiful. I get it. That was beautiful."

After Mario had left, Joey went behind the bar, poured another beer, and placed it in front of Duke. "See, Duke?" he said.

"See what?"

"I told you that you didn't get it. But Mario does."

"Get what? What the hell are you talking about?"

"There's that old expression, 'never try to bullshit a bullshitter.' Ever hear of that?"

"Yeah, I've heard of that but you're right—I still don't get it."

"I found myself in a little jam here today in a room full of Italians, a room full of professional bullshitters. So I gave them a story that was so much bullshit that they would all know it's bullshit. The point—which they get and you don't—is that by telling them this obviously made-up story, they would immediately know that this is my way of telling them that I am not about to tell anybody about my real background. Get it? Now they all know that there's something deep and dark and most likely a little scary about me. They don't know what it is, but none of them will ever question it again. They now know I won't tell my real story anyhow and, besides, they're afraid the real truth is something they don't really want to know."

Duke took another sip of beer. Jimmy ran his hands through his hair. "He might be right, Duke. In some dopey-assed convoluted way, he might be right."

"I don't know," said Duke.

"You're not Italian, are you, Duke?" Joey said.

Chapter 13

Even after the grand reopening, improvements at the Marconi Club continued. It quickly became clear that the tone and tenor of the club was reverting back to its roots. The most obvious improvements were all designed to appeal to the older members, specifically, the older Italian men who once used the Club as a daily get-away from their otherwise uneventful lives. The downstairs steam room was renovated and became operational in short order. The nine-foot pool table was refurbished, and two new card tables were purchased for the game room. Several large-screen TVs were set up—two over the bar and one in the sitting area near the old fireplace in the rear corner of the restaurant. The Marconi Club was being set up as an Italian version of a man-cave.

While the club was not open for dinner as it had been when Pat and Bobby Bocketti were in residence, it was open for lunch. Duke hired a daytime cook named Angelo Renna, who was the long-time general manager of The Villa de Ville—a once famous restaurant in the Troy Hill Section. The Villa, as it was known, had burned to the ground in what locals referred to as a "successful fire," given its waning popularity over the previous several years and the fact that it was never rebuilt.

Although in his sixties, Renna was not the type to be retired so he was happy to take the job for a few hours a day running the small kitchen operation at the club. He was really not a cook, but he knew enough about running a kitchen to handle a small lunch menu. He was delighted to take the job at the Marconi Club so that he could get back into a routine and be among old friends every day.

Every morning at eight-thirty, Duke would arrive to open the doors and make sure the nightly cleaning service had taken care of everything. He would fill and start the coffee urn located by the fireplace, put out the cream and sugar, place the daily newspapers he had brought with him on the coffee table by the fireplace, and turn on the TV.

By nine, some of the members would begin to come in for their free coffee. Several of the regulars took turns stopping at the Skylark bakery on their way to bring in pastries. Some would just sit and read the paper, others would watch TV, and a few would venture downstairs for a morning steam and shower. Generally, they just hung around playing pool or cards or sitting at the bar, solving all of the world's problems.

Around ten each day, Angelo Renna would appear, bearing the supplies he would need for that day's lunch. There was no actual lunch menu but each day Angelo would make a fresh pot of pasta e fagioli and a batch of chicken and rice soup. There would always be one hot and one cold sandwich available. The set charge for members' lunch was five dollars; draft beer and soda were one dollar; and there was, behind the bar, a vast but inexpensive choice of wines by the glass. The members could come early in the morning, have lunch, watch TV, play a game of pool or two, and stay all day for under ten dollars.

The club stayed open until seven p.m. By late afternoon, all but a few of the daily regulars had returned home and a second wave of members began to appear as they stopped in for a quick beer after work.

Bar tending was handled every day between three and seven p.m. by an affable but clearly rough-edged man in his early fifties named Tom Monacelli, who had spent his early years working on a tugboat team out of the Port of Albany. He had the appearance of a man who had spent hard time at sea although he almost never ventured beyond the Hudson

River. He was an unabashed NRA member and often spoke of his prized gun collection. He was fond of repeating the words of the former senator from Texas who once said, "I own more guns than I need but not as many as I want." He had a story for every occasion, true or not, and was one of those people who remembered every joke he had ever heard and somehow managed to tell it better each time he did. He went by the nickname Tugboat Tommy. Almost everyone simply referred to him as Tugboat.

Sometime around noon each day, Joey G. would come down from the upstairs apartment where he had taken up residence. He always wore a suit and tie and seemingly got a fresh haircut every day. Joey would greet each person, one by one. He had a talent for getting everyone to tell him everything about themselves without ever revealing much about himself. He would join them for lunch and then disappear into the back office, ostensibly to take care of some business. Occasionally, he would head out the door, saying, "I gotta go see somebody about something," and drive off in his black Lincoln Town Car.

With each passing day, the Marconi Club settled into a little routine all of its own. The members loved the new place and couldn't imagine how they had lived for so long without it. They were amazed by how all the renovations and improvements had been done to the club and that nobody was even being asked to pay dues. That oddity had become a frequent topic of quiet conversation around the bar and even around town, but nobody seemed to know how, or really why, this was all happening. Surely Joey was behind it all, they thought, but it was clear he was not going to say how or why, at least not yet.

And so it was when, on a routine Tuesday afternoon, that Al Clemente, a club regular, came in looking particularly glum.

Other regulars had taken up their usual places at the bar and were engaging in their two favorite pastimes: watching the OTB channel on one TV and CNN on the other.

"Tugboat, do you know Gerry Sickles?" Al Clemente said as he was pushing his empty beer glass ahead on the bar, signaling he wanted another.

"Who?" said Tugboat Tommy as he came to grab Al's glass.

"Gerry Sickles. You know him? He's the guy who lives next door to me with that no-good son of his."

"Don't think so," said Tugboat. "Why, should I?"

"No. Probably not. I was just wondering."

"I know him," offered Pete Tedesco, seated a few stools down. "I used to work with him at the paper mill. He's always been a bit of a hot-head. He worked nights at the mill and was always getting in somebody's face about something stupid."

"Yeah, I hear you," said Al. "He's got this teenage kid who's a druggie or something, and about three nights a week the kid and his delinquent friends are out in Sickles's backyard drinking beer and blasting their stinking music until all hours of the night. They're right across the fence from our bedroom, so it's impossible to sleep when they're out there. I tried talking to Sickles about it, and he told me if I didn't like the neighborhood I should move—belligerent bastard. Mary wants me to call the cops on them, but the guy is a nutcase. I know damn well that if I call the cops, they'll do nothing and things will only get worse."

"Sounds like Sickles," Tedesco said. "I understand your problem. You're right, though. If you call the cops on that psycho, the next thing you know you'll be calling the fire department to come and put out your house fire. He's gotta short fuse. He gets in trouble at the mill all the time. Be careful of that guy, Al."

"I don't know what to do about it, but it has to stop. I thought maybe somebody who knows him could help me out with this."

"Wish I could," replied Tedesco. "Wish I could."

Joey G. was seated at the corner of the bar, having a sandwich and reading the paper as this conversation took place. After overhearing it, he put the paper down and quietly approached Al, trying not to appear obvious.

"Al," Joey whispered and gave a motion with his head to get Al to come with him.

"What, Joey?" Al said over his shoulder.

Joey made the same come-with-me motion in Al's direction and began walking toward his office. Al got up and followed him in. Joey asked Al to take a seat and said he'd be right back. Al wondered what this was about. He had never seen anyone go into Joey G.'s office before.

Moments later, Joey came back with Duke who said nothing and sat in a corner chair. Al and all the members had seen Duke coming and going, but nobody had ever been introduced to him and nobody really knew who he was. To them, Duke was just another unexplained oddity in and around the club. Presumably Duke was a hired helper, but that's all anyone knew about him.

Joey sat behind the desk without introducing Duke or otherwise even mentioning him. "Al Clemente here has a little problem," Joey said to no one in particular. "Tell us more about it, Al."

"You mean the thing with Gerry Sickles? No, really, I can take care of that. No big deal, Joey."

Joey leaned back in his chair and put his feet up on the desk. "I've been hearing a lot around here about how, in the old days, when club members had problems other club members would step in to, you know, help them solve them. As you know, I'm very interested in maintaining the traditions of our club and was just wondering if, somehow, I can be of assistance with your issue with Mr. Sickles. We don't want you and your wife being kept awake all night."

Al was both surprised and intrigued by what Joey had just said. "You can help me out with this? That would be great, but believe me, I know you got better things to do than worry about me and Mary sleeping."

"This is not about sleep, this is about responding to a fellow member in need of something."

"You would do that?" Al said incredulously.

"Not saying I will or I won't. Let me just say that I'm going to leave you with my friend Duke, here. You tell him what you were saying at the bar, answer any questions he might have, and we'll see. If your problem goes away, that means my answer was yes. If it doesn't go away…"

Joey got up, shook Al's hand, and left him alone in the office with Duke. They talked for several minutes. When Al got back to the bar, Joey was gone. As Al finished his beer, Pete Tedesco leaned over to look down the bar at him.

"What was that all about?" Tedesco asked.

"Not real sure, Pete. Not real sure."

Just then, Tugboat Tommy walked by, stopped in front of where Al was sitting, and gave him a little wink. "Sleep tight," was all Tugboat said.

ↁↁↁ

The following night, a Wednesday, the ladies of The Settlement were going through their normal meeting agenda when Duke knocked on the door. Rita got up and let him in.

"Sit for a sec, Duke, will you? We're almost ready for you."

For the past several weeks, the ladies met as usual and had added a last item to their regular agenda—Operation Out 'n' In. Duke would come into the meeting at that point, brief them on developments at the Marconi Club, and present to them, for their approval, items relating to activities, expenditures, and future plans. It was the process they would follow for all decisions that needed to be made related to Operation Out 'n' In.

Duke's report that night was detailed and took over an hour. Among other things, he brought up Al Clemente's problem with Gerry Sickles. When they had concluded, Duke left and the meeting was adjourned. The ladies of The Settlement then went about their usual activities, none of which included going anywhere near the Marconi Club.

⌒⌒⌒

Gerry Sickles had just finished his night shift at the paper mill and was heading to his car in the lot behind the mill. It was just after seven a.m. Of the twenty or so men who were finishing their night's work, Sickles was one of the last to make his way toward his car. As he neared it, he stopped short, noticing three men standing beside it. One, a large Jamaican man, was leaning against the driver's side door of Sickles's car.

The other two were standing off to the side of the Jamaican.

As Sickles instinctively was about to run from what looked for all the world to be a holdup, he heard a voice come from immediately behind him. "Don't panic, Sickles, we just want to talk. At least this time."

He turned quickly. The man who had spoken was a rugged-looking individual who purposely and menacingly opened his jacket to reveal a shoulder holster and a hand gun.

Sickles was panic-stricken.

"Over here," the man said as he took Sickles by the arm to approach the others.

The nicely dressed and well-groomed man in the middle spoke as they neared. "Mr. Sickles, my name is Joseph Geracitano. My associates and I are here this morning to discuss with you a matter involving your son's behavior as it pertains to our client and your next-door neighbor, Mr. Al Clemente and his lovely wife Mary. Apparently, Mr. Clemente has tried to resolve this matter with you but to no avail."

Geracitano spoke in soft tones for several minutes while the others stood uncomfortably close to Sickles. Twice when he tried to interrupt, Sickles was told by Tugboat Tommy, the man with the gun, to just "shut up and listen." When he finished talking, Geracitano shook Sickles's hand.

The Jamaican slowly moved away from the car door. Sickles hastily got in, started the car, and drove off.

"Some tough guy," Donnie smirked.

"Thanks for coming, Donnie. You too, Tugboat," Duke said. "Donnie, you working today?"

"Yeah, I'm flagging at the road job up on Colvin Avenue. It's supposed to rain. I hate standing out in the rain getting splashed on all day. I gotta go. If I'm not there by seven-thirty my foreman will go ape-shit. See ya."

"See ya, Donnie," said Joey and Tugboat simultaneously as Moore headed toward his Chevy Blazer parked a few cars away.

"I didn't have my coffee yet," said Joey. "Wanna stop somewhere?"

"Coffee? No thanks," said Tugboat. "I'm going back to bed. This seven o'clock shit is not for me, man."

"Okay, I hear you," Joey said. "Duke, next time we need to deliver a message, can we make it sometime after noon so Tugboat can get his beauty sleep?"

"I'll see what I can do. Thanks for coming everybody," Duke said.

ᏋᏂᏋᏂ

"I'm telling you, the moron and his snot-nosed kid both showed up at my door last night," Al Clemente said to Pete Tedesco and a few others at the bar the next day. "I couldn't believe it. It scared the shit out of me when I saw them standing there ringing my doorbell. I told Mary to get ready to call nine-one-one. Next thing I know Sickles and the kid are apologizing up and down for making too much noise, and they're promising it'll never happen again. They actually apologized. Shocked the crap out of me."

"That's unbelievable," said an astonished Tedesco. "That guy never apologized for anything in his life. What the hell?"

Clemente moved closer to Tedesco as though to tell a

secret but everyone heard him anyway. "I know how that happened. The other day Joey G. heard me yammering about Sickles. He asked me all about it. I gave him details and, within two days, problem gone! That was no coincidence, my friend, no coincidence."

"Nice to see people still do good deeds in this day and age," Tugboat Tommy said as he passed by, wearing a knowing smile.

Al purposely waited around that day for Joey G. to come into the bar. He wanted to thank him personally. Joey had gone out earlier to "see somebody about something" and it was not until late in the afternoon that the Lincoln Town Car rolled into its reserved parking spot.

Joey came in through the front door, upbeat as always. "Ciao, fellow immigrants," he said with a wave.

The ten or so bar patrons all greeted him as he strode past the bar.

"Mr. Tugboat, sir," he bellowed, "beer for me and me mates. On me!"

"Hey, what's the occasion, Joey?" yelled out Marty Maroni from the far end of the bar as Tugboat Tommy set upside-down shot glasses in front of everyone at the bar to indicate they had a free beer coming.

"Occasion?" Joey yelled as he was hanging up his coat. "What the hell, you calling me a cheapskate? Like I need an occasion to buy you slugs a drink?"

"Aw, I'm only kidding, Joey," Maroni said, somewhat embarrassed. "I know plenty of cheapskates, but you're certainly not one of them. No offense."

"None taken, Marty. Besides, there is an occasion, actually. I just spent the past three hours with Jimmy Mariano down at the State Liquor Authority begging them to get off their asses and get us our liquor license back. 'Beer and wine are fine, but my men need liquor!' I told them. Jesus what a bunch of hard-asses they are down there," he continued while grabbing his seat at the end bar stool. "For a bunch of overpaid political appointees, they sure know how to jerk somebody around. I haven't dotted so many i's or crossed so many t's since I had to forge Vito Minetti's signature." He laughed.

They all laughed along as soon as they got his joke.

"Well, are we finally going to get some real booze going over my bar?" Tugboat asked.

"Next Wednesday!" Joey yelled.

After things had settled down, Al Clemente finally got up the nerve to approach Joey about the incident with Sickles. He had first written out and then carefully rehearsed his thank you all morning.

"Joey G.," he said as he put his hand on Joey's shoulder, "on behalf of my wife, I want to thank you for whatever it was that you did to help me with my problem the other day. It was wonderful and kind of you to take time from your busy day to do that for us. You surely are a fine example of the Italian spirit and camaraderie that this club stands for. I'm in your debt." He was relieved that he had remembered his rehearsed speech verbatim.

When Al finished, he noticed that everyone at the bar had stopped to listen. He was so intent on saying exactly what he had rehearsed, he was afraid that he had spoken too loudly.

Joey turned toward Al, stared for a moment, and gave him a great big smile. "Whatever are you talking about, Al? I'm sure I have absolutely no idea what you are talking about," he said in an exaggerated way.

Everyone enjoyed both the joke and its intent. They all knew that Joey had somehow fixed Al's problem but he was not about to "confess" to anything.

Al quickly felt relaxed that he had done and said the right thing with his thank-you speech. "I was going to get Mary to come to thank you too but I wasn't sure, you know? But believe me, Mary is grateful too. Very grateful."

"Do I have to plead the fifth, for God's sake?" Joey said loudly, continuing the ruse. "All right, all right. Listen everybody, I don't know what Al here has told you and, I repeat, I have no idea what Al is talking about. But let me just say that there are many, many benefits that come with being a member of the Marconi Club, and if any of you, for any reason, think this is an example, then don't forget to tell your friends about the benefits of membership. Oh, and one more thing, Al," Joey said as the bar quieted. "One more thing, before I forget."

"What's that, Joey?"

"You said earlier that you are in my debt. Did you not say you were in my debt?"

"I did Joey. I did say that. I am in your debt."

"Well, if you're in my debt, then buy me a damn beer, you cheapskate!"

Chapter 14

While things at the Marconi Club were going well, things at city hall were not, especially for Bruno Kreider. After the Marconi Day incident, he still had no idea of the faux pas he had made with the proclamation. Alex Cord, who had witnessed the whole event, knew that it would be no time before Kreider reached out to him to see what, if anything, he had found out about the club and its cast of characters. Cord soon received a voicemail message from Kreider asking for a meeting with him and the mayor at City Hall.

"Morning, Kathy," Cord said as he swung open the door marked *Mayor's Office*. Cord had always liked Kathy Gill. Despite being Michael Crotty's secretary, she was somehow able to stay above the fray and not be affected by all of the negativity and nonsense that went on inside that office. In fact, she had been secretary to the mayor for twenty-seven consecutive years, regardless of who the actual mayor was. She was Phillip DiMatteo's secretary during his short tenure in office and was as sorry as anyone to see Phillip step down. Cord actually admired Kathy for being able to work there for so long and not take on any of the heinous qualities of those who crossed her path each day. She was, he thought, just plain gracious, despite all of the decidedly ungracious people with whom she dealt every single day.

"Hello, Alex, how are you?" she said in a way that sounded like she actually cared.

"I'm well, Kathy. Glad spring is finally here."

"Oh, me too. Seems like the winter gets snowier and

colder every year. Let me buzz you right in, the mayor and Mr. Kreider are expecting you." With that, she reached down and pressed an old-fashioned buzzer which temporarily unlocked the door to the office. There was no open-door policy in Crotty's office.

Kreider was seated in his regular spot just off to the side of Crotty, who sat behind a ridiculously large desk. Crotty—rather, the city—had purchased it on his first day in office during his very first term. Cord remembered Crotty saying that it reminded him of the pictures he'd seen of the desk in the Presidential Oval Office. Every time Cord saw the desk, he was reminded that Michael Crotty's ego knew no bounds.

"Did you have fun with all the eye-talians the other night?" Crotty said before Cord had sat down.

"Fun? No, not really."

"Tough job you got there going to every circle-jerk in town every night."

"It's a living."

"I haven't seen your story in the paper yet."

"It's not a big deal. I filed it a couple days ago. It will run sometime soon. It will be buried somewhere."

"Alex, I told the mayor about how those bastards laughed at the proclamation." Kreider said this as though he had been stewing on it all week, which he had. "I think it's ridiculous that one hundred fifty people could all think it was a big joke that the mayor issued a proclamation in their honor."

"Doesn't surprise me, at all," Crotty said. "It was your stupid idea anyhow, Bruno. I knew those ingrates wouldn't appreciate it."

Kreider bit his lip as he always did. The proclamation was Crotty's idea, but he was used to getting blamed for everything that went wrong.

"You still don't know, do you?" Cord said to Kreider.

"Know what? What don't I know?"

"Ah, maybe we should just let it go. Chalk it up to experience," Cord said, not wanting to embarrass Kreider in front of his boss.

"No, tell me. You talking about the proclamation? What was wrong with it?"

Cord shuffled in his seat. He was clearly uncomfortable with where this conversation was heading. Still, he did not reply.

"Out with it, man!" bellowed Crotty. "Answer Bruno's question. Why did they all laugh at Bruno's proclamation?"

"April twenty-fifth, Bruno. The date of the event was April twenty-fifth."

"So?"

"So, for about a century, Italian Americans have recognized April twenty-fifth as Marconi Day. It's Marconi's goddamned birthday, Bruno. They actually call it Marconi Day. You were the only guy in the room who didn't know that, and you read a proclamation with about ten 'Whereases' and then declared the day to be something that it has already been for a century!"

Kreider turned red in the face.

"Are you kidding me? Bruno, are you fucking kidding me?" Crotty bellowed.

Cord recoiled at how loud this particular obscenity was. He wondered how many times Kathy Gill had heard such curses emanating from Crotty's office. He marveled at how little Crotty cared about his foul language, despite not knowing who might be within ear shot.

"Let me get this straight," Crotty continued while Kreider held both of his hands over his face. "Bruno, you go in front of a bunch of wops on Wop Day and tell them that we have decided to make it Wop Day. Is that what you did? You're a dope, you know that?" Keeping with the Crotty tradition of kicking people when they're down, he continued the attack on Kreider. "Wait, Bruno. That gives me another idea," he said mockingly. "Let's wait until December twenty-fifth and declare it Christmas Day in Troy. And if people like that, we'll declare January first New

Year's Day. We'll post fucking signs all over Times Square
in New York City. Maybe they'll have a big celebration on
New Year's Eve for years to come, and it will all be because of you, Bruno. I take it back. You're not a dope after
all. You're brilliant!"

"Okay, okay. Stop!" Kreider finally cried. "I'm sorry. I
didn't know. How was I supposed to know about Marconi
Day? I'm Scottish, not Italian," he said, launching a weak
defense if for no other reason than to stop Crotty's assault.

"You're only half Scottish," Crotty concluded. "Half
Scottish—half dope."

Crotty reached into one of the drawers in his desk and
pulled out a small glass and a half-empty bottle of Johnny
Walker. "Want a little pick-me-up, Alex?

"No. No thanks."

"Cord, Bruno tells me that you were trying to get some
information for us about what's going on at the Marconi
Club," Crotty said while pouring some scotch into the glass.
"Besides having Bruno inform you that it was Marconi Day,
did you find out any other information or was it all bullshit?"

"Well, the bullshit, as you call it, is what you will read
about when you see my story. Renovations, big party,
scholarships, new festivals, blah, blah blah."

"Can't wait to read it," Crotty said with as much sarcasm
as he could muster.

"But there was one interesting thing," Cord said.

"Like what?" asked Kreider.

"The interesting part is not what but who."

"Keep going," urged Crotty.

"Have you ever heard the name Joseph Geracitano?"

Crotty thought for a moment. "Geracitano? Nope. You
know that name, Bruno?"

"Never heard of him."

"It seems," Cord continued, "that he's the guy calling all
the shots there. It appears that he put up all the money for
the renovation. He was the star of the show. Jimmy Mariano

was the emcee, but Joseph Geracitano was the headliner."

Kreider had left the club that day before Geracitano was introduced and gave his speech. "Why? Who is he? He financed the renovation? Why did he drop all that dough into that rat hole?"

"That's the interesting part. Mariano pretty much gave him single-handed credit for saving the club. Geracitano gave this speech about why he did it and told some total crap story about his past and how he was saved from a life of misery by some doctor from Long Island who was a Marconi Club member. Somehow, so he says, he made a bunch of money on Wall Street and now wants to give back to the community by saving the Troy Marconi Club."

"You don't believe that story?" asked Kreider.

"Hell, no. I did a quick interview with him after and asked him more questions about his background. When he found out I was a reporter, suddenly he could not have been more evasive. I kept pressing him and what he finally did tell me was totally different from what he had said to everybody twenty minutes earlier. Nobody believes his story. I sure don't. I think it's all a front."

"Front for what?" Kreider asked.

"Obviously he didn't say, Bruno. Otherwise, it wouldn't be much of a front, would it?" Cord said derisively.

"All right, all right. Don't be a smart-ass. What do you think it might be a front for?" asked Crotty, essentially repeating Kreider's question.

"I honestly have no idea, none. But I'll say this. The guy's smooth. He pulled that whole thing off like he's done it all before. To tell you the truth, his story and the way he told it sounded like he was Mob or something."

"You think the Mob is behind the Marconi Club?" Kreider asked, sounding nervous. "You think this Geracitano guy is a mobster?"

"No, Bruno, I don't. Somehow, I don't see the Mob abandoning New York City, Chicago, or North Jersey to set up shop in Troy. No, I don't see that. I didn't say the guy was a mobster. I just said he acted like one."

"Why do you think that, Alex?" Crotty said. He was suddenly riveted on this conversation, something that rarely happened with Crotty. "What exactly did he do that makes you say that?"

"I can't say for sure, Mayor. It's just a vibe I get from this guy. It's nothing particular about what he said. Nothing particular about what he did. It's just the way he looks, the way he talks, and the way he carries himself. It kind of reminds me of somebody from the Sopranos. And, get this. When he told this story about his upbringing, half of it came straight out of that movie, *Goodfellas*. I don't know. It's just a feeling I got. I really don't have much more than that, Mayor. Honestly, it's just a gut feeling. That's all I can say. It's pretty clear to me, though, that the guy's not who or what he says he is."

Crotty got up from the desk chair and walked toward the window. He stared out, clearly deep in thought and seemingly distressed about what he had just heard. "What else, Alex?" he finally said without turning around.

"Nothing else really, just the Geracitano mystery-man thing."

"Thanks for coming," Crotty said.

Cord had been in enough meetings with Crotty to know that was the signal that he was being dismissed.

Crotty came back away from the window and started escorting Cord toward the door. He had gotten what he wanted from Cord and now had to make sense out of it. "Bruno, make sure we continue to keep Alex well informed about what's going on in city hall. We want to make sure our friend here keeps abreast, you know?"

"Will do, Mayor," Kreider said obligingly.

"Oh, and, Cord," Crotty added. "Keep us informed too. Especially about our mysterious friend, Mr. Geracitano. We'd love to learn more about him."

"Sure," Cord said as he left and said a cordial goodbye to Kathy on his way out.

"Always nice to see you, Alex," she said.

Back in the office, Crotty was clearly bothered by what he had just heard. "Gotta tell you, this concerns me," he said to Kreider as soon as the door closed behind Cord. "This concerns me a lot. The only thing worse than a bunch of fucking Italians being after you is a bunch of Italian mobsters being after you. Bruno, do you think maybe the Mob found out about what we did to DiMatteo and now they're coming after us?"

"No, Mayor. Absolutely not. Cord's been watching too many movies. Besides, we left absolutely no tracks on that DiMatteo trail. Only you and me and Danny know what really happened."

Kreider still did not know that Crotty had actually bragged about taking DiMatteo down to Cord that night in The Excalibar. Crotty, of course, was so drunk that night he did not remember.

"Just because some greasy punk comes to town with a bunch of money and starts acting like he's Michael Corleone, doesn't mean we should worry," Kreider added. "Alex Cord has been watching too many movies or something, that's all."

$\infty\infty$

In the tight-knit world of the Marconi Club, it didn't take long for a story of mystery and intrigue like that of the Gerry Sickles episode to become the number one topic of conversation. The quick and effective way in which Joey G. apparently dealt with Sickles created quite a buzz among the members. Also of keen interest to everyone was that Joey thought it was no big deal, that it was something he was happy to do. It was also apparent that this sort of thing was something he had done before. Each of the members, in their own way, began to think about their own problems and how Joey might be able to help solve them.

It didn't take long before several more members got an

"audience" with Joey in his office about their own problems. Seemingly no problem was either too great or too small to take to Joey. None of the members really knew who Duke was or what his role was, but everyone noticed that whenever there was a closed-door meeting with Joey, Duke entered just before the door closed.

After each such meeting, Joey would leave the troubled member behind with Duke, with instructions to give full details to him. Each time before leaving the office, Joey would say, "If your problem goes away, that means my answer was yes. If it doesn't go away..."

Every Wednesday night, Duke would arrive at The Settlement toward the end of evening and review the list of requests for help that came in during the week. The list grew longer each week and, to a great extent, more tedious. Duke, Rita, and Pat all felt that too much time and energy was being spent on trivial matters: "Cat stuck in a tree stuff," Rita called them. Yet no really big problems to solve came to them—none of the sort from which legends were made.

JoAnne and Chuck, on the other hand, were sympathetic to nearly every request that Duke brought in. In virtually every case, JoAnne and Chuck would sympathize with these pleas and suggest asking Duke to include these trivial things on the "to-do" list. Pat would usually agree while Rita just went along with them to keep the peace but made it clear that she thought that they were "trying to land a whale with a butterfly net."

Most of these requests Duke handled himself. They often revolved around minor money disputes over rent payments or shoddy auto repair work or overdue IOUs and the like. Generally, rather than get his crew involved in strong-arm tactics as he did in resolving Al Clemente's issue with Sickles, it was simpler to solve the problems by making small monetary payoffs. While the members were truly appreciative of these interventions, the desired effect was not being created. They were not creating the type of buzz around the club that the Clemente incident did. They were not building Joey G's reputation as a guy who can handle the tough stuff.

The ladies and Duke began to get a sinking feeling that Operation Out 'n' In had an Achilles' heel. If Joey G. was going to be known as a dangerous character who would cross the line if necessary, they had to go well beyond handling trivial issues. But none of the issues that had surfaced required the same level of "muscle" as they had applied to the Sickles matter. Operation Out 'n' In was turning into an expensive effort to do nothing more than get a few cats down from a few trees. They were stuck.

✁✃✁✃

"Read any good stories lately?" Rita asked Chuck one night at dinner.

"Nothing remarkable. No. Why?"

"Well, the last time we were all wondering how to solve a problem, Duke told us the story of the detective and the missing letter."

"*The Purloined Letter*," Chuck confirmed.

"Yes, that Poe story. I thought maybe there'd be some story out there that would give us a clue on how to land our whale. Moby Dick, maybe?" Rita joked.

"I wish there was. I can't recall any stories about a regular guy pretending to be a mobster. Usually it's the other way around. Mobsters generally pretend to be regular guys so they won't be noticed."

"What about Walter Mitty?" said JoAnne. "Chuck, you must know that story."

"I do. It's called *The Secret Life of Walter Mitty*. It's probably James Thurber's most famous story. They even made a couple of movies from it. They were all quite different from the original story."

"Except for the concept," JoAnne said. "The concept was the same, wasn't it? This guy is stuck in a dull life, so to make it more exciting he just made up a pretend existence, a bunch of them, actually. He was a regular guy, but he imagined himself doing amazing things."

"Yes, that's the main idea. The book and the movies are the same idea, they just have different made-up stories," confirmed Chuck.

"So, Jo," said Rita, "if I get where you're going with this, our problem is that the real-life issues that have been coming to us are too small, too dull. So, we take care of that by making up big problems and then solving them."

"Or maybe make up big problems and just pretend to solve them," Chuck added.

"That's what I was thinking," JoAnne replied.

"Like what?" Pat said skeptically.

They all sat for minute. Nobody had any ideas.

"Maybe Duke can help with this too," said Rita finally. "Maybe he can talk with his associates. I would think that their experiences may be better suited to this than ours. I'll give him a call right now."

The following morning, Duke, Joey, Tugboat Tommy, Donnie Moore, and Jimmy Mariano arrived at the club around seven a.m. They met in the office. Duke relayed the conversation he had with Rita the previous night. None of them had ever heard of Walter Mitty but were intrigued by the idea of making something happen or, more specifically, making something seem to happen. They spent several hours pretending to be Walter Mitty.

The next day, the usuals were at the bar after lunch when Joey G. came in the front door to join them for his regular late afternoon bowl of soup. He didn't seem to be his normally upbeat and jovial self.

"Somebody needs to give Renna a new recipe. I'm getting tired of the same soup every damned day," he said, clearly not in a good mood.

"Having a bad day?" Tugboat Tommy said as he was stocking the cooler under the bar.

"Yes, in fact I am. Actually, it's not me so much having

a bad day but I just talked to—well, it doesn't matter who I talked to. I just heard something that's making me crazy."

"I thought you didn't get mad, you just got even," said Tugboat as the conversation had gotten the attention of the others.

"What time does Judge Judy come on? I need to watch Judge Judy today. She's my role model—my inspiration," said Joey without responding to Tugboat.

"Judge Judy is your role model?" asked Marty Maroni, from a few stools down.

"Yes, she is," repeated Joey somewhat loudly, clearly agitated about something. "You know why? She takes no shit from nobody. That's why. Watch the damned show. That woman takes no shit from nobody. She can take care of two different bad guys in the same thirty-minute show. A half hour—including commercials—is all it takes her to set the bastards straight."

"Cowboy justice," said Tugboat. "Like the old cowboy movies. Every one of them has a good guy, a bad guy, a rope, and a tree."

"That's exactly right, my friend," Joey said. "That's exactly right." He did not finish his soup. He slapped the spoon down on the bar and marched upstairs only to return a few minutes later carrying a duffle bag.

"I gotta go see somebody about something," he said with a wave. "Be back in a day or two."

"Joey's got something up his butt today," Maroni said as soon as Joey left.

"I don't know who he's going to see, but I'm pretty sure I would not want to be that guy when Joey gets there," Tugboat agreed.

Joey was not seen at the club for the next two days. Word of the "cowboy justice" conversation and how Joey had stormed out, obviously on a mission, had spread around the club.

They had not seen Joey that aggravated before. They somehow all assumed that Joey was going to take care of some business and that, in the end, there would be a rope and a tree involved.

᙮᙮᙮

"Joey get back yet?" Al Clemente asked Tugboat Tommy who had just settled in behind the bar two days after Joey had stormed out.

"Back? What do you mean, back, Al?" Tugboat said.

Al and the others at the bar seemed confused by Tugboat's response. Most of them were there the day Joey left with his duffle bag and he had not been seen since.

"Back from wherever he went the day he stormed out of here," Al replied.

"I'm pretty sure Joey's been around here every day this week," Tugboat retorted. "You've all seen him here every day this week, haven't you, fellas? Haven't you, fellas?" he said slowly and loudly, spacing out the words so they sounded more like a statement than a question. It was clear that he was being coy but it was unclear why.

"Yeah, sure," Al said. "Of course. Now that I think of it, he has been here every day."

"Yeah," Maroni chimed in. "Every day so far this week."

Tugboat nodded and went about the business of setting up the bar. Nobody said a word as he did.

"Joey did call me, though," Tugboat finally said as if to continue the previous discussion. He was about to tell them, in code, about Joey's whereabouts. "He called me a little while ago to tell me he just got through talking with his sister Janice. She lives in Syracuse. She's eight months pregnant and a horrible thing happened to her husband. Seems last night as he was coming home late, somebody walked up to him in his own driveway and whacked him in the balls three times with a baseball bat."

"Oooh! Oh Jesus! Ouch!" came cries from various parts of the bar.

"Exactly!" Tugboat continued. "Funny how shit like that happens. Just two days ago, Joey got a call from Janice who was in hysterics because she found out that her husband was shacking up with another woman. Next thing you know, the guy's getting his balls busted—literally."

"Funny how that happens," Al said.

"Yes, it is," Tugboat said as he was pouring a beer. "And guess what? The guy can't even remember who did it. Amnesia or something. That's what he told the cops. Amnesia—probably from the shock of a baseball bat coming into contact with his balls."

"That would do it," Al said.

"In his own driveway?" Marty asked.

"Yep, right outside his house in Syracuse, in his own driveway," Tugboat continued. "It all happened pretty quick, I hear. The guy comes home, gets out of his car, and whack! He gets it right in the nuts with a Louisville Slugger. Apparently, it happened right around six last night when we were all here with Joey. You guys remember right? Around six last night, Joey was sitting right there when it all happened," he said, pointing to Joey's regular spot at the bar. "Remember?"

"Yep, I was here," said Al. "I was sitting right next to him. He was here having a beer sitting right between you and me, right Marty?"

Maroni looked perplexed at first but soon understood. "Oh—yeah, that's right. Yep, right here," he said, pointing to the empty stool to his left.

"It's good that we were all here with Joey when his brother-in-law got his nuts crushed. Otherwise, somebody may have suspected Joey did it, you know?" Tommy said.

Everyone at the bar nodded.

"Right here," said Maroni, pointing to the seat next to him. "Joey was sitting right here last night at six."

A short while later, the door swung open, and Joey barged into the room. "Ciao everybody," he bellowed.

The angry mood that he was in two days earlier had disappeared. He sat in his regular seat.

"Sorry to hear about your brother-in-law's accident," Marty said. "Tugboat told us the news. Seems like it happened all the while you and a bunch of us were here at the bar last night, right? Is your sister okay?"

"Janice? She'll be all right, I suppose. She's a tough Italian girl. She understands that things like this have to happen sometimes. She'll be fine as long as she knows her husband will soon be home to stay. I expect that will be the case from now on."

"At least until his swelling goes down," Tugboat added.

"Yeah. Anyways, listen, boys, I'm sorry to come and go so quickly but I gotta take a quick shower and then I gotta go see somebody about something," Joey said as he turned and went upstairs.

When he came down about thirty minutes later, he was showered, changed, and again carrying the duffle bag.

"Off again?" Tugboat yelled to him from behind the bar.

"Off again. I got a fresh rope in my bag here and I'm off to find some more bad guys and some more trees. Seems like stuff comes in bunches and I might as well take care of them all while I'm in the mood."

Joey was gone again, this time for two more days. The regulars at the bar noticed that Angelo Renna had replaced Tugboat Tommy behind the bar and some noted that Duke had not put out the usual morning coffee for the last two days. When asked about Joey's whereabouts, Renna would only say that Joey had called in a couple of times and that he and some friends he had with him would be back soon.

On Saturday, the club members were surprised to see a different car parked in the spot reserved for Joey. The black 2011 Lincoln Town car was replaced by a red 2011 Lincoln Town Car. On weekends, fewer members came during the early hours or for lunch but, by later in the day, the bar began to fill up. It was a different crowd from weekdays.

When Joey emerged from the office, he was accompanied by Jimmy Mariano. Mariano came to the club as often as he could, but he had an active family life and two young children. Since high school, Jimmy had worked as a long-haul trucker whose runs kept him on the road several nights a week.

He had a lot on his plate and a lot on his mind, but he tried to come into the club on weekends. He looked tired, as he often did, as he ordered a hot turkey sandwich at the bar along with his usual diet coke. Joey went directly upstairs and did not join Mariano and the others at the bar. On his way up the stairs, Joey heard John Marchi, a weekend regular, yell toward him. "New wheels, Joey?"

Marchi had noticed that in Joey's reserved parking spot the black Lincoln Town Car had been replaced by a red one.

"Not new, new," said Joey. "Just different."

"Same but different," Marchi joked. "Just get sick of the color?"

"Nah, the other one was too hot," Joey said with a wink.

"Air conditioner go, or just the black color made it hot?"

"It was just time for a different look," was all Joey said.

Jimmy Mariano had purposely taken a seat next to Bobo LaMarsh, who was not a regular but would come in on Saturdays to watch baseball. Unlike most club members, Bobo was not old-school Italian. He was a French Canadian who had lived in the shadow of the club for three decades. He couldn't care less about the club, its ideals, its heritage, or its mission. He went to the Marconi Club because it had inexpensive food and beer and because he could spend the entire afternoon at the bar, watch two baseball games back to back, and spend less than ten dollars. He was well known at both the Marconi Club and other local establishments as a guy who talked too much, drank too much, tipped too little, and had a very strong opinion about absolutely everything.

"Is it me, or does our rich friend there seem a little suspicious?" Bobo said to Jimmy.

"Rich friend?" Jimmy said. "You mean Joey?"

"Yeah, I heard he paid for all the renovations here."

"We could not have reopened this club without him, Bobo."

"I know, I know. And believe me, I'm glad it happened. If not for this place, I'd be sitting over there at that dive on Ferry Street, paying twice what I pay here to watch the same ballgame. I'm just saying. I've heard a lot of stuff about things he's doing that don't sound like they're on the up-and-up. You're the club president. I figured maybe you'd know a little more about him, that's all."

"Listen, Bobo, I don't want to say too much."

"I know, I'm just saying. Just saying, that's all."

Jimmy shifted in his seat and leaned toward Bobo. "Since you mentioned it, I gotta tell you, that's been bothering me too."

"See? I was right. I knew it. I knew there was something a little off about that guy."

"Shhh," Jimmy said. "Keep it down, okay? Listen, c'mon over here," he said, motioning to one of the tables off to the side. Angelo Renna placed Jimmy's hot turkey sandwich on the bar, which Jimmy picked up and carried to a nearby table. He motioned for Bobo to follow.

As they sat down, Jimmy started in on his lunch with Bobo right next to him.

"Bobo, can you keep a secret?" Jimmy said between bites. He knew that it was absolutely impossible for Bobo LaMarsh to keep a secret for longer than ten seconds, no matter what it was.

"Me? Jimmy, come on. Of course, I can keep a secret. If you tell me something is a secret, my lips are sealed forever."

Jimmy choked back a laugh when Bobo said this. He pretended to have some food caught in his throat. "Good. Look, since you brought it up, I've noticed the same thing about Joey G. as you have. I've been dying to talk to somebody about it. I honestly don't know what he's up to but, you know, I kinda feel responsible, being president and all. He single-handedly saved this club, but some of the stuff he's been doing—at least what I think he's doing—makes me very nervous."

"Like what kind of stuff?" Bobo was taking this all in, in large doses.

"You can't say nothing, Bobo."

"My word, Jimmy, you got my word."

Jimmy nodded at Bobo, pretending to be reassured of Bobo's ability to be a confidant. "For starters, a few weeks ago, I casually mentioned to him that we're having a little trouble with one of the subcontractors we had on this renovation job. I can't get into details, but the guy was threatening to sue us over some bullshit claim. He said we agreed to pay him for something he didn't do. It was total bullshit, but the guy was being a real asshole, and he lawyered up. I got this demand letter from his lawyer, telling me we owe the guy ten K but out of kindness they'd let it go for five. It was a shakedown, plain and simple. We didn't owe the guy squat. So I tell Joey about it, and he says, 'Kid stuff, Jimmy, don't even worry yourself over this.' Next thing I know, the subcontractor's lawyer calls me on the phone and says the whole matter was a misunderstanding and, at his client's instruction, the issue was being dropped. Just like that. I mean two days after I tell Joey about it—poof, problem solved."

"Maybe he just knew the creep, or the lawyer or something. Who knows?" Bobo said. "But I agree, it does sound a little coincidental. It also sounds a little bit like the Al Clemente story. Plus, I know that Gerry Sickles guy. He's a card-carrying psycho. For Joey to get him to back down so quick like that is pretty impressive."

"Hold on, it gets better."

Bobo leaned in. He couldn't wait to hear more.

"Did you hear what he just said about the car? Being hot?"

"Yeah, I did hear that."

"He was gone overnight, and I know where he was."

"Where was he? Where'd he go?"

Jimmy had all he could do to not laugh out loud at how gullible Bobo was being. "I saw him leave last night. He told me that he was going downstate to take care of something for Hap Anthony. You know Hap, right?'

"He's the guy with the paint store, right?"

"Exactly. Well, I happen to know that Hap was having a big battle with some other paint store guy somewhere downstate. Something about a big commercial paint job. I don't know…Orange County or maybe Putnam or wherever. Anyway, the downstate paint store guy was low-balling a bid and it was killing Hap because he knew there was no way the guy could do the job for the bid number he put in. It was a huge commercial job, and Hap's competitor put up a totally bogus bid that the guy would later jack up. Losing that bid was going to cost Hap a ton of money. A ton."

"Joey got involved in that?" Bobo asked.

"Let's put it this way. Hap told me this morning that he had talked to Joey about it. Then, the very next night, the downstate paint guy's store burned to the ground."

"Holy shit!" Bobo said. "Orange County, my sister lives in Orange County. Maybe she knows something about it. I'll give her a call if you want."

"No, don't do that. It would raise too much suspicion. Besides…Orange County, Putnam County…I forget for sure. Maybe it was somewhere on Long Island. It doesn't matter where it was, Bobo. I think Joey may have torched the place and then dumped his car or something maybe, thinking he got spotted."

"Jesus, you're right, Jimmy. His other car maybe got burned in the fire. He did say, 'hot.' I heard him say that to Marchi. He specifically said the other car was hot. Maybe he just got it painted red in case somebody spotted his black car. Oh, and I also heard about him whacking his cheating brother-in-law in the balls too. Did you hear that one? This guy's something, Jimmy. You're right to be careful with him."

"I hear you, Bobo. That's why I wanted to talk to somebody in case…you know…in case something else happens. But you can't blab to anyone about this in case I'm wrong."

"Or in case you're right!" said Bobo.

"Exactly! I'm in a tough spot here, and if you get any ideas how to handle it, let me know. Now you better go, I don't want anybody to wonder what we're talking about. And, Bobo, don't say nothing to nobody about this, okay?"

"Right, Jimmy, right."

By the very next weekend, stories about Joey and his mysterious deeds abounded. Not surprisingly, they included the paint store story that Jimmy related to Bobo and no one else. Also, as could be expected, the tales of Joey's deeds seemed to get more and more dastardly each time they were told. Several completely different and even more sinister tales of his escapades cropped up almost daily. At the Marconi Club and beyond, with each passing day, a new rumor about Joey surfaced, and an old one was embellished upon. In short order, the reputation of Joey G. as someone who could and did make things happen was solidly in place.

Around The Settlement, they began to refer to Joey as Walter Mitty.

Chapter 15

It was shortly after ten a.m. when Chuck went to the back door to let Duke in. He had just finished his morning activities to open the Marconi Club and had several things to do at The Settlement that day. He sat down at the table with Rita and JoAnne while Pat and Chuck busied themselves about the kitchen.

"That new landscaper is coming today to give us a proposal," Rita said casually to Duke. "Please make sure he understands everything we want and get a detailed quote. I don't want any misunderstandings like we had with those idiots last year."

"Copy that, Miss Rita. But before the guy comes and I get busy, I know it's a couple of days before our next meeting, but I want to tell you that the stuff we've been doing is really working."

"You mean the Walter Mitty stuff?" asked Pat.

"Yeah, the Walter Mitty stuff."

"See, Duke, I told you reading more books is a good thing," Chuck said, reminding Duke about her consistent urging to get him to read more.

"I'm trying, Miss Chuck. But I've been a little busy lately."

"Never mind that," Rita said abruptly. "What do you mean, Duke?"

"I mean it's really working. Joey, Tugboat and even Jimmy have all been, like, world-class actors. I'm telling you if they gave out awards for spreading rumors, they'd each win one. As far as I can tell, everybody's thinking that

Joey and his gang are like the Gambino Family. The thing with Al Clemente worked great. The stories about Joey's brother-in law, the new car, the paint store fire are all over the place and everybody's eating this stuff up. And the way Jimmy handled that set-up with Bobo LaMarsh was a thing of beauty. That was Tugboat's idea, and it's working like a charm."

"Apparently Mr. LaMarsh was a good choice?" said Pat.

"Definitely. That stuff Jimmy told him could not have spread faster if it was on the six o'clock news. Plus, there are about ten other stories about Joey's escapades that are going around that we didn't even plant ourselves. According-ing to Tugboat, who hears everything, Joey has allegedly been involved in money laundering, hijacking cigarette shipments from North Carolina, and running a high-stakes poker game every Monday night in Staten Island. You know that story that's been on the news about that Wall Street guy getting kidnapped? As far as everyone at the Club is concerned, that guys is probably tied up in the trunk of Joey's car."

"Do you think we have enough to get started on the next act?" asked Rita.

"You know, I think so, ma'am. That's what I'm sayin'. I think we just might."

"Let's do it," Pat said. "We're running out of time," she urged.

"We are," Rita said. "Duke, if you think we have enough momentum, let's pull the whole cast together and get the next act going Wednesday night. Jo, you call Alex Cord and your group. Duke, bring in your whole team."

"Giddy-up!" Duke said excitedly.

ᏨᎧᏨᎧ

It would be hard to imagine a more disparate group had ever sat around a single table than the one that crowded around the dining room table of The Settlement that night.

Rita and Pat, two middle-class Italian girls who grew up together in South Troy sat on one end flanked on one side by JoAnne, a fifty-five-year-old former pharmacy owner, and a former Catholic nun named Chuck. Also, at the table was a loyal handyman named Duke; an aptly named former tugboat worker; a menacingly large Jamaican man; a retired restaurant manager named Angelo; Jimmy, a long-haul trucker; and a dapper-looking middle-aged Italian who went by the name of Joey—which everyone there knew was an alias. Across from them sat newspaper reporter, Alex Cord; a beer distributer named Fippi; a shoemaker named Mo; and Dan Robbins, the former city council member who had been pushed out of office under threat by the Democratic Machine.

They all knew why they were there that night, but only a few in the room knew the actual connection they had to each other. It was the first time they had all gotten together in the same room. They each understood their individual role, but only Duke and the women really knew how everything fit together. They were all anxious to find out precisely how it was all connected, and over the next two hours, they did.

Rita and Duke gave a detailed overview of Operation Out 'n' In and the progress to date. Alex Cord took detailed notes while the others listened intently to the report. There was a spirited discussion in which everyone engaged and included numerous suggestions regarding what Chuck referred to as the "plot outline."

The ladies and even Duke were delighted with the tone and tenor of the conversation. It was clear that everyone in the room was not only fully engaged but fully supportive of Operation Out 'n' In. The meeting lasted far longer than anyone had anticipated, mostly due to the many "improvements" to the plan that were suggested and discussed. In the end, the group was of one mind and now that they all had heard how all the pieces fit together, they were more excited than ever to be a part of it.

"On behalf of my husband," JoAnne said as the meeting was concluding, "I can't thank each of you enough for what you are doing. To me, this is not about vengeance, it is about justice, justice for Phillip and for all of the people of this city who have lived too long with this problem. My deepest appreciation goes out to each of you for your part in seeking justice."

"And revenge," Rita declared.

ɛ∕ɔɛ∕ɔ

The following morning, Alex Cord's car entered the parking lot behind city hall. One of the little perks he had received from the mayor was a reserved parking place in the always-crowded lot. It was marked by a sign which read, *Reserved for Special Visitors.* Kreider would remind Cord every so often that he would remain a special visitor so long as the mayor liked what Cord was writing. The spot was a few spaces away from the one marked *Secretary to the Mayor.* Kathy Gill arrived precisely at eight fifty-five a.m. as she always did. Cord greeted her as she got out of her car. "Good morning, Kathy."

"Ah, good morning, Alex. What brings you here so early? I don't remember seeing your name on the calendar."

"It's not, but I have to talk to the mayor or at least Kreider as soon as possible. I thought I'd get here a little early and try to catch them first thing. Think I can get to them this morning?"

"I'll check when I get inside. I don't see why not. They're probably still at the diner, though."

They walked in together and Cord hung up his jacket as Kathy glanced at the day's calendar. They were alone in the office.

"There's nothing on the calendar and they should be in pretty soon. Before they do, though, I'm glad you're here. I wanted to tell you this personally but haven't had the right moment."

"Oh?"

"I'm quitting, Alex."

"What? Whoa, I didn't see that coming."

"Believe me, it's been coming since Mr. DiMatteo left. I was going to quit last year but hung on when it began to look like doofus was going to lose the last election."

Cord was taken aback by her use of that term to describe Crotty. He had never heard Kathy Gill utter a disparaging word about anyone, let alone her boss.

"What's it been, twenty-five years or so? This place is going to fall totally apart without you."

"More, actually, and I finally realized I've had enough," she said. "Working for Mr. DiMatteo, even for that short time, made me realize how badly I've been treated by Crotty all this time. He and Kreider are always, always, always in a foul mood. I'm sick of it. And I'll tell you the truth, Alex, they're both getting worse every day. I'm not the kind of person who needs to be treated with kid gloves or anything, but I'm also not the kind of person who deserves to be treated like they treat me either."

"I'm surprised you lasted this long."

"It was actually my husband who convinced me to leave. I guess I use up all of my patience being outside Crotty's door all day and end up being a bitch to Walt when I get home."

"I can't imagine you being a bitch."

"Just ask my husband, he'll tell you. I thought I'd better quit before he gets fed up with the horror stories I tell him about what goes on here every day and comes over here, and kills somebody."

"Well for what it's worth, even Crotty will realize how good you are after you're gone. When are you leaving?"

"I was kinda hoping he'd get run out of office again in the next election but it looks like he's going to be unopposed. Kreider gave me a pretty nice bonus to stay until after the election. I was going to tell him to go scratch, but I can use the money."

Cord was surprised at Gill's frankness but understood how somebody could feel that way being around Crotty every day.

"How did Crotty take the news?"

"With his usual grace. He said, 'Don't let the door hit you in the ass on the way out.'"

"Jesus," Cord said, shaking his head.

"I need to run this stuff down the hall," she said, grabbing up one of the stacks of mail she had just sorted. "They should be here soon. Don't let them tell you they're too busy. They have nothing this morning. Oh, and, Alex, that conversation a minute ago was just between you and me, okay? I just remembered that you're a reporter."

"Of course, Kathy. I didn't hear a word that you said."

Cord sat alone in the office, thinking about what he had just learned. He wondered how Kathy had been able to comport herself for so long, seemingly unaffected by city hall politics or by Crotty's constant rudeness. Clearly, based on what he had just heard, Kathy hated Crotty as much as the next person. She had just kept it inside all this time. His mind wandered for a few minutes as he thought about how this new-found information about Kathy could somehow help with Operation Out 'n' In. In the midst of those thoughts, the office door swung open.

"Look what the cat dragged in, Bruno," Crotty mumbled as he entered the office and noticed Cord sitting in the waiting area. Kreider followed close behind. "Remind me to upgrade the security," Crotty said as he unlocked the door to his office.

Kreider stopped. "What brings you here, Alex?"

"You and the mayor got a minute?"

"For what?" Kreider said gruffly.

Cord remembered Kathy's comment about them always being in a bad mood. "I thought you were interested in me keeping you informed about Mr. Geracitano. But if you're not interested any more…"

Kreider motioned to Cord to follow him into the

Mayor's office. Crotty was inside hanging up his navy-blue blazer.

"Mayor, Alex says he has some information about Geracitano."

Crotty suddenly abandoned his earlier dismissiveness toward Cord. "Oh, really? Well, come on, Alex, come sit down."

Cord sat in the chair in front of the mayor's overly large desk. Kreider took his regular spot next to the mayor. Crotty sat behind his desk and put his feet up on it. "So what did you find out, my friend?"

"I thought you'd like to know that I've been busy trying to learn more about Mr. Geracitano. I have some new information that may suggest that my earlier feelings about him may, in fact, have some merit."

"You mean about him being a mobster or just a bull-shit artist?" Kreider injected hurriedly.

"Call it what you will, Bruno."

"Shut up, Bruno," Crotty demanded. "Go on, Cord, go on."

"Geracitano has been busy lately, and it seems that, co-incidentally, some bad things have been happening to some people as a result."

"What's your source, Cord?" Kreider said with suspicion.

"I said, shut up!" Crotty yelled. "Let the man talk. But where are you getting this information?"

Kreider shook his head behind Crotty's back. "Good question," he muttered.

"I have what you might call a mole inside the Marconi Club. He's a member who hangs around there a lot—a lot! The guy hears everything. The word is all over the club about what Geracitano has been up to."

"Who is it? Who's your mole?" Kreider asked.

"Come on, Bruno. Don't ask me that. It's a guy. A friend. A member of the club who I bump into all the time at Siena College basketball games. We were talking at half-time the other night, and I casually asked him a couple of general questions about the Marconi Club. Right away he started spouting off about Geracitano—Joey G. they call him."

"Joey G.? That sounds like a mob name to me. Doesn't it, Bruno? Joey G. Tell me that's not a fucking mob name," Crotty said.

Kreider didn't answer. "Spouting what, Alex?"

"We couldn't really talk at the game—too many people around. But he said that there's a bunch of strange stuff going on. So I met the guy last night over at the Red Door. I went in alone, like I do a lot, and ordered a pizza at the bar. He came in, pretended like we just bumped into each other. We shared a pizza, and he told me all about Joey G. I'm not going to give you the guy's name, Bruno. I can keep this going with him as long as he thinks it's all confidential. Otherwise, he'll just clam up. It seems our Mr. Geracitano is a pretty scary guy."

"Okay, fine," Kreider agreed. "No names. What did he say?"

For the next twenty minutes, Cord related to Crotty and Kreider the stories that had been circulating around the club. He told them of Al Clemente, the hot car, the suddenly dropped lawsuit, the paint store bombing, the brother-in-law and the baseball bat.

He even made passing reference to few of the stories that had come up from out of nowhere. He knew the words, "kidnapping" and "hijacking" would especially get their attention.

Crotty and Kreider were enthralled.

"That's the short version," Cord said when he had finished. "There's more but it all paints the same picture."

"You sure this is not all bullshit, Cord? Why is this source of yours telling you all this?" Kreider asked, this time more inquisitively than as a challenge.

"No, I'm not sure of anything, Bruno. I didn't personally see any of this happen. But a lot of what my guy said is all over the street. I've heard about this stuff from several different people."

"Okay, Alex, I won't ask you for your source. I understand that," Kreider said almost apologetically, "but these are pretty serious accusations, and we need to verify this."

"When did you become the cops? Talk to Chief Roberts if you want to run the guy in. I suggest, though, that you save your energy. There may be a lot of stories about Geracitano floating around, but they're just stories. I doubt you'll find any evidence."

"Hold on, Alex," Crotty said, "we're not looking to arrest anyone. We appreciate you telling us what you've heard. We only want to know about this sort of thing going on in our city. It helps us…helps us to govern."

"Any ideas how we can verify any of this stuff, Alex, besides your informer friend?" Kreider asked.

"I can't tell you my source's name, but I can tell you that there's a guy named Bobo LaMarsh who seems to know a lot about what's going on. He's just a yokel, but he's a talker. Guys like that are always my best sources. They say stuff because it makes them feel important or something, like they're insiders. I don't know. Maybe have one of your people chat with him. Maybe you should just go to the source." Cord got up from the chair. "Look, Mayor, I don't really care if you believe this or not. You guys keep begging me to tell you what I'm hearing, and that's what I'm doing. If you don't want to hear the answers, then stop asking me the questions, okay? It's none of my business what you do with this information. If you guys want to really find out what Geracitano's up to, maybe you should ask him yourself. I gotta go."

"Relax, Alex," Kreider said. "It's not that we're questioning you. It's just that these stories are—"

"Whatever," Cord interrupted. "I gotta go."

Kathy was back at her desk when Cord was leaving. The door to the mayor's office closed behind him.

"Nice talking to you, Kathy. Sorry to hear the news,"

Cord said softly. "I'm going to miss you. We'll talk again soon."

"Not much more to say."

Cord put his jacket back on. "Maybe," he said as he left.

\&∼∾

Back in the office, Kreider was pacing and Crotty looked out the window as he always did when he didn't know what to say or do. Neither said anything for several minutes.

Finally, Kreider said, "Maybe we should."

"Should what?"

"Like Cord said, maybe we should talk to this guy and find out what he's up to."

"Yeah? And how exactly are we going to do that? 'Excuse me, Mr. Joey G., my friend here and I want to know whether or not you're a mobster. We're just dying to find out if you're in town to get back at us for doing in your fellow wop, Phillip DiMatteo. And by the way, I've also been meaning to ask you if you're an arsonist or a hijacker.' Is that what you're thinking we'd say to him, Bruno?"

Kreider did not answer right away. He continued to pace. "Maybe we could just pay him a social visit. You know, welcome him to our fine city, congratulate him on reopening the club, stuff like that. We can invite him in for a real soft chit-chat and check him out. It will make him feel like he's a big-shot. We can at least see if he tells us the same story he told Cord in his little interview. Who knows, sometimes guys like that like to talk too much, you know?"

"Maybe. And who's this LaMarsh guy Cord was talking about?"

"Never heard of him."

"Your detective buddy...what's his name?"

"Chip Murray?"

"Whatever. You can trust him, right? I mean trust that he'll do stuff for us without it getting back to Chief Roberts."

"Sure, I can. He does all sorts of stuff for us. He owes me big time. If it wasn't for me, he'd be directing traffic somewhere."

"Have him find this Bobo LaMarsh guy and scare the crap out of him so we can find out more about our friend Joey Geronimo or whatever in hell his name is. In the meantime, I'll think about how we can meet with Mr. Mobster himself."

☙❧

Two days later, Kreider took a call on his cell phone as he drove to pick up Crotty to go to breakfast. He was just finishing the call with Detective Murray when Crotty got in the car.

"That was Chip Murray. He tracked down and then shook down that LaMarsh guy like I asked him to."

"What happened?"

"This is classic. Murray tracks the guy down in the Congress Street OTB Parlor, the guy's inside wasting his money, minding his own business. Murray grabs him by the arm, flashes his badge, and tells LaMarsh to step outside. He takes him around back and tells him he's under arrest as an accomplice of one Mr. Joseph Geracitano. Of course, LaMarsh freaks out and starts babbling like a fool that he's innocent and had nothing to do with all that stuff Geracitano has been doing. So Murray tells the guy he believes him and will let him go if he tells him all he knows about Geracitano. Well, LaMarsh couldn't throw Geracitano under the bus fast enough. He spills his guts to Murray right behind the OTB. No Miranda rights, no warrant—no nothing."

"You're shittin' me, right?"

"No! True story. So after the guy spills, Murray says he's going to let him walk but if LaMarsh says one word about any of this to anyone, he'd come back, slap him in cuffs, and fit him for an orange jump suit."

"Christ, I can't believe he did that. Is this Bobo guy a moron, or what?"

"It doesn't matter. The guy's dumber than a box of rocks, and Murray scared him out of his mind. He isn't going to talk about this to anyone. Besides, Murray knows I've got his back. He's not worried about it."

By then, they had arrived at the diner. When Crotty got to the booth, Kreider related everything that Bobo had told Detective Murray about Geracitano. The stories sounded just like those they had heard from Alex Cord.

"So, it appears that our mob friend really has been busy," Crotty said as he finished his breakfast. "We need to talk to this guy."

That afternoon when Kreider returned from lunch Crotty was sitting at his desk with his feet up and his arms behind his head. He had an amused look on his face.

"You look comfy."

"Guess who I just talked to, Bruno?" Crotty said as he stared at the ceiling, still grinning.

"I hope it was Charlie Meadows. I've been waiting for his answer on the campaign donation. Every year, it's like pulling teeth to get that guy to part with his money. He's richer than a damned Arab sheik, but he makes me jump through a hundred hoops to get a donation."

"Relax. We don't need any of his stinking money. How much we gonna spend running against nobody anyhow? We've got loads of money, Bruno, forget that. Come on, guess who I just talked to," Crotty said again like a little boy with big a secret.

"Okay fine, Mayor. I give up, who did you just talk to?"

"You better sit down," Crotty continued the buildup as Bruno took his regular seat. "None other than Jimmy Mariano."

"What? Jimmy Mariano called?"

"Yep, shocked the crap out of me too. I'm sitting here, minding my own business, coincidentally thinking about his buddy, Mr. Geronimo, or whatever his name really is—"

"Geracitano. His name is Geracitano, not Geronimo. He's an Italian, not an Apache."

"Whatever. Anyway, it was like it was fate or something. I'm stewing over the shit going on at the Marconi Club, and next thing I know the club's president is on the phone."

"What'd he want?"

"It appears as though he's in the middle of some scrape with the IRS people who are busting his balls because somehow after the club closed, the dumb asses over there forgot to keep filing their annual tax forms."

"Taxes? Wait. They don't even have to pay taxes! It's a social club or something like that. They don't pay income taxes. Hell, they don't even pay us any property tax."

"Yeah, that's what Mariano thought, too, but guess what? They may not have to pay taxes but they still have to file anyway. Apparently if they don't file the forms every year, the tax man gets cranky."

"What's that got to do with us? We can't do anything about that."

"I know that. But I didn't tell Mariano that. He wants to meet. He wants our help."

"Why would we do that? My guess is that nothing would suit you more than to see those guys at the Marconi Club get their asses in a sling. Besides, we've got no yank with the IRS."

"Right you are, my friend, on both counts. But Mariano asked us to meet and he asked if he could bring Geronimo."

"Geracitano? He wants to bring Geracitano to us?"

"Yep. As soon as I heard he was bringing the wop king-pin with him, I couldn't say yes fast enough. Now we don't need to come up with some bullshit story about playing nice-nice with these guys so that we check them out. They're coming to us and, better still, they're looking for a favor."

"Apparently, the IRS is out of Geracitano's league when

it comes to fixing things," Kreider said. "I can't wait to hear this!"

Crotty got up and high-fived Kreider.

"You know," Kreider said a moment later, "there's not a damned thing we can do to help them. This is a federal thing."

"I know that. Did I say anything about actually helping them? No, I did not. Need I remind you that the last time one of our Italian friends—Mr. DiMatteo—got in a scrape with the government, good things started to happen for us. Maybe it will happen again and this time we may not even have to get our hands dirty. This time, the less we do, the more trouble they'll be in."

"Beautiful!" said Kreider. "When are they coming?"

"I told Kathy to clear the deck for tomorrow at ten. Can't wait!"

☙❧☙

The following day, Crotty and Kreider rushed through breakfast and arrived at the office early. They barged right by Kathy Gill's desk and went into the office.

"When Mr. Mariano shows up, buzz him right in," Kreider said to her.

Inside, Crotty and Kreider went over how they would play this meeting. Crotty generally preferred the good-cop-bad-cop game with him, of course, being the good cop. At exactly ten a.m., the office door buzzed and Kathy showed Mariano and Geracitano in.

"Mayor, Mr. Kreider," Jimmy said upon entering, "I'd like you to meet Joseph Geracitano."

Joey shook their hands and Kreider showed them to the two seats across the desk from Crotty.

"Joey. Call me Joey," Geracitano said.

They all settled in. Bruno asked if they wanted coffee but both declined.

"Jimmy, long time no see. How have you been? You're creating quite a buzz around the neighborhood with your big opening over there."

"Thanks, Mayor," Jimmy said.

"Oh, and before I forget," Crotty added, "I want to apologize for that little slip-up my friend Bruno made with our proclamation."

Bruno shook his head. He had hoped that would not come up.

"No. No apology necessary, Mayor. We were all appreciative of your kind gesture."

"Okay, good. Now, Jimmy, on the phone you told me about some issue you were having with the tax people. I feel for you, my friend. I can see how it was just an honest mistake you made in this instance and I'm sorry it has gotten messy on you."

"Mr. Kreider is aware of the issue?" Jimmy asked.

"Oh, yes. I briefed him after you called," Crotty said. "In fact, that's why I asked Bruno to join us today. He's going to be my go-between when we talk to the IRS about this matter. Believe me, we want to help, but I have to tell you this is not going to be easy. Those feds can be very difficult sometimes. Some are real hard-asses. But we'll do everything we can to help you. Bruno will be calling you soon to get all of the details, no need to discuss all of that right now. We'll see what we can do to help."

Crotty was trying to speed along the IRS discussion. He was anxious to change the topic and find out what he could about Geracitano.

After an uncomfortable pause in the conversation, Joey spoke for the first time since they had sat down. "That's it? Meeting over? That's it? Don't call us, we'll call you is what you're saying? I come all the way down here for two minutes?"

"No, no, no Joey. Not at all," Crotty said. "Hold on. We'll take as much time as we need. It's just that I don't need all the details right this minute. If you're in any kind of trouble, we're here to help. And we will. Take it easy, my friend."

Joey's abrupt questions were a clear signal to Crotty and Kreider of his no-nonsense approach to things. But neither was expecting him to get that hot that quickly.

"Jimmy, Joey." Kreider jumped in. "We're going to do everything we can to help you with this. We will," he added. "But do you mind if I ask what brings you here, Joey? Jimmy has told us about the IRS problem, but I'm curious. What is your role in this?"

Joey gave a rather menacing look at Kreider. "Curious?"

Jimmy reached over and put a hand on Joey's arm as though to stop him from answering. "Let me answer that," he said. "Mr. Geracitano has been quite instrumental in providing the means necessary for us to reopen the Marconi Club. He has invested a great deal of time and a significant amount of his own money to help us get back on our feet after the terrible tragedy we experienced with Bobby Bocketti."

"Shame," Crotty said. "Absolute shame that was."

"Yes, it was," Jimmy continued. "Anyway, now that we're operational again, this tax matter has become a deep concern to the club and, of course, to Joey. He's got a lot invested in our well-being, and I thought it appropriate that he personally be here to discuss this problem."

"Of course," said Crotty. "And excuse me for not saying this earlier to you, Joey. I think it's a wonderful thing you're doing for the club. A wonderful thing. I hope you feel welcome in our city, and I personally hope that we can be of service to you on this matter and others for many years to come."

Joey sat back in the chair. He had noticeably edged forward when Kreider questioned why he was there. He apparently was calm again.

"Thank you, Mr. Mayor. I appreciate that very much." Joey then looked directly at Kreider and added, "Does that answer your question, Mr. Kreider?"

"Bruno, call me Bruno."

"Well, does it answer your question—Mr. Kreider?" Joey repeated.

It was clear that a game was afoot. While Mariano and Crotty were being pleasantly businesslike, Geracitano and Kreider began to spar.

"It answers one of my questions, Mr. Geracitano," Kreider shot back.

"Maybe we should get going," Jimmy said as he leaned forward.

"No, wait, Jimmy. It seems that Mr. Kreider here has some more questions," Joey said. "What's on your mind?" he said to Kreider. "I come here in all good faith to have a business conversation with you, Mayor, and within two minutes, your pal here is getting in my grill. I don't understand that. Where I come from, that's a little impolite."

"Where do you come from Mr. Geracitano?" Kreider shot back, giving no ground.

Crotty jumped up from behind the desk. "Now let's hold on, everybody. I see no need for us to get all sideways here. Let me make a suggestion." He walked around to the front of the desk where Jimmy and Joey were still sitting. "Bruno, Jimmy looks like he could use a cup of coffee. Why don't you and him take a stroll down to the cafeteria and have some coffee while Joey and I get to know each other a little." Crotty motioned his head toward Kreider as if to coax him to leave. Kreider and Jimmy got up and left. As they were going out the door Crotty said, "I think a ten-minute coffee break will do it." After the door closed, Crotty returned to his desk chair. "Joey, first let me apologize. Bruno gets a little too aggressive sometimes. He means well, but sometimes he forgets his manners."

"So, I see," said Joey. "I'm glad you're a man who appreciates good manners, Mr. Mayor. I think good manners are important. Especially in the business world."

"Couldn't agree more," Crotty said. The tension had left the room. "Can we talk, Joey? I mean really talk."

"That's why I came here, Mr. Mayor."

"Good. That's why I asked Bruno and Jimmy to give us a moment together."

"I gathered that. But, sir, if I may be frank, I can't help but think that your guy Bruno there was going to ask me some questions and that you have the same questions but thus far have been too polite to ask."

"Nobody has ever accused Michael Crotty of being too polite before."

They both laughed a bit at the joke.

"Fact is, Joey, your perceptions are quite right. There is much we'd like to know about you but, unlike my associate, I want to be certain that you are approached with these questions in the proper way, with proper manners."

"I see. I thought that Jimmy and I were coming here to talk about taxes not to be attacked by one of your grunts."

"Yes, I know and I apologize again about that. And we did talk about your tax matters, and I assure you we'll do anything we can to help."

"And now?"

"And now I'd like to use our little time together to chat about some of the things I've been hearing about your...your activities."

Joey sat up slightly, turned in his chair, and grinned knowingly at Crotty. It was a signal that the rules of engagement were about to change yet again. "We can be frank, right Mr. Mayor?"

"I love a frank conversation."

"Good. So, let me say this as frankly and as well-mannered as I can. I know that by now you probably have been hearing a lot of things about me, about my background, about my activities, and about the fact that nobody can quite figure out what I'm all about. You, being an astute man and the mayor of this city, are curious about these things and would like to know more. Am I getting warm?"

"You should be feeling the heat any time now."

"Whoa, Mayor. Feeling the heat is not something I ever

want to feel. You know what I'm saying?" Joey laughed.

It took Crotty a second to pick up on the little joke but when he did he enjoyed it. "I like your sense of humor, Joey. That was a good one. Let me rephrase that."

"Yes, please do."

Crotty laughed some more. "You in a hurry, Joey?"

"I got all the time you need, Mr. Mayor."

"Wait one sec," Crotty said as he pushed a button on the old-style intercom on his desk. Kathy Gill's voice was on the other end. "Yes, Mayor?"

"When Mr. Mariano and Mr. Kreider come back from downstairs, tell them to wait and don't let them come in here until I come out."

"Will do, Mayor."

"Now, Joey, where were we?"

"Well, sir, you were about to ask me to explain some things of interest to you. And I was about to tell you what you wanted to know, but I was going to answer in such a way that I could easily deny everything if I need to later. I think that's where we were," Joey said with a smile. "I think you politicians call it plausible deniability."

"And what do you call it?" Crotty said.

"Me? I call it smart."

For the next several minutes, Crotty asked Joey questions about his past, but mostly he asked about Joey's apparent ability to get things done. Joey answered each question in a completely non-incriminating way and let the mayor's imagination cement his reputation. He didn't confirm any of the stories—he didn't deny them either.

About fifteen minutes into this conversation, Kathy Gill buzzed the mayor's intercom.

"I said I didn't want to be interrupted," he blared.

"Mr. Mariano wanted to let you and your guest know that he has to get to work. He apologizes but he has to leave."

"Oh," Crotty said into the intercom. "Jimmy, we'll get back to you on that other matter. Thanks for stopping by."

"Joey, we good?" Jimmy asked from the other end.

"We're good, Jimmy. Catch up with you later," Joey yelled back.

Crotty took his finger off the button. "I hope I'm not keeping you too long, Joey."

"No, no, not at all. Jimmy was my ride, though," he said with a little chuckle.

"Oh, shit," cried Crotty, "I'm sorry."

"No big, Mayor, I'll call over to the club and have one of the guys come get me."

"Nonsense, I'll arrange to have you driven back. Ever been in an official city vehicle before?" Crotty said, immediately realizing how silly that sounded.

"Nope, not even one that says 'Police' on the side."

"You're a funny guy, Joey."

After several more minutes of conversation, the meeting seemed to be winding down. They had gotten as much as they were going to get from each other. It had gone extremely well from both of their perspectives, however different those perspectives were.

"I can't thank you enough for coming by to see me, Joey. I've enjoyed it thoroughly. It was nice to get to know you a little better," Crotty said as he got up from behind the desk.

"Thank you, Mayor. If you don't mind me saying, you're not as bad a guy as everybody says you are. Just kidding," Joey said as he shook Crotty's hand.

"You're a funny guy," Crotty said again.

Joey was tempted to do his Joe Pesci imitation and give Crotty a hard time about the "funny guy" comment. But he thought better of overdoing the *Goodfellas* routine again. Besides, his mission was nearly accomplished, and it was time for him to get out. "Mayor, I like to do little wrap-ups after I have a business meeting. Sometimes people hear the same thing but they hear it different, know what I mean?"

"Good idea, yes, I know how that can happen. Let's hear your wrap-up."

"I think we agreed that you were going to use your resources to help the club out with our tax issue and that you and I might have little meetings once in a while just to chat about some potential business opportunities for me. Oh, and you agreed to leave your ill-mannered assistant home when we did that. In return, I agreed to consider making a sizable donation to your deserving campaign fund and that my services would be made available to you in the future if, and when, you think I might be of help to you in some way."

"That sounds right," Crotty agreed. "I think you hit it right on the head with your summary."

"And finally, I think we both agreed that we weren't going to discuss this with anyone," Joey added.

"Discuss what?" Crotty said with a wink.

"Exactly," Joey said.

They were laughing as the door swung open and the two emerged into the outer office. Kreider was pacing around the outer office, looking quite irritated. He got even more irritated when he saw what a good time Crotty and Geracitano seemed to be having.

"Kreider, call down and get somebody up here to drive Mr. Geracitano back to the Marconi Club," Crotty demanded. Joey had fully intended to call the club for a ride but when he saw how angry Crotty's offer made Kreider he couldn't resist.

"You in charge of transportation too, Mr. Kreider?"

"Jesus, come on you two," Crotty said loudly before Kreider could respond. "Kathy, you call up the car. Bruno, come in here now. Goodbye, Joey."

"Pleasure, Mayor."

Kreider was fuming and slammed the door as he followed Crotty back into the office.

"You need to calm down, Bruno. What the hell's wrong with you? We were supposed to find out about this guy, not piss him off. You took the bad-cop thing too far this time."

"Calm down? That guy is nothing but a punk. Why should I calm down? And what in hell were you two having such a good laugh over when you came out? Busting my balls over the Marconi Day thing again?"

"Bruno, Bruno, Bruno. Take a deep breath and listen to me for a second."

"Fucking punk," Bruno muttered.

"You're wrong, Bruno. He's not a punk. He's a guinea wop bastard, but he's not a punk. Punks are small time operators—this guy is the real deal. Say whatever you want but after spending a little time with this guy, I'm telling you he's the real deal."

"So what's with the love fest? How is he the real deal?"

"Bruno, you would have been proud of me. For once, I wish we actually did tape conversations in this office. If you had heard that conversation, you'd realize how I played that dumb bastard. I played him like a violin."

"So, you don't think he's coming after us anymore? You think he's no longer a threat? One meeting with the guy, and you think he's your pal?"

"No, I don't think any of that. What I think is that he's a downstate guy who has a lot of experience doing a lot of things that some people think are mob stuff. I don't care what you call it. But listen to me. In our little conversation, I learned a few interesting things."

"Interesting how?" Kreider said.

"Look, I can't tell you everything, but I did find out something interesting about why he landed here in Troy. It seems that he got a little sideways with his bosses—who knows who his bosses are, but he specifically referred to them as his bosses."

"So?"

"So, it seems that it had something to do with an unauthorized activity he was involved with. He made some reference to having some influence on the outcome of a downstate election or something like that. He didn't say specifically how he did it, but it's clear that he wasn't talking about selling cookies to support a candidate."

"He told you that he rigged an election?" Kreider asked.

"Of course not! He didn't say that, but I gather from our conversation that, apparently, he took it upon himself to somehow affect the outcome of an election but, for some reason, that did not sit well with his bosses. Evidently, they were plenty pissed off that he did that without their blessing, and he was worried about getting whacked or something. What I gather is that because he's second-generation mobster or something like that, out of respect for his family, they decided to just exile him instead of...you know...instead of something worse."

"You're saying that he rigged an election and was going to get killed by the mob for doing it but got exiled to Troy instead. Is that what you're saying?" Kreider said incredulously.

"Something like that. He was a little vague about the details. But yeah, something like that. Bruno, stop being so naive. Shit like that happens. Especially downstate. Anyway, I assumed from what he said that he had to leave town in a hurry. He decided to set up shop at the Marconi Club. It's a front. Remember? That's what we thought. That's what Cord thought too. But it's not a front for political stuff like we were worried about. He's here on business. He doesn't give a good crap about Marconi or festivals or scholarships or any of that. He also doesn't give a crap about Phillip DiMatteo or any of that shit we pulled. He's interested in having a base of operation for his business."

"What kind of business?"

"The kind of business he's good at—monkey business. He asked me a bunch of stuff about how certain things work in this city. Things like sanitation, protection for business owners, liquor distribution, even produce. He asked about produce, for God's sake. I didn't know the mob was into selling fucking tomatoes but I suppose if there's some way to make a quick buck, he's interested in it."

"Jesus, Michael, if half of this is true, this is dangerous stuff. Why are you getting involved with this guy?"

"I'm telling you, Bruno. I think this guy can make things

happen. Big things, and it's never a bad idea to have some-body on your side who can handle big stuff when shit hits the fan. Agree?"

"And you agreed to help him with his so-called business interests and what else?"

"I told him we'd help him with the tax issues, and we'd keep the cops away from their stinking club. That's it. Oh, and I also told him we might be able to help him get a city contract or two."

"We can't do that! We can't do any of those things."

"No shit, Bruno. But, apparently, he doesn't know that! He did his homework and he knows that we play a little fast and loose with the rules sometimes. I know we can't do anything about the IRS or even the cops for that matter. But he thinks we can! That's all that counts."

"And when he finds out we can't?"

"We'll worry about that later, Bruno. All I wanted to do was set him up, and you and I both know we can throw him a bone or two with a couple of no-show contracts. I put the trap right under his foot and the dumb bastard is going to step right on it. Let him think we can help him and as long as he does, we've got him right where we want him."

Chapter 16

Thinking about the meeting he had attended at The Settlement, Fippi Casella had a strange feeling of deja vu as he cleaned up the lunch room at his beer distributorship. It brought back old memories of when, in that very room, the Gang of Twelve had successfully plotted to overthrow Michael Crotty. He had flashbacks of the feelings of excitement that he and Phillip DiMatteo and the others had enjoyed the night of the election.

As Fippi set up the meeting table, Mo Wheeler—who had led those earlier meetings of the Gang—came in the door accompanied by Dan Robbins, the former city council member who had been forced to resign to make room for Michael Crotty's return to the council. The three, now strange bedfellows indeed, made small talk as they waited for the two remaining invitees.

At just after seven p.m. they were joined by Alex Cord and Ed Abrams, the chairman of the New York State Working Families Party. Abrams had traveled from Brooklyn, his life-long home and headquarters of the upstart political party. Abrams had met earlier that day with Alex Cord at the *Troy Register* newspaper office, ostensibly for an interview that was part of a story Cord was going to do on the state's various political parties. In fact, the conversation at this meeting was one of several Cord had with Abrams over the previous few days on an entirely different matter.

Abrams briefly explained to the others the relatively modest history of the party and its platform which centered, not surprisingly, on the concerns of working families: jobs, education, health care, and the like. While the party had high ideals, it was a minor political party which specialized in supporting candidates for the sole purpose of offering voters an opportunity to vote for someone other than the endorsed candidates of the Democratic or Republican parties. The Working Families Party took root in New York State and a small number of other states which maintain so-called "electoral fusion" laws that allowed for the cross-endorsement of a single candidate by multiple parties. With electoral fusion, a candidate's votes from any number of party endorsements were combined. It was a way for voters to support minor party candidates and not waste their vote on a candidate facing opposition by another of the major parties. Occasionally, the party would run its own candidate, but mostly it used electoral fusion to support one already running on a different slate.

"I have to tell you, gentlemen, that the proposition that Alex has put out there is a pretty interesting one," Abrams said after his overview of the party and its goals.

"You're familiar with the politics of our city?" Wheeler asked.

"I surely am," Abrams assured them. "We have not gotten involved in any of your races here but I, for one, was delighted when Phillip DiMatteo ran Michael Crotty out of office. I only wish that we had been smart enough to endorse him. Regardless, it's politicians like Crotty who we dream about getting rid of. We're all about running and endorsing candidates so that people can have honest and responsible elected officials to vote for. Since I first spoke with Alex about this, I've done a good deal of research on Troy politics over the past several years, and I think this idea has a lot of merit."

"Tell them why you think that, Ed. Tell them what you told me earlier," said Cord.

"We've studied this a little. For the past twenty or more years, this city has been locked in a situation where there has been virtually no hope of getting rid of incumbents, no hope of getting rid of the corruption that the Democrats here revel in and that keeps getting them elected. As a result, Troy elections have been foregone conclusions. Few good people even run for office and very few people even bother to vote in elections. The situation with Phillip DiMatteo was an aberration and won't happen like that again in my life-time, especially given what happened in the end.

"Frankly, I have already spoken with our party leader-ship, and we think this proposal has some promise. And I won't lie to you guys, we're excited to get out in front of this. We think this is our first opportunity to successfully have one of our candidates get enough momentum to actu-ally win an election and we love the fact that nobody will see this coming. If nothing else, it will be great PR for us."

"Are you aware that we're not really going to cam-paign?" Robbins asked.

"Yes, and to be totally honest, our party does not have the resources to financially support a campaign like this at the local level anyway. So, to some extent, that works better for us. Right now, it appears that Michael Crotty and the rest of them will once again be unopposed by anyone. It's our hope that if there are no other candidates coming from the other parties, we may get their cross-endorsement if we put someone out there and convince them that electoral fu-sion can work here in Troy. And we love the idea of being first in the boat. If this works, it will be a real momentum builder for our party. I still think it's a long-shot against this machine, but a grass-roots effort against a political machine is what we're all about. Win, lose, or draw, it's a win for us. So, we're in."

"Okay. But we're still pretty new at this," said Wheeler. "What's next?"

"We can't give you much money or people on the ground or anything, but we can do all the necessary filings and paperwork for you. We'll get you on the ballot. We can help with strategy and maybe with getting some press. Mo, you and Fippi and Dan are going to have to sign a bunch of paperwork to get on the ballot, but we'll handle the details. We've still got a few weeks to make the filing deadlines. We'll do it all, and when we're all set, we'll come back and march it all down to the state board of elections, hold a press conference and off we go."

They spent the next hour discussing strategy. The potential candidates, especially Wheeler, had many questions. In the end, they all sensed that their scheme had a chance of reaching their goals, none of which necessarily included winning the election.

"Do we have a deal?" Cord said while looking at the three would-be candidates.

"Deal," each said and shook hands with Abrams.

"I'll be in touch," Abrams said. "I got a long drive ahead of me. Goodnight—candidates," he said with a smile.

After Abrams left, the others sat, each deep in their own thoughts.

"Alex, this is still all about Operation Out 'n' In, isn't it?" Casella said, breaking the silence. "We can't really win, can we?"

"I don't see you guys winning," Cord answered.

"I don't really care one way or the other," Robbins said. "I just want to make Crotty and Burgess squirm a little."

"I already promised my family I wouldn't win this, so you better be right Alex," Wheeler said.

"Well, Mo, I don't think you're going to win but this is politics—stuff happens."

"Wrong answer, Alex," both Mo and Fippi said at the same time.

℘℘℘

"Mayor's office," Kathy Gill said into the phone in Crotty's outer office.

"Kathy, it's Alex Cord, how's things?"

"Same old, same old."

"Sorry to hear that. Anyway, can I have a word with the mayor?"

"Hold a sec, Alex, I'll see if he's awake," she joked.

Cord noted to himself how openly hostile toward Crotty she had become since she decided to leave.

"Excuse me, Mr. Mayor, Alex Cord is on line one and wants to speak with you."

She could hear Crotty say to Kreider, "It's Cord, you take it."

Kreider took the phone from Crotty. "Put him through."

"Mayor, this is Alex Cord, thanks for taking my call."

"It's me, Bruno."

"Bruno, I have something I want to talk to the mayor about."

"What is it?"

"No offense, Bruno, but I want to make sure the mayor knows this is coming from me."

Kreider put the call on the speakerphone.

"What's up, Alex?" he heard Crotty say.

"I just got some information I thought would be of great interest to you, sir. I wanted you to hear it from me."

"Don't worry, Alex, you'll get full credit," Crotty said in a condescending tone. "What's so important?"

"I just got a call from a buddy of mine at the board of elections. He tells me that you may actually have to run a campaign this year."

Kreider's eyes flashed. "What are you talking about? The Republicans have already decided they're not running anybody against us."

"Maybe so but the Working Families Party has just filed three candidates. They filed the paperwork this morning."

"Working Families Party?" Crotty said incredulously. "Who or what is that?"

Before Cord could answer, Kreider said, "They filed somebody? You sure? They usually just endorse some loser who's already running, and nobody else is running. I don't understand."

"Apparently, that is not the case this time," Cord replied.

"Nobody else is running against us," Kreider said. He found this information astounding. "They're putting up their own candidates? They never do that. What in hell is going on?"

"It gets better," Cord said.

"They never do that," Kreider repeated, sounding even more incredulous each time he spoke.

"Better? You said it gets better. What do you mean?" Crotty asked.

"They've put up Mo Wheeler as a candidate for mayor. They're running Fippi Casella for an at-large seat and—are you ready?—Dan Robbins is running in the sixth ward, your old district."

There was total silence on the other end.

"You guys still breathing?" Cord said.

Crotty said nothing and walked toward the window to gaze out.

"We're still here," Kreider said. "What else you got, Cord?"

"Isn't that plenty for one day?"

"Is that it, Alex?"

"Is the mayor still listening?"

"I'm listening," Cord heard Crotty say.

"Mayor, I want to explain to you that I have to write this story. I can't not write about this."

"Don't make this out to be something big when it's not," Kreider jumped in.

"Yeah, that's right," Crotty agreed, who had gotten nearer to yell into the speakerphone. "It's just three yokels trying to get their fifteen minutes of fame. They got no shot at us. I know that and you know that. Don't go giving this bullshit story legs it doesn't deserve."

"I won't, Mayor. But I'm the political reporter, so I have to write it."

"Fifteen minutes of fame, Cord. That's all you give them," Crotty said as he hit the button to end the call.

Kreider sat quietly, staring at the ceiling as he tried to make sense of it all. He had not seen this coming. With so little time left to file for candidacy and the Republicans already deciding not to run a candidate, both he and Crotty has assumed there would be no opposition in the November election and no need to even campaign.

Crotty stood at the window again. "Do these idiots have short memories or something?" he bellowed. "Do they not remember what happened to them the last time they tried to get cute with us? Is Wheeler looking to have to run out of the YMCA naked again? Is Casella trying to get all of his shitty little trucks sabotaged again? What the hell!"

Kreider did not answer.

"And Dan Robbins? Are you kidding me? Do we have to take him out to the fucking woodshed again? Is he just stupid or what?"

"Hold on a second," Kreider finally said. "Let's not get all nuts over this. I have no idea what they're thinking, but remember, this is the damned Working Families Party. They have never run a successful campaign for dog catcher, let alone against a machine like ours. This is all bullshit. I'm not going to lose any sleep over this, and you shouldn't either."

"Ah, Jesus," said Crotty. "The last thing I need is to have to campaign. I hate running around this town every night going to rubber-chicken dinners, and playing nice-nice with a bunch of idiots."

"Well, Mayor, let me say this. Before I even think about us launching a campaign, I'm going to need to see a lot more out of these morons. Just getting a lousy nomination from a fifth-rate party doesn't mean a damn thing to me."

సౌసో

Kreider had already read the morning paper before picking up Crotty for breakfast the next day. He gave Crotty an update at the diner on Cord's article about the new candidates entering the race that was in the paper. "First, I have to say that Cord did a good job with the story. If there was any slant to it, it was how much of an uphill climb these guys have against us. It basically suggested that this was just some sort of a statement rather than an actual campaign."

"What page was the story on?" Crotty asked.

"Three. Down in the left corner. About five column inches."

"Okay, good. Remind me to give Cord a pat on the head."

"The best part was this," Kreider continued. "According to the story, these guys are not going to campaign at all. I don't think their fame is even going to last fifteen minutes. Fifteen seconds is more like it."

"No campaign?" Crotty said. "Mo Wheeler wants to win an election against me and he's not even going to campaign? I don't get this at all."

"That's the point," said Kreider. "They don't expect to win. They're just trying to make a point."

"What point?"

"Who knows? But Wheeler is quoted in the story as saying that all they want to do is give voters a choice. They're running only because they allegedly don't think there should be an election without at least two candidates."

"That's it?" asked Crotty.

"That's it," replied Kreider as Donna refilled his coffee cup.

"Morons," Crotty mumbled.

ⒺⓈⒺⓈ

Kathy Gill sat nervously alone at one of the metal tables at the far end of the city hall cafeteria. She was, as she always was at ten-thirty a.m., on her morning coffee break. She had fifteen minutes before she was due back in the office. As soon as she sat down, Alex Cord entered the cafeteria and casually got a cup of coffee from the vending machine. He pretended to happen to notice Kathy, waved, and went to her table.

"Sleep well?" he said.

"Not a wink, as you would imagine."

"I like your home. Thanks for your time last night."

Kathy was edgier than he had ever seen her. She didn't look up. She sat breaking a wooden coffee stirrer into smaller and smaller pieces.

"Your husband seems like a nice guy," Cord continued. "I imagine you two had a lot to talk about after I left."

"Until about midnight," she said. "Actually, he did most of the talking."

"And?"

"You know, after all these years of Walt listening quietly to me complain about Crotty and seeing how much I grew to despise everything about what goes on here, I think he's more interested in this than I am."

"If you need more time to think about it—"

"I don't need more time, I just need some assurances that if somehow your plan, whatever it is, doesn't work, I won't get caught up in a huge problem. I know how vicious Crotty can be. Walt wants me to cooperate, but we're both concerned about retribution. I've got a pension to worry about, Alex, and health benefits. If Crotty finds out I'm involved in whatever it is you're up to—"

"That's completely understandable," Cord said sympathetically. "He won't. I give you my word."

"It would help if we knew what the plan actually is, you know."

Cord recognized that Kathy and her husband were being asked to get involved in something they knew little about. "I know, Kathy. But I really can't tell you. Besides, the less you know about where this is heading, the better off you'll be."

"Walt's biggest question to me was whether or not we can trust you."

"Also quite understandable. He doesn't know me at all." There was a long pause in the conversation. Cord did not want to push too hard. "Do you?" he said.

"Do I what? Trust you?"

"You and Walt. Do you trust me?"

"That's what scares me, Alex. I do."

"Look, Kathy. I'm not going to lie about this. I don't know exactly what's going to happen, and you're the last person I want to see hurt in any way. But I need your help. What I need from you is very simple, simple but very important. It will be easy for you to do, won't directly implicate you in any way, and will go a long way toward…" His voice trailed off.

"Toward what? Getting my revenge?"

"Yours and a lot of other people."

"Walt left it up to me, depending on exactly what you wanted from me. We want to help."

"That's all that I can ask for."

During the remaining five minutes of her coffee break Kathy found out what Cord wanted from her.

"That's it? That's all you want me to do?" Kathy asked when he had finished.

"That's plenty," he replied. "I know you don't know where all this is going but those things are important. Even if the whole plan turns sour, what I'm asking you to do simply cannot be traced back to you."

She got up from her chair. "I gotta get back," she said. "You stay here for a few minutes after I leave." She gathered up her empty coffee cup along with the tiny pieces of the broken stirrer and tossed it all in the nearby trash container. "I'm in," was all she said as she walked by Cord on her way out.

Later that afternoon, Crotty and Kreider were in a rare good mood when they returned to the office after lunch. They had been talking about their unexpected good fortune as they drove back to city hall.

Earlier that day, as he was instructed to do, Kreider had

phoned Jimmy Mariano to get details about the Marconi Club problems with the IRS. They wanted to at least pretend that they were going to try to help.

"Okay, now that we're alone," Crotty said as they had entered the office and closed the door, "give me all the details. This is incredible!"

Kreider was animated and clearly happy with himself for how he handled the call with Mariano. "So, I start asking him about the tax thing," he began to elaborate. "Now remember, I'm just making this call because I had to. I expect I'll take two minutes and pretend to gather all this information from him about their taxes so that we can do absolutely nothing," he said, laughing out loud. "It was a total bullshit call."

"Then he told you?"

"Well, fortunately, I just started the call by telling him I'm following up on the tax issues we discussed. About two seconds later, he says how thankful he is that we took care of this so quickly! At first, I thought he was just talking about me calling to get information then the dumb bastard proceeds to tell me how he got a letter this morning from the IRS saying that the whole thing was an error and the file was being closed. He then starts gushing about how thankful he and Geracitano and the whole club are to us for taking such prompt steps to get this taken care of. Mariano was praising you up and down and saying how much Geracitano was impressed with your ability to get this done."

"What the fuck happened?" Crotty said incredulously.

"I have no idea," Kreider said. "No idea. I don't know, and I'm sure Mariano doesn't know, but somehow the problem went away. Whatever happened, those dopes think we're responsible for making it happen, and they couldn't be more grateful."

"This couldn't be better," Crotty said.

"And then he makes me promise to let you know that Geracitano says that he is in your debt. Then he makes some vague reference to how Joey never, ever forgets a debt."

"And you said?"

"I played it cool and told him that it was our pleasure to help. I didn't want to ask too many questions, like we didn't know how this happened. I just went along with it and pretended that we take care of shit like this all the time. Mariano was gushing so much about it, I had all I could do to not laugh out loud. We got what we wanted and didn't have to lift a finger."

"See, Bruno? I told you. Even if you know you can't do something, you should always pretend that you can. You never know, my friend, you never know. And you never know when having a guy like Geronimo in your debt will come in handy. This is beautiful! See? I told you, didn't I?"

❧❧❧

Two days passed and Kathy Gill was alone in the office, opening the morning mail. Crotty and Kreider had a morning meeting with Danny Burgess and would not be back for hours. She came across an envelope addressed to Crotty which had the Marconi Club's return address. She immediately knew that her role in Alex Cord's scheme had begun.

She slit open the top of the envelope then took out a handwritten note and a cashier's check made out to Michael Crotty in the amount of $10,000. She stamped the note with the mayor's office official date register and went to the copy machine. She copied the note and the check, clipped both originals to the envelope as she did with all incoming mail, and put them back into the stack she was working on.

She then reached into her desk drawer and pulled out a stationery pad containing sheets of white note paper on the bottom of which was printed, *From the Desk of Mayor Michael Crotty*. She placed the photocopies of the note and check along with the single piece of Crotty's stationery into an envelope, which she put into her purse, and went about the rest of her otherwise-normal day.

After returning from the meeting, Kreider was going through the stack of mail in the mayor's office as Crotty talked on the phone with a constituent.

"These jerks think if they make one stinking little campaign contribution, that you'll take care of all of their stinking little problems for them," Crotty complained as he hung up the phone.

"Or the other way around," Kreider said, holding up the note and check that had just come in.

"Huh?" said Crotty.

"Seems that our friend Mr. Geracitano does things the other way around," Kreider said as he handed the envelope to Crotty.

"What's this?"

"Read it."

"Ten grand!" Crotty gushed, looking at the check made out to him personally. "What's this all about?"

"Read the note," said Kreider.

Dear Mayor,

I can't tell you how grateful I am for your part in taking care of the tax matter we discussed. Very impressive. Enclosed is what I hope will be the first of many examples of gratitude that you and I will show toward one another in the days ahead. You will notice that the check is made out to you personally in the event that your campaign may not need it.

Gratefully yours,
Joey G.

"This guy is a piece of work," Crotty said after reading the note.

"I'm a little surprised he was so forthcoming in his note," Kreider said suspiciously.

"Bruno, I told you this guy was the real deal. Relax, this

is the way they do things. They do things personally, with manners. He knows what I'll do with this note and this money," Crotty said as he walked over to the corner of the office to put the note into the shredder. Crotty then picked the cashier's check up from his desk. "It's made out to me. I'm just going to deposit this in my personal account. We've got plenty of campaign money already."

Chapter 17

It was a hot and steamy early July day. At that time of year, things normally tended to be pretty quiet around Troy City Hall. A majority of the workers were on vacation or just took personal days leading up to the long Fourth of July weekend. Because of the steaming heat in the non-air conditioned city hall, and the fact that almost no one else was in the building, the door to the mayor's outer office was wide open.

Kathy Gill was at her desk. She was not permitted to take vacation in the summer months. "We need to keep a skeleton crew here in the summer," Crotty reminded her every year, "and you're the skeleton."

She could hear the sound of footsteps on the marble flooring as council president Danny Burgess and council member Larry Monk came toward the office. Monk was the member from the sixth ward who was handpicked by Crotty to fill his old seat and was now being opposed by Dan Robbins. They were there for a strategy session with Mayor Crotty and Bruno Kreider. Like Crotty, they did not like the fact that they were being opposed in the election and thus had to consider actually running a campaign for re-election. As the unofficial political strategist for Troy Democrats, Kreider had called the meeting, mostly to assure the others that the Working Families Party candidates would not be a real threat, but he had mentioned that there might be a bit of a problem they had to at least talk about. As usual, when things weren't going their way politically, they blamed Kreider.

"You need to get this joint air conditioned, Michael," Burgess said as he sat down in Crotty's office. Burgess, having been around Troy politics for as long as anyone could remember, was the father figure among Troy Machine Democrats. Nothing happened in Troy politics without his support. As such, he was one of the very few who got away with calling Crotty anything but Mr. Mayor. It was clear, even to Monk, the newest member of the council, that Burgess—not Crotty—was in charge.

"Give us the bad news, Kreider," Burgess began.

"Who said anything about bad news?" said Kreider.

"Well I'm in this sweltering building today because you called a meeting. Presumably you would not have called a meeting on this bitch of a hot day if not for bad news. I'm telling you, Bruno, if Casella or anybody else gets my leadership spot, you're going to have a lot of explaining to do. Now be a good boy and tell me exactly what the problem is and exactly how you're going to get us out of it."

"Is there really a chance that I could lose my seat?" Monk said.

"You just shut up and listen," Crotty said abruptly to Monk. He was clearly in as foul a mood as Burgess.

"All right, everybody. Calm down," Kreider said. "We're just here today for an update and maybe a little planning."

Kreider went into some detail on the Working Families Party and stressed their long history of running failed candidates. He stressed that neither Mo Wheeler nor Fippi Casella nor Dan Robbins was actually doing any campaigning and that he still believed that their candidacies were just a symbolic gesture.

As Kreider continued his assessment, Crotty erupted. "For Christ's sake, Bruno, tell them!"

"Tell us what?" Burgess demanded. "I still don't see the problem."

"It's just that we've heard there may be a little problem brewing—no big deal," Kreider said, trying desperately to keep Burgess calm. "It's just that the newspaper guy, Alex Cord, told me the other day that he had done some quiet polling which suggested that the race may be tighter than we'd like. Honestly, I think it's all bullshit, but I thought you should know what he's saying."

"Cord has polling data and you think...what?...he's lying or something? Let's see the damned data," Burgess roared.

"No not lying. Exaggerating maybe. You know how reporters are. They make things sound worse than they really are. Personally, I think he's just asking the wrong questions of the wrong people. I think he's just asking a bunch of people who won't vote in the first place if they'd like a choice, and they sort of just instinctively agree. Cord promised he'd keep this quiet, at least until we have a chat with him about it. I wanted you guys to hear it from him, not just me. That way you can ask him any questions you might have."

"So, a reporter is coming here?" Monk asked. "Is that wise?"

"Larry, listen," Crotty said condescendingly, "if we didn't think it was wise, do you really think we'd be asking him to come?"

"Cord's always good to us," Burgess said. "We'll see what he's got."

The intercom buzzer sounded. Kathy Gill announced that Alex Cord had arrived.

"Send him in," Kreider said.

Cord spent the next few minutes telling them in detail about a poll he had conducted. Burgess, in particular, quizzed him on his methods, the questions he was asking and the results he was getting. Cord had known that Burgess would want to drill him. He was prepared for that.

"Why are you doing this, anyway?" Monk asked.

"Ignore him, Alex," Crotty said. "But why are you doing this?"

"My first poll a few weeks ago surprised me a little,"

Cord explained. "I went into this thinking you guys would be polling at ninety percent, but you all came out roughly the same—somewhere around sixty to sixty-five percent."

"That's still enough, isn't it?" Monk said.

"Yes and no," Cord said. "Certainly, that's an okay number in straight up races but for the at-large seat, it makes getting the highest vote count a little trickier since there are more seats and more candidates. Mr. Burgess could get more than fifty percent of the votes, but since people will vote for three at-large seats, somebody else could get even more votes and the person with the most votes becomes council president. If this Casella guy looks like a spoiler, he could come out on top and Mr. Burgess here loses the leadership position."

"Fuck!" Burgess yelled.

"And sixty-five, even for the mayor or for you, Mr. Monk, is not a number that should make you very comfortable. Not with this much time left before the election."

"Alex, you said you took this poll weeks ago and that you were going to do another poll—maybe a little more scientific or something. Anything changed?" asked Crotty.

"I'm glad you asked, Mayor. And it's good that you guys are all here today so I can tell you all at once."

"What changed, Mr. Cord?" Burgess said.

"I did a second poll just like the one I told you about. I had presumed that the results would be similar since I asked the same question of the same demographic. The good news is that I was right. All three of you are actually doing a little better. Your opponents have done absolutely no campaigning and, frankly, most of the people I polled didn't even know they were running."

"So, what's the bad news?" Kreider asked.

"The bad news?" Cord hesitated. "The bad news is that I have it on good authority that there will be cross-endorsements coming."

The room sat silent. None of them had expected this. Monk had no idea of what that even meant. He had never heard of cross-endorsing. "Help me out here," he said. "I don't understand."

"Spell it out for us, Alex," Kreider said. He wasn't sure Crotty knew what it meant either. Kreider knew what it meant and it frightened him.

"In New York and a few other states, there is an election rule which says that a political party does not have to run its own separate candidate. They can simply endorse a candidate who is put on the ballot by another party. And when the votes get counted, a candidate who is cross-endorsed gets the total of all the votes cast for him on all of the party lines. It's sometimes called electoral fusion."

"Oh," Monk said. "That's bad, isn't it?"

"Where did you find this guy?" Burgess said to Crotty, motioning at Monk.

Kreider sat with both hands rubbing his face. He was trying to assess the damage. Everyone else was trying to process this information. Cord said nothing more.

Finally, Kreider said, "Alex, you've been reporting on politics for a long time. How much of a difference do you think electoral fusion will make with our candidates?"

"Hard to say. On the one hand, the people who said they may vote for your opponents will probably do that, no matter what line the candidates appear on. Those people can still only vote once so a cross-endorsement won't mean anything with them. On the other hand, there may be some Republicans or Independents or Conservatives out there who would not have bothered to vote at all without a candidate endorsed by their party. But if those parties decide to cross-endorse somebody and these otherwise non-voters actually come out to vote—"

"The polling numbers you came up with will get worse for us," Burgess said, finishing Cord's sentence.

"Could happen that way," Cord said.

"Can you even guesstimate what that may mean in this case?" Burgess asked.

"You're putting me on the spot, Mr. Burgess. This has

never happened around here before so we have no history to look at."

"Guess," Burgess said impatiently.

"Guess? Could be a fifteen to twenty percent difference," Cord replied.

"Which could get them over what they need," Crotty added.

"And me way under what I need," Burgess agreed.

There was a prolonged silence in the room. Crotty got out of his chair and went to the window to stare out.

"What are we going to do about this?" Monk said urgently.

"For starters," Burgess offered, "we should thank Mr. Cord for coming today and let him get back to work."

Cord knew he was being dismissed so that they could talk in private. He got up from his chair, nodded at each of the men in the room, and left the office.

After he had closed the door behind him, he went by Kathy Gill's desk.

"Hot day," Kathy said.

"Getting hotter by the minute. Stay cool," he whispered.

"You too," Kathy replied as she reached down into her purse to pull out an envelope containing the photocopies she had made a few days earlier of Geracitano's date-stamped note, the $10,000 check made out to Crotty, and the sheet of Crotty's personalized note paper. She handed the envelope to Cord on his way out.

ເອເอ

In August, the County Republican Party announced that it was taking the unusual step of cross-endorsing Wheeler, Casella, and Robbins. Later that same day, the Conservative and the Independent parties did likewise. Each of the parties, desperately tired of seeing Democrats being elected in Troy year after year, had been contacted by and had met with Ed Abrams, the WFP Chairman. While there had never before been such collusion among the parties, the scenario Abrams presented to them seemed a far better alternative than having their own candidate get trounced again by the Troy Democratic Machine or having no candidate at all.

Each put out statements in support of Wheeler, Casella, and Robbins as a way of giving the people of Troy a choice, an opportunity to vote for a candidate other than that of the Machine. They were tepid endorsements, but endorsements nonetheless.

Even with these endorsements, the three candidates still did not campaign. The buzz among those who followed politics in the city was that these candidates had made a calculated and brilliant move by not campaigning. Addition by subtraction, as one pundit called it. The very fact that they were not campaigning was more appealing and noteworthy than any real campaign could have been. The less they campaigned, the more popular they got, and the more the Democrats worried.

Meanwhile, the old-line Democrats fought back the only way they knew how—they began calling in all of the political favors they had built up through their years of corrupt dealings. Crotty, Burgess, and Monk, much to their deep dismay and dislike, hit the campaign trail. They attended nightly gatherings at every Rotary meeting, Elks Club dinner, Church bazaar, and pot-luck supper they could find. They reluctantly dug into their campaign war chest to run local television spots which depicted their opponents as too inexperienced to handle the complexities of city hall. They made not-so-subtle references about how Crotty and the Democrats had saved Troy from the disaster of Phillip DiMatteo's administration.

The Democrats were relying heavily on turning out the vote from among the city employees, contractors, vendors, and the like—all of whom owed their livelihoods to the Machine. The Democrats never missed an opportunity to insinuate that the way of life that so many people of Troy were dependent on would come down to voting Democratic in November. They called in every chit they had as they felt their long-held grasp on not only the mayor's seat, but the city council leadership as well, was in jeopardy.

No one was more surprised by these developments than the man who had essentially orchestrated this political maneuver himself, Alex Cord. As he sat alone in his apartment each night, he marveled to himself that he was, for the first time in his life, something more than just a reporter of the news. Not only had he been deeply involved in concocting this entire political scenario in the first place, but it was his pushing of the buttons which set in motion these incredible developments.

He was fully aware that his role in Operation Out 'n' In was completely contrary to the notion that reporters should report the news, not create it. He no longer cared about that. He was now just *pretending* to be a reporter. He had a greater goal of somehow righting the years of wrongs he had witnessed and, he believed, abetted with his indifference. He wanted things to be different this time.

As he always did, Cord attended the annual Labor Day Parade in Troy. All along the parade route on River Street, locals crowded the sidewalks to see the high school marching bands, scout troops, fire trucks, floats, and representatives of virtually every other organization which called Troy home. Of course, with this being an election year, the city's politicians were out in full force. They rode in convertibles at the tail end of the parade as though to somehow take credit for the entire event.

At the very end of the parade, Troy Council President Burgess and Councilman Monk rode in a Cadillac convertible along with the parade grand marshal, who just happened to be Mayor Michael Crotty. They smiled and waved, and occasionally the Cadillac would stop so that they could shake some hands and kiss some babies.

In years past, the politicians were normally greeted with at least reserved adulation from the people along the route. This time, Cord was both amused and astounded when he heard a smattering of boos coming from the crowded sidewalk as the convertible rode past.

Cord had completely made up the story of having conducted polls which showed that Crotty and the others were in trouble. No polls had actually been done, but the cross-endorsements that came from the various political parties caused him to wonder what an actual poll would show.

He decided that, on the day of the parade, he would pass among the crowd and randomly ask the exact same set of poll questions he had told Crotty and his cohorts about during his meeting with them at city hall. He went around randomly asking bystanders if they were likely to vote in the upcoming election and, if so, he polled them on their preferences. By the time he had finished, he had what he believed to be a fair sampling. In his apartment that night he tallied his results and was genuinely shocked to find that the estimates he had given to Crotty and the others about voter preferences were actually fairly accurate—almost exactly what he had told them. Even his guesses about the effect of cross-endorsement were within a point or two in each of the races. This time Cord had done a legitimate poll showing both Crotty and Burgess running slightly behind.

ᘓᘓ

While the drama at city hall was escalating life at The Settlement went on as usual. An outsider looking in on the daily goings on would be hard pressed to see any evidence that this setting of serenity and normalcy was the nerve center of a plot to take down a corrupt political machine—unless of course, that outsider happened to be in The Settlement dining room on Wednesday evenings.

Every Wednesday night, the ladies received a detailed briefing from Duke Bennett and occasionally from Alex Cord on Operation Out 'n' In and planned their next steps.

On the Wednesday night after Labor Day, Duke, Mo Wheeler, Alex Cord, and Joey G. joined the meeting. Cord was anxious to tell them about the parade and the actual polling he had done. He had kept the results to himself until that time.

"So, Alex, you're saying that we could actually win this election?" Wheeler asked.

"I'm saying exactly that! But don't let me mislead you. This was not a statistically valid sampling. It was just me asking a bunch of random people about their voting preferences. I'm not going to sit here and tell anyone that if the election were held today that you guys would win—but you might."

"This is amazing!" said Chuck. "This is a scenario that none of us expected. Now what do we do?"

"What difference does it make?" said Rita. "I don't see how it makes any difference, except that maybe now Crotty will finally get really desperate. He was getting desperate anyhow, wasn't he, Alex?"

"Yes, I think he was. He doesn't know that my earlier poll information was made up. This real poll doesn't change that."

"So I repeat. What difference does this make?" Rita persisted.

"I think the difference is that maybe we can get what we want without actually having to play it all out," said Chuck. "Maybe this can just run its course and we win the election outright."

"That may be true," Pat agreed. "We still don't know if we can pull this off in the first place, and if it somehow backfires..." Her voice trailed off. "Maybe we should just wait and see if we can win the way it stands now. That way we may still get what we want and nobody will know what we've done. If Alex's poll is right—"

"No, I don't want to stop now," interrupted Rita with a hint of disappointment in her voice. "The fun is just beginning. If the poll is wrong, we did all this for nothing. I think we keep going."

"I'm still pretty nervous about the rest of our plan.

There's a lot of things that can go wrong," said Pat.

"I agree. A whole lot could still go wrong," agreed Chuck.

None of the men said anything. They were all aware of and respected the fact that in the final analysis this was not their decision.

"I wish you didn't even take that stupid poll, Alex," Rita said.

"I thought you all should know," Cord said defensively.

They all looked toward JoAnne.

"Jo, we need you to weigh in on this," said Rita.

"Oh. I don't know," JoAnne said nervously. "I really don't know. I think I need to hear more. Yes, we usually hash out these decisions among the four of us but this time I'd like to hear from the others. Duke? Mo? Joey? What do you guys think? Alex, you've been closer to this than anyone lately."

The four men just looked at each other. They each had a lot invested in this, but they all knew that they were only actors in this drama.

"I'm good with whatever you ladies want to do," offered Duke. "I think that the way this is turning out, we can still be winners, no matter what we decide. But to tell you the truth, I was kind of looking forward to the rest of this."

Alex Cord cleared his throat. "I tend to agree with Pat and Chuck. It's still not clear to me that we can actually get the rest of these dominos to fall where we want and when we want. Don't get me wrong, I love our plan but honestly—it may work and it may not. This plan has a lot of moving parts and any number of things can go wrong. Personally, I think Mo and the others may win. If we keep going and something goes wrong, it all could backfire on us. If that happens, we lose all around. I'm okay with us pulling the plug. What do you think, Mo?"

Wheeler was taking this all in and still digesting the entire notion that he might actually be the next mayor. "I'm still in a state of shock over this and the possibility of becoming mayor. You guys never told me that this possibly could happen," he said with a chuckle as he tried to lighten the mood. "And I gotta be honest, I'm still more than a little concerned that Crotty and his crooks will be looking for revenge. I guess I might even feel better if they were locked up in a cell somewhere. But I can see both sides of this." He was clearly not going to weigh in on this decision which he, as well as the others, thought belonged to JoAnne. "I think I'm going to recuse myself from this discussion. Whatever you ladies want to do is fine with me."

"Spoken like a real politician," chided Rita.

There was then a long silence.

"Joey? We haven't heard from you," Chuck said.

Joey smiled and shook his head as though he did not want to say what was on his mind.

"Say it, Joey," JoAnne said. "I can't tell what you're thinking but I'm sure you have a strong opinion. Tell me what you think."

"It's your call, Mrs. DiMatteo," he said.

"Tell me," JoAnne repeated as a demand more than a request.

After a long pause, Joey folded hands in front of him on the table and looked toward the ladies at the far end. "Okay, I'll tell you what I really think. Let me first say that, in the beginning, I got involved with this because I thought it would give me a chance to play a role that I think I was born to play. It was right up my alley, and I thought it would be a kick—like a lark. So, I thought, why not? It sounded like fun and, besides, I had nothing going on anyway so I went for it. But that was before I met all of you great people, that was before I met you, Mrs. D. and before I really knew why you were doing this. Sure, I kind of heard the reason but I really didn't understand. I didn't understand the real point. It almost didn't matter to me then.

"I've had a lot of fun with this and made a bunch of new friends, including all of you nice people. Plus, you've been kind enough to pay me nicely to do this, which has come in real handy since I'm otherwise out of work for the time being. I couldn't be happier, no matter what happens next. But since you asked me, I gotta tell you—maybe it's just me—maybe it's my nature or something like that—but I like to finish things that I start, especially things that I think are worthwhile doing.

"To be perfectly honest with you, Mrs. D., when I first heard what you had in mind here, I thought you were all nuts. I thought it was nuts, even for me, to pack up and move upstate, for God knows how long, to play a part in the wildest scheme I ever heard of. And believe me when I tell you that I've heard many, many wild-assed schemes in my life. Oh, sorry ma'am, excuse my French."

"That's quite all right, Joey. We all hear worse from Rita almost every day," JoAnne said understandingly. "Go on. You were saying…"

"Yeah, anyway, I was saying that this was before I met any of you and way before I learned what a creep Crotty actually is. This was before I really learned about your story and about your husband and the crap these dirtbags pulled on you and your family. What happened to you was horrible. I think what they did to you is the kind of thing that cries out for a response. After I understood what this was really all about, it became something more to me. It became a worthwhile cause. And after all we've gone through, I still think the same thing. Getting revenge on these guys for what they did to you is definitely worthwhile in my book. And as I said before, I like to finish things I start."

"Thank you, Joey," JoAnne said. "Well said."

"And may I say one more thing, Mrs. DiMatteo?"

"Of course."

"I hear everybody always refer to this whole thing by what I guess is a code name or something. You call it Operation Out 'n' In. Am I right?"

"We do," JoAnne said.

"Well as I understand it, the Out means out of office; the In means in jail. Am I right about that also?"

"That's right," Rita exclaimed, sensing where Joey was heading.

"So, as I see it now as we all sit here tonight," Joey continued. "I think we have a good chance of running that creep and his scuzzy friends out of office already but where I come from, we finish the job and make sure the in—in jail—happens too. I think it's worthwhile. My opinion? We shove these dirtbags into jail where they belong."

There was a stillness in the room as though the cloud of any question had just cleared.

"Spoken like a true Italian. I couldn't agree more," Jo-Anne said. She smiled at Joey and then at everyone seated around the table. "Let's finish what we started, shall we? Out n' In it is. Plus, I still want my apology."

"Also spoken like a true Italian, Mrs. D.!" Joey said.

Rita stood and applauded.

Chapter 18

On his way to pick up Crotty the follow morning, Kreider's cell phone rang.

"Bruno? This is Alex Cord."

"What gets you moving so early, Alex?"

"I've been stewing on this since Labor Day, and I've decided to play things your way. When I get information regarding the election, you get it first, before anything shows up in the paper."

"What do you have, Alex?"

"Can I meet you and the mayor at the diner this morning?"

"The mayor usually likes breakfast before starting work."

"Trust me, Bruno, he'll want to see this right away. I have a story I have to run with—have to. You and I know how much the mayor hates being blindsided. He's definitely going to want to see this before it gets in print and it's going in today."

"I'm picking him up right now. We'll be at the diner in ten minutes."

Cord had made the call from the diner parking lot so he could get inside before Crotty and Kreider arrived. He went inside, sat at the mayor's booth, and began to spread out the notes he would be using. The notes laid out each question he had asked potential voters on Labor Day with detailed responses broken out by voter demographics. Cord had spent most of the night getting it in shape to present.

Crotty barged into the diner and went directly to the

booth without going through his usual glad-handing with everyone there. Kreider scurried in immediately behind.

"What is it, Alex?" Crotty grumbled after squeezing himself into the booth. "What's so damned important that it can't wait until after I eat?"

With that, Cord laid out a detailed synopsis of poll results which strongly suggested that Crotty, Burgess, and Monk were all in trouble in the upcoming election. He used actual results but had skillfully presented the data so that it would, at least upon first look, paint the most dire picture possible to Crotty and Kreider. If someone were to dig down and carefully examine all of the data, they would see a slightly different picture, but Cord knew that Crotty would not actually do that. Cord had the actual polling results, but he revealed only that part which accentuated the problem areas for Crotty and the others.

Cord concluded his summary by saying, "According to my data, which I think is pretty accurate this time, it appears that you and Burgess are in trouble."

"This shit keeps getting worse, Bruno," Crotty grumbled when Cord had finished the presentation.

"Can I keep this?" Kreider asked, reaching for some of the pages of data Cord had shown to them. "I want to show Burgess."

"Sorry, Bruno, you can't keep any of this. This is my only copy," Cord said, taking the notes away from Kreider. He had specifically decided to meet that day in the diner because he knew Kreider would want a copy. If they had met at city hall, Kreider would insist on a copy. There was no copy machine at the diner.

"Then make a copy and drop it off later," Kreider insisted.

"I'll see about that, Bruno. I can't have this getting out there before my editor sees it, though. He'd have my ass if he even knew I was showing you this."

"You can trust us, Alex," Kreider said.

Cord had all he could do not to laugh at that statement.

"Back off, Bruno," Crotty said to Cord's relief. "We got the bad news. Let's not spend all day staring at a copy of it. We gotta figure out how to deal with it, not just sit around staring at numbers. Thanks for this, Cord. We owe you. Thanks for coming."

With that, by way of a Crotty dismissal, Cord packed up his papers and left in a hurry.

After Cord left, Crotty finished his breakfast without saying a word. Kreider was silent too. Crotty wiped his mouth, downed the rest of his chocolate milk, and said, "This is not good, Bruno. I think it's time for us to go off the reservation. It might be time to call in the army on this."

"The army?" said Kreider.

"The Italian Army," Crotty replied.

Kreider was perplexed. He had to think a moment about what Crotty had just said. It then occurred to him that the so-called Italian Army was a reference to Geracitano.

"Whoa, Mayor. You're not thinking of getting you-know-who mixed up in this, are you? Are you crazy? I don't think that's a good idea at all. We can't trust that guy. I still think he's a bullshit artist. We can't go all the way out on that limb because of some half-assed poll. We'll keep campaigning. It will all work out."

Crotty leaned in toward Kreider across the booth. "We've been campaigning. I'm sick of it. You got a better idea? You saw the poll. You heard Cord. We're fucking losing, Bruno. Besides, the more we campaign, the worse it gets. That's unacceptable!" Crotty slammed his fork on the table. "It's time we take care of that."

"What do you think Geracitano is gonna do, vote one thousand times?" Kreider said in a whisper.

"I don't know what he's going to do, but what I do know is that this guy's the real deal and can make shit happen. He's gotten mixed up in politics before and he as much as told me flat out, he can do it again."

"What makes you think he'll get involved in this in the first place?"

"He's a businessman, Bruno. He's a businessman who has manners. A businessman who has shown us that he believes in returning favors. If we handle his needs, he'll handle ours. He still owes us for the tax thing, and we can sweeten this even more."

Kreider rubbed his eyes and shook his head. "I can't believe I'm even hearing this."

⌘⌘⌘

After leaving the diner, Cord went to the newspaper office to complete work on a different story. When he finished an hour later, he decided to call Joey to fill him in on the meeting with Crotty.

"What's up, Alex?" Joey said, picking up the call from Cord.

"I think I got their attention with the poll results," Cord said.

"I think so too."

"What do you mean, you think so too?"

"I mean just five minutes ago, I got a call from someone named Kathy Gill. She said she's with the mayor's office."

"Kathy? Yes, that's Crotty's secretary. Why did she call you?"

"She tells me that the mayor has room on his schedule to meet with me about the matter I had asked him about a week or so ago. It kind of caught me flat-footed. I wasn't real sure exactly what she was talking about, so I just agreed to meet and figure out later what it was all about. I'm guessing he's not talking about the tax issue."

"He bit on it, Joey!" Cord exclaimed.

"Seems so. Now we get him to swallow it."

"Jesus! I can't believe this is really happening. When's the meeting?"

"Tomorrow at three."

"Beautiful! Now, where are you? I need to get you that poll information so we can really scare the crap out of him.

Remember, we talked about this possibility. You need to know the numbers I told them about. That's important."

"That's a bit of an issue, Alex. I'm heading out of town right now, and honestly it's even going to be tough to get back by the time I have to meet with him tomorrow."

"Oh, that's right. I forgot it's Monday. You go to see your mother every Monday night."

"Yeah, that's right. She and I have dinner together at her house every Monday night, no matter what. I'm on my way to Staten Island right now, in fact. Usually, I just come back first thing Tuesday morning but tomorrow morning she's got an appointment with her doctor—something about changing her nerve medication. I gotta go with her. The last time they changed her Xanax dosage, she instantly got whacked out. I'm gonna go with her to make sure the doc doesn't do something stupid like that again. I should still be able to make the meeting with Crotty but not by much. You'll have to figure out some way to get me that information at the last minute."

"What if the doc is late, Joey? That happens all the time."

"I'm going with my mom, Alex. End of discussion."

Cord quickly noticed Joey's voice getting a little testy.

"Of course, Joey. Of course. I'll think about how to get the info to you and call you in the morning. Have a good dinner with your mother."

"Always do, Alex. Call me tomorrow."

☙☙☙

Joey Geracitano arrived back in town and arrived at the mayor's office at two-thirty the next day for his three p.m. appointment. "Good afternoon Mrs. Gill?" Joey said to Kathy as he entered. They were alone in Crotty's outer office.

"Hello Mr. Geracitano, she said softly.

"I think the mayor is expecting me in thirty minutes. I

also understand from Alex. Cord that you have something for me to read while I wait."

"Yes, yes I do," Kathy said, picking up a magazine from her desk and handing it to Joey. "Mr. Cord said he thought you'd enjoy reading this."

"Thank you," he said, taking the magazine and moving toward a secluded spot in the rear of the waiting room. He sat and leafed through the magazine to a place where there was a loose typewritten page. Keeping the magazine open to that page, he studied the page carefully for the next thirty minutes. At exactly three p.m., he put the page in his pocket, got up, and handed the magazine back to Kathy.

"I'll buzz you in now, Mr. Geracitano. Have a good visit."

"Is Kreider in there?"

"The mayor is alone."

"Perfect."

Inside, Crotty was quite cordial in his welcome, overly so, Joey thought.

"You'll notice that I remembered to keep Bruno out of our discussions," Crotty said by way of introduction.

"I appreciate a man who honors my simple requests," Joey said as he shook hands with Crotty and settled into the chair in front of Crotty's giant desk.

"I have to tell you, sir, I know you're a really busy guy with the campaign and all, so I'm very flattered that you wanted to see me today. And if I might say so, sir, I couldn't help but notice that you went to some pains to have this invitation come by—shall we say—a roundabout route. You could have called me directly. I told you to call me any time."

"I thought it may be important that it not be common knowledge that it was my idea for you to come here today, Joey. I wanted this to look like a routine constituent call. Should anyone notice you're here, we can just say you asked to stop by on some governmental matter."

"I fully understand, Mr. Mayor. But just in case that actually happens, what might my governmental matter be?"

"I'm sure you'll think of something," Crotty said.

"So, I take it this is not a routine matter. Tell me why I am here today, Mayor."

This time Crotty was prepared for Joey's directness. "Joey, I enjoyed our conversation of several weeks ago, especially the part when you told me of the business goals you were trying to achieve here in our city. I admire a man with goals."

"Thank you. I enjoyed our visit too."

"Anyway, I was thinking about your interest in hearing more about any city contracts that your enterprise might fulfill if only you had a chance to participate in the selection process."

"Ah, Mayor, again you impress me with your eye for detail. I'm honored that you remembered. And to be truthful, yes, I am interested in such things."

"Good, good. Well, Joey, just the other day something came to my attention that I thought an entrepreneur like yourself may be interested in."

"And that would be?"

"Towing."

"Towing, sir? Did you say, towing—as in pulling stuff?"

"Yes, that kind of towing. It seems that our towing contract is up for renewal soon and, for a variety of reasons, I think the current vendor needs replacing."

"I'm sure I don't understand what that entails, Mr. Mayor. Excuse my ignorance."

"Of course. Let me tell you how this works here in Troy. Almost every day, one or more of our departments are called upon to have a car removed. Often, it's a DWI where the driver is arrested and somebody has to come to tow the car to a lot somewhere. Naturally the service has to get paid to do the towing and then they are allowed to charge a fee for storing the car, usually overnight."

"Naturally," said Joey.

"Or on other occasions, people might be parked in what

we have labeled as tow-away zones all over the city and the same need exists. The car gets towed, stored until the fine gets paid, and then the owner has to pay a bill for towing and storage before getting the car back. It's quite common. And, as you can also imagine, when it snows in our city, the streets need to be plowed. Invariably people forget about alternate-side street parking during snow emergencies and unfortunately somebody has to come and tow the cars so that the streets can be cleared. Now I shouldn't be divulging this to you, but in case you're interested, towing is big business in this town, thousands of dollars. And, as I mentioned, we might have a need for a different vendor to provide this service. Given your apparent wide range of interests and abilities and our cordial relationship, I thought I would make you aware of this potential."

Joey saw an opening. "Thousands of dollars." he said derisively. "Did you say thousands of dollars?"

Crotty sensed that Joey was not impressed. He wished he had made up a bigger number. "Could be a lot more," was the best with which he could counter.

"This is all presuming you get elected, correct, Mayor?"

Crotty did had not known exactly how Joey would respond to this whole idea but this was not at all what he expected. "Excuse me?" he said.

"Mayor, can we be honest with each other?" asked Joey.

"That's the only way."

"Good. Then let me tell you where I think this is all leading, and then you tell me if I'm far off. You're in trouble in the upcoming election and if, somehow, I am able to assist you in actually getting re-elected, then you're offering me some nickel and dime towing service deal in exchange for my help. Am I getting warm?"

Crotty was back on his heels. Yes, Joey could be direct at times, but Crotty was not prepared for this. He thought this meeting would just be a little friendly sparring session, but Joey took the gloves off instantly. For a moment, Crotty wished Kreider was with him. Maybe he was misreading

Geracitano's aggression. Maybe this was just his style. Crotty was clueless as to how to respond so he decided to keep it cordial.

"I'm sure I have no idea what you're referring to, Joey. Do you think I'm worried about being re-elected? Well, surely, I'm not. I have no idea why you would say that, especially since I'm just trying to do you a favor. Now, if this idea doesn't suit you, then—"

"Favor?" Joey said, interrupting Crotty. "Mayor, Mayor, Mayor. Stop it. You're beginning to insult me. Favor, my ass! I don't think you're trying to do me a favor at all. Here's what I do think, Mayor. I think you are losing in the polls to some dork named Wheeler by about seven to eight points, and you're scared shitless about losing. I also think your partner in crime, Danny Burgess, is in the same boat, except he's losing worse than you are. Even if he does get a seat, he's losing the council president position for sure because Casella is going to win the most at-large seat votes. Burgess is at least eleven points behind Casella, and I assume Burgess is climbing up your ass to do something to save his. I also think that your dim-witted little protégé, Larry Monk, is down by five points and that there are not enough Democrats in this city who actually intend to vote to make up the difference in any of your races. I also think that the cross-endorsements by the other parties will end up with you and Monk getting ousted and Burgess losing his leadership position. That's what I think." Joey had nailed every statistic Cord had slipped to him in the note.

"No, Joey, wait. Hold on. All I'm trying to do is—"

"Hold on, my ass," Joey said, again cutting Crotty off mid-sentence. The full-court press was on. "You're getting your ass kicked by some schmuck named Wheeler, so you're offering me thousands of dollars to bail you out. Thousands of dollars! I spend more than that on dry-cleaning in a month."

Crotty was stunned by this reaction and by the fact that Geracitano had hit the numbers almost exactly as Cord's poll had indicated, even the part about the likely Democratic voter turnout.

"Did you get this information from Alex Cord? How do you know this?"

"From who? Cord? That reporter guy? Come on, Mayor, give me a little credit, will you? Alex Cord? Jesus," Joey scoffed. "Look, I've got my own eyes and ears on the ground. I've got my own insiders in the news bureaus all over this town. I don't get my information from cub reporters like Alex Cord. I get it from reliable sources. I have a great interest in keeping up on things like this. One never knows when such information can come in handy. Besides, that shit I just told you is all over this town. I'm sorry you're the last to know."

"What other polls are you talking about?" Crotty asked, pressing for information. "What do you mean it's all over town?"

"With all due respect, Mayor, isn't this the sort of information you should be getting from your advisors? Maybe you need to get rid of that butt-hole, Kreider. I can't believe your number one advisor is totally in the dark on stuff you're now hearing from an outsider like me. Do you actually pay that guy? Jesus!"

Crotty was clearly overmatched. He had no idea how Joey knew all this. He was stunned that his towing ruse had so easily been figured out. It was clear that Joey instinctively knew that his offer for the towing contract was a ploy to get help with the election. In five minutes, Joey had the whole thing figured out.

"Look, Mayor." Joey's tone suddenly changed. It was lowered, measured, and calm. He was thoroughly enjoying shoving Mayor Crotty all over his own office, but he sensed enough was enough. "I'm sorry for jumping ugly with you here. I just get a little annoyed when people underestimate me. It seems, you know, disrespectful."

"I mean no disrespect, Joey, believe me."

"Sure, Mr. Mayor, sure," Joey said. "Mayor, let's stop

jackassing around here. Let me say this as simply as I can. If you want my help in the election, just say so. And if you do want it—and if I do agree to help you—then we'll talk about how you can return the favor. But believe me, Mayor, if that is what you want, you're going to need to stop insulting me with some bullshit towing idea. You're fishing in some deep, deep water here, my friend."

Joey got up from his chair and began to walk around the room as though he was thinking this through. Crotty said nothing. When Joey sat back down a moment later, he laughed a little.

"What's funny?" Crotty said.

"Mayor, do you remember that movie, *Jaws*? Did you see *Jaws?*"

"Uh, yea I saw that. You mean that shark movie.? What's that got to do with anything?"

"Yeah, the shark movie. That's the one. Do you remember in that movie the first time we get a look at the size of that fucking great white shark? Remember? It comes out of the water and almost bites Roy Scheider's head off. The thing is enormous! It scared the crap out of him and everybody in the movie theater. Do you remember that? They were scared shitless. And do you remember what he said after he saw the size of that shark?"

Crotty's head was spinning. "Uh, no. I don't remember."

Joey leaned in toward Crotty who was still seated across the desk. "When he saw the size of that enormous shark, he looked at the other guys with his eyes popping out of his head and calmly said, 'We're gonna need a bigger boat.'"

Crotty got up, headed for the window, and stared out as Joey was enjoying that line again.

"We're gonna need a bigger boat," Joey repeated. "Now that's funny, funny stuff, don't you think? Funny, but at the same time also very, very true."

The mayor didn't respond and remained motionless at the window.

A moment later, Joey was suddenly standing right beside

him. He spoke in a calm and friendly tone. "Mayor, I knew that sooner or later, a day like this would come. I knew it. It always does with guys like you and me. Sooner or later, guys like you and me always end up in a conversation like this. I know you need help, and I'm here to tell you that I can help you land that shark. But, Mayor, let me tell you that this is a big shark. It's a really big shark, and you're gonna need a bigger boat."

"Tell me what you mean. Quit talking about boats," Crotty growled, getting frustrated.

"I mean that if you really want outside help winning this election, I can make that happen. But if you want that help, the payback will be big, and you'll probably be in my debt for a long time. But I think you can handle it. I'm a fair guy, Mayor. I never ask anyone to do something they can't do. I would never do that."

Crotty walked back to his desk and sat with a thud. "You can't expect me to agree to buy something when I don't know what it will cost. Nobody does that."

"Fair point," Joey replied calmly. "You make a fair point. But right now, I can't tell you exactly what this will cost. It's complicated. See, Mayor, my work is often a lot like yours."

"I don't see how that's possible," Crotty said.

"No, really, it is. Most of the time all I do is arrange things. I make things happen but I don't actually do anything other than get other people to do what needs to be done. My job is a lot like yours, like you were saying with the cars being towed. You arrange for that to happen, but you get other people to do it. I know you're not out there driving any tow trucks in the snow. Am I right?"

"Joey, I don't even drive my own fucking car!"

Joey smiled. "Exactly," he said. "So, in the instance that I think you and I are discussing, I can arrange for this to be done, but I'm not actually going to do it myself. As a result, I'm going to be owing somebody else, more than one somebody else most likely. What you need can be done, but

I'm sure you'll appreciate that it is…shall we say?…a complicated matter."

"I have access to some money but—"

"Whoa, Mayor. Stop! This isn't about you paying money. In my world, and that of my associates, having politicians in our corner is far more valuable to us than what they can actually afford to pay us. We can make more money off of you than we can from you. Believe me, we've done that math many times over."

All the cards were now being put on the table, and Crotty was getting his bearings. Joey was talking about IOUs, a subject that Crotty was very familiar with. "So, you help me get re-elected and I owe you something, somewhere, sometime. Is that how it works?"

"Is that not how it always works? Have you not been doing the same damned thing your whole political life?"

"It is a game I've played before," said Crotty.

"Right again, Mayor. Except that, this time, maybe we're talking about 'same game, different table limit.' But, essentially, you're right. Blackjack, for example, is played exactly the same way, whether you bet a dollar or a million. No matter what the stakes, it's still the same game, with the same rules, played the same way."

"Good analogy," Crotty said. "I get that. Can I ask you a couple of questions?"

"Ask away."

"Now don't get offended, okay? I just want to understand a few things about this—this potential."

"Ask."

"How are you going to get this done?"

"How? That's a little like asking a magician to reveal how he does a trick, is it not?" Joey said, clearly joking. "But it's a fair question. I'll give you the short answer because, honestly, I don't understand all the details myself. That said, having participated in similar endeavors in the past, I can tell you that elections are fairly simple to fix if you have the right tools and somebody who knows how to use them."

"Tools?"

"Yes, tools. But think a little beyond hammers and wrenches, Mayor. It's done by fucking with the computers that do the vote counting. I'm not a computer guy so I can't begin to tell you about bugs or hacking or stuff like that. I just know people who do know all that stuff. They refer to it as malware. Personally, I wouldn't recognize malware if I found it on a hanger in my closet."

"Me neither," said Crotty. "But whatever it's called, you mess with the counting done by the computer, right?"

"I don't, no. I just told you that. I don't mess with anything. I got people who do that. It's been done before, and it can be done again. I happen to know that for a fact. Even an experienced politician like you would be shocked to find out how often this happens. I also know that it can work in Troy."

"How do you know that? How do you know it can work in Troy?"

"I told you that I knew this day was coming. And when I found out your campaign was headed down the sewer pipe, I took the liberty of having one of my colleagues look into how the system works in this city. Guess what? It just so happens that it works here just the same way it works in several other cities where elections have been…shall we say?…pre-determined. To certain guys who know what they're doing, using the right tools, it's a piece of cake. If you want more details, I can get them for you, but we're not kicking tires here. I'd need to know that you're serious before I reveal any of the hard tricks to you."

"Can this work with more than one candidate?"

"You're not going to bat for that idiot Larry Monk, are you?"

"No, fuck him. Just me and Danny Burgess. Can you help both of us?

"That question I can answer. The answer is yes. It takes a little more work, but it's not a problem at all. I'd be glad to give you a two-fer 'cause you're such a sweetheart. Actually, now that I think of it, if you want Monk to win, I'll throw him in the mix too. It would be an actual three-fer. Can't beat that. That's up to you, I really don't care."

"Okay, fine, last question. As you apparently know, the poll numbers are still pretty close. I'm behind, but I can still win and so can Danny. If you do get involved and we do win, how will we be sure we won because of you and not us just winning on our own?"

"Excellent question, Mayor. Excellent! One that I would have asked myself if I were in your shoes."

Crotty oddly felt proud that he was at least asking the right questions and relieved that Joey was apparently not irritated that he was asking them.

"Here's my answer to that excellent question, Mayor. You'll know. I guarantee it. Again, we can talk specifics later. And again, I can't give up all my secrets on our first date. But believe me, you'll know."

"I have to be honest with you, Joey. I've been involved in my share of shady deals in my time, but this one is way beyond what I'm used to. It scares me a little just talking about it."

"Mayor, that is quite understandable. It's a big step—a very big decision. Listen, I think maybe I've given you about as much to think about as you can process in one afternoon. You know where to find me. If this is something you want to do, let me know. If not, fine. We'll still be friends. Guys like you and me need each other, if not today, then some other day. We'll always be friends," Joey said with a smile.

Crotty did not respond.

Joey began to move toward the door. "Oh, Mayor, one last thing. Think long and hard about this before you decide. Take your time, but whatever you decide, be sure. Once you pull the trigger on this gun, there's no getting the bullet back. It doesn't work that way. This is way too complicated to be jerking around with it. One answer—one time. In or out."

With that, Joey left, thinking how glad he was that he had not said, Out n' In, instead of in or out.

Crotty was relieved when he heard his office door close. He could not remember ever being so scared in his life. His hands were shaking and his heart was racing a mile a minute. He went back to the window where he stood, staring out, for the rest of the afternoon.

ℰↄℰↄ

The next morning Kreider was quiet, almost silent, as he picked Crotty up at his house and sat through breakfast without saying a word. On their drive to the office, Crotty finally said, "Okay, Bruno, you haven't said two words all morning. What's the problem?"

"The problem?"

"I know you're pissed off at something, what is it? You're pissed that I went solo at that meeting yesterday afternoon, ain't you?"

"That's your prerogative, Mayor. I don't have to be in every meeting with you. But in this case—this particular meeting—I would have thought you'd want me there. That's all."

"Bruno, look. It's clear that you and Mr. Geracitano don't see eye-to-eye. He thinks you disrespected him and you know the way Italians are. You can do almost anything to them without them getting pissed, except disrespect them."

"Oh, he's Mr. Geracitano now? Since when? When did you stop calling him Geronimo?"

"See? That's what I'm talking about. You and him are never going to get along. But he and I have developed an understanding. We both respect each other, so whatever dealings we have in the future will be on that basis. I thought that if you were involved, he and I would lose that mutual respect we've developed."

"Do you mind at least telling me what happened at the meeting? Can you fill me in? I still think this guy's really dangerous and you're playing with fire dealing with him."

"I'll tell you what's really dangerous," Crotty said, raising his voice. "What's really dangerous is coming into an election behind in the polls. Dangerous is me risking losing this race and Danny losing the council presidency. If we lose this, those bastards will have a blueprint to do it again and again. Not only will we get ousted, the rest of the council members will get picked off next election and the next, and we'll be done forever. We can't let that happen, Bruno!"

As they rolled into the mayor's city hall parking spot, Kreider turned off the car. "Before we get out. You still didn't tell me what happened in the meeting," he said.

Crotty did not answer. Instead he just got out of the car and went inside. "Bruno, I'll tell you what I think you need to know and when I think you need to know it," he said once they had gotten in the office and closed the door.

Kreider said nothing. He was still annoyed about not being in the meeting. After about ten minutes of silence between them, Crotty said, "Geracitano can help us win this election."

"Help us? How?"

"Let me correct myself. Geracitano can make us win this election. He can guarantee it."

"Come on, Mayor, be serious."

"Serious? Did you just tell me to be serious?" Crotty bellowed. "Nothing is more serious to me than winning this election, Bruno. Nothing! I'm the one seriously working on winning it while you spend your day with your thumb up your ass."

"He's going to rig the election. Is that what you're telling me?"

"If I tell him to, yes. And if you really want to continue

to be involved, then you'll just have to accept that. If you don't accept that, then you're going to miss a whole lot more meetings between now and November."

"Have you actually agreed to that?" Kreider asked, fearing the answer.

"Not yet. Not just yet."

Kreider sighed audibly. He was caught between trying to steer Crotty away from Geracitano on the one hand and getting shut out of whatever deal Crotty would cut to get reelected on the other.

He knew that if Crotty dealt with Geracitano alone, somehow, he would screw it up. That always happened, and this time the stakes were too high.

He thought that if he could be a part of whatever it was Crotty was doing, he might be able to avert potential disaster. He decided that his best approach was to stay involved as long as possible by playing along. "What can I do to help, Mayor?"

"That's the sprit, Bruno!" Crotty exhorted.

"Tell me at least what you're thinking about and how I can help."

"Do you know much about computers, Bruno?"

"Computers? Uh, a little."

"Good. Now go get us some coffee. When you come back, we'll talk."

For the next half hour Crotty gave Kreider chapter and verse on the meeting with Geracitano. At times, Kreider felt like he was having an out-of-body experience. He and Crotty had been involved in many underhanded deals before, many of which were completely illegal, yet this one was on an entirely different level.

"So, Bruno, what I need right now more than anything," Crotty said toward the end of his discussion with Kreider, "is to find out if what Geracitano said about how this is done makes any sense. He told me that if we were serious, we could find out the details. Somehow it involves computers. He's not a computer guy any more that I am but this thing is all about screwing with computers. Moleware...or something like that...he called it."

"You mean, malware?"

"Yeah, maybe. Mole, mal—whatever. Anyway, if we find out that it does make sense, then it only stands to reason that he's done it before. Otherwise, how would they know this stuff? Right?"

"I don't know if any of this makes sense, but I agree that's a first step."

"Geracitano said he would get me in touch with a guy who can explain it all, but you, not me, need to have that conversation. I don't know shit about computers."

"But Geracitano won't deal with me," Kreider said.

"I know that, but I already got it all figured out."

"I hope so, Mayor. I hope so."

☙☙☙

Duke and Joey were in the office at the Marconi Club when Joey's cell phone rang. Joey had given his number to very few people so he was hoping it was Crotty.

"No, Mayor, no trouble at all," Duke heard Joey say. Duke could hear only what Joey was saying but gathered the gist of the conversation from what he overheard.

"I did say that, yes....So, does this mean you're getting more interested? Interested enough to take the next step?...Excellent!...Good, sure. That should not be a problem....I can do that but it's going be a little tricky having that conversation....I knew you'd understand. Give me a day or so. I'll call back on your cell and leave a message about how we can do that....Yep, nice talking to you too, Mayor."

"He bit on it?" Duke asked anxiously.

"He's still nibbling, but I think he's about to take a big bite. He wants to know how we do it. You were right, Duke. It's amazing how predictable this dope is."

"I'll get Adam going on this," Duke said.

"He's what? Your cousin or something?"

"Yeah. He's a computer geek. He's one of those Geek Squad guys."

"Geek squad? What the hell is a geek squad, some sort of nerdy commando team or something?"

"No, Joey. Those are the guys who work at that computer electronics store in the mall. They're all tech kids who know all about computers and electronics. They help people like you and me who know nothing about that shit."

"Never heard of it," said Joey.

"He's twenty-two years old, and he somehow knows all about this stuff. He's a whiz at it, he really is. I already talked to him about this. He got a bunch of information about voter fraud from the internet, and he can make it sound good because he can talk the talk."

"And he'll get the phones too?"

"That too."

☙☙☙

The following morning just after dawn, Bruno Kreider's car stopped in front of the Marconi Club. He left it running as he got out and hurried up the front steps, looking back over his shoulder, hoping not to be seen. There in the corner, as planned, was a small box containing a pre-paid cell phone—the Bat Phone, as Joey had called it. Joey had explained to Crotty that this was necessary to make sure their conversations could not be recorded or traced. Crotty was instructed to use it to call yet another pre-paid phone. Both phones should be disposed of after the call. Crotty loved the Bat Phone reference. He was duly impressed by this cloak-and-dagger approach. Another sign that Joey had done things like this before, Crotty thought.

Joey had told Crotty that he did not want Kreider involved. He chuckled to himself, knowing that it would, of course, be Kreider who would call since Crotty knew nothing about computers, and he would never trust anyone other than Kreider to be involved in a scheme of this magnitude.

Kreider grabbed the package and drove off, taking notice that no one had seen him.

At eight a.m. sharp, he called the only number programed into the phone.

"This is Adam."

"This is Bill," Kreider said. "Do you know why I'm calling?"

"I do. You have some questions about vote computations. What do you want to know?"

"Yes. First can you give me the overview?"

"Are you a computer guy?" asked Adam.

"I'm up on things."

Adam wanted to make a quick determination of how tech-fluent the man on the other line actually was. That way he'd be able to assess how detailed he'd have to be in his explanation. "So you know about ciphertext?"

Kreider had never heard that term before. "Well, sure, but go ahead and tell me what you're referring to, so I know we're on the same page," he responded, thinking that was a cleverly deceptive answer.

Adam was not fooled. "Encryption, then? You know what encryption is?"

"Oh yeah, encryption. Like scrambling messages. Codes." Kreider groped for some way to sound informed.

"Never mind. Here's the skinny," Adam said as he quickly assessed that the man on the other end knew little about computers and nothing about programming. He could just use the dumbed-down version. "The voting system in most cities, like Troy, is called a Public Network DRE Voting System," Adam began.

"Right, I'm aware of that," Kreider said, again attempting to sound knowledgeable.

"Right. Anyway, as a direct open system, votes are electronically captured at the voting place and sent through an open network to a central computer which basically takes the data coming in, counts it from all of the polling places, and spits out a total vote count. They all work pretty much the same."

"And you can hack the counting computer?"

"We don't actually hack the computer. That's where all of the firewalls are. That's where they set up all of their safety procedures. Those are pretty hard to hack unless you can physically get at the machine, which is usually not possible unless you have an insider with access. You don't have an insider we can use, do you?"

"Ah, no. No insider."

"Too bad, that would make this a whole lot easier."

"Can it still be done?"

"Oh, yeah, not a huge problem really, it's just easier if we can get our hands on the computer that does the counting. With DRE voting, all you need to do is inject a program between the voting places and the calculating components at the main computer. When votes get uploaded from the polling places, the program intercepts the transmission, manipulates the numbers, and then sends it along to the main computer. It's a little bypass mechanism. It's ridiculously simple, actually, and happens so fast nobody knows it's happening."

"So the results are calculated off of the data you changed?"

"Yep. And we change it in a way so that it looks just like a regular vote count. Except we pre-program the outcome."

"I can't believe it's that easy."

"Well, that part is. But there's one trick."

"Which is?"

"You need to get somebody with access to the system to download the program that lets us cut off the data before it gets counted."

"How do we do that? How are we going to get somebody at the election office to download a program for us?" Kreider said.

"It's really not all that hard. Pay attention. Every one of these places is operated on a LAN."

"LAN?" Kreider asked.

"You don't know what a LAN is?" Adam asked derisively.

Kreider caught himself. "Oh, you said LAN. I thought you said YAN."

"Yeah, whatever. As I was saying, these places are all on a network so that all of the computers in the place are linked. All you need to do is get somebody—anybody—on that network to open up an email that contains our program, and it automatically downloads to every computer on the network, including the one used to count the votes. All you need is one email opened by somebody in the LAN and you're into all of the computers connected to it. Not hard, and the program's invisible and doesn't affect anything other than the DRE system, virtually impossible to spot unless you're looking for it."

Kreider was taking this all in and was shocked to hear how simple but effective this sounded. "So I send an email with the hidden program to somebody at the election office. It doesn't matter what the email is about but when they open it, the bug gets into the whole system. Am I following this right?"

"You got it. Can you send the email to somebody's computer that's on the LAN without anyone getting suspicious? We have to make sure somebody trusts the sender enough to open the email, otherwise, there is no download."

"Yeah, sure. I email those guys a lot, especially around election time. And the program is invisible?"

"Absolutely, in fact, after the official vote is certified by the election commission, the program self-destructs. It disappears without a trace."

"How does it know when to do that?" Kreider asked incredulously.

"The law says that they have two weeks to do the official certification. So, we just write the program so that it erases itself in fifteen days. Poof! It's gone. Nobody knows it was there, and nobody can find it later." Adam said.

Kreider went from being skeptical to being fascinated. "So you set up the vote count ahead of time?"

"There is a pretty sophisticated algorithm which changes the input data so that it comes out to a pre-determined outcome."

"What will it be in our case?"

"You can make the outcome anything you want. The program doesn't care. I sure as hell don't care. You just program in the percentage you want each candidate to end up with, and the program puts in vote counts that will come out to those percentages."

"Amazing!"

"Pretty simple, actually." Adam felt he had done what he needed to do and wanted out of the call as soon as possible. "Any other questions?"

"Ah, no. No, I think that's it. If I think of any more, can I get back to you?"

"That's not up to me," Adam said.

"Oh, sure, I forgot," said Kreider.

"And, Bill? One more thing."

"What's that, Adam?"

"As soon as you hang up this call, ditch the phone. It will never be used again. Rivers are always good places for that."

"Got it."

Chapter 19

H ow does that Tom Petty song go?" Joey casually asked Duke as they sat in the Marconi Club office. "Oh, yeah, something about the waiting being the hardest part," he said, answering his own question.

It had been two days since the phone call between Adam and Kreider. Adam had given Joey and Duke a complete report on the call and, in Adam's opinion, "Bill" was convinced that the election rigging scenario was completely plausible. But neither Kreider nor Crotty had followed up.

Everyone involved in Operation Out 'n' In knew that they were running out of time if their plan was going to work prior to the election. The trap had been set, but Crotty still had not taken the bait.

"Even if he does think we can pull this off, I don't know," Duke said. "I have a feeling that this is making Kreider way too nervous. I'm afraid he's going to talk Crotty out of it."

"We need something to push Crotty over the edge," Joey replied.

"Like what?"

"I have no idea, Duke. At this point, I have no idea what else we can do that doesn't look suspicious."

೧౧౧

As it was, Duke was right in his assessment. Bruno Kreider did report to Crotty that he was duly impressed by the conversation he had with Adam, but a final decision had still not been made. Kreider, thinking that this was an insane and dangerous plan, was still hoping that Crotty would back off.

"The guy sounded to me like he really knew what he was talking about," Kreider said to Crotty. "But I still don't like it. Too many things can go wrong, and this is not like the old days when we just stuffed the ballot box with votes from dead or fictitious people. We know how to do that kind of stuff. This is way outside our comfort zone. Even if Geracitano can pull it off, I don't like this."

Crotty still wanted to go through with the plan. "Bruno, I don't see how screwing with the computer count is fundamentally any riskier than screwing with the votes that get put into the computer," he reasoned. "As you just pointed out, we've done that a zillion times before. Whether you mess with one vote or all of them, the risk is the same, Bruno. In fact, from what I understand, this seems less risky than a lot of the things we've done. A lot less risky. Tell me how this is different. When we fixed votes before, we had to trust a lot of people to not rat us out. This time we only need one or two other guys to clam up, and the last time I checked, mobsters were notoriously good at not remembering things when the shit hits the fan."

Kreider felt oddly at a loss to answer that. In his own twisted way, Crotty had made a fair point. Exactly how one rigged an election was not the point. It was either rigged or it wasn't. "I hear you, Mayor," he said. "This just feels different to me on a lot of levels. I still don't like it."

"And I still don't like losing," Crotty said, almost to himself.

He stood by the hour looking out his office window, paralyzed by indecision. He desperately wanted to be reelected, and he was horrified to think of what would happen if Danny Burgess lost the council presidency.

Yet, for years he had relied on Kreider to help him think through difficult problems. He recalled many instances when his own instincts had been wrong and Kreider had kept him from making big mistakes. But he could not tell the difference between Kreider's normal fear of taking chances and his ability to see things clearly, more clearly than Crotty almost ever did.

∼∽∾

While Crotty stewed over what was perhaps the most important decision he would ever make, Alex Cord was getting more worried with each passing hour. He tried to go about his normal routine, but he was totally preoccupied with wondering whether Crotty would agree with the idea of rigging an election. The wait was torturous to him. He busied himself meticulously assembling all of the notes he had been taking since the plot began. It would be his ultimate task to put the story together, the story which, he hoped, would put an end to the corrupt tenure of Michael Crotty and his cronies and hopefully land them in jail.

Cord was confident that they could already bag Crotty on the "pay-to-play" transaction between Joey and Crotty over the tax issues. He was sure that Crotty had cashed the check for his own benefit, and that it would be easy to trace. He could also just divulge Crotty's drunken Excalibar confession, but he was sure that Crotty would somehow explain these things away. Without conclusive evidence of the vote-rigging plan, the whole Operation would likely fail. With each passing hour, Cord sensed that something more was needed to push Crotty over the edge. *One more push*, he thought. But he did not know where that push would come from.

It came in a way not even Cord could have imagined.

∼∽∾

As the waiting game played out at the Marconi Club, at The Settlement, in Alex Cord's apartment, and at city hall, a series of unprecedented and secret meetings were being held between and among the local leadership of the political parties that had cross-endorsed Wheeler, Casella, and Robbins. They had done their own polling and had a sense that their candidates could actually win the election, which was less than two months away.

They were particularly confident that Fippi Casella could become the highest vote getter from among all of the candidates in the at-large council seat election and thus unseat Burgess as council president. Even if Burgess was re-elected, if Casella outpolled him, the council leadership would be in Casella's hands, more importantly, out of the hands of the Machine.

It had never been done before but, given these circumstances, the Republican, Independent, and Working Family parties decided to jointly pay for a television ad blitz over the last weekend in September. The ads would support Wheeler, Casella, and Robbins but, more pointedly, they would focus on taking down Danny Burgess. Burgess, they thought, was the real head of the snake that needed to be cut off.

They prepared and aired an absolute attack ad which focused on getting rid of corruption in city government and in no uncertain terms put a bulls-eye on the back of Danny Burgess. The ad, depicting Burgess as a puppeteer pulling the strings of his corrupt underlings, ran on all of the local television channels from Friday through Sunday. It ran with such frequency that virtually everyone in the city saw it numerous times.

The effect was so noticeable that even the *Troy Register* newspaper, long known for supporting the Democratic Machine, had to make mention of it in its Monday morning editorial. Although the editorial stopped far short of endorsing any of the insurgent candidates, it certainly made it clear that the re-election of Burgess, and perhaps Crotty too, was very much in doubt.

By Monday morning, after the weekend-long barrage of

anti-Burgess TV ads, the entire Democratic ticket was on its heels. Danny Burgess, in particular, was infuriated when he barged into Crotty's office.

"Open that goddamned door," Burgess demanded of Kathy Gill as he marched directly toward the closed door into Crotty's office.

Kathy was startled by this entrance. "I'll let him know you're here, Mr. Burgess," she said while picking up the phone into Crotty's office.

"Put down the phone and buzz that door open right now!" he yelled.

Kathy was not about to get in the way of this and did as he instructed her to do.

Inside, Crotty was standing at the window and Kreider was on his cell phone. Both were startled by the door being buzzed open without first being phoned in by Kathy.

"Well, Michael, did you enjoy your weekend? I sure did. I love being called a crook on TV every fifteen fucking minutes," Burgess said loudly as he stormed into the office.

"I didn't exactly get treated like a choir boy either, Danny."

"How long are we going to get our asses kicked before we fight back?" Danny said to Kreider. "Did we know this was coming?"

"Nobody saw this coming. They've never done anything like this before. Never," said Kreider.

"Michael, you and me need to talk—alone," Burgess said ominously.

"We've always hashed these things out together," said Kreider defensively.

Burgess stared directly at Crotty, who had returned from the window. "Michael, get him out of here," he snarled.

"Bruno, go take a walk around the block. I'll call your cell," Crotty said. He did not really want to face Burgess alone, if for no other reason than Kreider always served as a convenient whipping-boy when things were going wrong. But Crotty knew Burgess was already in a foul mood and he

surely did not want to get into an argument over having
Kreider stay.

Kreider grimaced. He was not happy that he was being
kicked out of what he knew would be an important conversation, important to the upcoming election, and important to
his own status as the party's chief political strategist. He
also did not trust Crotty being alone when strategy was being discussed. "I won't be far. Call me," he said as he left
the room.

Crotty was barely listening while, for the next ten
minutes, Burgess went into a tirade about how over the
years he had personally been responsible for keeping the
Machine together and had personally stuck up for Crotty,
time and time again. He went on and on about how he had
orchestrated the moves which ended up returning Crotty to
power after Phillip DiMatteo's victory. He reminded Crotty
that if they lost both the mayoral race and the council presidency, there'd be no coming back from that for either of
them.

Crotty knew all of this, but he just let Burgess vent. As
he half-listened, he contemplated whether or not to tell Burgess about what he now thought was a sure-fire way of getting them re-elected. He wasn't sure if he should tell Burgess of the vote rigging scheme.

Burgess knew nothing of Joey Geracitano, and he had no
idea that Crotty was seriously considering rigging the election. Crotty was thinking that if he brought the whole thing
up at this point, Burgess might get even more enraged and
might put a stop to moving forward with the plan. Yet it
was clear that Burgess was putting the pressure on him and
Kreider to solve the problem. Crotty did not know what to
do as he stared out the window during Burgess's verbal barrage.

"Are you listening, Michael?" Burgess yelled after his
monologue was followed by a long silence.

"Of course, I'm listening, Danny. I always listen to you.
I just don't know what you want me to do."

"Michael, I'll make this easy on you. What I want you to do is to get together with Kreider and pull every rabbit out of every hat you've got. Call in every favor you have out there. I want you to do anything you have to do to have us win this election."

"Anything?" Crotty asked, trying to fully understand Burgess's comment.

"Anything and everything," Burgess said. "Michael, I am well aware of some of the ways we've used in the past to get the votes we need. I'm aware that not all of them have been…shall we say?…textbook good government stuff. I know we've had dead people vote for us. I know we've had people vote who didn't even exist. I know we've used unorthodox methods to convince people to vote for us. I know all this. I'm not proud of it, Michael, but I learned a long time ago that, in politics, if you think you're the right person for the job, then you do anything you can to secure that job. In politics, the end always justifies the means. The end justifies the means, Michael! Do whatever you have to do. Just do it!"

"I understand," Crotty answered as Burgess stormed out.

Crotty did not immediately call Kreider after Burgess left his office. He wanted a little more time by himself to consider what he had just heard. He kept repeating to himself Burgess's words about the end justifying the means. He remembered his conversation with Kreider about there being no real difference between rigging a single vote and rigging an entire election.

"Do whatever you have to do, Michael," Burgess had told him.

Crotty pulled out his cell phone. He did not call Kreider. He called Joey Geracitano instead.

"This is Joey. How can I help you?" Crotty heard as the call was answered.

He had given some thought to how he would tell Geracitano he wanted to move the proposal forward without saying it on the phone. "Mr. Geracitano, Mayor Crotty here.

You and I spoke the other day about your associate's ability to help us with our software issue."

Joey paused then said, "Oh, the software issue. Ah, yes. I understand that your computer consultant called ours to discuss the proposal a bit more."

"Yes, that's right. And I'd like to see if we can continue this discussion."

"I see," said Joey. "You recall that I mentioned that this particular program we discussed was a complex one and that we needed to make certain the project would definitely move forward before we involved our developers any further."

"Yes, that's right. I remember that," Crotty said, confident that he was being sufficiently discreet. "Well, I think we're prepared to go with it. I just want to discuss some minor details and perhaps get a little more clarity about what the actual cost for this project may be. Assuming we can come to a gentlemanly agreement on these things, I'm prepared to engage your services."

"Yes, of course."

"How do you suggest we go about having that conversation?" Crotty asked.

Joey was excited. The bait was being taken and he had been preparing for this moment for some time.

"In anticipation of your favorable consideration, I have already spoken with my associate about doing just that. He and I would be most happy to meet with you late tomorrow night."

"Your associate?" Crotty asked. He had expected this to be just between the two of them.

"Yes, as I think I've mentioned, my role here is as more of an intermediary, so to speak. The final arrangements need to be discussed directly with the project manager."

"Who is that?"

"Nobody you know. He insists on meeting all of his clients before he does any programming for them."

"Oh. In that case, I may bring my...uh...my computer

guy with me," Crotty said, instinctively not wanting to be outnumbered.

"Fine, but only one other person. My programmer doesn't like crowds," Joey said.

"Exactly where and when shall we meet?" asked Crotty.

"I'll leave details at your office by three tomorrow."

"Good, I'll wait to hear from you," Crotty said before ending the call.

Kreider had not taken an actual walk around the block as Crotty had told him to do. He just waited on the sidewalk about a block down the street from city hall. He rushed back up to Crotty's office when he saw Burgess leave. Kathy Gill buzzed him in just as Crotty finished the call with Joey.

"Why didn't you call?" Kreider said as he entered.

"I was talking to Geracitano."

"What? Oh, Jesus! Don't tell me."

"The decision has been made, Bruno. Danny endorsed it," Crotty said, already trying to absolve himself.

"Wait. Are you telling me that Burgess blessed this? He knows what's going on, and he green-lighted this?" Kreider was astounded. He knew Burgess never left any tracks when it came to dirty politics.

"Yes, Bruno. That's exactly what I'm telling you." Crotty did not want to say that Burgess had not actually agreed to rig an election but he did want Kreider to think that.

"Then you're both out of your minds. This is lunacy!" Kreider yelled.

Crotty was not in the mood to be reprimanded. "I'll tell you what lunacy is, Bruno. Lunacy is sitting around like you've been doing watching us lose this fucking election. That may be okay with you, but it's not okay with me, and it's definitely not okay with Danny. He's got a serious case of ass rash over those fucking ads this weekend, and I'm the one he's taking it out on. And I'm the one who's going to take care of this problem."

Crotty was as agitated as Kreider had ever seen him.

"Bruno, I already set the thing in motion. Now you've

got two choices, and I strongly encourage you to think carefully about what you say next. You can either walk out that door right now and never come back here again, or you can do what I pay you to do and help me win this election by seeing this through with me. Make your choice and make it right now. Either way, Danny and I are winning this election. With or without you."

Kreider and Crotty stared at each other, neither saying anything. Crotty had made up his mind. Kreider had a horrible feeling about the entire matter but knew his only hope of salvaging it, and likely his job, was to stay close to it.

"I'd rather do this with you, Bruno," Crotty said in a conciliatory, almost pleading way.

"Under one condition," Kreider finally said.

"Don't ask for too much, Bruno. I'm not in the mood."

"No matter what happens next, you can't cut me out of it again."

"Okay, fine," Crotty said. "But don't get in my way, Bruno. I'm doing this." He sat in his chair and rubbed his eyes. "This is going to work out, just like it always does. You'll see."

Kreider could tell that with those words Crotty was trying to reassure himself more than anything.

∞

They spent most of the next day waiting for instructions from Geracitano about the meeting. They knew that it was likely going to be that evening but did not know where, when, or how. They each sensed how nervous the other was and neither said much of anything all day.

At just before three p.m., a young man appeared in the office wearing tan pants and a white oxford shirt which had "Will" embroidered over one pocket and "Premier Courier Service" over the other.

"May I help you?" Kathy Gill said as he entered.

"Courier letter, ma'am, for Mayor Crotty. You just need

to sign this," Will said as he handed Kathy a delivery receipt for signature and an envelope addressed to the mayor with the Premier Courier Service return address in the corner. She signed and took a copy of the receipt.

As soon as the courier left, she quickly opened the envelope and took out its contents. Inside was an unsealed second envelope with no outside markings at all and a handwritten note inside. She photocopied the note, put it back into the unmarked envelope, which she then sealed. She placed the courier envelope, the delivery receipt, and photocopy of the note into her purse.

She phoned into Crotty's office.

"Some kid just dropped off an envelope with no markings on it at all and said you were waiting for it."

"Bring it right in," Crotty said over the intercom.

Crotty tore into the sealed envelope and read the handwritten note. He immediately handed it to Kreider after he had finished reading it.

Parking lot. Lock #4—East Gate. River Road. 9:30 tonight. Make sure you're not followed. J.G.

"This is scaring the crap out of me," Kreider said as he put the note into the shredder.

Chapter 20

Completed in 1825, the Erie Canal ran from the Hudson River near Troy, New York, due west to the waters of Lake Erie some 360 miles away. To travel this route, one had to navigate a significant elevation change, some 566 feet in all, along its long route.

Moving from a higher to lower elevation—and vice versa, of course—along the canal was accomplished via a series of so-called "locks." Along the Erie Canal there were fifty-seven such structures, each approximately one hundred feet long, forty feet high, and twenty feet wide. The locks operated today much the same as they did in the 1800s.

A watercraft approached a "lock," which consisted of massive high-rising cement walls on either side and an equally massive set of steel double doors on either end. A lock tender opened the set of doors, or gates as they were called, at one end, and the craft entered the lock. The doors were closed behind it. To rise from a lower to a higher elevation, tens of thousands of gallons of water were let into the lock from below, causing the boat to rise to the level of the canal leading out the other side. At that point, the opposite end doors opened and the craft gently sailed out of the lock. To travel from a higher to a lower level, the process was simply reversed.

At the origin of the Erie Canal, just north of Troy, there were six such locks, each consecutively numbered. At each, there was a small parking lot at either end, used mostly by lock tenders and by the occasional visitor who stopped by to watch the locks in action. To some, it was still a sight to watch and a monument to the engineering genius of another age.

At the top of each gate, or double doors, there was a three-foot-wide metal grate walkway, which was the only way to get to the guard house located on the other side of the lock.

Along the concrete side walls of each lock there were tie-offs for the boats to use to steady themselves while in the lock and a single metal-framed bench, presumably there for use by the occasional sightseer.

Since the locks only operated during daylight hours, at night the entire area around each was quite desolate, lit only by a small light atop each of the guard houses. As such, the locks were scary and dangerous places to be at night.

Such was the setting when Bruno Kreider turned left off River Road and slowly entered the parking lot at lock number four at nine-thirty p.m. They were not in the mayor's official car, rather they came in Kreider's personal vehicle. This venue was surely no place for a vehicle bearing the vanity license plate, *MR MAYOR*.

Kreider had picked Crotty up at his home some thirty minutes earlier so that they could drive to the lock via an extremely circuitous route, being careful to not be followed as Joey had instructed.

There was a single light on a high pole at the end of the lot near an imposing set of cement steps which led up to the top of the lock. The parking lot was empty when they arrived.

"There's nobody here," said Kreider.

"You sure this is the right lock?" Crotty asked.

"Positive. Lock number four. I drove by during the day so I could make sure and just to see what the place looked like."

"Where the fuck are they?" Crotty said nervously as Kreider turned off the ignition and his car lights. They sat saying nothing. Their eyes were adjusting to the darkness but it was still hard to see anything.

After a few moments, from the base of the stairs leading up to the gate some hundred yards away, Crotty noticed a flashlight go on and off and then on and off again.

"There," said Crotty. "Over there by the stairs."

As Kreider looked toward where Crotty was pointing, he saw the flashlight again. On, off. On and off again.

"I think that's them. They probably want us to go over there," Crotty offered.

"This is too creepy for me," Kreider said. "We have no idea what we're walking into."

"They're just being cautious. We don't want to be seen with them any more than they want to be seen with us. Let's get this over with," Crotty said as he got out of the car and slowly walked toward the stairs. Kreider quickly followed and caught up as they were about halfway there. They began to make out two figures standing in the dark.

"There's two of them," Kreider whispered.

"Joey and the mystery man," Crotty whispered back.

In a few more steps, Kreider stopped short and grabbed Crotty by the arm to stop him.

"Neither of them looks like Geracitano."

"It's too dark to tell," Crotty said but still he took no more steps toward the men. They waited about twenty yards away.

"Don't stop now, Mayor," came a voice from the staircase.

Crotty and Kreider stepped cautiously forward until they saw the two men more clearly. One was a large Jamaican man, the other a smaller but sturdily built man wearing a jacket.

"You guys looking for a programmer?" said Tugboat Tommy.

"Cut the shit," Crotty said. "Who the fuck are you guys? Where's Geracitano?"

The two came closer. "Easy, big shot," said Donnie Moore in an ominous Jamaican accent. "This ain't city hall, so your tough-guy talk doesn't mean shit here."

"Mind if my friend here feels you up a little?" said Tugboat Tommy.

"For what?" asked Kreider.

"It makes him happy, okay?"

Donnie gave a brief pat-down to both Crotty and Kreider.

"Do we get to do the same?" Crotty asked.

"Don't bother," Tugboat answered as he opened his jacket to reveal a gun in a shoulder holster.

Crotty and Kreider were frozen in fear.

"Your keys," Donnie said to Kreider.

"My what? Keys? You want to take my car keys? No way!" Kreider protested.

"Relax, runt," Tugboat said, "you'll get your shitty little car back. It will be in the lot at the other end when we're done here. The keys will be on the front seat. Mr. Geracitano and his guest will be picked up here so you need to leave from a different place. Quit asking questions and give him your keys."

"Do it, Bruno," Crotty said. "Let's get this done."

"See? That's how you got to be mayor," said Tugboat as Kreider was giving the car keys to Donnie. "You're the mayor because you make good decisions. Come with me for a little walk."

Donnie Moore took the car keys and started walking toward Kreider's car. Tugboat motioned for Crotty and Kreider to follow him. He proceeded up the cement stairs. There were about twenty-five stairs up to the first landing and then another twenty-five to the top. As he and Kreider followed Tugboat up, Crotty stopped at the first landing. He was totally out of breath.

"Wait, hold on. It's too dark to see these steps," he said.

"Each step is right in front of the next one," Tugboat said impatiently. "If you need a fucking rest, just say so."

"Let's go," Crotty said, starting up the second flight of stairs. His struggling grunts were the only sound as they made their way slowly up.

At the top of the stairs, they could see the faint light on the guard house across the lock. It was just enough light for Crotty and Kreider to see that they were standing only a few feet from the emptied lock number four. They were terrified as they looked down and could see the glimmering water some forty feet below.

"If you don't like heights, I suggest you keep your head up," Tugboat said with a snide laugh.

He pointed ahead toward the metal grate crosswalk with single pipe on one side for a handrail, on the other side, nothing but a forty-foot drop into the canal. The crosswalk led across the top of the gate to the other side.

"Mr. Geracitano is over there. You might want to grab on to that handrail," said Tugboat as he did his best not to laugh at the abject fear in the eyes of both Crotty and Kreider. "It's a long way down."

Tugboat proceeded to quickly and casually walk the twenty yards across the abyss not even bothering to hold the rail. When he got to the other side, he turned to see Crotty and Kreider hanging on to the handrail with both hands as they slowly sidestepped their way across, making sure not to look down. He chuckled to himself and waved as he looked along the side wall between the gates to the metal bench where Joey G. and Angelo Renna sat waiting.

"Look at those two," Angelo said as he watched the two silhouettes inch their way across the canal. "Too bad we don't have a video of this. It's hysterical watching those two get across."

"They'll be in sight of the surveillance camera as soon as they get across," answered Joey.

"It might be sunrise by the time they get there. The light won't be necessary," Renna joked. "This is priceless."

Joey laughed. "I learned a long time ago that if your opponent is scared shitless, the fight is pretty much over before the first punch gets thrown. We did this for effect."

"I think it's working," Angelo said.

Back in the parking lot, Donnie Moore got in Kreider's

car and drove north the short distance to the parking lot at the other end of lock number four. As he entered, he saw Duke get out of his pickup, which was parked next to Joey's red Lincoln. Duke's cousin Adam also hopped out of the pickup as Donnie parked next to them and turned off the car.

Without saying a word, Donnie handed the keys to Duke. Adam pulled a small recording device and a roll of tape from his jacket pocket. He switched the device to sound activation mode and then climbed into the back passenger side of Kreider's car. He peeled off several inches of tape and secured the device to the underside of the passenger seat.

At the same time, Duke took the car ignition key from Kreider's key ring and pulled out a large piece of molding clay from a cigar box. He made two impressions of the key, placed the clay in a plastic bag, and put it into the cigar box to make certain the impressions would not be damaged. He then put the key back on the key chain and tossed the set of keys on the front seat.

Duke took the box containing the key impressions with him as he got back into the pickup where Adam was already waiting in the passenger seat. He gave a thumbs-up toward Donnie as he and Adam drove off. Donnie followed them out of the lot and drove Joey's Town Car back to the lot on the other end of the lock where he would wait for Joey and Angelo.

It took several minutes for Crotty and Kreider to sidestep their way across the top of the lock gate. Tugboat was waiting for them in front of the small guard house, which was a simple wooden structure, approximately ten feet square with a single door and a window on either side. It was where the lock tender went about the business of opening and closing the lock gates and activating the raising and lowering of the lock water level. It had a small light on its roof and a hard-to-notice surveillance camera on the eave facing the gate crossing.

Tugboat made certain to wait for Crotty and Kreider directly beneath the light and in full view of the camera. "Congratulations," he said as they arrived on the other side. "Shall we continue or do either of you need to change your underwear?"

"Remind me to nominate you for smart-ass of the year," Crotty said. He was already totally unnerved and annoyed by this entire episode, and he had not even gotten to Joey yet.

"Thank you, I will," Tugboat replied. "If you're ready, then," he continued while pointing along the lock wall, "Mr. Mayor, as you look down there maybe you can make out a little park bench. Your hosts are there waiting for you now. When you finish, don't come back this way, but keep walking along the lock until you get to the other gate. Cross back over to the other side and go to that parking lot. Your car will be there with the keys on the front seat."

"We got to cross that fucking bridge again? You bastards are just screwing with us, aren't you?" Crotty said.

Kreider was still too scared to speak.

"Shall we?" Tugboat said as he led them toward the metal bench where Joey and Angelo awaited in the darkness about fifty yards away.

As they approached, they could see the silhouettes of two figures getting up from the bench. With no lighting along the 100 yard stretch between the lock doors, the area where the bench was located was extremely dark.

With approximately twenty-five yards to go, Tugboat stopped. "Mayor, you go ahead. Mr. Kreider, you stay here with me."

"What? Why?" Kreider protested.

"I said, you stay here. Why? Because that's what Mr. Geracitano wants."

Crotty said nothing but kept walking toward the two men. He paid no attention to Kreider's protest.

When he got to the bench, Joey was first to speak. "Mr. Mayor, I'm so glad to see you. And listen, I'm really sorry about this meeting spot. Can't ever be too careful. Don't you agree?"

Crotty was surprised by Joey's demeanor. He had expected the "all-business Joey" and instead was greeted by the "mister-congenial Joey." It unnerved him that none of this was going as he had expected.

"Of course, Joey. I agree. Can't ever be too careful."

"And please don't be overly concerned about the hardware my associate there is packing," Joey said, pointing toward Tugboat. "It's like a security blanket to him. You know the way some guys are."

"No problem," was all Crotty could muster.

"Good, good. Now, Mayor, before we go another minute, I want to introduce you to the man I've been telling you about. Mayor Michael Crotty, I'd like you to meet Don."

"Don?" Crotty said. "Don what?"

"Just call me Don," Renna said as he held out his hand to shake with the mayor. Even as close as they were, it was so dark that Crotty could just barely make out the face of the man he had come to meet.

"Now that I've made this introduction," injected Joey cheerily, "let me leave you two alone while I go back there and chat with my friend Bruno."

Joey walked away leaving Crotty and Angelo Renna—or Don, for this purpose—alone.

"Sit, Mayor," Renna said as he motioned toward the bench. Crotty could barely even see the bench.

"Can I call you Mike?"

"I prefer Michael."

"Fine, Michael it is. Michael, I understand that you want me to rig your upcoming election."

Yet another jolt for Crotty. Joey's niceties were immediately followed by Don's directness. "I see you're a no-nonsense guy, Don."

"I thought we were here to talk about your election. If you came to watch the boats go by, you're too early."

Crotty quickly understood that Don intended to forego any small talk, which was fine with him as he really wanted to get this all over with.

"Since we're being direct, Geracitano tells me that you can guarantee a victory in the upcoming election and that you've done this sort of thing before."

"That is correct. On both counts."

"I asked him a couple of questions earlier about how this would work but did not get complete answers. May I ask them of you?"

"I'll give you complete answers as long as you actually need to know what it is that you want to know. I'll be the judge of that."

"Okay. Fine. I have a few questions. How do I know that you can actually pull this off, and how will I know that if I do win, it will be because of something you did? I could very well win on my own."

"Before I answer, Michael, let me say this as tactfully as I can. We've done a lot of careful checking into this. I assure you that you're not going to win this election without my help. And insofar as it's of importance to you that Mr. Burgess and Mr. Monk also win, I can also say with all assurances that they are not going to win either—not without my intervention. None of you has a chance without me. Michael, we both know that, if you thought you could win without my help, you wouldn't be here now, would you?"

Crotty did not respond. Clearly Don's last comment was accurate. This was about the last place Crotty would be if he wasn't desperate.

"Be that as it may, let me try to answer your questions, Michael. Of course, you can't truly know that we can actually pull this off. No matter what I tell you, you won't know with absolute certainty that we can do this until we actually do it. Maybe I can best answer your question with one of my own. Why the fuck would I be here if I wasn't able to do this? I have made a long trip here tonight, and I've got lots better things to do than come all the way here to bullshit you for some unimaginable reason."

Crotty was sorry to have asked that question. Don's answer made total sense to him.

"Now, as to your second question, regarding how you will know for certain that it was us determining the election outcome and not you winning on your own, that's a reasonable one to ask and quite simple for me to answer. You tell us exactly what you want the vote count to be and that's what it will be. When you wake up the morning after the election and you see that the vote count is exactly what you asked us for, you will know it was us who made it so. Surely that should convince you, would it not?"

"I suppose it would," Crotty mused. "And so, all I have to do is tell how many votes I want and that's it?"

"Not the count, the percentage. It's done by percentage since we have no way of knowing how many total votes there will be."

"Sure, of course," Crotty said. "That makes sense." *These guys do have this down pat*, Crotty thought.

"We can make the percentage anything you want. However, it's in both of our interests that the percentages you select be realistic. We don't want to make it so one-sided that it raises suspicions. We suggest you make it a slim victory but not so slim as to trigger a recount. A recount would render the same result but we don't want anybody looking into this too closely before the program gets erased. Just a precaution, mind you. We recommend between eight and eleven percent."

"That makes sense," Crotty said.

"Your third question?" Renna said. "Those were only two questions. You said you had a few."

"Okay, yeah. Suppose we agree to this. My last question then is, how much will this cost me? I need to know what this will cost," Crotty said sheepishly. He did not want to sound like he couldn't handle payback but Kreider insisted that he find out what the real cost of this would be. "You know, I'm a business man like you are, Don, and I want to make sure I can repay all of my debts."

"Ah, payment is always the real issue, isn't it, Mayor?"

"It is with me."

"Understood. As to that matter, I have discussed this at length with Mr. Geracitano. He would expect that within a reasonable period of time, you see to it that his enterprises enjoy the benefits of a service contract of some sort that would net him six figures annually at a minimum. He would also find it most beneficial going forward if he could be assured, in the event of any issues that may arise involving any criminal investigations, that, as mayor, you would intervene on his behalf. Having some leeway in conducting business without such interference is very important to Mr. Geracitano. That will be your total obligation to him since he already feels in your debt for some tax matter you helped him with earlier."

"That's it?" Crotty said excitedly. He had paid a higher price for deals many times before in exchange for things far less important than him winning the election. This was a no-brainer to him! He expected a far greater demand from Don. Then he caught himself, "I mean, that's a lot to ask, but I think it's manageable and fair. So, let me understand. I get Geracitano some six-figure contracts and keep the cops and the DA off his ass. That's it, right?"

"That's right. Joey has determined this to be equitable."

Crotty was ready to take the deal right that minute until the thought occurred to him that Don had said that this was the payoff for Joey but not Don himself.

"Wait. Hold on. That's Joey's take. What about you?" he said, fearing the answer coming next. "What do I owe you?"

"Me?"

"Yes, you, Don. I got the idea that Joey's role in all of this was over once you and I sat down. You told me what I would owe him but what do I owe you—"

"For my part?" Don interrupted with a slight chuckle. "You're quite right in your assessment of who is doing what here, but not in who is doing what for whom. I'm not doing this as a favor to you, I'm doing this as a favor to Joey. If I do get involved, you owe him, and he owes me. That's how it works. You owe me nothing. Joey takes care of my services. He and I discussed this long before tonight. We have a suitable arrangement in mind, but to be brutally frank with you, Michael, that's between Joey and me. What I get out of this for my trouble is not your concern."

Crotty was trying to process what he was hearing. He was expecting a huge payoff obligation but from the deal Don just presented, he was going to get what he wanted and could easily handle the payback. This was way better than he thought it would be. He wanted to get the deal done before anything changed.

"Okay, let's do it," Crotty said. "I'm in."

"No turning back after we leave this place, Michael. Understand?" Don said as he rose from his seat on the bench.

Crotty got up as well and vigorously shook Don's hand. "Yes, I understand."

"One more thing," Don said.

Crotty's heart sank. He knew this was going too easily to be true. "What's that?"

"You have to let us know what you want the vote tally to be so that you can be sure we did our job correctly, remember?"

Crotty was relieved that Don was not dropping in a last-minute demand for payment. His mind was spinning from all that had happened in the past few minutes, and he had never talked with Kreider about the vote count issue.

"Oh yes, of course," said Crotty. "Can I get back to you on that?"

"Sorry, Michael, no. Once we leave here, there will be no communication between us again. Not ever. We need the percentages now."

"Can I talk to Kreider for a second about that?" he asked, while pointing to Kreider who was still standing several feet away with Joey and Tugboat.

"You stay here. I'll let him know you want to talk. But make it quick, Michael. We've been here a little too long already." Don said as he left Crotty at the bench and went over to where Kreider was standing.

"Mr. Kreider, the mayor would like to speak with you, subito."

Kreider looked at Don. But he did not move. "Subito?"

"Subito—right now, hurry up," Don said impatiently. "Come on, man, I don't have all night."

It was the first time Kreider had gotten close enough to see Don, although it was still quite dark where they were standing. Kreider heard what Don said, but he stood for another second and stared intently at him before going to meet Crotty. For a brief moment, he sensed that he had seen that face before. He went over to where Crotty was waiting.

"Bruno, the deal is done. I'll tell you all the details later but for now, we need to tell them what voting percentages we want."

"What? Jesus, Mayor, you did it? This is crazy! You gotta stop this right here, right now. This whole thing is nuts."

"It's too late. We now have one minute to give them the numbers. We tell them the vote percentage we want, and they rig it that way. But we have to tell them right now. Think about it, but hurry up."

"All the percentages?"

"Me, Danny and Monk. But make them realistic. Come up with the numbers right now," Crotty said as he waved to Don to come back.

Don led the way, followed closely by Joey and Tugboat.

"You have the numbers?" Don said.

"Bruno will give them to you."

Don turned to Tugboat. "Pen and paper."

Tugboat reached into his jacket pocket, pulled out a pen and a small piece of white note paper folded in half, and handed it to Bruno.

Kreider wrote the names of Crotty, Burgess, and Monk as well as their opponents and next to each wrote a number.

He showed Crotty, who quickly squinted at the numbers in the dark.

"Fine," Crotty said as he started to hand the paper to Don.

"Your autograph please," Don said to Crotty.

"Autograph?"

"Just so there's no misunderstanding later, Michael," Don replied. "Initial each line and sign your name at the bottom."

"Fine," Crotty grumbled as he initialed and signed.

Don took the sheet of note paper and stuffed it into his pants pocket, all the while making sure that the words, *From the Desk of Mayor Michael Crotty*, imprinted on the other side of the fold would not show.

"You go that way. Remember, your car is in that lot now," Tugboat said, pointing along the canal toward the other gate to lock number four.

Don, Joey, and Tugboat walked the other way and were soon out of sight in the darkness. Before going back across the gate, Joey looked into the security camera and took an exaggerated bow. They hurried back down the cement stairs. Donnie was waiting for them in the lot, and they piled into the Town Car.

"Everything go okay?" Donnie asked as they drove off.

"Fucking beautiful!" Tugboat said. "That was sweet."

"Angelo, you missed your true calling, my man," said an elated Joey. "You should have become a mobster, not a cook."

"I'd appreciate it if you would refer to me as Don Renna," Renna said with a laugh.

"Donnie, how'd it go on the other side?" Joey asked.

"All good," Donnie said. "We were in and out of there in under a minute. Duke's got the car key imprint and will go to Artie Costello's to get a duplicate made first thing in the morning. I'm going with him. After we get the key, we'll stop by Kreider's car in the city hall lot to grab the recorder out of it. I'm guessing Adam's tape is rolling as we speak."

"Not yet probably," Joey said. "It's going to take those two candy asses fifteen minutes to get back across the lock and into their car."

"This was a thing of beauty!" Tugboat said.

Joey was almost right. It took Crotty and Kreider nearly ten minutes to grope their way back to the other gate house, cross in front of the security camera on the other guard house, and slowly shuffle their way back across the lock gate. They hurried down to Kreider's car, neither saying a single word on their way back. Crotty was delighted that he had pulled this off without getting hurt, or worse. Kreider was in a virtual panic, struck not only by the events of the past half hour but even more so by the fact that he and Crotty had just conspired to rig an election.

"Thank God the car's here," Crotty said as they arrived at the lot.

Kreider grabbed the keys from the front seat and started the car. As they pulled out of the lot onto River Road heading back to Troy, the sound of the car engine activated the recorder taped underneath Crotty's seat.

"What time is it?" Crotty said. "I need a drink. Let's stop at the Excalibar."

"I don't think so. Not me."

"Come on, Bruno. You can relax now, it's over. It's over. We pulled this off, and other than getting the shit scared out of us, we came out without a scratch. We should be celebrating!"

"I'll just drop you off, Mayor. I'm not in the mood."

Crotty just sighed. "Fine." As they crossed the bridge leading back to Troy, Crotty said, "That scotch is going to taste good tonight. You should join me, Bruno. We should be happy. You look like you're facing a firing squad. Lighten up a little."

"I can't believe that you just arranged to rig an election. I still can't believe this."

"Well, my friend, that's exactly what just happened. On the morning after this election, you'll be glad I did," Crotty said as the recording device under his seat rolled.

Kreider drove on, hardly hearing Crotty. He was still trying to process what had just happened. He was troubled by any number of things which made no sense to him. Why did they have to give up their car? Geracitano and his group could have easily just parked in the other lot without the switch which they said was necessary. Why did they keep him and Crotty separate all that time? Why did they insist on Crotty's signature on the paper with the vote count? Why did they bring that smart-assed guy with a gun? Why did they have to go to the top of the locks to meet? None of this was adding up to him.

He was especially haunted by the image of Don. In that brief moment when he and Don spoke and crossed paths on top of the lock, he had gotten a close look at the alleged mobster from downstate. It was dark up there but Kreider felt sure that he had seen the man before. As he drove toward Troy, he kept picturing Don over and over in his mind trying to recall where he had seen that face before. How did he know that face?

Then it came to him. The Villa de Ville! He had seen "Don" before at The Villa de Ville restaurant. He remembered the face when he connected it with the expression Don used at the lock, "subito." Kreider had eaten dinner several times years before at The Villa de Ville. He remembered the busy restaurant and the man who was clearly in some sort of managerial role. He remembered him as the guy who was always frantically commanding the waiters and the bus people to hurry things along. "Subito," he would always say to them, trying to get them to hurry up.

It was a word that he had never heard before hearing it at the restaurant and had never heard since, not until "Don" said it to him at the lock. He even remembered after one such night at the restaurant he actually went online to look up the translation for "subito," which he assumed correctly was an Italian word. It means quickly or right away, he recalled. The man calling himself Don used that same expres-

sion to Kreider moments before when he wanted him to
hurry up. That word—that face. The man calling himself
Don was once the manager at The Villa de Ville. How
could that be? This made no sense to Kreider. In fact, nothing he had witnessed over the previous half hour made
much sense to him, unless...

"Tell me what happened over at the bench, Mayor,"
Kreider said as he drove into the downtown section of Troy.
The Excalibar was still several blocks away.

"I think you know," said Crotty.

"Tell me anyway. I'm not sure I understand anything
you do any more."

"Bruno, we were going to lose this election. I was going
to lose, Danny was going to lose, and Monk was going to
lose. Now, all I have to do is push a few bullshit contracts
to Geracitano and call off the cops if they start sniffing
around and that problem is solved. I've been doing shit like
this all my life, Bruno, and there's certainly no reason to
stop now. It's done. The fix is in and there's no stopping it
now. So can we just move on?"

Kreider's car turned the corner onto Third Street. He
drove right by the Excalibar.

"Wait, I'm going in," Crotty said as Bruno drove past
the bar. "What are you doing?"

Kreider pulled into a parking place on the street about a
block away.

"Bruno, if you're not coming in, then at least drop me
off in front of the place. I've done enough walking for one
night. Drive me around the block, will you?"

Kreider put the car in park and just sat staring out the
windshield. He was still trying to answer all of the unan-
swered questions he had about what had just transpired. He
had never trusted Geracitano, never fully believed the tall
tales about why the Marconi Club had been reopened, never
really thought that Geracitano was some dark mob figure,
never really believed that an election was this easy to rig.
And now he could not piece together any scenario in which

a guy who once worked at a tiny restaurant on the outskirts of Troy could turn out to be a mobster from downstate.

As he sat there in the dark with Crotty, he knew that Crotty would not listen to his concerns. Crotty would not, and now probably could not, undo the actions that had just taken place. Kreider knew nothing good would ever come of this—not for Crotty, not for Burgess, not for Monk or the Party, and certainly not for him. All these thoughts whirled in his head as he sat at the curb with Crotty yelling at him to drive back around the block. He then had a singular moment of clarity.

"Mayor, I'm done," he said finally.

"Done? Done what? What are you talking about?"

"I want no part of this anymore. I want no part of this vote rigging. I want no part of your petty crimes. I want no part of your bullshit. I want no part of you. I'm done."

"Bruno, hold on. You're just a little shaken by this whole thing at the locks. Go home and calm down. You'll see this differently tomorrow. Better yet, come and have a drink with me. You'll see I'm right about this. You'll see this will all work out."

"I quit, Mayor. I'm resigning right here, right now. For the record, I'm against what you're doing, and I want no part of it. Get out of the car, Mayor. I'm done."

"Bruuuuunooooo, come on," Crotty pleaded.

"I'm done. Out," Kreider said.

Chapter 21

Duke and Donnie could not explain why Bruno Kreider's car was not in the city hall parking lot the next morning. Kreider never missed a day of work, so when he hadn't arrived by ten a.m. Duke made a frantic call to Joey.

"He didn't show up. I have no idea why or where he is but he didn't show up."

"We gotta get that recording," Joey said.

"I know, I know. But he's not here. We don't know where his car is."

"Stay there. I'll call Alex. Maybe he knows."

A short while later, Cord pulled up to the apartment complex where Kreider lived. He had once done an interview with Kreider there. Kreider's car was not in the lot. Cord rang the bell to the apartment. He had no idea exactly how he would explain his presence there but he had to find Kreider—more specifically, his car. There was no answer as he rang the bell several times.

He pulled out his cell phone and dialed Kreider's number. There was no answer. He called city hall. Maybe Kreider had somehow gotten there without Duke or Donnie seeing him go in.

"Mayor's office."

"Kathy, this is Alex."

"Hi, Alex, how are you?"

"Fine, thanks. Can you talk?" he said abruptly.

"It's just me here. The mayor is in his office, slamming things around."

"Kathy, is Bruno there?"

"No, and I'm not expecting him any time soon."

"Why? What do you mean?"

"Crotty came in about an hour ago and was going totally ballistic. Somebody else had to pick him up this morning, and he didn't get his breakfast. He's not happy."

"Where's Bruno? I gotta find him. Why did you say you're not expecting him?"

"Mr. Warmth screamed something to me on the way in about Kreider quitting."

"Quitting? Bruno quit?"

"So I've been told, and Crotty's been throwing stuff around the office all morning. He's on the phone with Burgess right now. They've been talking for a long time. Do you know what's going on, Alex?"

"No, not exactly, but I have to find Kreider. He's not answering his cell. I'm at his apartment now, and he's not here either. Any idea where I can find him?"

"I really don't know where he is. But obviously something is hitting the fan today. Usually, when that happens, Bruno just falls off the face of the earth."

"Do you know where he goes?"

"Not really, but I know that he has a cabin on Lake George. I always presumed that's where he goes when he goes underground."

"Do you have an address?"

"You need him that bad?"

"I do, Kathy, I really do."

"Alex, please don't tell me this is falling apart. You sound frantic."

"No, no, everything's fine, but I have to find Bruno."

The address Kathy gave Cord was located on a tiny dirt road just north of Bolton Landing, a village on the west shore of Lake George. Cord met Duke and Joey at the Marconi Club and told them he was going up to Lake George to see if Bruno—more importantly, Bruno's car—was there. Getting the recording from Kreider's car was critical to the plan. They knew it would contain the admission from Crotty they needed. It was just past noon when Cord and Duke headed off to the cabin, some sixty miles north of Troy.

A little over an hour later they turned down a winding dirt road, located off the main road which runs the length of the thirty-two-mile-long lake, to the address that Kathy gave Alex. At the end of the tree-lined dirt road, they saw three small cabins which fronted on the lake. Kreider's car sat behind the cabin at the far end.

"That's his car," Cord said, pointing toward the farthest cabin.

"Maybe I can just swoop in there and grab the recorder without him seeing me," Duke said as Cord stopped near the end of the dirt road. Duke took the duplicate key for Kreider's car from his pocket.

"Make it quick," Cord said.

As Duke neared the car, Kreider appeared on the back porch. "What do you want?" he yelled toward Duke.

Duke stopped in his tracks and looked back at Cord who was still in the car. Plan A was not going to work, Kreider had seen Duke. Plan B was for Cord to pretend he wanted to talk with Kreider about a story he was writing for tomorrow's edition. While they were inside, Duke would grab the recorder. It was a lame idea, but that's all they had.

Cord got out of the car.

"Bruno, it's me, Alex Cord." he yelled across the driveway.

"Alex? What are you doing here? And what's that guy doing sniffing around my car?"

"I want to talk with you, Bruno." Alex had just a few seconds to come up with an explanation for not only what he was doing there, but also what Duke was doing there.

Kreider walked off the porch. Instead of walking toward them, he proceeded to slowly walk around the side of the cabin toward the lake. He waved to Cord to follow. Cord followed him out to the small dock that fronted the property.

"I was expecting you, Alex," Kreider said as Cord reached him. They began to walk out onto the dock toward two Adirondack chairs situated at its end.

"Me? You were expecting me?"

"Well, honestly not you, exactly. But I figured somebody would track me down. I'm actually relieved, in a way, that it's you."

Cord had no idea what Kreider was talking about. "I don't understand, Bruno."

"Oh, I think you do. It's not there, you know."

"What's not there? Bruno, what are you talking about?"

"The recorder. It's not in the car."

Kreider had found the recorder so, Cord assumed, he must be aware of the plot. "So you and Crotty know about—" He paused, knowing he had to choose his next words very carefully.

"Just me," Kreider said. "Crotty is oblivious as always."

"How did you figure it out?"

"I actually haven't figured it out, Alex. Not really. I came up here last night, and I sat right out here until sunrise," Kreider said as they reached the wooden chairs. He sat in one and motioned to Cord to join him in the other. "There were too many things about last night that didn't make any sense. Lots of thing didn't add up. I got to thinking about them moving my car for no logical reason. It occurred to me that they may have taken it so somebody could bug it or something. The recorder was not that well-hidden, Alex."

"Did you destroy it?" Cord asked, fearing that he already knew the answer.

Kreider reached into his pocket and pulled out the device.

"Nope. It's all right here. I didn't even listen to it. I remember that car conversation with Crotty last night almost verbatim. I didn't need to hear it."

"Who were you expecting, Bruno? You said you were expecting somebody, just not me."

"I actually was expecting the police or, worse."

"Worse?"

"Alex, I know there's some sort of scam going on. I'm just too stupid to understand what it is yet. And honestly, at this point I really don't care. It's clear to me that the fiasco at the locks last night was—" Kreider stopped himself. "You know all about that right?"

"I do, Bruno."

"I don't know how you're involved in this, but right now it doesn't much matter to me. I know I'm screwed. I'm just glad you showed up and not some SWAT team or a bunch of mobsters to chain me up and throw me into the lake. I got pretty scared there, for a minute, when I saw that guy you came with sneaking around. I figured he was looking for the recorder."

Cord was still uncertain exactly what Kreider knew or, more importantly, what Crotty knew. Kreider had just used the term "scam," but what did they know? He fell back on his reporter training. Kreider had begun to spill his guts. Cord didn't want to stop him by asking specific questions just yet. He just needed Kreider to talk. They sat together, looking out over the peaceful lake as two kayakers paddled by about a hundred yards off shore.

"It's beautiful here, Bruno."

"So you're in on this too, Alex? Good work, by the way. I've been thinking about this all night and all morning and not once did I imagine that you were involved. I just assumed it was the cops or the feds or somebody who finally caught up with all the shit Crotty's been pulling. Honestly, I was still a little worried that this was some sort of mob operation, but the more I thought about it, especially after I recognized that guy last night pretending to be a mob boss, I figured it was all a sting—feds most likely. Obviously, that Geracitano guy is involved in this but, Alex, not once did I suspect you. Please don't tell me this is some undercover reporter thing. It's not some *Sixty Minutes* thing where you're going to shove a camera and mike in front of my face and start asking me about rigging elections, is it, Alex?"

Cord still did not want to expose too much. He needed to know how much Bruno knew. And he had to find out what Crotty knew. He was worried that the plan was falling apart. "Bruno, if you knew you were about to go down, why didn't you destroy the tape?"

"I quit, you know," Kreider said. "Last night, I told Crotty I was done. Done with this bullshit and done with him."

Cord almost said that he knew this but was concerned about implicating Kathy Gill. "Quit?"

"I know now that somehow this whole thing is a set-up. I don't know who or what, but I know it's a set-up. I told Crotty I was out and I quit. I should have done this a long time ago, just as soon as I knew where it was heading. I tried to talk him out of doing this but I couldn't. And then last night when all this was happening, I knew I had to get out."

"Does Crotty know it was a set-up?" Cord finally asked.

"No, he's too stupid. He's oblivious. All he can see is getting re-elected and continuing to screw everybody in the city, pad his own bankroll, and have his fat ass kissed by everybody all day."

"But you still didn't destroy the tape?"

"I was about to. I went down to the lake this morning and was all set to throw it in, but then I remembered the conversation Crotty and I had in the car. I remembered that I told him I was quitting. In some strange way I thought that if the feds or somebody were going to bring this all down, the fact that I bailed on the scheme might help me somehow. Maybe it'd be a defense, you know? In some strange way, I thought the tape might actually help me."

Cord was relieved to hear that perhaps it was only Kreider who had figured this out and the plan could still work. The tape was still in play, but Cord still had not yet heard what was on it.

"Tell me the story, Alex. I know I'm screwed anyway

and, at this point, not knowing what's going on—what's going to happen to me—is worse than anything."

As they sat on the dock together, Cord began to feel an odd sense of sadness for Kreider. They had been through a lot together over the years, and while Kreider had annoyed Cord to no end on hundreds of occasions, he still felt bad sitting next to a man who had just figured out that his life was about to be destroyed.

Cord told him the story. Without going into all of the specifics, he told Kreider all about Operation Out 'n' In.

"That's quite a plan, Alex. My congratulations to all of you. Is it going to work?"

"Yes, Bruno, I think it is."

"Good. I'm actually glad. I know I'm going down too, but honestly I'm glad this is finally over."

They sat for a time, saying nothing, looking out at the end of the dock. It was a beautiful setting which, in a way, seemed to mellow each of them.

"You know, Alex, I didn't start out thinking I was going to be a part of something this ugly—this illegal. I actually thought being a civil servant was a good thing, not just a term crooks use to describe themselves. Somehow over the years, I just got caught up in it all. One little favor turned into a bigger favor. Then there were some bribes here and a little payola there. At some point, I stopped thinking about the ethics involved, and it all became normal. That's certainly no excuse. It's just how it happened, that's all. It's hard to explain."

"Of all the people in this world, I understand that better than anyone," Cord said to Kreider and, in a way, he was saying it to himself. "I got caught up in it too, Bruno. Maybe I just realized it before you did. That's why I got involved in this in the first place."

"How so?"

"I've watched Crotty and the Machine pull this shit for years and years. And because I didn't report it—not honestly anyway—and always gave you guys what you wanted from me, I got closer and closer to it all. In a way, I wasn't a reporter, I was an accomplice, just like you. By letting them get away with it, by saying nothing and by actually feeding them information they could use to do more dirty stuff, I became just like them. I became a part of the problem. Then I stood by and watched Crotty cause Phillip DiMatteo's death and the ruination of his wife. I said nothing about it, and I wrote nothing about it. In a real sense, I actually helped Crotty ruin their lives. Just like you, Bruno, I knew I had to get out. I decided to quit too. But then I was presented with an opportunity to at least make amends."

"By getting back at us?" Kreider said.

"By helping to get some measure of revenge for Phillip and JoAnne DiMatteo. I've gotten to know her really well over the past few months. You can't find a nicer person. And in some small way, I feel that helping to bring this all crashing down on Crotty is my small way of apologizing. And if this helps JoAnne DiMatteo to deal with all of her pain, it's all worthwhile to me. It's good that Crotty is going to pay for what he did to them."

"It is, Alex. I know it is. I know that now."

Cord stood up and stretched while he looked out over the lake. "I should go, Bruno."

"You'll want this," Kreider said as he pulled the recorder from his pocket. "Nail his fat ass to the wall."

"Thanks, Bruno. Good luck."

"Before you go," Kreider said as they began walking back. "I can help put an exclamation point on this."

"What do you mean, Bruno?"

"Let's you and I go for a little boat ride," Kreider said as he pointed to the small boat with an outboard motor tied to the end of dock. "We still have a few hours of sunlight. Being out on this lake as the sun goes down is the most peaceful place on earth."

"What did you mean when you said you could put an exclamation point on this?"

"Give me a little time and I can tell you stories about

what those bastards have done that will make them fall even
harder," Kreider said as he handed the tape recorder to
Cord. "We'll go for a little boat ride, have a little dinner,
and I'll tell you more about Crotty's escapades than even
you can imagine."

"You would do that?"

"I need to apologize too, Alex, just like you did."

A few minutes later Cord was back at his car where
Duke had been waiting.

"What was that all about?" Duke said as Cord got in.

"Long story, Duke. Long story."

"The tape was not in the car. I looked everywhere."

Cord pulled the recorder from his pocket and gave it to
Duke.

"What the hell?"

"Duke, I'll tell you all about it tomorrow. Listen, I'm
staying here tonight. You take my car back to the club. Tell
Joey everything is under control and the game is still on.
Tell him I'm staying up here tonight to get some more nails
to pound into Crotty's coffin. Kreider will bring me back
tomorrow, and I'll fill you all in then. Everything's good."

Cord pulled a notepad from the back seat of his car and
joined Kreider on the front porch of the cabin. Kreider
handed Cord a jacket. They walked back down the dock,
climbed into a small motorboat, and headed slowly down
the shoreline.

For the longest time, nothing was said about the whole
operation. Instead Kreider pointed out the scenic and historic spots along the lake as though they were just two old
friends taking a pleasant ride on the lake. Crotty's name
never came up and Cord oddly felt that it was one of the
most peaceful and pleasant times he had spent in a long
time.

Later, back in the cabin, as the sun set over the lake and
a gentle breeze blew across the tops of the pines, Kreider
spent several hours providing a virtual avalanche of details
of corruption orchestrated over the years by Crotty and

Burgess, things that even a hardened political reporter like Alex Cord found astonishing. It was as though Kreider had been waiting years to tell someone about all of this.

Nearing ten p.m., Kreider finally said, "I'm sure that after I get some sleep, I can think of a lot more to give you."

"Bruno, I think we've got enough here already to put these guys away for a long, long time."

"Are you Catholic, Alex?"

"I am—sort of."

"Me too—sort of," Kreider said as though his mind was far, far away.

"Why?" Cord asked.

"I feel like I've just spent the last several hours in confession. It feels good, actually."

"Well, Bruno, I'm certainly no priest, and I'm in no position to absolve you of your sins. But I think that when this all plays out, your penance may be manageable."

Kreider laughed a little. "Did you say penance or sentence?"

"For your sake, Bruno, I hope it will be both."

☙❧☙

Richard Lewis was the forty-seven-year-old editor of the *Troy Register* newspaper. He had started as a reporter with the paper after graduation from Syracuse University's Newhouse School of Public Communications. Lewis was once the paper's political reporter and, in fact, it was Alex Cord who replaced him in that position when Lewis was named editor. Lewis was a thoughtful and congenial man who penned most of the paper's editorials himself and kept actively engaged in the community as well as with all of the newspaper staff. He was well-respected and well-liked, and he believed in keeping an open line of communication, especially with his reporters. He and Alex Cord had an excellent rapport and working relationship.

So it was not unusual for Lewis to agree to meet with

Cord about a story Cord was working on. Normally such meetings involved a reporter "pitching" a story line to an editor. What was unusual about this meeting was that the story had already been written. Cord had handed it to Lewis on Friday evening and asked for a meeting to discuss it at Lewis's earliest convenience. It was also unusual for Lewis to call Cord at his home that same night, leaving a message on Cord's answering machine to meet at the newspaper office the very next morning. Cord was uncertain whether Lewis's interest in meeting on a Saturday morning was a good sign or not.

Alex Cord walked nervously down the hall toward the editor's office as the sound of his footsteps echoed in the empty corridor. On Saturday mornings, the newspaper office was a quiet place. Lewis's door was open and he was alone inside.

"Is that you, Alex?" came Lewis's voice from inside.

"Good morning, Richard," Cord replied as he entered and saw Lewis sitting alone at a rectangular coffee table off to the left of his desk. Cord could not help but notice the copy of his story sprawled out across the table.

"Tell me this is some sort of joke, Alex."

Cord sat across the table and reached into his jacket pocket to pull out an envelope. He tossed it down on the table atop the sheets of paper which contained his story.

"There's more?" Lewis asked.

"It's my resignation letter," Cord said, pointing to the envelope. "It's effective yesterday."

"Consider it accepted. Effective yesterday," Lewis said.

Lewis tossed the envelope aside without opening it. He gathered up the sheets of paper, arranged them in a pile and tapped them a few times on the table arranging them in a neat stack. He did not appear angry, as Cord had feared. He appeared more somber than anything.

"Presuming that this is not a joke, Alex, I have two questions for you. First, when exactly did you lose your mind?"

Cord sighed and closed his eyes. He had known this

would not be easy. "Presuming your question is not a rhetorical one, I'd say I lost my mind a few months ago. I know this is nuts, Richard."

"Then my second question is this. Do you really think we can print this?"

"Honestly, I think you can, but I don't think you will. I understand how radioactive this is for you, especially in your position. Have you talked with Bill?"

Cord was referring to Bill Fagan, the CEO of Century Publications, the publisher of the *Troy Register* and several other newspapers across upstate New York.

"I did. I gave him a Cliff Notes version over the phone last night after I read it. He practically fired me for even thinking about printing this. You know how newspaper publishers feel about taking on the establishment. Jesus, Alex, you know how this works!"

"I do. And I understand, Richard. I really do, but this story has to be told. It has to get out."

Lewis raked his hands through his hair and shook his head. "You're way off the reservation, Alex. Way off the reservation. The *Register* and other newspapers don't make the news, they report the news. If you had simply uncovered this somehow and not been a part of it, we'd put it on the front page. But you didn't uncover it, Alex. You helped orchestrate it! A newspaper can't just create an incident and then write about it. This isn't even an incident! This is a corruption scandal of epic proportions. This is going to go national as soon as it gets out. You know we can't print a story that one of our reporters created."

"But you know we have to!" Cord said, immediately realizing that he had raised his voice at Lewis and was in no position to do that. "Sorry, Richard," he said. "I'm sorry. I'm a little tense." They both took a breath and Cord pressed on. He was prepared for this. "Richard, I know I crossed the line. That's why I handed in my resignation."

"And that's why I accepted it, Alex. I don't want you to quit, but I know you well enough to know that if we don't print this, it's still somehow going to get out, so you have to resign anyway. I get that."

"Richard, the mere fact that you even called Bill suggests to me that you gave it some consideration. You thought it was possible. Am I right?"

"What I thought was that this story is so explosive that I needed Bill to weigh in. That's what I thought."

"And he said no? No as in never?" Cord asked, but already knowing the answer.

"I mean no as in never. Look, this is not a newspaper story anyhow. It's not a report on news, it's an exposé. Bill is absolutely right. I agree with him. For about a million reasons the *Register* should not and cannot print this. Not now, not ever."

Cord sat without responding. Lewis got up from the chair and walked around the room. The two said nothing for several seconds.

"Sorry to put you in this spot, Richard. I really am. But these crooks have to pay for what they did, not only to Phillip and JoAnne DiMatteo, but to all the other people they've screwed and will continue to screw if somebody doesn't stop them."

"That, I agree with," Lewis said.

Cord's heart leapt. He felt that somehow there was still hope. Lewis had agreed with him that the story should be told.

"Let me ask you some questions about the story itself, Alex. But we're still not printing it!"

"What do you want to know?"

For the next several minutes Lewis quizzed Cord on the story details. He asked about how reliable all of the evidence was, he asked how credible Kreider's tales were, he discussed with Cord the nature of legal entrapment, and they discussed the potential for a slander suit.

Cord had brought much of the evidence with him: the note and check from Joey as payoff for alleged help with the IRS; the courier message; the sheet with voting percentages with Crotty's signature on his own letterhead; the recording from Kreider's car, in which Crotty admitted to it all; and, lastly, the promise from Bruno Kreider that he would swear in a deposition to myriad other incidents of corruption, pay-to-play, and election fraud.

They agreed that the legal prohibition against entrapment did not apply outside of governmental or police actions, and that slander would not be an issue if the story was totally accurate. And they discussed how compelling the testimony of people like JoAnne, Rita, Pat, and an ex-nun would be as the story unfolded in the media and even in court.

Cord was energized by the detail into which Lewis probed. The mood in the room changed from one of hostility to an actual discussion of the story's merits. It seemed to Cord that Lewis was trying to find a way to help.

"I have to say, Alex. Despite the fact that you annoyed me to no end by dropping this hot potato in my lap, this has to be the coolest scam I've ever heard of."

"Thanks, I guess," Cord said with some relief and a slight smile.

"Why not just turn this over to the DA or the feds or some law enforcement people? Let them handle this. Why write this story at all? Why not just let the cops handle this?"

"We thought long and hard about that, Richard. We really did. But you know how the legal system works. Crotty's crew will lawyer up. Any indictments will get sealed shut, and this will go on forever. Who knows? They'll try to suppress all this evidence, and it could be dragged out for years. In the meantime, these guys could all get elected again. You know that! The legal system is way too slow, Richard, and full of too many potential loopholes. If we put this story out there," Cord pressed on, "the sheer mockery they will get for being totally hoodwinked by four ladies from South Troy will get them laughed out of town. The people of this city will believe this, with or without a trial. Then the courts can take as long as need to get these guys locked up. In the meantime, they'll never get re-elected. They're going down sooner or later, Richard. We want them to go down now—the election is only a few weeks away."

Lewis took it all in.

"And besides, Richard," Alex continued. "Don't you think we owe it to JoAnne DiMatteo to have her be the one who takes Crotty down on her own terms?"

Lewis came back to sit across the coffee table from Cord. He leaned over, picked up the story pages, leafed through them, and said, "I do, Alex. I do think we owe her that. But I'm still not printing your story," he concluded as Cord let out a long sigh of frustration.

"Okay, Richard, I know when I'm beat. I understand. I really do."

"I didn't say you were beat, Alex."

"We're running out of time before the election, Richard. I don't see how we can do this without the story being printed."

"Bill called me back this morning. He called me at home and asked me to send him your full story. So I got it over to him. He read the whole thing and called me again. Now, Alex, I need your word that what I'm going to tell you next never, ever leaves this office. Not a word, Alex. Not a single word to your comrades, not to anybody, not even to Jo-Anne DiMatteo. Nobody, Alex. Nobody can ever find out that I'm going to tell you next. You owe me that."

"My word, Richard. You have my word. And yes, I owe you a lot."

"Does the name David Kennard mean anything to you?"

"No."

"He's a Princeton guy who graduated with Bill."

"Our Bill?" Cord asked.

"Yes, Bill Fagan, our publisher. In the early eighties Fagan and David Kennard together founded the Princeton student newspaper called the *Orange Weekly*."

"You're kidding, right? We're going to print this in a

student newspaper?" Cord asked incredulously.

"No, Alex. They've both moved on from their student newspaper days. Bill Fagan will not let this get printed in the *Troy Register* but he thought that his old friend David Kennard might be interested. Kennard is the editor of *The New York Monthly*.

Cord leapt from his seat. "*The New York Monthly* magazine is going to print this? Jesus, Richard that's fantastic!"

"Not so fast. I'm telling you that Bill called Kennard. This sort of exposé is not a newspaper story, but it may be the kind of story *The New York Monthly* would love. They do a ton of this in-depth writing and especially love political intrigue. Kennard is intrigued."

"Intrigued? How intrigued? What does that mean?" Cord was excited again.

"Hold on. He's only agreed to read the story. They normally don't even read unsolicited manuscripts like this, but he agreed to look at it as a favor to Bill. Bill emailed the story to him about an hour ago. He's probably reading it right now. I have no idea what he's going to say or when. Remember it's Saturday morning. I expect he won't keep Bill hanging too long but who knows. So why don't you go home and sit tight. If I hear anything, I'll call your cell."

"You're the best, Richard. Jesus God Almighty, you're the best! And Bill too!"

"All we did was ask Kennard to read and consider it. The rest is up to him. No matter what happens here, Alex, remember your promise. Nothing can ever be said about my or Bill's involvement."

Cord was so excited he couldn't think straight. The scenario that was in play was even better than he had ever hoped for. Having this story appear in *The New York Monthly* would give it far greater notoriety than it would get from the *Troy Register*. It would be a national story overnight. He was dying to tell the others what happened at his meeting with Lewis. The ladies at The Settlement and his fellow conspirators at the Marconi Club knew about the meeting and were waiting patiently for word from him, but he was not about to call them yet. Besides, he remembered, Lewis had sworn him to secrecy about *The New York Monthly* potential and Bill Fagan's intervention, so he could not tell them about that in any case. Joey, Rita, and Duke had all called his cell phone but he purposely didn't answer the calls. So far all he had was a rejection from Lewis and a potential for an outlet for the story. It was just a potential. He had to wait.

The time dragged on and finally he felt he had to say something to the others. He called Rita but only to say that the decision had not been made, that he was waiting for a call back. Cord returned to his apartment. He busied himself with minor edits to his story. As far as he was concerned, it was ready to print, but he had to keep himself busy doing something while he waited to find out who, if anybody, was going to print it.

His cell phone rang late in the early afternoon. The display read, "Richard Lewis."

"Did he say yes?" Cord blurted without even saying hello.

"No," Lewis replied as Cord's heart sank. "But that's to be expected, Alex, so relax."

"Expected? How? Why? Did he actually say 'no' or do you mean no, he did not say 'yes'?"

"Alex, these guys are pros, and they don't know you or anything about you. Kennard told Bill he was interested in the story, but they would have to vet you and the story before making any decisions."

"Of course," Cord said after he realized that a national publication would never just print such an incendiary story without checking out every detail.

"But, Alex, they're hot on it. Kennard wants to see you Monday morning in his office in New York City. Can you get there?"

"Get there! Of course, I can get there. I'll start walking right now if I have to."

"Of course, I forgot you don't have a job."

"Don't remind me."

"I'll email you exactly where and what time Kennard will meet you but it definitely will be Monday, probably at their New York City office. You'll need to bring all of your evidence. All of it: notes, videos, audiotapes, everything. This is going to be an inquisition, Alex. He'll probably have a herd of fact checkers with him so do your homework. You'll have one shot at this. One."

"I'm all over it, Richard. Christ, I can't thank you enough. And Bill too. Thank you, thank you."

"And one more thing."

"What's that?"

"Bring JoAnne DiMatteo."

"JoAnne? They want to see JoAnne? In New York?"

"That's what he said. Bring her."

"Why?"

"Because Kennard said so."

"Okay. I will. No problem."

"Good luck, Alex. And remember what I said about keeping Bill and me out of this. After this hits, if it hits, our paper will cover this story like no other. But we can't be implicated in this in any way. That's critical, Alex. No exceptions. Hear me?"

"Of course. I understand. I promise. I owe you big time."

"Good luck, Alex. I'm pulling for you. If you ever need a reference…"

"I think this will be my last story ever, Richard, but I appreciate the offer."

Chapter 22

Duke's pickup truck rolled up the driveway of The Settlement at seven-thirty a.m. on Monday morning. Cord was in his car waiting for Duke to arrive. They each got out of their vehicles and Cord followed Duke around to the kitchen door in the back.

Pat heard them coming and opened the door.

"Good morning," she said cheerily.

As they entered, Rita and Chuck were at the breakfast table.

"Early start for a reporter isn't it, Alex?" Rita said.

"Ladies," he simply said.

"JoAnne will be down in a minute," Chuck added. "You have time, have a cup of coffee. We have thermal cups so you can take them with you and some muffins."

"Is there anything you don't think of?" Duke said playfully.

"Not that I can think of," Chuck replied with a wink.

"You're looking pretty spiffy today, Alex," Rita noted as she saw Cord wearing a dark blue suit rather than one of the assortment of sport jackets he normally wore.

"Big day," he said.

"And you too, Duke," Pat offered.

"Sorry I don't have a suit," he said apologetically as he wore a solid red tie on a white dress shirt and a pair of khaki pants.

"Nonsense, you look very nice, Duke," Chuck offered.

As they sat drinking their coffee, JoAnne appeared in the doorway. She was dressed meticulously in a black and white print dress with a black patent leather belt and matching shoes. She carried a leather handbag which somehow exactly matched the pattern in her dress. Her hair and makeup were perfect.

"Whoa, Jo! You look like a million bucks," Rita said.

"Two million!" Pat added.

"Stop it," she said sheepishly. "Is this really okay?"

JoAnne always took great care with her appearance even when just staying around the house, but none of them had seen her "dress up" like this since the days of the Marconi Club dinners.

"If you don't mind me saying, ma'am, I think you look fabulous," Duke said.

"Thank you, Duke. And you do too. Are we ready?"

"Let's do it," Cord said.

"Oh, by the way, Alex," Rita said almost as an afterthought, "you never told us how this meeting came to be. Last we heard you were pitching this story to your editor. Now you're off to pitch it to *The New York Monthly*. How'd that happen?"

Cord was hoping to not have to answer that question. Richard Lewis had made it crystal clear to him that neither he nor Bill Fagan could be implicated in any way.

"Rather not say, Rita. Let's just say I got lucky. Stuff happens."

"Since you went in to see your editor about him running the story and you came out with a trip to New York, can we assume there is a connection?" asked Rita.

Cord finished the last of his coffee and looked at Rita. "I know we've never had any secrets with any of this so can I just ask you not to ask me about that? I don't want to lie, but I swore not to answer that question."

"I think we all understand, don't we?" JoAnne said, effectively bailing Cord out. "Shall we go to New York?"

After getting good-luck wishes from the others, JoAnne, Alex, and Duke went into the garage, piled into Joe Black, and began their trip to Manhattan, about 150 miles to the south. Almost as soon as they were underway, Alex began to pour over his notes which he had spread out in the back seat. He knew that the magazine staff would engage him in a detailed vetting of the story to make certain that every detail was not only accurate but able to be proven. He had been awake most of the night preparing.

JoAnne was lost in her own thoughts. She was quite uncertain as to what her role would be in the events of the day but knew that, before it ended, the ultimate success of Operation Out 'n' In would largely be determined. Little was said along the route as each was lost in contemplation about what lay ahead and how it would all end.

About two and one-half hours later, Duke drove Joe Black through the Lincoln Tunnel out into the bright sunshine of the crowded streets of Midtown Manhattan. He followed the exit ramp north two blocks to 42nd Street and then drove east the remaining three blocks crossing 8th avenue, 7th Avenue and then Broadway to their destination at 6 Times Square, the address of the Newman Building.

The building, a fifty-eight-story skyscraper—the tenth tallest building in Manhattan—was named after its largest tenant, The Newman Corporation, which was the publisher of nearly twenty different national magazines, including *The New York Monthly*. The other tenant occupying the lower twenty stories was Marshall & Saint John, the largest law firm in the State of New York.

JoAnne and Alex instinctively looked up at the skyscraper as Duke let them out at the curb in front of the building's entrance. They both were born and raised in small towns in upstate New York but neither was intimidated by or otherwise in awe of Midtown Manhattan. Alex had been there on several occasions while covering stories for the newspaper. Likewise, the DiMatteos had visited the city often. JoAnne and Phillip both loved the museums: The Guggenheim, MoMA, and "The Met," which was Phillip's personal favorite. And several times a year, they would travel into the city for dinner and a Broadway show. They had gone to see the annual Radio City Music Hall's *Christmas Spectacular* on many occasions.

JoAnne could not help but think back fondly of those days as she stood on the sidewalk in front of the Newman Building, less than two blocks away from Sardi's, the iconic restaurant on 44th Street where she and Phillip always had dinner when they were in town.

"Good luck," Duke called out from the car as he drove off toward a nearby parking garage to wait.

"We'll call your cell phone," JoAnne yelled back as she and Alex entered the building.

As was sadly the case with most office buildings in Manhattan, especially since the events of 9/11, Newman's entrance foyer was tightly guarded. Security personnel checked everyone who entered for their ID badges. Visitors, like JoAnne and Alex, had to check in at the front desk, show identification, and be listed in advance as having an appointment at one of the offices upstairs. They were photographed, issued a "visitor" badge, escorted through a metal detector, and shown to the elevator leading to the offices above.

David Kennard's office at The New York Monthly was on the thirty-fourth floor. The receptionist welcomed JoAnne and Alex and led them to a conference room, beautifully equipped with a modern table surrounded by twelve leather chairs, a sixty-inch television monitor built into the wall just above a state-of-the-art multimedia system, and a marble-topped credenza situated in front of the large panel windows offering a spectacular view north toward Central Park. The receptionist invited JoAnne and Alex to help themselves to the continental breakfast which was awaiting them on the credenza.

They declined the offer and instead just stood looking out the floor-to-ceiling windows over the busy city below against the backdrop of a clear blue sky. They both were incredibly nervous.

"Hi, I'm David Kennard, thanks for coming," Kennard

said as he bounded into the room and first shook JoAnne's hand and then Alex's. "Coffee?" he said as he prepared a cup for himself and sat across the table from them. He was smiling, animated, and incredibly well dressed. JoAnne thought he looked just like Pierce Brosnan in *The Thomas Crown Affair*, one of her all-time favorite movies.

"No thank you, Mr. Kennard," JoAnne said. "And thank you for taking the time to see us. I can't imagine a busy man like you taking the time to meet with us."

"Please call me David."

"Only if you call me JoAnne," she replied.

"JoAnne, it's my pleasure. I want you to know how much I appreciate you coming all the way down here to meet me today and especially on such short notice."

"I love the city," JoAnne said with as pleasant a smile as Alex Cord had ever seen. She was absolutely charming. He was really happy that she was there and hitting it off so well with Kennard.

The three—but mostly JoAnne and Kennard—engaged in several minutes of small talk about the city and both talked fondly of Christmas time in New York, especially at Radio City.

Soon Kennard smoothly turned the talk to the matter at hand. He explained his fascination with the story which he had read over the weekend. He apologized profusely to Alex for what was to come—i.e. a strenuous pouring over the details to authenticate all of the incredible facets of this, what he called, "a ruse of epic proportions."

"I have to tell you, this story is a tough one for me as an editor," he said. "On one hand I love it, on the other, if it's not one-hundred percent accurate..." His voice trailed off.

"I understand that completely," Alex said. "I understand how important unfailing accuracy is here."

"Good, good. I'm glad you understand. That way you won't be offended by the third degree my staff will be putting you through here today."

"I expected nothing less," Alex replied.

"Mr. Kennard," JoAnne said, "if you don't mind me asking, why did you want to see me today?"

Before he could answer there was a slight tap on the glass door followed immediately by the entry of three men and four women who randomly took various seats at the table. Kennard dutifully introduced JoAnne and Alex to the group which he had obviously assembled to vet the story they each had first read that very morning.

Kennard apologized for what he called this "herd" of people: Marsha Solomon, features editor; James Arnoff, general counsel; Sarah Jane Walcott, staff writer and regular contributor of political pieces; Zak Witcomb, head of copy; and three additional staffers who were introduced as "fact checkers."

It was clear to Cord that Kennard had assembled an "A-Team" to vet the story. On the one hand he felt that this was a good sign of how seriously his story was being taken. On the other it was an ominous sign of how taxing his day would be. He felt prepared.

"If we were to use this story, it would be a real departure from how we normally do business," Kennard said. "We'd surely prefer to have a lot more time with this and give this a lot more thought but I'm well aware that it needs to get out before the upcoming elections. I believe that at least half of my staff here thinks I may have lost my mind to even consider it. The other half is sure I've lost my mind," he said jokingly.

JoAnne noted that this attempt at humor was not met by even polite laughter. It appeared that his comment may have seemed more accurate than amusing to the group.

"Mr. Cord," Kennard said as he rose from his seat, "I'm going to leave Marsha Solomon in charge of this little inquisition. Mrs. DiMatteo—JoAnne—you asked me a short while ago why I requested that you be here today. Let me answer your question in my office."

He escorted JoAnne out of the conference room. She felt badly about leaving Cord to face the others alone but Kennard was in charge and clearly had a plan. She was still more than curious as to why he had insisted that she come.

As they went down the long corridor leading to his office, Kennard stopped frequently to comment on several of the more famous magazine covers and cartoons that adorned the walls throughout the maze of offices. These lithographs gave a visual history of this iconic publication, dating back to 1935.

Down another hall the walls were covered with black and white photographs of some of America's most famous authors and critics who had written for the magazine: Dorothy Parker, Ring Lardner, F. Scott Fitzgerald, Ogden Nash, James Thurber, John Updike, Truman Capote, and many others. JoAnne enjoyed the tour so much that she temporarily forgot why she was there. She wished for a moment that Chuck and Duke were with her to see the pictures of the authors.

From his office, which cornered Broadway and 43rd Street, Kennard pointed out many of the historic landmarks of the City below and they sat for a long time at a small coffee table talking about JoAnne's life at the Fam Pharm and her recollections of her visits to Manhattan with Phillip.

Kennard, she observed, had an incredibly charming way of mixing friendly banter with the business at hand as he adroitly slipped in several detailed questions about Operation Out 'n' In. While his questions were many and varied, they were all presented in a way such that it would never appear that JoAnne's veracity was being tested. She was taken not only by his polished style but also by his deft touch in making the vetting of her seem more like a trip down memory lane.

Shortly after noon, Kennard and JoAnne left the building, walked three blocks east on 43rd, and entered Grand Central Terminal. JoAnne had traveled through Grand Central several times in the past but never really stopped to admire its grandeur. She was totally enthralled by the "nickel tour" her host gave her of the building's interesting history and landmarks. He talked as though he were a tour guide, offering up little-known details about the opal clock and the ornate ceiling of the main terminal, the "Kissing Room" at the entrance to the famous Biltmore Hotel, FDR's private passageway, and the Whispering Gallery outside the famous Oyster Bar restaurant.

He led her into the restaurant and was recognized and greeted by a man wearing a white tuxedo shirt, black pants, suspenders, and a black bow tie who knew Kennard by name. While the restaurant was already quite crowded, the man escorted them immediately to a quiet table at the rear of the restaurant.

Upon Kennard's recommendation, they ordered a light lunch and then talked more about New York and also about Operation Out 'n' In.

After a slight lull in the conversation as the waiter cleared the table, JoAnne said, "You're not going to publish Alex's story, are you?"

Kennard was surprised by JoAnne's question, which sounded more like a statement. He was quite impressed that JoAnne had made this correct assumption based on what he felt was no evidence to that effect given by him.

"No, JoAnne, we're not. How did you know that?"

"Then why are we here? Why am I here? You certainly did not have to spend all this time with me and invite me to lunch to break the news. I'm quite sure that an editor of your stature has issued thousands of rejections over your career. Surely you don't invite all those people to lunch just to give them a rejection notice."

"No, surely I don't," said an amused Kennard.

"I met you a couple of hours ago not really knowing why you invited me here in the first place. And now I surely don't understand since you are not going to publish Alex's story. If you're not going to print our story, why have you spent so much time with me and why are your people grilling Alex about the details?"

"If you must know," Kennard said with a smile, "I wanted to see for myself if you are actually as impressive in real life as you are in the story."

"And?"

"More so," Kennard said.

"You flatter me, but I still don't understand," JoAnne replied. "I truly appreciate you spending all this time with me, I really do. I've had a wonderful visit with you, and you have been extraordinarily kind. But now, I think it's time for you to be honest with me."

"So it is," he said as they were leaving the Oyster Bar, emerging out onto East 42nd Street. Once on the street, he stopped and said to her, "I said I was not going to publish Alex Cord's story but I did not say I would not publish yours."

"But I didn't write a story, Alex did."

"Not by you—about you! JoAnne, I've read Alex Cord's story, and it's truly an amazing one for a lot of reasons. But to me the allure—the real significance—of what went on in Troy is not that yet another sleazy politician got caught up in corruption. That sort of thing unfortunately happens all of the time, same story, different creep. My magazine is not about catching or even exposing criminals. We're more interested in stories of extraordinary actions, occurrences which happen once in a lifetime, stories of a kind which not only interest our readers but inspire them at the same time. We don't write to shock or appall our readers. We leave those things to the tabloids. I'm far less interested in a corrupt politician going to jail than I am in you and your friends actually standing up against corruption. To me, the real story is not what you did. The real story is how and why you did it!

"Alex Cord's story is all about exposing corruption and taking down a few garden-variety politicians. He wrote it like it was a blueprint for prosecutors to follow to take down Michael Crotty. He wrote it like a news story. We don't do news. We do stories of interest, of bravery, of extraordinary deeds and occurrences. I don't think Alex Cord has written that story. The story I'm interested in is about you, JoAnne. It's about you, your friends, and that crazy bunch who helped you—and about Phillip."

JoAnne slowly turned and started walking alone down 42nd Street. Kennard followed a short distance behind. He knew JoAnne needed a moment to herself. When she reached the Madison Avenue intersection, she stopped and turned back to Kennard. He went into a quick trot to catch up with her. She was crying. Noticing that, Kennard felt awful about bringing up Phillip's name.

"I'm sorry," he said sincerely. "I shouldn't have mentioned Phillip."

"We didn't do this to be written about. We don't care about any of that. We all did this to take down the man who killed my husband. You want to write a human-interest story. I want Michael Crotty to pay for killing my Phillip."

JoAnne surprised herself at how loud she had said that. What surprised her even more is that for the first time she had said those words out loud.

They walked, saying nothing, for the remaining few blocks back to the Newman Building. Once alone inside the elevator heading back to Kennard's office, he said, "I needed to talk to you today to make sure I understood the real story, to make sure we both understood the real story."

As they walked down the hallway to Kennard's office they passed the windows to the conference room where Cord was still pouring over the details with the magazine staff. The table was strewn with the debris of the catered-in lunch, as well as the myriad exhibits, notes, and documents that Cord had brought to substantiate every detail of his story. Kennard poked his head in the door as they passed.

"Almost done?" he asked.

"Give us thirty minutes to wrap this up," answered Marsha Solomon.

"Perfect," Kennard said as he led JoAnne back to his office.

Once inside, Kennard entered into a side door which

opened to a nearby closet. He reached up to a shelf, took down a package wrapped in plain brown wrapping, and gave it to JoAnne.

"I'd like you to have this. Open it," he said.

JoAnne slowly unwrapped the package. Inside was a framed and autographed lithograph of the *New York Monthly* cover drawn by famed artist Paul Berg in 1986, often entitled *The New York Monthly's View of Christmas*. It depicted a crowd of people entering Radio City with snow falling. It was perhaps the most famed cover in the publication's history.

"What a wonderfully thoughtful gift," JoAnne said, totally taken aback by Kennard's continued kindness. "This has to be extremely rare and valuable—it's even signed by the artist."

"It is and it seems totally appropriate that you have one of these. I thought of it when you told me about your visits to New York and to Radio City. JoAnne, no matter how this ends up, I want you to remember me as someone who appreciates what you did and respects how you did it," he said.

"This gift is wonderful. You're so kind," JoAnne replied. "May I donate it to the Marconi Club? I hope you won't think me ungrateful. I think it will go well there, in a place of prominence. This whole thing was a collective effort, and this should be shared."

"Of course," he said. "I assumed you would want to do that."

JoAnne sat quietly for a while still processing what amounted to the counter offer made by Kennard regarding the story.

"So, as I understand what you're saying, you will only take our story if you can rewrite it."

"Assuming my staff is totally comfortable with the details that Mr. Cord provides them, yes. That is correct."

"Then let me ask you one more question. If we do that, do you think we can still reach our real objective?"

"Taking down Crotty?"

She nodded.

"Yes, I do," he said without hesitation. "I have already discussed this with our general counsel, Jim Arnoff. You met him in the conference room earlier. Jim and I both think that there is plenty of evidence here that Mayor Crotty has conspired to commit voter fraud. This is a federal criminal matter which, if presented with this information through the proper channels, the US Attorney's Office will quickly turn into an indictment. Our suggestion is to turn the evidence over to the feds and let them handle the arrest and prosecution. We want to rewrite the story to focus on how and why you exposed Crotty. That way, the real story will be told and Crotty will pay for what he did to you and to Phillip. In the meantime, these creeps will never get elected while the courts take their time getting them convicted."

"Oh, dear," JoAnne said. "That scares me a little. I don't think we ever contemplated getting involved with lawyers, especially a swarm of federal attorneys."

"Mr. Arnoff will be happy to connect you with an experienced attorney from the Marshall and Saint John law firm downstairs. They're quite good. They have plenty of experience in dealing with criminal matters and know their way around the US Attorney's Office. My suggestion would be for you to have them act on your behalf in turning over the evidence and shepherding this thing through. We have them on retainer, and I'm sure that if we ask nice, they'll take this case pro bono. It will be great exposure for them, and they'll do everything right. That way you won't have to deal with any of the mess this whole thing is going to create, no matter how it comes out. They'll take care of all that."

"I see," JoAnne said. "But this is surely catching me by surprise. May I have some time?"

"Of course, you may. Take as much time as you need and by all means talk to the others. The story still belongs to you. If you prefer to go elsewhere with it, of course you can do that, and I wish you nothing but the best. But if you think our idea has any merit, let my staff rewrite the story. If you don't like what we do, I give you my word we won't print it."

ᏋᏗᏋᏗ

It was just before noon four days after the trip to New York City. Chuck and Pat were in the kitchen laying out a buffet lunch as Rita and JoAnne set places around the dining table. Duke was bringing in extra chairs to provide seating for twelve.

A FedEx box had been delivered, as scheduled, early that morning. The package contained twenty copies of a draft *New York Monthly* story written by staff writer Sarah Jane Walcott. Walcott, one of the staffers who met with Alex Cord several days before, had been assigned to rewrite his story. The package, addressed to JoAnne, also contained a hand-written note from David Kennard which read:

JoAnne,
My thanks to you and your associates for giving us this opportunity. It is our sincere hope that you find that we have done justice to your amazing story. My offer to provide assistance toward securing experienced legal guidance with your follow-up stands whether you allow us to print your story or not.
Please call me the moment you have decided how you would like to proceed.
Sincerely,
David
P.S. The pleasure of our meeting earlier this week was all mine.

By noon, all of the participants in Operation Out 'n' In were in The Settlement's dining room, milling around the table. They were all well aware of why they were there. Jo-Anne made it perfectly clear to everyone that the decision as to how to play the end-game would be a collective one. The Marconi Club had closed for the afternoon, even Donnie and Adam took time off from work to be there. Every one of them had a vested interest in how the story would play out.

They all went to the kitchen, served themselves plates from the buffet, and took seats around the dining table. JoAnne sat at the head of the table flanked by Rita, Pat, and Chuck. Duke Bennett and Jimmy Mariano sat next to each other across from Tugboat Tommy and Angelo Renna. At the other end sat Joey G. with Alex Cord to his right, Donnie Moore and Adam to his left.

"Thank you all so much for coming on such short notice," JoAnne began, "and before I say another word, I want to thank you all sincerely for everything you have done. We've had a remarkable journey to get to this point and without the help of every single one of you, we would not be here today. You've all been amazing. Phillip and I thank you all. Now does anyone have anything they'd like to say before we begin?"

"Mrs. D?" Joey said while raising his hand slightly to be recognized.

"Yes, Joey."

"Mrs. D, I couldn't help but notice that there are exactly twelve of us here. I don't know if that was done on purpose or not but I wonder if we should be calling ourselves 'Gang of Twelve Two,'" he said with his usual panache.

"Interesting observation, Joey," JoAnne said with a smile. "I'm quite sure that the number is coincidental, but I think that name would be an appropriate one. I think Phillip would approve. But speaking of attendance, for clarity, let me explain why Mr. Wheeler, Mr. Casella, and Mr. Robbins are not with us today. While they have been apprised of our situation, they have recused themselves from further direct involvement in Operation Out n' In due to their candidacies in the upcoming election. With that, let's get started."

JoAnne nodded to Pat who walked around the table passing out the copies of the story, which came in at just over 11,000 words, standard size for a *New York Monthly* feature story.

"Take your time reading this and enjoy your lunch," Jo-Anne said as they all stared at the cover page:

In Sheep's Clothing
How a group of crafty ladies and an odd cast of characters pulled the wool over the eyes of corruption
By Sarah Jane Walcott

For the next hour the sound of turning pages was all that could be heard in the dining room of The Settlement, save for the occasional clinking of knives and forks as the group devoured both their lunch and the story. Alex Cord was the first to finish and was noticed rising from the table deep in thought as he stretched out his arms.

"I have to read faster," Duke said as he noticed Alex getting up from the table. "I'm not even close to being done."

"Take all the time you need, Duke," JoAnne reassured him.

As each person finished, they got up from the table and walked around the room in silence. Duke was the last to finish. "I was reading this real carefully which is why I was so slow," he said almost apologetically.

"Duke, you stretch your legs for a moment while we clear the table. Let's reconvene in ten minutes, everyone," JoAnne said. "In the meantime, let's not talk about our thoughts so that we all can hear everybody's comments at the same time." After they had all returned to the table, JoAnne began. "It seems we have followed our plan well up to this point, but now we have a choice to make. It's time to decide how to play this out. The question before us now is do we stick with our original plan or go with the one the magazine has presented to us?"

"Or something else entirely," added Rita.

"Let's talk," said JoAnne.

As the discussion ensued, everyone at the table said their piece. JoAnne purposely sought out the opinions of everyone and again made it clear that all input was welcomed and wanted, the final decision would be a collective one.

By late afternoon, the Gang of Twelve II members went their separate ways. They were all exhausted and energized by what they had seen, heard, and agreed upon.

Chapter 23

With only a few weeks remaining until the November election, Michael Crotty went about his business at city hall. He cut back his campaigning, much to the chagrin of Danny Burgess and other Democrats, who were still quite fearful of the potential of losing to the "fusion" candidates. Crotty seemed to everyone to be oddly relaxed. Only he seemed to think that his election victory was a foregone conclusion.

He was somewhat concerned by the resignation of Bruno Kreider, but since that night in front of the Excalibar, Crotty had neither seen nor heard from him. He knew that Kreider had gone underground at his cabin on Lake George. The fact that Kreider had apparently said nothing to anyone about the resignation convinced Crotty that Kreider was not going to be a problem. Kreider, he thought, had as much to lose as anyone if their plan was revealed. The official story coming out of the mayor's office was that Bruno Kreider had experienced some sort of stress-related medical condition due to pressures of his job and was simply taking a hiatus.

Upon hearing that Alex Cord had left the *Troy Register* newspaper, Crotty had attempted, through Kathy Gill, to reach out to him but to no avail. Crotty did not like that the flow of information he normally got from Cord had stopped, but given the "arrangement" he had made with regard to the election outcome, he actually cared little about these things. None of that mattered any longer, he thought. Don would take care of everything.

Despite the pre-election tension surrounding city hall and the fact that he had lost both his closest advisor and his source of political intelligence, Crotty didn't appear to have a care in the world. That is, until one evening as he left city hall and made his way to the parking lot, where he was supposed to be picked up by his new driver and taken home as usual at six p.m. As he turned the corner onto the side street adjacent to city hall, he noticed two men coming directly toward him. He slowed his walk when he recognized them from the night at the locks. Donnie Moore and Tugboat Tommy blocked his way along the sidewalk as they neared.

"Can I help you fellas?"

"Nice night, isn't it, Mayor?" Tugboat remarked.

"Can I help you fellas?" Crotty repeated.

"Actually, we're here to help you, Mayor," Donnie said.

"With what?"

"We're here to help you remember that you have a deal that you have to keep."

"I'm sure I have no idea what you're talking about," Crotty said curtly as he tried to pass.

Tugboat moved to his left to block Crotty from passing. "We want to remind you," he said, "that once you make a deal with Don, going back on that deal is something that he doesn't like."

"Look," said Crotty, "I still don't know what you're talking about, but whatever it is we can't talk about it on the street."

Donnie handed him a piece of paper with a phone number on it. "Call this number tomorrow morning at eight a.m. sharp. Use a secure phone. If you don't call, my friend and I will be back. You don't want that."

Crotty took the paper. Donnie and Tugboat then began to walk past him, each menacingly brushing Crotty's shoulders as they did.

Crotty was panicked. He really didn't have any idea what they were talking about but clearly there was something going on with the plot. Something was wrong. He hurried to meet his driver, got home, and spent the rest of the evening worrying and wondering what the problem was. At around ten p.m., he couldn't stand it anymore and called the number.

Duke looked at his cell phone as it sat beside him on the couch. "I knew it!" he said out loud. "You can't get any more predictable than this slug."

"You called it," Donnie said as he turned down the sound of the baseball game they were watching at Duke's apartment. Donnie answered the phone. "It's not eight a.m. sharp, and you're not on a secure phone, asshole. Now do what you're told," Donnie said in the most threatening voice he could muster.

Crotty recognized the Jamaican accent from the night at the locks but before he could get a word in, Donnie ended the call and turned off the phone.

"You like scaring people, don't you?" Duke said with a little grin.

"I like doing what I do best," Donnie said, tossing the phone back to Duke.

At eight-oh-two the next morning, Duke and Joey sat in the office at the Marconi Club. The phone had not rung at eight a.m.

"What do you make of that?" Duke said. "He couldn't wait to talk last night and now, no call?"

"My guess?" said Joey with a smirk. "My guess is that the dumb bastard is still trying to figure out how to get a secure line."

At the same time, Crotty had finally arrived at the diner and convinced Donna to lend him her cell phone. It wasn't "secure," he thought, but at least it wasn't his own phone. He went into the men's room and locked the door behind him. He dialed the number.

"Good Morning, Mayor," Joey said.

Crotty recognized Joey's voice. It was not the same voice he heard when he called the previous night. "Joey? Is that you?"

"You're late. Being late is a thing which I honestly don't much care for."

"What the hell is going on? I thought we were not going to speak again before the election."

"That was before we got the disturbing news of your change of heart, Mayor."

"What change of heart? What the fuck are you talking about?"

"Your change of heart. I received a voicemail yesterday from your dip-shit buddy that you were calling off our deal. Going back on a deal, I might remind you, is simply not allowed."

"Off? What? What dip-shit buddy? Joey, I don't have a clue what you're talking about, but I assure you I'm not going back on any deal," Crotty said in a panic.

"Kreider. Your dip-shit buddy Kreider left me a message that he appreciated our willingness to help with your election problem but that our assistance would no longer be required. You didn't even have the balls to tell me yourself. You had Kreider leave a message. I don't appreciate that either."

"Joey, there's been some kind of mistake. Kreider is full of shit!" Crotty yelled. His voice echoed loudly from his spot in the men's room stall.

Hearing the echo, Joey said, "Where in hell are you anyway? Are you trapped in a fucking cave or something?"

"Never mind where I am. I'm telling you Kreider is lying. I haven't even seen him in weeks. He doesn't work for me anymore, and he's certainly not calling off any deals for me. I didn't authorize that! I don't know what he's doing."

"Interesting story, Mayor."

"It's true. I swear!"

"You know, I want to believe you, but this is very upsetting to me. Don't get me wrong, I couldn't give a crap if you get elected or not, but since I'm the one who introduced you to Don, I feel somewhat, you know, responsible when you break off a deal with him. This doesn't shine such a good light on me in Don's eyes. So, like Don, I too am quite perturbed."

"Don? You told Don the deal was off?" Crotty shrieked.

"Of course, I did. And it probably won't come as any surprise to you that he is not in the least bit amused by this turn of events."

"But I didn't call anything off. This is all a big mistake. I have no idea why Kreider did that, but he's not speaking for me. Just tell Don that! Tell him that, Joey. The deal is still on!" Crotty again heard his voice echo in the stall.

He then heard someone banging on the men's room door from the outside.

"Hey, you gonna be in there all day?" came a voice from outside the men's room.

"Beat it!" Crotty yelled as the knocking continued.

"Did you just tell me to beat it?" Joey asked incredulously.

"No Joey, not you. Some other asshole. No wait! Not other—I didn't mean to say that. Jesus, this has got me all fucked up. Come on, Joey. You gotta believe me. You gotta tell Don this is all Kreider's fault."

"Well, it would be nice if things were that easy, Mayor, but in the real world, things don't work that way. Maybe they do in your world but since you decided to enter ours, I'm sorry to tell you that it just doesn't work that way. What the fuck is all that banging?"

Crotty was beside himself. The guy outside was banging on the door and yelling, making it hard for Crotty to hear what Joey was saying.

"Go away!" he yelled. "No, not you, Joey. I didn't mean you." This was going all wrong. Not only was the election scheme going sour but at the same time he had incurred the wrath of Don and Joey. He knew he had to repair both of these problems immediately. "Joey, what do I need to do? I still want the deal, and I certainly don't want to get on the wrong side of you and Don."

"No, Mayor, you surely don't want that. Let me think,"

Joey paused for a long moment for effect. "Here's where it currently stands. Don and I and some of our friends had planned to stop by your house tomorrow night."

"What? My house? You were coming to my house?"

"Yes, we find that in cases such as this, it's best to meet with people nose-to-nose—much more effective."

"Jesus!"

"Indeed," Joey said. "If you've got any markers out with the guy upstairs you might want to think about calling them in."

"I'll meet with him. I'll explain everything. Just not at my house—don't come to my freakin' house!" Crotty yelled. "My freakin' wife will have a stroke if you guys show up there. Jesus!"

"Wait," Joey said, not being able to resist. "Did you say 'wife'? You mean someone actually married you?"

"Joey, I wanna meet with Don, just not at my house."

"Oh, for certain, Mayor, you'll need to meet with Don. What he does after hearing your explanation is anybody's guess, but he's going to need to hear this from you person- ally. He's like that. Frankly, I don't blame him. Neither of us likes mixed messages.

"Fine, no problem. I'll tell him this is all Kreider's fault."

"He's coming in tomorrow night."

"Tomorrow night is fine. Just not at my house, okay? And not at that fucking lock either. That place gives me the creeps."

"All right, Mayor. I'll see what I can do. I'll talk to Don and give him an update. Let's just make it simple this time. The Marconi Club closes at eight. Don and I will meet you there at nine. Maybe we can still salvage this."

"The Marconi Club? I can't be seen going in there. I don't think it's such a good idea for me to go the Marconi Club, do you?"

"Oh, you don't? Interesting. Let me tell you what I think, and then let me be as polite but clear as I can be. At this point, neither I nor Don could give two shits what you think. What I think is that you should do what we tell you to do and then maybe, just maybe, we can get through this without anyone getting hurt," Joey said, his voice taking on a tone suggesting to Crotty that this was no time to annoy him further.

"Okay, okay. I'll be there. No problem," Crotty back-pedaled.

"Good answer, Mayor. If anything changes, I'll be in touch. Otherwise, tomorrow night at nine at the Marconi Club. Oh, and Mayor, nine means nine. Don't be early, don't be late. Don hates that. In fact, we both hate that."

Crotty spent the rest of the day and the next rehearsing what he would say to Don. After each rehearsal, he felt somewhat better about having a chance to salvage the election and, perhaps more importantly, to spare himself from the ire of Don and Joey and whatever other characters might be involved. He was furious at Kreider for somehow getting back into this. He couldn't imagine how or why he had done that but would deal with him later. For the moment, he had to focus on getting back in Don's good graces.

He was confident that by the time his meeting was over, all would be smoothed over. Joey was a hothead but Don, Crotty thought, was more businesslike—at least that's what he hoped.

⁍ʘ⁍

It was rare for Crotty to take his personal car out of his garage. It had been a long time since he had even thought about driving himself anywhere. He thought though that driving his personal car would be better since there would be little chance that it would be recognized if it was parked near the Marconi Club. He had not heard back from Joey, so he assumed the meeting with him and Don was still on as he arrived in the vicinity of the club.

He remembered the warnings about not getting there too

soon or too late. His plan was to park on the street about a block away from the entrance. At exactly eight fifty-nine he'd walk down the street to the club and press the bell at exactly nine. He reasoned that Don and Joey would be impressed by his punctuality. He had told himself repeatedly to not do or say anything that would even come close to annoying either of them. He would just explain that Kreider had gone rogue or something, and all would be forgiven. He had his speech all prepared.

Angelo Renna and Joey sat at the bar by the front entrance and smiled at each other as they heard the bell ring at exactly nine p.m.

"Showtime!" Joey said as he went to the door. Renna snapped himself into the role of Don and went into the office to wait. Joey knocked loudly twice on the large wooden sliding doors which led to the dining room. The doors were closed tight.

Joey said nothing to Crotty as he opened the front door to let him in. As they made their way into the bar area, Crotty stopped for a moment to take in the area.

"Nice place," he said.

"Take a good look. You may never see it again," Joey replied. "Follow me."

"What do you mean, never see it again?" Crotty was scared senseless. "What does that mean?"

The door to the office was open as they arrived. Crotty could see Don sitting inside behind the desk. He and Joey were dressed in expensive black suits. He thought for a moment that his blue blazer and gray slacks made him look raggedy.

Don looked especially dapper with his patterned yellow pocket handkerchief and matching tie. The thought occurred to Crotty that they were dressed to kill. Thinking of that expression made him even more nervous.

"Don, so glad to see you again," Crotty said, feigning a pleasant greeting. In fact, his hand was sweaty and visibly trembling when he put it out to shake Don's. Don did not reciprocate and stayed sitting behind the desk.

"Sit down, Mayor," was all he said.

Joey sat next to the mayor, across from Don—uncomfortably close, Crotty felt, as his shoulders was almost touching Joey's.

"Joey here tells me that you've now had…what, yet another change of heart?" Don said.

"Oh, no sir. No change of heart. I hope Joey told you that it was Bruno Kreider who said we didn't want the deal and that Bruno is no longer on my staff. He was not speaking for me and, under no circumstances, did I ever even think of calling the deal off. No, sir, I'm still on board and never once did I think of—"

"Shut up, Crotty!" Don roared. "You're babbling like a fucking idiot. I hate idiots."

Crotty's entire body tensed up.

"I've dealt with shit-heads like you many, many times in my life and do you know what they all have in common?" Don asked with a lowered tone of voice.

Crotty's mouth was so dry he had difficulty answering. "No, sir."

"They all think they're big shots until somebody like me comes along and pokes them in the chest a few times and then within two seconds they turn into babbling fucking idiots. They all think they want to play in the big leagues but when they get there and the first fastball comes whizzing by their heads, they run into the dugout, looking for mommy."

Crotty was not about to say anything again until asked.

"Here's what I think happened, Crotty," Don continued. "I think you either got scared or got to thinking you could win this election on your own and told your asshole pal, Kreider, to see if he could kill this deal. Then when Joey told you that was not going to happen and we were pissed, you threw Kreider under the bus."

Crotty was still frozen. He said nothing.

Joey leaned over and said softly to Crotty, "This is

where you need to say something—something really good."

Crotty was sweating and hyperventilating so much that Joey leaned away. He thought Crotty might actually vomit. "I swear, Don. That is not what happened," Crotty finally blurted out. "I never wanted to go back on our deal. Kreider went rogue on me. I swear on, on..." He couldn't find the word. "I swear it. This is all Kreider's fault. I still want the deal, I give you my word."

"Ooooh," Joey said as though Crotty had just said something wrong. "You shouldn't have said that."

"What?" Crotty asked. "What's wrong with what I said?"

"Your word? You give me your word?" Don yelled, rising from his chair. "You're nothing but a fucking two-bit crooked politician who has spent your entire life on the screw. You lie for a living and I'm supposed to take your word?"

Joey practically wanted to give Angelo a standing ovation for so thoroughly terrifying Crotty. He only regretted that the others weren't there to witness it.

"It's not my fault," Crotty said, lowering his face into his hands.

Renna couldn't tell if Crotty was sweating or crying, his face was red and covered with moisture.

"Maybe—" Joey said and then paused. "Don, permit me if I may. Perhaps I can be of some assistance with this. Perhaps we can take a moment to analyze where we are and see what we can do to get out of this."

Don sat back in his chair. Crotty was slightly relieved that Joey appeared as though he was trying to help. At least Don seemed to have calmed down.

Joey got up from his chair, paced around the room for a moment. "As I see this," he began, "whether or not Mr. Crotty here is being totally honest, he says he still wants the deal, but unfortunately he doesn't fully comprehend the problem."

Renna understood the meaning, Crotty did not. "No, Joey, I don't think so either. As a matter of fact, I don't think dumb-ass here does understand the problem."

"What's the problem?" Crotty asked. "What problem?"

Don and Joey got up from their seats. Joey looked at Crotty and said, "You never did understand any of this did you? Maybe it's time somebody explains this all to you."

"Maybe instead of explaining the problem, we should show him the problem," Don said. "Come with us."

Crotty was totally mystified by what they were talking about.

Don and Joey left the office, leading Crotty through the bar toward the dual sliding wooden doors that led to the dining room. The three stood in front of the doors, pausing for effect.

"The problem, you fat stupid fool, is right behind these doors." Don said, gesturing to Joey to open them.

"Behold the problem!" Joey said with as much fanfare as he could muster, opening them.

Crotty just stood there in the doorway—frozen—trying to process what he was seeing. First he noticed Donnie Moore and Tugboat Tommy standing at either side of the entrance. He was startled as they took him by either arm. They escorted him in and sat him in the lone seat at the end of a large squared-off table. Angelo Renna closed the wooden doors and he and Joey took up places on either side. Crotty then saw, facing directly across the table, Jo-Anne DiMatteo, Rita Russo and her sister Charlene, and then Pat Bocketti. He tried to make sense out of seeing Alex Cord sitting next to Jimmy Mariano. Across from them sat Duke Bennett and his cousin Adam.

"What the hell is this?" Crotty roared. He looked around the room of people and tried to make some connection—any connection. As his mind swirled he could not even fathom what was going on. He knew that something horrible was about to happen. He had no idea what it was but he wanted no part of it.

"I'm not staying here," he grumbled as he began to rise

from his chair. He then felt behind him the hands of Donnie Moore pressing on his shoulders and pushing him back into the seat.

"Sit tight, stupid," Donnie leaned over and said to him. "Your long night has just begun."

With that, JoAnne slowly rose from her seat. "The problem that my friends were referring to," she said softly, "is that you have been had. The problem with you winning a rigged election is that there will be no rigging of your election. In fact, by the time this night is over the election will be the farthest thing from your mind. You're finished, Mr. Crotty. You and your corrupt friends from city hall are all finished. You're all going down."

Crotty again instinctively jumped up from his chair. This time Donnie placed his large hands onto Crotty's collarbones and squeezed them until Crotty yelled, "Ow! Stop," as he sat back down. "You can't keep me here," he yelled. "You can't do this!"

"We can and we will," JoAnne said. "You're staying right where you are until you tell me you're sorry."

"What? Say I'm sorry? Sorry for what? Are you kidding me? Sorry for what? This is bullshit!"

"Hey, watch your language," Joey yelled. "There are ladies present. Now tell the lady you're sorry."

"What should I be sorry for?"

"You should be sorry for many, many things, Mayor Crotty," JoAnne said slowly and calmly, "sorry for stealing money from the people of this city and sorry for all of the people whom you have hurt and the lives you have destroyed by being corrupt. Tonight, you should be especially sorry for trying to rig an election. But most of all and what I really want to hear you say is that you're sorry for ruining my life and for killing my husband."

"Say it, fat boy!" whispered Tugboat into Crotty's ear.

"All right, all right, hold on here," Crotty said trying to gather himself. "Is that what this is all about? You want an apology? For what I don't know. I didn't steal anything from anybody, and I certainly did not kill your husband. I don't know what you're talking about, but you've obviously gone through a lot of trouble to arrange all of this so if an apology is what you want, then fine—I'm sorry. There, happy? I'm sorry."

"Say it like you mean it, you scum," Rita demanded from across the room.

Crotty felt like he was having an out-of-body experience. He knew that somehow everyone in the room had pulled a hoax on him, but at that point his only instinct was to extract himself from this situation. He had to get out of there and then figure out later what to do next.

"Okay, fine. I'll play your game if that's what you want," he said condescendingly. "Mrs. DiMatteo, while I admit to nothing, if I have done anything to offend or harm you, your husband, anyone else in this room, or in this city, I humbly apologize. I'm sorry."

"That's what I wanted to hear," JoAnne said as she smiled at Crotty.

"So, are we all happy now? Now let me go, or I'll have you all arrested," Crotty demanded.

"Odd you should mention that," Alex Cord said.

"Cord, you moron, what are you doing here?" Crotty demanded.

Joey rose. "Mrs. D, are we good to go now?"

"Well," JoAnne said, "I don't think his apology was all that sincere but, considering the source, I'll take it. I got my apology. And so, now it's time for us to—" JoAnne stopped herself.

"I'll say it," Rita jumped in. "Now it's time for our revenge."

Everyone in the room smiled—except Crotty, of course.

"So I guess that wraps up this portion of our fun. Let's move on," Joey said in a loudly spirited voice as he sprang from his chair. "It's time to let the mayor go. He's still got a long night ahead of him. I think we can let him figure out the rest. Lord knows he'll have plenty of time to think about it. Mr. Mayor, on behalf of all of us here I'd like to say goodbye, stupid, and good riddance."

Donnie and Tommy got up and reopened the double doors.

Crotty sprang from his chair and began to barge out of the room. "You're all going to pay for this. You'll see. You can't get away with—"

Crotty stopped in his tracks when he saw Police Chief Jackie Roberts standing outside the doors with two uniformed officers to one side and Assistant US Attorney Mark Owen on the other.

"Roberts! Am I glad to see you," Crotty exclaimed. "These bastards have kept me here against my will. Haul all of their asses in. I'm pressing charges. This is all bullshit!"

"Funny," Roberts said as he quickly approached Crotty. "Your friend, Danny Burgess, said something just like that when we hauled his ass in about an hour ago. Now be a good boy and put your grubby hands behind your back. You're under arrest."

Roberts took great pleasure in slapping handcuffs on Crotty while Owen quickly read the charges and issued the standard Miranda Rights statement. Crotty didn't say another word. After Roberts used the term, "under arrest," he didn't hear anything Owen said. He didn't need to.

While Crotty was being handcuffed and read his rights, the entire Gang of Twelve II passed by, went out the front door, and assembled themselves at the top of the front steps. Roberts took Crotty, with his hands cuffed behind him, out the front door making his way through the Gang. Halfway down the steps, he stopped.

A photographer for the *Troy Register* newspaper had somehow been notified about a photo opportunity. His camera flash went off, time and time again, as he captured the moment for publication in the next day's edition.

The photo chosen for the paper showed Chief Roberts leading Crotty down the Marconi Club steps in handcuffs against the backdrop of twelve people on the landing behind, all smiling and simultaneously waving goodbye to Michael Crotty.

Epilogue

Many believed that the arrests and indictments alone might not have been enough to defeat Crotty, Burgess, and Monk in that election. Troy was, after all, still a heavily Democratic city and the old Machine was still able to turn out the vote. The arrests that night of both Crotty and Burgess were met by their initial pleas of not guilty, and the two quickly made bail after their arraignment the next morning. Through their attorneys, they each issued statements claiming total innocence, suggesting that they had been illegally entrapped. They adamantly denied each of the claims against them, vowed to countersue for slander, and predicted vindication in the courts and victory in the upcoming election.

Indeed, it was the story in *The New York Monthly* that appeared a few days later that actually doomed them and brought election victory to Wheeler, Casella, and Robbins.

The feature story written by Sarah Jane Walcott chronicled the events of Operation Out n' In from start to finish and painted a sympathetic if not admiring portrait of four totally different but single-minded ladies from a small town who assembled an equally disparate group of accomplices to take down one of the most tenured political machines in the country.

Most of the evidence in the legal proceedings against Burgess and Crotty was sealed in the indictment, pending trial, and thus not made public prior to the election. The story, however, which was written as a tribute to ingenuity rather than an exposé of corruption, offered in-depth details of the plan to take down Crotty and his regime. Those details, appearing shortly before the election, made it quite clear that Michael Crotty and Danny Burgess were totally corrupt and that Crotty, especially, was a complete fool for falling for such a ruse. In the eyes of the electorate, with or without a trial, he was not only guilty but stupid as well.

After the *New York Monthly* story hit, the firestorm of publicity it generated in the national media sealed their fate. Crotty became the national poster boy for both corruption and stupidity. The front page of the tabloid *New York Daily* that ran the day after the story broke showed the photograph of the handcuffed Crotty doing the so-called perp walk down the Marconi Club stairs. The caption read, *Fat, Dumb, and Unhappy*.

Mo Wheeler won in a landslide to become mayor of the city of Troy. Fippi Casella and Dan Robbins took seats on the city council; Casella became council president after bringing in the largest vote count from among the at-large candidates. Mo's first act as mayor was to visit with Kathy Gill and convince her to stay on as secretary to the mayor—an offer she gladly accepted.

Several weeks after the election, when presented with all of the evidence, including the deposition of Bruno Kreider who had agreed to testify against them, Crotty and Burgess entered pleas of "No Contest" to be filed in exchange for sentencing considerations.

Michael Crotty was sentenced to five to seven years in federal prison for multiple counts of bid rigging, accepting bribes while in office, and conspiracy to commit election fraud. On his way to prison, he proclaimed to the assembled reporters that he would be vindicated and would someday return as Troy's mayor. When one of the reporters reminded him that his sentence included a lifetime ban from holding any public office, he replied on camera, "It did?"

Danny Burgess was sentenced to one year in federal prison as an accomplice in most of the corruption charges but not for election fraud. While he too was prohibited from ever again holding public office, his sentence was reduced for agreeing to cooperate in the prosecution of Michael Crotty.

Bruno Kreider received immunity from prosecution in exchange for his agreement to testify. He retired to his camp on Lake George; changed his name; and took a job at Hague Marina, renting boats and jet skis to summer tourists. He never again set foot in the city of Troy.

Alex Cord retired from journalism and had initially planned to do some freelance writing. But he couldn't resist taking the job offer he received from Assemblyman Don Cantori to become chief of staff to the New York State Assembly Committee on Ethics in Government. The irony of that appointment was not lost on anyone.

Tugboat Tommy Monacelli and Angelo Renna stayed on at the Marconi Club and enjoyed telling stories about their part in the episode, especially the night at the locks, which got more and more hysterical every time Tugboat told it. Renna, of course, was forevermore known as Don.

Donnie Moore was given an honorary Marconi Club membership and during the impromptu induction ceremony presided over by President Jimmy Mariano, he proclaimed himself to be the world's first Jamaican member of the Marconi Club. The crowd loved it when Donnie ended the ceremony by singing what amounted to a Reggae version of "That's Amore."

Duke Bennett became an instant hero and received many job offers in the aftermath but after Rita convinced Joe White to offer him a salary increase and a large "performance bonus" for his role in Operation Out n' In, he gladly agreed to remain with the ladies at The Settlement.

Joey G. packed up his bags and left town immediately following the night of Crotty's arrest. He was anxious to get back to the apartment in Soho he still shared with three struggling fellow actors. Shortly after his return, he was able to parlay the notoriety of the *New York Monthly* article into securing the role of a mob boss named Gyp DiCarlo in the touring company of the musical Jersey Boys. His Aunt Pat was enormously proud to see the name Joey Bocketti listed in the playbill he sent her on the evening of his first performance.

The story of political corruption indeed had gained national notoriety, but even more so did the story of the ingenuity and determination of JoAnne, Rita, Pat, and Chuck. Their fame lasted far more than fifteen minutes, but, for their part, the ladies of The Settlement shunned all of the publicity. Despite repeated offers and invitations, they never granted a single interview or made any public statements about Operation Out n' In. Instead, they each went back to their routine of simply enjoying each other's company and life in general. Every Wednesday night they met to do the business of The Settlement and to discuss new and exciting ways to support good causes and to have some more fun.

The Marconi Club remained open and flourished as a place for like-minded people to come together, share in their Italian heritage, and enjoy an inexpensive lunch. The many tourists, who stopped in to see the site where much of Operation Out n' In took place, loved hearing the stories of derring-do told at the bar—some of which actually happened.

About the Author

Ken Bessette began creative writing as an English major and writers' forum member in Upstate New York. His interest in being a novelist was piqued after participating in an all-night poker game with author, James Dickey, of *Deliverance* fame. Bessette later earned a masters degree while teaching high school English and wrote his first novel after enduring too many harsh New York winters and moving to South Florida.

Much of his earlier creative writing came as a cruciverbalist (from Latin "crux" = cross and "verbum" = word). His crossword puzzles have appeared in national syndications, as well in the *New York Times*, the *Wall Street Journal, the LA Times,* and *USA Today.*

His favorite author is Fitzgerald although his favorite author he would have liked to have hung out with (if only he had been living in Key West during the 30s) is Hemingway. When not writing crosswords or fiction, Bessette spends an inordinate amount of time learning about Impressionist Art and the French Revolution for no apparent reason. His goal as a novelist (and puzzle writer, for that matter) is to create a work that people will become briefly but totally immersed in, enjoy thoroughly, and then wait restlessly for his next publication.